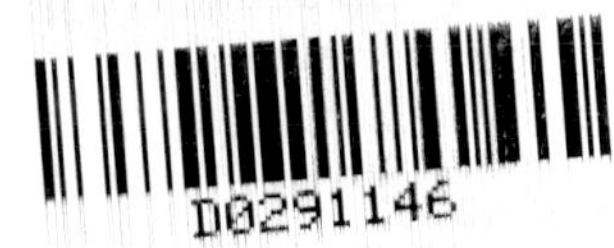

THE MESSAGE ON THE QUILT

The Quilt Chronicles

STEPHANIE GRACE WHITSON

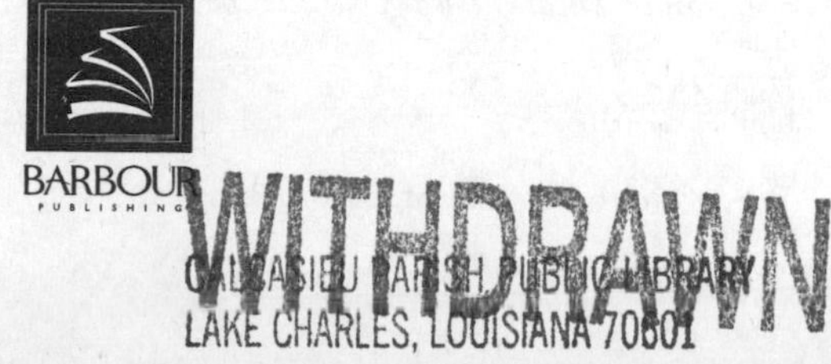

BARBOUR PUBLISHING

Print ISBN 978-1-61626-443-7

eBook Editions:
Adobe Digital Edition (.epub) 978-1-62416-040-0
Kindle and MobiPocket Edition (.prc) 978-1-62416-039-4

All scripture quotations are taken from the King James Version of the Bible.

This book is a work of fiction. Names, characters, places, and incidents are either products of the author's imagination or used fictitiously. Any similarity to actual people, organizations, and/or events is purely coincidental.

Cover design: Müllerhaus Publishing Arts, Inc., www.Mullerhaus.net

Published by Barbour Publishing, Inc., P.O. Box 719, Uhrichsville, Ohio 44683, www.barbourbooks.com

Our mission is to publish and distribute inspirational products offering exceptional value and biblical encouragement to the masses.

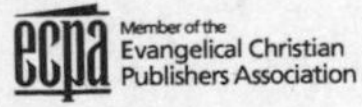

Printed in the United States of America.

DEDICATION

Dedicated to the memory of
God's extraordinary women
In every place
In every time

CHAPTER 1

Emilie Rhodes couldn't remember a single time in all of her eighteen years that she'd failed to charm Father out of a sour mood. But there was something about his grip around her wrist today that sent a chill up her spine as he pulled her out of the press room. Something about the insistence with which he propelled her along the narrow aisle that ran the length of the newsroom. And something about the posture of the handful of men bent over their work like acolytes bowing before an icon. Not a single one looked up as Father and she passed by. Not even Tom Tomkins, who'd always treated Emilie like something of a mascot for the *Beatrice Daily Dispatch.* As for the typesetter she'd been helping—when Emilie glanced back at him, Will Gable looked unusually concerned. If Will was worried. . . Emilie shivered.

Father released her as soon as they crossed the threshold to his office. He closed the door firmly and pulled a shade down, obscuring the sign on the window that read EDITOR IN CHIEF, *BEATRICE DAILY DISPATCH.* Emilie found her voice just as he reached for the second of the shades mounted above the two large windows that usually afforded him a view of his universe.

"Don't you want to be able to see when Mr. Shaw arrives?" When Father looked surprised, Emilie shrugged. "I heard you and Uncle Roscoe discussing who to feature in the inaugural Chautauqua edition. Y–you said you were meeting with Mr. Shaw as soon as he arrived on June 24th. Tuesday. Today." When Father merely continued to lower the last of the shades, she defended herself. "I wasn't eavesdropping. I was helping clear the dining room table. We all heard you. Talking about Mr. Shaw. Something about 'spell-binding pathos.' You wanted to be the first to speak with him. To beat out the *Journal* with an interview."

For a moment, Emilie thought she might have succeeded in diverting Father's attention from the fact that she'd disobeyed him. But all he did was open the door and call to Tom Tomkins. "Let me know if Mr. Shaw arrives before I've finished my business with my daughter. And whatever you do, don't let him get away." He closed the door firmly and, without so much as a glance in her direction, marched around his desk and sat down.

Emilie knew he'd sat down only because she heard the chair creak. She hadn't dared to look at him. Instead, she clutched her ink-stained hands before her and waited to be told what to do. After what felt like eons, Father cleared his throat and told her to sit down. She perched on the edge of the simple oak chair shoved into the corner. As she looked down at the jobber's apron she'd donned earlier, a hank of hair tumbled into view. She reached up to tuck the ash blond strands back into place, but the ink stains on her hands made her hesitate. Instead of repairing her coiffure, she curled her fingers into her palms and dropped both hands back into her lap. Maybe Father hadn't noticed her hands.

Of course that was a false hope. Father noticed everything. "Exactly what," he said, accenting the *t*s in both words, "do you think you were doing just now?"

"Will— " *No, don't call attention to Will. You'll get him in trouble.* She lifted her chin and made herself look at Father, concentrating on the tip of his immaculately groomed handlebar mustache. "I was setting type."

"I am familiar with the process," Father snapped. "Allow me to rephrase the question. Exactly what do you think *you*—the accomplished daughter of Mr. William T. Rhodes and Mrs. Henrietta J. Rhodes—were doing—especially in light of recent conversations in regard to your notion of a 'career in journalism.'"

Emilie swallowed. "I want—" She reached up to scratch her nose, then realized with horror that she'd probably just blackened it. Leaning down, she rubbed it with the hem of the apron, taking note of the new black smudge that had just joined a host of others. She took a deep breath. "I want to understand the process," she said.

"The process." He elongated the sound of the *o*.

Emilie had learned to judge the state of Father's temper by his pronunciation, and that long *o* was a bad sign. A very bad sign. Still, she persisted in trying to make him understand. "I want to do more than just write a column announcing church ice cream socials and Ladies' Aid meetings. I want to write real news someday. Why can't you understand that? You praised everything I wrote when I was away last year. So did my teachers. They said I have a real talent, Father. I want to use it. And I don't just want to write. I want to understand every part of what it takes to produce the paper." Finally, she dared to look at him. "Some of my earliest—and best—memories are of visiting you in this very office." She shrugged. "It's in my blood. I don't see why you can't understand that."

Father removed his watch from his vest pocket. He glanced down at the watch before looking over at her. "Let's talk about that word *understand*, Emilie Jane. Apart from the issue of the news, I wonder. . . Do you *understand* that it's rude to keep people waiting?" He held the watch up so that she could see the time. "Or did I *mis*understand your mentioning a four o'clock rehearsal over breakfast this morning?"

Emilie focused on the watch: *Four fifteen. Oh, no.* She reached behind to untie the apron. "I lost track of time." She pulled it over her head, newly aware of just how much of her coiffure had been affected by her afternoon in the press room. "If I hurry—"

"If you hurry," Father snapped, "you will still have kept your cousins waiting. You will still have demonstrated a rude disregard for their schedules for the day. And ultimately, *they* will 'understand' that you were thinking only of yourself. Again." He snapped the watch closed and tucked it back in his vest pocket. Then he rose, came around the end of the desk, and reached out to tap the back of one of her hands. "And Mother, Emilie Jane. What will you say to make her *understand* these hands of yours?"

Emilie uncurled her fingers and inspected the distressing amount of filth beneath her fingernails. It was as if Father's touch had deflated her resolve. She sighed. *I won't say a thing. Why would I bother? Nothing I say changes anything.* She seemed to have been born with a talent for behavior that horrified Mother and consequently upset Father. She preferred balls to dolls and had little patience with the culinary arts. Doing a sewing stint made her want to scream, and she was never content to just sit on the grass and watch Will Gable and Bert Hartwell play baseball. She wanted to play. In recent months she had steadfastly maintained friendships with several young men while just as steadfastly resisting Mother's attempts at matchmaking. Just last week she'd declared that it was wrong for women not to have the right to vote—and come very close to suggesting there was something wrong with a woman who didn't agree with the idea of women's suffrage. An embarrassing moment, since Mother didn't support the idea of women's suffrage.

Poor Mother. The voting discussion had been particularly distressing because it took place in the company of Aunt Cornelia, Mother's only living relative. Aunt Cornelia could bask in the joy of three perfectly genteel daughters. Any parent would be proud to claim those three, while poor Mother's fate allowed her only one child—and a faulty one, at that.

The sound of Father clearing his throat brought Emilie back to the moment and the subject of her ink-stained hands. "Dinah will know what to do," she said. It wasn't the answer Father wanted, but it was the best she could do. And it was true. Aunt Cornelia might not envy her sister her only child, but she did envy Mother Dinah Brooks, the best housekeeper in Gage County.

As for Emilie's cousins, also known as the popular ladies' trio, the Spring Sisters—they were the least of Emilie's worries at the moment. April would scold, but more out of a sense of duty as the oldest than from any real anger. Junie would roll her eyes and mutter something about "Emilie being Emilie again." And May, the middle child, would understand. May always understood, because she shared Emilie's desire to become something more than ornamentation for a man's life—even if May was more subtle about her leanings.

With a sigh, Father stood and stepped over to his office door, pausing with his hand on the brass knob long enough to say, "Get that apron off. I'll have Hartwell see you home. He can wait while Dinah helps you get cleaned up, and then he can drive you out to the assembly grounds for your rehearsal."

"You don't need to bother Bert. I can—"

"Do not tell me what I do or do not 'need' to do."

Obviously Father wasn't open to suggestions. The best thing Emilie could do was to keep her head down and do as she was told. Even if it was 1890. Even if she was eighteen years old. Not that Father seemed to remember that very often.

"I'd take you myself," he continued, "if I hadn't arranged to meet with Mr. Shaw about that column." He cleared his throat. "Unlike others, *I* do not make a habit of missing appointments." He paused. "Hartwell can be counted on to get you home—and not to snicker behind our backs." He opened the door and called for Bert.

Emilie dared a look at Father as he waited for Bert. At the set of his jaw. The glum expression. The disappointment. Over her.

The only child her parents would ever have. Even if Father had gotten over the disappointment of her not being a boy, he was still disappointed. And why? Because she couldn't even manage to be the next best thing—a lady like Mother. And this time, Father wasn't just upset. He was ashamed of her. He wanted her out of the newspaper office as quickly as possible, and he was calling on someone who wouldn't "laugh behind their backs." As she ducked her head and waited for Bert, Emilie blinked back tears. It was one thing to be a disappointment, and quite another to think you might have been the cause of people laughing at your parents.

"This conversation is not yet finished," Father said. "We'll continue it when you return from rehearsal. In my study at home." He sighed. "I thought giving you the Ladies' News column would—help, somehow. Now I see that it's only put more ideas into your head." Taking a deep breath he said, "Be thinking of who you'd recommend to replace you. The column performs a worthy service to the community—but I realize now that it was a mistake to put you in charge."

The air grew close. Crumpling the soiled apron into a ball, Emilie sprang to her feet and blurted out a promise. "No, Father. Please. I—I didn't think—"

"Indeed, you did not. For such a bright girl, you seem—" At the sound of a familiar, shuffling gait approaching the office, Father broke off and stepped back to admit Bert Hartwell.

Bert had a unique walk. It was more of a shuffle, really—a shuffle caused by a poorly set broken leg suffered six years ago when Emilie and Bert were twelve-year-olds chasing each other in and out of the trees along the banks of the Blue River one Sunday afternoon. It was long before the city had staked out ninety acres and designated it for a ten-day extravaganza called the Interstate Chautauqua. Back then, the woods meandering along the clear river were just a favored spot for family outings. Now they provided the perfect site for a regional event that drew thousands of visitors to Beatrice to hear lectures and attend reunions, to savor concerts and endure sermons. But back before all of that, twelve-year-old Bert Hartwell had taken a dare from his best friend, Emilie Rhodes.

"Bet you can't climb that tree," she'd said. And now Bert shuffled.

The scent of his cologne preceded Bert into the office. Emilie scrubbed at her nose with the soiled apron. It came away with still more evidence of her hours setting type. What she must look like! She glared an unspoken message in Bert's direction. *Don't you dare laugh.* He gulped and looked at Father, who was giving instructions in the no-nonsense way he had that sounded of authority—and yet of kindness.

Kindness. How Emilie wished Father would have flavored his words to her just now with even a hint of that. Perhaps he would have even been proud of a child taking an interest in the business—were that child named *Emil.* What a difference two letters could make.

"You can take my buggy instead of collecting one from the livery," Father said. "I'll walk home after I've concluded my business with Mr. Shaw. The fresh air will do me good. Please wait through the rehearsal and see that Emilie goes directly home when the ladies are finished."

"Yes, sir," Bert said. "You can count on me."

"I knew I could." Father waved them both out of his office.

When Emilie glanced back, he was rolling up the window shades to once again reveal the part of his world over which he had absolute control.

—∿—

"Whew," Bert said as he helped Emilie into the buggy hitched in the alley behind the newspaper office. "I haven't seen him that angry in a while."

"You haven't seen him around *me* in a while," Emilie said, suddenly aware of the fact that she was still holding on to the soiled printer's apron. They made their way toward Sixth Street and then north, past the construction site of the new county courthouse and, finally, to North Seventh and the new home Father had had built for Mother only last year. When Bert pulled the buggy to a halt beneath the porte cochere, Emilie didn't wait for his help before jumping down. "You might as well come in," she said. "I'll hurry, but it's still going to take a few minutes. Dinah made lemon pie yesterday. I'll tell her to get you a piece."

Bert followed her along the narrow porch that extended from the front of the house, around the curved corner turret to the porte cochere, and then all the way to the back, where it widened to create a modest sitting area just off the kitchen.

Dinah liked to sit there in the evening, knitting while she waited for her husband Calvin to finish his work in the barn or elsewhere on the half-acre property. But this afternoon, Dinah was standing at the sink, trimming the tops off a bunch of carrots. Emilie peeled off her gloves and went to her side. Holding out her hands, she said, "Help. And can Bert have the last piece of pie, please?"

Dinah spoke to Bert first. "It's right there under that cloth." She pointed at the worktable on the far side of the kitchen. "All you need is a fork." Dinah peered down at Emilie's hands. "What you been doing?"

"It's printers' ink. Will Gable was showing me how to set type. And I'm late to rehearsal with the cousins." She shrugged. "And Father caught me, and he's fit to be tied." She bit her lower lip. "He asked Bert to drive me. And to bring me home later."

Shaking her head, Dinah trundled into the pantry, returning with a small tin, which she set on the counter. The foul-smelling mixture she ladled out of the tin and into Emilie's open palm removed the ink from her hands as she scrubbed. Dinah helped her remove the smudges from her face and soon all traces of the ink were gone, except for the dark lines beneath her nails.

"You gonna have to soak your hands to get rid of those," Dinah said.

"I will when I get home tonight. For now, gloves will have to do. I'll just have to hope the cousins don't notice while I'm playing." Planting a quick kiss on Dinah's leathery cheek, Emilie raced up the back stairs and into her room. One look at herself in her dressing mirror and she almost understood why Father had been so upset, especially when her imagination recreated the smudged face and a filthy apron.

Repairing her hair would take too long. Pulling a dozen hairpins out, she let it tumble down around her shoulders, then quickly drew a brush through it and tied it back with a green ribbon. Grabbing a straw bonnet, she headed back downstairs, landing in the kitchen just as she heard her mother call Father's name from the front hall.

Emilie sent a panicked look in Dinah's direction. "I thought she was at a library meeting."

"Must have finished early." Dinah headed into the pantry with the tin of cleanser.

Tugging on Bert's sleeve, Emilie headed for the back door. When Bert hesitated, she hissed, "Dinah will explain that it was us and why we had to hurry off. Come on!" Cramming the last piece of pie into his mouth, Bert set the pie plate in the sink and followed her outside. Once he had the buggy moving, Emilie said, "I've already heard Father expounding on what a disappointment I am. I don't need a sermonette from Mother, too."

—∾—

As the late afternoon train pulled into Beatrice, Nebraska, "The Man of Many Voices" rolled up his old quilt and tucked it inside the canvas duffel he'd had made especially for the road. He'd spent the last few hours trying to find a way to make his six-foot frame comfortable so that he could nap, and as he stood up to retrieve his travel bag, his back and shoulders complained. Stretching, he pulled the travel bag down from the luggage rack overhead. By the time the train came to a stop, Noah Shaw had clipped the duffel in place and was standing out on the platform, ready to jump down and head for the Paddock Hotel. To his chagrin, the fellow passenger he'd been trying to avoid for most of the trip joined him as the brakes squalled and steam spewed into the air.

Ma had raised him to behave like a gentleman, and so, whether the term *lady* applied in this situation or not, he motioned for the garishly dressed woman to precede him down the stairs. "May I help you with your bag?"

"You may." With a toss of her bewigged head and a dramatic sweeping of her skirts, the woman who'd introduced herself earlier as Madame Jumeaux descended to the platform. She'd said her name with a flourish and a tone that made it obvious that Noah was expected to recognize it. When he didn't, she'd condescended to excuse him. After all, she'd said, his was largely a Midwestern career. One couldn't expect everyone in "that part of the country" to be informed "as to the larger theatrical scene on the coast."

Noah grabbed the woman's valise and tucked it under one arm as he grasped his own bags and followed her off the train. As soon as he'd alighted, he set her bag down. "May I summon a porter to assist you?"

"He can assist us both," she said. "I assume you're staying at the Paddock? It is, regrettably, the best they have to offer." She waved a gloved hand. "I suppose it's not so bad. One must temper one's expectations to the venue."

A screech rang out as a freight car door slid open a short distance up the tracks. Noah turned to see a dark figure scurry out of the far end of the station, a wheeled cart in tow.

"That will be our trunks," madame said.

"Yours, perhaps." Noah indicated his valise and the duffel. "I travel light."

Madame's painted lips parted in a prim smile. "How clever of you. Impossible for an actress, of course. One's costumes and associated regalia." She put a gloved hand on his arm. "Shall we walk together?"

"I regret that I must decline," Noah said. "I've an appointment." He made a show of pulling his watch out of his vest pocket. "And I'm afraid I'm already late." He tugged on the brim of his hat. "Have a good evening." He pretended not to notice that the woman was about to say something. Instead, he headed off up the street—as if he knew where he was going. As if the exact location of the *Beatrice Daily Dispatch* wasn't a complete mystery.

CHAPTER 2

Emilie was quiet for most of the drive to the Chautauqua assembly grounds. Thankfully, Bert knew her well enough to let her simmer without forcing conversation. He was driving the buggy beneath the largest of the four wooden arches that marked the entrance before she voiced one of the worries that had been niggling at her for most of the twenty-minute drive. "What do you think Father will do to Will for letting me help set type?"

Bert didn't answer for a moment. Instead, he let Father's pride-and-joy buggy horse cool down, ambling along the winding road that led to the open-air auditorium called the Tabernacle. When he did speak, his tone was confident. "It's more important than ever to get the paper out on time during Chautauqua. Folks are estimating there could be as many as ten thousand people on the grounds—and that's on an average day. Who knows how many will come to hear Reverend Talmage that last Sunday? I imagine Will's safe—although he's probably had his ears pinned back by now. When it comes right down to it, though, there's too much business to be missed if the *Daily* isn't running smoothly over the next couple of weeks. You don't need to worry about Will."

"Too much business to be missed." Too much money at risk. Bert was right. Father was, first and foremost, a businessman. He wouldn't let anything stand in the way of all those newspaper sales.

"Come prepared to suggest your replacement." In the wake of relief on behalf of Will Gable came a wave of dread at the memory of Father's implied threat to take the Ladies' News away from her. She couldn't let that happen. She wouldn't. She'd find a way. But she'd have to think about that later. Worrying over it would make her hands tremble. And then she'd miss notes at rehearsal, and Cousin April would scold even more than she would anyway because of Emilie's being late.

Glancing toward the Tabernacle in the distance, she said, "Do you really think the crowd will be that large this year? Will was working on the program today, so I had a chance to see the schedule. Ex-President Hayes isn't coming. I know Reverend Talmage is popular, but I can't imagine him being as big a draw as a former president."

"Never underestimate the power of a good sermon." Bert looked over with a grin. "And besides that, I hear that the Spring Sisters and their lovely accompanist are to be featured a half-dozen times." He pulled the buggy up alongside the Tabernacle stage. "At least I *thought* we had the Spring Sisters. But there's clearly no one waiting to rehearse. Do you think they got tired of waiting?"

"Who could blame them?" Emilie gazed past the empty stage toward the row of cottages in the distance. "They could be helping Aunt Cornelia settle in. You wouldn't believe what she hauled out here last year for the series. She even brought an icebox. For a ten-day campout. Can you imagine?"

Bert smiled. "Well, just because a person is camping is no reason to suffer needlessly, eh? I seem to recall that your parents' cottage was fairly well furnished last year, too." With a flick of the reins, he headed the buggy around the back side of the Tabernacle and toward Cottage Row.

"In case you don't remember it's the pink one with the diamond-patterned roof," Emilie said. "I don't see the girls, but there's definitely something going on."

Mother had been the first of the town ladies to come up with the idea of erecting a cottage out here. Once it was known that Mrs. Rhodes had come up with such a clever alternative to tent camping, a flurry of activity along the Blue River had resulted in an entire row of diminutive cottages. Some boasted gingerbread, while others had expansive porches or whimsical gazebos.

As the buggy got closer, Bert said, "Looks like the ladies have some kind of competition going this year." Workers swarmed like bees around several places. One was getting a fresh coat of paint, while a team of men installed window screens and shutters on another. But none was getting attention comparable to Aunt Cornelia's. Burt gave a low whistle as they pulled up. "Well. Would you look at that?"

Emilie just shook her head. "It was bound to happen. Mother and Aunt Cornelia may be sisters, but it's always a contest between those two. We have a porch around ours, and last year everyone congregated over there. Especially after Mother talked Father into having hammocks put up all around. Aunt Cornelia would never let a porch and hammocks go unanswered."

"But. . .a tree house?" Bert gazed up into the massive oak tree that shaded the pink cottage. Carpenters had already built a platform around the trunk. Now, two were adding a simple railing between uprights obviously intended to support a second story. The beginnings of winding stairs circled the tree trunk.

Aunt Cornelia stepped through the front doorway and hurried over. "You didn't get the message? 'Etta said she'd tell you."

"Tell me what?"

"The piano hasn't been delivered to the Tabernacle yet. You'll have to practice at the house. The girls are waiting there." Aunt Cornelia pointed at carpenters at work on the tree house. "Isn't it lovely? And after they've finished the observation deck, I'm having them lay a lovely veranda across the open space between our cottage and the tree." She smiled. "I just might have your uncle bring the parlor piano out for the duration." She waved a hand in the direction of the new construction. "It's the perfect setting for evening entertainments, don't you think?"

Emilie muttered something she hoped sounded positive before turning to Bert. "I guess it's Aunt Cornelia's next." She bid her aunt good-bye, and Bert urged Dutch into a smart trot. As they slowed to cross the bridge across the river, Emilie said, "I hope you didn't have plans for an early supper."

"The only plans I have is to do whatever it takes to give a good report to my employer after I return his buggy, his horse, and his daughter later this evening."

"A report? You'll be expected to report?"

"Not in the way you mean. But he'll probably work it into a conversation at the newspaper office tomorrow." He nudged her. "Don't look so glum. All I plan to say is that I personally escorted the lovely Miss Emilie Rhodes to her destination and that she looked every inch a lady, right down to the ribbon in her hair which was, I happened to notice, exactly the shade of her green eyes." He glanced her way. Shrugged. "You're right. Needs editing. Too much detail."

"My eyes aren't green."

"They tend toward green when you're upset. And when you wear that color."

Emilie glanced down at her gray-green skirt. The realization that Bert could describe her ensemble made her feel strangely. . .strange. Did her eyes really tend toward green when she was upset? No one had ever said anything like that to her before.

They'd made their way back into town and were passing by the Paddock Hotel and Opera House before Bert spoke again. "He wants what's best for you, Em. He gets angry because he cares."

She snorted in disbelief.

Bert was quiet for the rest of the drive. Emilie had just climbed down, and Bert was hitching the buggy when a voice sounded from the screened porch up on the second floor of the two-story white farmhouse.

"Bert Hartwell, is that you?" And a giggle.

"You didn't tell me the Penners were going to be at your rehearsal," Bert groused.

Emilie looked over at him. "Because I didn't know." There was no time to say anything more, as the front door opened and the Penner twins bounded down the porch stairs, followed closely by Emilie's three cousins. The twins fluttered about Bert as he finished tying off the buggy reins.

April, the eldest of the three Spring sisters scolded. "You're late."

May, the middle sister and Emilie's best friend interrupted. "But it's actually kind of good that you were."

"I wouldn't be this late if I'd known we weren't practicing at the Tabernacle." Emilie directed her defense at April, then looked over at May. "And why is it good that I'm late?"

April pressed her point. "Mother told Aunt Henrietta at the library meeting, and Aunt was supposed to tell you to come here."

Ahnt. In recent weeks, it was as if that miniscule garnet engagement ring on April's finger gave her a right to pontificate to her younger sisters and, by reason of association, to Emilie. Emilie scowled. "Well, *Ahnt* Cornelia may have told your *Ahnt* Henrietta, but no one told me, because I wasn't home this afternoon to get the message. And for your information, *Ahnt* Cornelia didn't seem upset with me at all." She looked back to May and repeated her question. "And why is it a good thing that I was late?"

Junie, two years younger than Emilie and suffering from a long-standing crush on Bert Hartwell, didn't give May a chance to answer. "Where were the two of you?" She gazed toward Bert, still trapped by the giggling Penner twins.

"Relax, Junie." Emilie tugged playfully on the thick blond braid trailing down Junie's back. "I was working at the newspaper office, and I assume Bert was doing the same, although I didn't really see much of him—until Father ordered him to drive me home." She leaned close. "He has to stay all evening. Apparently he's to be my keeper. Father ordered him to deliver me home."

Junie blushed bright red. "I bet he's hungry. I could get him a sandwich from the kitchen. Do you think he'd like that?"

"I'm certain he would."

"Actually," April said as Junie headed inside, "we're all on our own for supper. Mother summoned Papa out to the cottage." She raised her voice so that the Penner sisters—one hanging on to each of Bert's arms—could hear her. "We'll have to rustle up our own supper."

The Penner on Bert's right arm sighed dramatically and leaned forward just enough to see her sister. "That's our cue to leave, Fern. We don't have permission to stay for supper."

"I'd invite you to stay," April said, "but we really do need to concentrate on our music." She glanced in Emilie's direction. "We've gotten such a late start."

"Oh, bother." Fern let go of Bert. She patted his shoulder. "We'll save you a seat on the front row for the opening exercises."

Bert muttered something noncommittal, disengaged, and headed up the stairs and onto the wide front porch, where he waited to play doorman.

As soon as the Penner twins were out of earshot, May spoke up. "Finally. I thought they'd never leave." Her blue eyes sparkled as she said, "With April getting married this fall, this is her last chance at independence. So"—she clasped her hands before her—"we've reserved a tent for the entire Chautauqua. And we paid the extra dollar to get a floor installed. Won't it be wonderful?! Just the four of us. We can go boating on the river or take a moonlight cruise on the riverboat or walk in the moonlight or read or play music or—do nothing at all. No parents, no servants, no chores, no cares. For ten whole days!" She reached for Emilie's hand and pulled her along into the house.

As they all passed the doorway into the formal dining room, Junie called Bert's name. "I—I made you a sandwich. I hope you like it."

Emilie smiled. Dear Junie. She'd made a sandwich, all right. And set the table with Aunt Cornelia's good china, right down to a crystal wine glass. Filled to the rim with milk.

"It's only roast beef," Junie said. Her expression dared her sisters to say a word. They didn't.

"It looks wonderful." Bert gave a little bow to the others. "Ladies, if you'll excuse me." And he headed into the dining room.

The look of joy on Junie's face made Emilie want to hug Bert for being so kind. Instead, she followed April and May into Aunt Cornelia's kitchen, wishing with all her heart she didn't have to disappoint her cousins. But there was no way on earth Father would let her stay in their tent during the Chautauqua. Not after today. He didn't even trust her to get herself home from music rehearsal. *"Be thinking of a replacement for the news column."*

Suddenly, a knot of sadness and apprehension took over the empty space in Emilie's midsection that she'd been planning to fill with Aunt Cornelia's scrumptious roast beef.

—∾—

Noah laid his fork and knife down. He bit his lower lip to keep from frowning. The roast beef was succulent, the gravy smooth and flavorful, the candied sweet potatoes better than any he'd ever tasted. A succulent meal in the Paddock Hotel dining room ruined. By four little words.

"May I join you?"

If only he'd been seated facing the door that opened onto the hotel lobby. Maybe he could have escaped. But he hadn't and couldn't, and so he forced a smile, rose, and pulled out a chair for Madame Jumeaux. Across the table, instead of beside him.

"I hope you won't mind my being so forward." A veritable cloud of scent rose as the woman settled on her chair. "Life on the road does teach one that it is sometimes necessary—and pleasurable—to circumvent convention."

The combination of cheap perfume and musty gown made Noah take a step back. Thankful for the expanse of table between him and Madame Jumeaux, he muttered something noncommittal and returned to his own chair.

"Don't let me be the cause of you having to eat a cold meal." Madame made a show of removing her lavender kid gloves and laying them atop the table. When a waiter approached with a menu, she fluttered her eyelashes and waved it away, ordering coffee, toast, and a poached egg. She touched his elbow. "And do emphasize *soft*-poached," she said. "The last time I was here, the cook was calling white stones soft-poached eggs."

"Yes, ma'am." The waiter nodded. "I'll see to it."

The waiter retreated, and Madame folded her hands in her lap and smiled at Noah. "A profitable meeting at the newspaper, I assume?" She tilted her head as she waited for a reply. When Noah said nothing, she gave a little laugh. "Please forgive me, Mr. Shaw. I've been forced to acquire a certain boldness over the years. A lady traveling alone—you mustn't let it bother you. I don't mean to pry like some gossipy spinster."

Noah glanced down at his plate. He'd been ravenous not two minutes ago. Ah, well. Tomorrow was another day. He took a sip of water. "Are you pleased with your accommodations? You expressed doubts, as I recall."

Madame gazed about them. Gave a little shrug. "I've had worse. And better." She sighed. "Much, much better. But then you don't want to hear about that."

She was right. He didn't. He didn't want her at his table, either. Dining with an overly painted aging actress wasn't exactly the best way for a single man to maintain his reputation. "I think you'll be pleased with the food," Noah said, nodding down at his plate. "This is delicious."

The waiter approached, a plate in one hand, a coffeepot in the other. Madame waved the coffeepot away. "I'd forgotten the late hour. Just bring me a cup of hot water with a splash of lemon." The waiter set the plate before her and headed back to the kitchen. Madame leaned forward as if sharing a confidence. "Lemon is good for the instrument, you know." She bent one wrist, lifted her chin, and swept the air along her powdered throat.

"So I've heard." Noah set his glass down. "And now," he said. "I'm afraid I'll have to leave you to enjoy your meal in private. There is still one thing to which I must attend before nightfall." He wasn't quite certain what that thing was, other than to escape. An inner warning sounded every time Madame Jumeaux came near, and he'd learned to heed inner warnings. He'd encountered plenty of lonely ladies in his travels, and he didn't mind a friendly conversation, but there was an air of desperation about this woman that made him wary.

"But you haven't finished your meal." Madame pointed at his plate. "A man of your considerable"—her gaze swept over him—"physique cannot possibly be satisfied with so little."

Noah folded his napkin and rose. "I am quite satisfied," he said. With a bow, he took his leave. Exiting the dining room through the door that opened onto the street, he feigned a certainty that he did not feel. Once out on the street, he hesitated just long enough to glance through the window and catch a glimpse of Madame reaching across the table with fork in hand to stab a strip of the roast beef Noah had left on his plate. She moved quickly. The roast beef deposited on her own plate, she repeated the action, this time with a spoon, downing a spoonful of his sweet potatoes before attacking the roast beef waiting on her own plate.

Frowning, Noah headed off up the street. How had he missed

it? Cheap cologne. A wig arranged in the long curls that hadn't been in style for a very long time. And, now that he thought about it, those lavender kid gloves she'd laid on the table had been quite worn. As was the carpetbag he'd carried off the train for her earlier today. With a sigh, Noah realized that he'd misunderstood—out of pride. He hadn't seen her in the dining car on the train. Not once. Madame Jumeaux wasn't desperate for a man. She was *hungry*.

Noah paused and looked back toward the hotel. How was she paying for a room in the finest hotel in Beatrice? He looked off toward the west at the spectacular sunset and thought of Ma and her love of the evening sky. Ma would have expected better of him with regard to Madame Jumeaux.

Taking a deep breath, he muttered an apology. *I'm sorry, Ma.* She'd never turned anyone away from their door. It didn't matter that it was just the two of them. It didn't matter that she worked long hours and late nights providing for them. Ma had said that sometimes they might be entertaining "angels unawares" when they were kind to those in need.

I'm so sorry. His conscience pricked, Noah decided to walk for a while. He headed off toward the Chautauqua grounds where he'd spend the greater part of his time over the next ten days. As he walked, thoughts of the Artist who'd painted this evening's magnificent sunset led to another apology. *I am sorry, Father. I was only thinking about myself. I missed the face of hunger behind those painted cheeks.*

Pausing before crossing the bridge across the river flowing just to the south of the city, Noah Shaw, "The Man of Many Voices," decided something. Tomorrow, he would invite Madame Jumeaux to dine with him. He would thank her for all the advice she'd given "her fellow thespian" on the train. At the time, he hadn't really appreciated her rattling on. Now he realized that he should have listened and seen with his heart.

CHAPTER 3

When the waiter returned for Noah Shaw's plate and headed to the kitchen, Grace Jumeaux followed his retreat with profound regret. So much delicious food left on that plate. And those sweet potatoes. She couldn't remember the last time she'd tasted something that mouthwatering. She stared down at the poached egg on her plate. *Eggs.* She was so sick of eggs. She couldn't face them tonight. Not after getting a few bites of roast beef and sweet potatoes. She lifted the cup of hot lemon water to her lips.

"Is the egg not to your liking, madame?" The waiter had returned. "The kitchen is about to close. If you require another—"

"No, no." She waved him away. "It's fine. I've just realized I'm not really all that hungry." She took a nibble of toast before picking up her worn kid gloves and pushing herself away from the table. Relief washed over her when she peered out into the lobby and saw that the night clerk wasn't at his station. She hurried to the stairs.

"Madame?"

Too slow. She pivoted about. He was too young. No chance of charming him. She would have to try something else. Tilting her head, she responded with a little frown. "*Oui? Vous m'avais appellé?*"

"I was directed to ask you about your room."

"*Pardon?*" The man hesitated. Good. It usually took only a few French words to get them to give up.

He smiled. "*Vous ne parlez-pas anglais, madame? Ça ne fair rien. C'est mon plaisir de vous assister en français.*"

Madame pursed her lips. Who would have thought a night clerk in Beatrice, Nebraska, would speak French. *Dommage.* She gave him her most gracious smile. "Please excuse me. It wasn't that long ago that my company was touring *en Europe.* Sometimes I forget that I'm back home." She didn't move from the stair. "You were saying?"

"I was instructed to inquire about the room."

"It's lovely. Thank you so much." She turned to go.

The young man raised his voice. "About payment?"

She looked back at him. Frowned. "Is this some new policy? The last time I was here. . ." She feigned confusion. "I am so sorry, monsieur, but I was not aware that payment in advance would be required."

"It isn't—usually. But with the Chautauqua coming and rooms in such demand—" He paused. "We don't raise our rates for the event, but we do request payment in advance. There's a waiting list, you see."

"Of course," Madame said. "And I shall be happy to accommodate you. I am only waiting, you see, for my most recent remuneration to be converted into American dollars and wired to the bank here."

"I understand, ma'am, truly I do. And I hate to inconvenience you, but the manager indicated that you were aware of the policy. He instructed me to say that if you can't pay in advance, then. . ."

At least he feigned embarrassment. Or maybe he was embarrassed. It was hard to tell. Madame lifted her chin. She glowered. "Are you implying, young man, that there is a problem with my staying at this hotel?"

"No, ma'am. There's no problem, it's just that—"

"Tell your manager that I shall speak with him in the morning. At which time I will request that my trunks be removed to a more accommodating hotel." With a toss of her false curls, Madame

Jumeaux stormed up the first flight of stairs. Out of breath, she forced herself up the second flight and to the end of the hall. Finally in her room, she leaned against the door, fighting off tears and waiting to catch her breath. Dreading the desk clerk's knock on the door. Thankfully, he wasn't so loyal to the management as to pursue a poor woman up two flights of stairs.

Trembling, she pulled her wig off and placed it on the stand atop the open theatrical trunk crowded between the foot of the bed and the wall. Lighting one of the gas lamps by the door, she stared at herself in the mirror above the washstand. She hadn't planned on knocking on Josiah's door quite yet. But if the hotel manager was going to be that pushy. . .well. She didn't really have a choice. She might be a good actress, but there was no "more accommodating hotel" in her future. Since paying for that egg she hadn't eaten, she had exactly twenty-five cents to her name. Enough to pay her way onto the Chautauqua grounds for one day. But now she needed a place to stay.

She hoped seeing her again would soothe whatever anger Josiah might have felt about her selling the house and leaving town. After all, it had been twenty years. He had to have known she wouldn't last long living alone in a one-horse town while he traipsed all over kingdom come chasing after Indians. He'd said he was born to be an Indian fighter. Well, good for him. She'd been born for the stage. And didn't a woman have as much right as a man to seek her destiny?

For all the good it had done her.

As she stood in the dim light, staring at the trappings of her last twenty years as a vagabond, Grace was tempted to wonder what her life might have been like if only—no. Once again, she looked in the mirror and spoke aloud to the tired woman staring back at her. "You made a choice to live a dream. And you had some wonderful times, old girl. So stop the pity party. You've hit a rough patch. That's all it is. Josiah will keep his promise." She lifted her chin, even as she pressed one palm to her growling stomach and repeated, "Josiah will keep his promise."

He had to. According to the one letter she'd received some years ago, he'd become a Bible-thumper. And she had nowhere else to turn.

—∾—

The idea of sharing a tent during Chautauqua put conversation and supper ahead of the Spring Sisters rehearsal. And then there was the matter of the state of Emilie's hands, which of course could not be hidden from view when it came time to eat. As Emilie had expected, Junie said something about "Emilie being Emilie," April merely shrugged, and May understood.

"Don't worry," she said. "Uncle Bill will have calmed down by the time you talk again."

Uncle Bill. Emilie didn't think Father had been called "Bill," by anyone but May, even as a boy. But then May had a way about her. If only Emilie could borrow some of her charm. By the time Bert drove her home, she'd calmed down a bit. But then the house came into view, and Emilie saw that the old-fashioned hurricane lamp in Father's study window was lit. Her grip on the edge of the wagon seat tightened. Had Father merely lingered in the study while relaxing. . . or was he waiting up for her? As the buggy slowed beneath the study window, Emilie thought she saw the fringe on one of the window curtains move a bit. As if someone were standing there, watching. *Oh no.* If Father had waited up. . . *Oh no.*

"Didn't expect to see a light in the old man's study," Bert said. "I hope everything's all right."

"He's waited up for me." Emilie swallowed in a vain effort to keep her voice from quavering. "H–he told me to be considering my replacement for the Ladies' News. I was hoping the late hour would at least delay that conversation. Hoping he'd rethink it."

"Maybe he has," Bert said, "and he's just waiting to tell you."

Dear Bert. Such a good friend, always hoping for the best. "Maybe." Emilie forced herself to agree, even as her heartbeat ratcheted up. Maybe, but probably not. The second Bert pulled the buggy up at the side stairs, she moved to get down. "Thanks for babysitting."

"My pleasure. Tell the old man I bedded Dutch down. Make sure he knows I gave him fresh water and forked hay into the crib in his stall."

"The 'old man' thanks you." Father's voice sounded from the other side of the screen door. "It's late, Hartwell. If you'd rather ride back to town, you are most welcome to saddle Royal once you've seen to Dutch." He paused. "Emilie won't need him for the next few days."

The next few *days*? Whatever that meant, it sent a frisson of nerves up Emilie's spine. She'd planned to ride Royal over to the Chautauqua grounds tomorrow. First, for an on-site rehearsal as soon as the piano was delivered to the Tabernacle. But also to help the cousins get settled in their tent.

She was supposed to help them make the sign that named the temporary abode the "Bee Hive." And after that, who knew? The grounds would be a fascinating place tomorrow, with a veritable army of men raising camp tents and dining-hall tents, wiping down and installing benches at the Tabernacle, and more. Emilie had planned to spend the day there, not only to have fun, but also to give Father time to calm down. To see reason in regard to his threat about the Ladies' News. Swallowing, she repeated her thanks to Bert.

Bert murmured, "You're welcome," and headed on up the drive toward the carriage house at the back of the property.

Father motioned her inside, then closed and latched the screen door and the heavy inner door behind them before leading the way to his study. The aroma of cigar smoke lingered in his wake. If he'd had a relaxing evening at home, maybe all was not lost. But that flickering hope died the minute they turned the corner into Father's study. Mother was waiting there, standing next to one of the chairs she'd proclaimed "hideous" the first time she'd seen it. Father had a pair of them, one tucked into each of the two corners of the study. They were upholstered in black horsehair. The hideous part was the fact that each chair's framework had been constructed with horns from longhorn cattle.

If Mother had spent the evening sitting in one of those despised chairs, things were very bad indeed. As Emilie offered a greeting, Mother wound a half-finished sock around the knitting needles in her hand and bent to tuck them into a bag sitting on the floor. She sat back down, and motioned for Emilie to do likewise.

Father settled in the swivel chair behind his desk. "I know you're wondering about not having Royal tomorrow. Mother has agreed to chauffeur you. She'll wait until you've finished your farewell column and then drive you to my office so that you can submit it on time."

Farewell. Emilie glanced Mother's way. "B–but the cousins and I have rehearsal at the Tabernacle as soon as the piano arrives."

"Not to worry," Mother said with a forced smile. "We'll go straight out to the grounds from your father's office. I can drop you at rehearsal—"

"After which," Father chimed in, "you'll head over to the cottage and offer Mother your assistance getting our camp set up."

Emilie swallowed. "She has Dinah to help her. And I—I told the cousins I'd help *them* set up housekeeping. They've rented a tent."

Mother frowned. "Why on earth would they do such thing? Cornelia's ordered all kinds of improvements to their cottage."

"I know." Emilie forced a conspiratorial smile. "Bert and I saw. And you are so right about her and 'improvements.' She's having a two-deck tree house built around the big oak out back. And a porch laid out between the tree house and the cottage. She even mentioned having Uncle Roscoe haul the upright piano out for 'evening entertainments.'"

Mother shook her head. "Cornelia will never stand for the girls jumping ship after she's had all that done."

This was good. A conversation that deflected attention away from this afternoon and the *Dispatch* print shop. "May said the three of them wanted to do something special since this is their last summer together. What with April getting married." She plunged ahead. "Actually, I'm grateful you both stayed up. The cousins were hoping you wouldn't object to my joining them over at the campgrounds. They're quite enthused about their plans. They've even paid to have a floor installed in the tent. And they're going to name their camp the Bee Hive. Hang a sign above the tent flap and everything."

Father tugged on the tip of his mustache. Emilie knew the gesture well. He was hiding the beginnings of a smile. Given half a chance, Father would help his nieces paint the sign. He was probably already designing it in his mind's eye. If only Mother weren't here, it would be easy to talk him out of his dark mood over her foray into the press room today.

But Mother was here, and she wasn't deferring the conversation to Father. "So that's why you're so late," she said. "I was worried it meant there was a problem with the music." She settled back in the chair.

"The Spring Sisters sound wonderful," Emilie said. She relaxed a little. "April's chosen the perfect repertoire for the week. And they're all in good voice. We'll do the family proud." She began to remove her gloves, but then remembered the ink beneath her nails. She laced her fingers together instead—hoping she looked more relaxed than she felt. "I'm late because April insisted we all have a light supper before we practiced." She chattered on. "The Penner twins were at the house when we first got there, and you know how they are. The way they were hanging on Bert and flirting, poor Junie was fit to be tied. She really does care for Bert—even if she is only sixteen. I hope Bert's paying attention. They'd be a great match."

When Mother didn't seem inclined to discuss the romantic possibilities looming before her nieces, Emilie veered back to coming events. "We'd just finished practicing when Uncle Roscoe brought a copy of the Chautauqua program in. I stayed so the cousins and I could talk over the offerings and decide what we might attend together."

They had actually spent more time planning which sessions to skip, but that was just semantics. Emilie took a deep breath and looked over at Father with a bright smile. "Did the meeting with Mr. Shaw go well? Are you going to feature him in the *Dispatch*?"

Father ignored the question. Instead, he looked over at Mother. Emilie followed his gaze. Something passed between them. Finally, he said, "The hour is late, and I see no reason to belabor this." He cleared his throat. "I have decided that this week's Ladies' News will be your final foray into journalism." He paused. "When you write the article, be certain to include sincere good wishes to your successor."

Successor. The word landed like a blow. "B–but—you said we'd talk—you—"

"And we *are* talking," Father said. Again, he looked at Mother. Was it Emilie's imagination, or was he pleading with her to say something?

Mother spoke up. "We understand that you will be disappointed, and we do not take that lightly, dear. One of the most difficult things any parent faces is the necessity to do the hard things that cause momentary conflict but that will, in time, yield long-lasting benefit for a beloved child."

Father nodded. "That is the very principle upon which I based my support when you wanted to attend the Female Seminary in Rockford. Your mother had her doubts, but I argued that a short season of pain at being separated from her only child would yield lasting benefit for you."

Pain at being separated? Emilie rejected the notion. Mother hadn't felt pain. She'd been relieved. Not one of the letters she had sent to Emilie in northern Illinois had said a thing about missing Emilie. Not one.

Emilie took a deep breath. She turned away from Mother so that Father could see the tears brimming in her eyes. "I learned to think for myself. That's a benefit, isn't it? You haven't forgotten what you said the day I left, have you? 'Don't be led along like a bleating sheep,' you said. 'Make up your own mind. Examine the facts. Form your own opinions.'"

The tears didn't do any good. Father was clearly more concerned with Mother's feelings and opinions tonight. "When I said those words, I did not mean to encourage rebellion. I was envisioning my daughter taking her place among the leading women in our community. Well-equipped to tread in her mother's footsteps—with newly acquired grace." He sighed. "I have perhaps encouraged you too much when it comes to the subject of independence." He glanced over at Mother. "And I most certainly did not encourage thoughts of a career in journalism."

Words tumbled out. "Since when is it 'too much' to want to learn? To want to be engaged with what's going on in the world?"

"*The world*," Mother said, "as you seem to define the term, is not something with which a lady concerns herself, Emilie Jane. And it's time that you accepted the simple facts of your birth." She sighed and shook her head. "Sometimes I think you resent being born a woman. I don't understand why you must always challenge everything. The boundaries protect us, Emilie. Why can't you see that?"

Resentment and simmering anger bubbled up. Emilie wanted to scream. What did Mother know of the world? She lived beneath a glass dome where everything was sunny and rosy and ladies made afternoon calls and conducted fund-raising bazaars to support causes. They threw money at problems. They never got their own hands dirty doing real work. Angry tears threatened. She blinked them away. And then, quite deliberately, she removed her gloves, laid them in her lap, and crossed her hands in a way that exposed the honest results of the afternoon's experience setting type.

Two spots of color appeared on either side of Mother's aristocratic nose as she looked at Emilie's hands. She rose from her chair and went to the doorway leading into the back hall. "Come to the kitchen when you and Father are finished discussing the Ladies' News," she said. "I'll prepare what you need to take care of that."

"I don't need your help," Emilie said. "Dinah told me what to do."

Mother sighed again. "All right, then. I'll excuse myself and leave the two of you to discuss the rest of this business." She crossed to where Emilie sat and bent down for a good-night kiss, murmuring, "I'll ask Dinah to make cinnamon biscuits for breakfast."

The faint aroma of Mother's perfume softened Emilie's anger. As did the mention of cinnamon biscuits. Mother always apologized through Dinah's cooking. Perhaps there was still hope, especially if she was going to leave and give Emilie a chance to talk to Father alone.

But Father called for Mother to wait for him. As he rose from his chair, he said, "If you have any notes that would help with the next column, you can bring them with you in the morning. I'll see that Mrs. Penner gets them."

Mrs. Penner? With a sharp intake of breath, Emilie said, "Mrs. Penner? As in—Fern and Flora's mother?"

"Do we know any other Mrs. Penners?"

"She was quite pleased to be asked," Mother added with a gentle smile.

"Of course she was." Emilie snorted. "You've just handed one of the worst gossips in town a captive audience." She glowered at Mother. "This is all *your* doing, isn't it?"

Father broke in. "Mind your tongue, Emilie Jane. Whatever her faults, Mrs. Penner is a tireless and devoted member of your mother's Ladies' Aid Society—and one of Mother's oldest friends. And do not seek to lay blame at someone else's feet. *You* are the one who stepped into that print room today and emerged looking like some hapless immigrant mill girl."

Emilie swallowed. She blinked back tears. She'd lost. She could have made Father see reason—if only they could have spoken alone. Just the two of them. But Father was already at Mother's side, preparing to retire with her. "My penchant for sparing you the consequences of your choices over the years has not served you well," he said. "I see that now, and I'm moving to correct that mistake." He forced a smile. "Once you've calmed down, I doubt you'll be all that disappointed, anyway. You weren't really happy writing the Ladies' News. And to be quite candid, a lighter hand and a more. . .*feminine*, for lack of a better word, tone will not be a bad thing for the column."

The words hewed a new wound. Father had just said that her journalistic voice wasn't feminine. A lighter hand would be more fitting for the Ladies' News. A *different* hand. And Father never "lacked for a better word." He always said exactly what he meant, which was one reason he and Emilie got along so well. She hated the way women talked around things instead of about them.

All was silence in the study, while Emilie fought the urge to raise her voice. To cry. To beg. None of which, she knew, would move Father, and all of which would only serve to assure Mother that they'd just done the right thing. Mother had no inclination to come out and be honest about what she thought—or felt—about things. She called honest arguments "unseemly emotional outbursts."

Taking a deep breath, Emilie willed her voice to remain calm and steady as she rose from her chair, her gloves clutched in one hand. "I should see to my hands."

Something in Father's expression shifted. Was that relief shining in his eyes? He gave a little nod.

Mother spoke again. "In time, you'll see that this was for the best, my dear."

Emilie turned to go, pausing just long enough to look back at Father. "When I was setting type today, I heard that the daily print run will increase by thousands during the assembly." She swallowed and allowed the bitterness she felt to sound in her voice. "Thousands of people could have read my work. How could you take that away from your own daughter and give it to Hazel Penner? How could you?"

She made her way out into the hallway and into the kitchen. Father called after her in a gentle voice she hadn't heard in a long time. She heard Mother murmur something. She ignored them both, moving from pantry to kitchen table to stove and back again until she had everything she would need. She warmed water and mixed Dinah's concoction, then dipped all ten fingers into a bowl. And as she sat there staring at the squares of pale light cast onto the kitchen floor by the moonlight streaming in the windows. . .she wept.

CHAPTER 4

Noah Shaw (born LeShario) loved walking at night. It was a habit borne of necessity, for once he'd appeared on a small-town stage, "The Man of Many Voices" effectively surrendered anonymity. To have any chance of privacy, any chance of simply enjoying new surroundings, he'd learned to do so by moonlight.

Standing out in a crowd wasn't a new phenomenon. It wasn't even all that bad. He owed his career to it. Being tall for his age had landed him his first dramatic role—Abraham Lincoln in a second-grade school pageant—and in every school pageant thereafter until Ma died.

When his voice dropped into the lower registers and his schoolmates were still squeaking and squawking, that saved him more than one fight after school. The average boy from Missouri might not like the idea of Italian last names and dark Sicilian coloring, but no one was going to pick a fight with a boy who sounded like a full-grown man, who towered over them, and whose dark eyes warned them away. *"I'm not looking for trouble, but if you start some, I'm not the type who runs."*

In point of fact, Noah LeShario had rather enjoyed being different—until, at the age of eleven, he fell head-over-heels in puppy-love with blond-haired, blue-eyed Sally Bennet, a newcomer to St. Charles, Missouri. Sally took a shine to spindly Eldridge

Mason, who had his very own pony, which he rode to school every day. No one had ever been allowed to so much as touch the creature until Sally. Once Eldridge showed her how to give his pet sugar cubes, the two of them spent nearly every recess near the tethered pony. And Noah knew jealousy for the first time.

The day he finally rounded up the courage to try to lure fair Sally away from both the pony and its owner by offering to help her practice her part for the upcoming school pageant (in which he would, of course, be Abraham Lincoln), Sally snubbed him. Later that day, Noah heard her snickering about it with Eldridge Mason. "Surely if he only used soap more frequently," she sneered, "some of that brown would wash off."

The wound opened by those words festered, until one day Noah decided to take action. He'd seen how Ma lightened lace and fabric and how she removed stains. Maybe the recipe would help him look more like fair-skinned Ma—and less like he needed a bath in the eyes of Sally Bennet.

Buttermilk made no difference at all. Lemon juice failed, too.

Ma caught him just as he was dipping a rag into oil of turpentine. "What do you think you're doing!"

Noah ducked his head. "I don't want to be Sicilian. I want to be American. And I want to look like you."

When Ma finally got the whole story out of him, anger flashed in her blue-gray eyes. She cupped Noah's chin in one hand and leaned down to stare into his dark eyes. "You got your good looks from one of the best men who ever walked this earth—a man who died saving my life and yours, too. Don't you ever let me catch you trying to erase God's handiwork again, do you hear me?" She couldn't say any more. Tears choked off her words.

The idea that he'd made his little mother cry broke Noah's heart. He flung his lanky self into her arms and choked out an apology. That night after Ma was asleep, Noah crept across the room they shared above a bakery to retrieve the small mirror atop her dresser. Moving over to the window, he looked at himself in the moonlight. *I look like Pa. He was brave.*

After that night, Ma began to talk about the past more often. In the evenings, she'd sit with handwork in her lap and tell stories "from the old days" while she sewed. About heading west to start a new life and camping under the stars at night. About the other argonauts on the trail. About the soldiers who guarded the way. About Pa dying and a freighter taking pity on her and letting her ride with him back to Nebraska City. About working her way home to Missouri on a steamboat called the *Laura Rose*. About losing everything and being lonely and then—having God bless her with a baby boy who looked just like his Pa. In time, Noah realized that he didn't really like Sally Bennet anymore. Eldridge Mason could have her.

Noah was thirteen when Ma took ill. She was only sick for a few days, but pneumonia settled into her lungs and took her life. Noah was sent to live with a distant cousin he'd rarely seen, even though she lived in nearby St. Louis. It didn't take Noah long to understand that Cousin Beulah would do "her Christian duty," but she despised it and would rejoice on the day it was once and for all fulfilled.

A year later, being different came in handy again. Noah might have been only fourteen, but he was over six feet tall and strong as an ox when he stowed away on a freight car one night, bent on riding as far away from Cousin Beulah and her black snake whip as possible. Before long he was loading and unloading freight cars. Helping unload a theatrical troupe in Kansas City introduced him to Professor Harry Gordon, and Professor Gordon introduced him to Shakespeare and Whitman, Dickens and Coleridge, Byron and Shelley and Keats. And now, ten years and what felt like a lifetime later, Noah Shaw had educated himself and found a life in which his big voice and his height and even his dark looks all gave him an advantage.

Using Mother's maiden name had been Professor Gordon's idea. "There is no reason to give people an excuse not to hire you, my boy. It's as wrong as it can be, but that statue to liberty they put up in New York harbor a few years ago hasn't done a thing to change the average American's opinion of the tired and poor if they happen to be Italian or Irish." He'd pronounced it Eye-talian, to make his point. "As long as Eye-talian means the same thing as Papist, that's two strikes against a man. What was your mother's name before she married?" He'd waited for Noah to respond and then nodded. "There you have it. Be Noah Shaw. It's a good English name. Protestant, too. Oh, I know it could be Irish or Scot, but you just let people think your roots go deep in the land of the Bard himself. That's perfect for a theatrical career."

Noah had felt guilty about it for a while, but then he decided there was nothing wrong with paying tribute to a woman by using her name. Pa had loved her, too. He'd understand. And so here Noah Shaw stood in southeastern Nebraska, at the place where the prairie met the edge of Beatrice in Gage County, gazing up at a clear night sky. He was looking forward to the moonlit walk about the Chautauqua grounds and along the banks of the Blue River. He'd be able to listen to the same night sounds he imagined Ma and Pa hearing about twenty-five years ago when they'd camped on the banks of this very same river.

Once he'd stepped through the arched entryway to the Chautauqua grounds, Noah paused and looked up to locate the Big Dipper in the night sky. Next he found the Bear, which spread out from the Dipper, and then Orion and the Pleiades. He smiled. Ma had embroidered the Big Dipper and the Bear on the surface of the quilt rolled up inside the duffel back in his hotel room. It was his only physical connection to her. He wasn't certain which he valued more, the quilt or Ma's stories about the things she'd embroidered on it. He didn't know how old he'd been when she began calling him her "Little Bear." That had transformed to "Bear" when what she called his "growly voice" emerged. They'd laughed about it, and she'd drawn a real bear standing on its hind legs and added it to the quilt she was making for him.

An owl hooted. As Noah glanced in the direction of the sound, he caught a moonlight glimpse of a great bird swooping down out of a tree and landing in the tall grass up ahead. Ma had embroidered an owl on his quilt. A wagon wheel and flames of fire. It was almost as if the old bedroll was coming to life as he imagined wagons camped nearby and campfires flickering over by the river.

When he finished here in Beatrice, he'd be headed to the Long Pine Chautauqua, some three hundred miles north and west of here. He wondered if he'd have a chance to see a live buffalo out that way. They were almost extinct now, but Ma had told him about seeing herds that spread across the prairie like a dark wave. What that must have been like!

He stood still and closed his eyes, listening to the sound of the prairie at night. And he said a prayer for this season, which was about much more than monologues and storytelling. This season was a quest. Somehow, somewhere in the broad expanse of the western sky, Noah LeShario Shaw hoped to find the piece of himself that had always seemed to be missing.

At the sound of footsteps on the wide porch just outside the kitchen door, Emilie snatched her fingertips from the bowl of warm water on the table before her. She stood up, hoping the sound of her chair scraping the floor wouldn't carry to the bedrooms upstairs. Drying her wrinkled fingers, she went to the door and peered out, smiled, and opened the door to Bert.

"You should be home by now." She glanced past him toward the drive and the hitching post. "And where's Royal?"

"As if I would take your horse and leave you trapped here all day tomorrow." He hesitated. "I couldn't head home until I knew you were all right."

With a glance behind her, Emilie stepped out onto the porch and closed the door behind them. "They've taken the Ladies' News column away."

"Oh, Em." Bert reached for her hands and gave them a quick squeeze. "I'm so sorry."

She almost leaned in to have him comfort her, but instead she squeezed back and let go. "I'll be all right." She took a deep breath. "It's just a detour."

"But you loved writing for the paper."

Emilie shrugged. "Father said something tonight that made me realize it was the *idea* I liked—not the assignment. It wasn't really much in the way of real news. Just a list of events. Apparently Mother disapproved of even that—much more than I realized." She paused. "This was going to happen sooner or later. Father as much as told me that tonight. 'Actions have consequences,' he said. And he couldn't spare me anymore. Not if he wanted to keep the peace at home." She paused. Forced a little laugh.

"He gave the column to Mrs. Penner. If she can do it, why would I even care about their taking it away?" Still, her voice wavered and she had to bite her lip to keep from crying again. Because she did care. Even if it wasn't much, it had been hers. Her name in print.

"Well, don't give up," Bert said. "People everywhere are going to read Emilie Rhodes someday. I just know it."

Emilie kissed his cheek. "You are the best friend a girl could ever hope for."

Bert pointed up at the moon. "Nice night for a walk."

"It is," Emilie agreed, "but Father laid down the law. And now that my fingers are all prune-y from getting the ink out from beneath my nails, I have to get upstairs and write that farewell column." She glanced toward the carriage house. "You really should save your leg and ride Royal home. Mother has plans to keep me tied to her apron strings all day tomorrow. I won't need him."

"I have a feeling you'll think of a way out of it—and wish you had your horse. Besides, like I said, it's a nice night for a walk." Bert paused. "You're sure you're all right?"

Emilie thought for a moment, surprised that she could honestly say she was. "Not that I didn't have a pity party a little while ago, but I'm all cried out." She took a deep breath. "I'll be fine. And I'll see you Thursday evening at the opening ceremonies."

"Save me a seat."

"I thought the Penner twins had that taken care of."

Bert cleared his throat. "Friends do not let friends get hornswaggled by the Penner twins. Save me a seat." He stepped off the porch and headed into the night, whistling as he walked.

Back inside, Emilie hurried to pick up after herself in the kitchen and then tiptoed up the back stairs and into her room. Once she'd lit the lamp at her desk, she spread out the assorted bits of paper in the folder Father had handed her earlier: cryptic notes from this member of that committee and that chairman of this board. Ice cream socials, quilting bees, silent auctions, Ladies' Aid meetings, chorale recitals, and of course the opening exercises for this year's ten-day Interstate Chautauqua.

Now that the Ladies' News wasn't hers anymore, organizing the bits of paper and rewriting the information made Emilie feel weary. There was so little room for creativity in any of it. Which was probably why she'd charmed Will Gable into showing her more of the "behind the scenes" workings of the paper. . .and come out of the press room *looking like some hapless immigrant mill girl.*

Father's words still smarted. She couldn't think of another time when he'd spoken to her with the harsh tone he'd used today. At least not for an entire portion of a day. He always relented, and he usually gave her what she wanted. Hadn't April Spring said as much when they were growing up? *Emilie Jane Rhodes, you are so spoiled.* Apparently that season of life was over.

Thoughts of the Spring Sisters set her mind to whirling once again about the Bee Hive. She had to find a way to join them. She looked down at the announcements submitted for the Ladies' News. Doing an exemplary job with her farewell column might be a good start:

The Ladies of the First Methodist Church remind everyone attending the upcoming Chautauqua that Stewart Boarding Hall on the grounds will once again offer fine fare daily. The ladies are organized and ready to assuage the hunger of as many as three hundred diners at each meal. Homemade pie will be offered on a first-come, first-served basis for each luncheon. Cake at the evening meal. Come one, come all, and know that you are supporting a good cause. Proceeds will support various mission efforts at home and abroad.

—w—

Elocutionist Miss Ida Jones will offer daily instruction in the Elocution Room at WCTU Hall located on the grounds of the upcoming Chautauqua. Daily lessons will commence at ten o'clock each morning. Miss Jones will also offer private tutoring sessions in French, German, and elocution, beginning on Thursday, June 24, and continuing through July 12, whereupon she must depart in order to benefit those attending the event scheduled in Long Pine, Nebraska, the end of this month. Miss Jones is widely known for her unique method of instruction, and our Interstate Chautauqua is indeed fortunate to have her stop in our fair city. Inquire at the Paddock Hotel to reserve an appointment for private instruction. Many will undoubtedly wish to take advantage of the opportunity to purchase Miss Jones's privately published "Favorite French Phrases" and "German for Gentlemen."

—∞—

Miss Ida Jones will give her renowned lecture:

"Resolved: That woman has as much influence in the nation as man"

Check the special Chautauqua Edition of the Daily Dispatch *for further details.*

After penning the announcements about Miss Ida Jones, Emilie sat back. Father might veto the idea of highlighting that last announcement, but surely the ladies who read the *Daily Dispatch* would appreciate the newspaper's emphasizing such a topic. She pondered the lecture title. It was hard to imagine anyone believing that a woman could have as much influence as a man. The women she knew didn't have any influence at all—at least not when it came to things that really mattered such as politics and business.

She looked back up at the Methodist ladies' announcement about pie and cake and "mission efforts at home and abroad." As far as Emilie knew, that was the only acceptable way for women to have influence in the nation—or the world, for that matter. No one looked askance at a woman selling cake so that she could send money to missionaries in China—or to the Pawnee students attending the boarding school in Genoa up in Nance County. The latter was one of Mother's pet projects. Mother thought the single missionary ladies who served on Indian reservations heroic. Wasn't it interesting that a woman who thought it was perfectly all right for someone else's daughter to socialize with Indians declared her own daughter's writing for a newspaper unacceptable. How ironic. How hypocritical.

Emilie looked over the announcement again. How did Miss

Jones manage to travel the lecture circuit and still maintain the kind of reputation that encouraged Chautauqua boards to invite her to speak? How wonderful to be free to travel from place to place: to teach and speak about things one cared about; to be independent, with no one to answer to but oneself; to make a living from words. Whatever Emilie did over the next few days, she would make it a point to attend Miss Jones's lecture and to linger afterward to ask a few questions.

Inspiration struck. *I could request an interview.* In fact, she could interview all the women teaching or speaking over the next ten days. She could give them a chance to express their views to the thousands of ladies who'd be coming from all over this part of the country to attend Chautauqua. Emilie's mind raced from one possibility to the next, and then, as quickly as she'd gotten excited about the idea, things came to a grinding halt.

If Father wouldn't let her continue with the Ladies' News, there was no possibility of his publishing interviews. That was, after all, real news. Something that people might actually read. Something that could give Emilie a chance to use her writing talent. If she'd ever had any. She glanced over at the trunk that held the books and papers from her year away at Rockford. Excellent marks on school papers might not translate to newspaper interviews. But then again, who was to say they wouldn't? She wouldn't know until she tried.

What had Bert said just moments ago? *"People everywhere are going to read Emilie Rhodes someday."* She reread the announcement about Miss Jones. Taking a deep breath, she put her final Ladies' News in the folder for Father. And she decided that somehow, in the midst of delivering it and going to rehearsal and helping Mother get set up out at the cottage, somehow she would manage to interview Miss Jones and take the resulting article to Father. Somehow she would convince him that the female portion of his readership would be fascinated to read interviews conducted by a woman. She smiled.

Another View. The perfect title. And if Father refused to publish it—well, the *Beatrice Daily Dispatch* wasn't the only newspaper in town.

A new challenge reared its head. Father had already interviewed a Mr. Shaw. If she wanted the scoop concerning Miss Jones, she would need to conduct the interview as soon as the woman arrived at the Paddock Hotel. All the speakers stayed there, but there'd be no chance of preempting Father if Mother ruled Emilie's every waking moment tomorrow, and she was depending on help with the cottage.

Getting the place ready for habitation was no mean task. Dinah's husband Calvin had hauled camp cots and cleaning equipment out there today. He'd probably done some cursory cleaning, but Mother would never be satisfied with that. She would insist that cobwebs be swept and walls be washed and floors be scrubbed. After that, Mother and Dinah would set up the "camp kitchen." They didn't really cook at the cottage—Dinah stayed at the house and made "picnic food" and delivered it every day. Still, Emilie had no doubt that Mother would think of all kinds of things for her to do.

With a sigh, Emilie plopped down on her bed. There had to be a way to make things work—to help Mother and still get that interview. She looked across the room at the folder lying atop her writing desk. At least the Ladies' News was done. She and Mother could get an early start. Except for the fact that Mother never got an early start anywhere.

And then. . .Emilie smiled. Bert had left her Royal. She could leave at sunrise if she wanted to, riding into town to leave a note for Miss Jones with the night clerk at the hotel and then going on to the grounds. She could have most of the scrubbing and cleaning done before Mother so much as drove up in the buggy. They could be finished by early afternoon.

It was perfect. Father would be pleased that she'd written the final Ladies' News without any further protest. Mother would be pleased with Emilie's hard work. And then—then Emilie would be free.

She returned to her writing desk and wrote a note explaining that she'd gone on ahead. Mid-note, she looked out her window and realized that the moonlight was so bright it was casting shadows as it shone through the trees. Why spend the next few hours tossing and turning in anticipation of the day ahead? She could leave right now. All she would need was a change of clothes for rehearsal with the Spring Sisters. She could fit everything in a carpetbag.

Emilie finished the note to her parents. Next, she penned an interview request to leave at the Paddock on her way through town. And then she packed a bag.

CHAPTER 5

Noah stood beneath the roof of what the locals called "The Tabernacle." Not much was visible in the night, but as he meandered across the fresh sand spread over the ground—benches would likely be hauled in and arranged tomorrow—he imagined the thousands of people who would crowd those benches.

He made his way past the uprights supporting the permanent roof and finally up the stairs and onto the stage. Glancing off toward the Blue River, he once again imagined campfires glowing in the night. He closed his eyes and listened. Frogs croaked and locusts buzzed. A lone coyote howled. A chorus of barks answered.

Taking a deep breath, he walked to the edge of the stage and looked out, imagining a sea of faces looking back at him. Expecting... expecting what. Would they want to be challenged? Encouraged? Comforted? Convinced? He was glad he'd have a day to wander the grounds before he actually had to mount this stage and face the audience. It would give him time to get a sense of things. Not every audience wanted Shakespeare. Of course if the G.A.R. had a strong presence, he would definitely do the St. Crispin's Day speech from *Henry V*. Depending on how many young people frequented the evening assemblies, he might tell Twain's story about the jumping frog. Boys especially enjoyed that one.

Tonight, though, Noah wasn't really in the mood for humor.

Taking a deep breath, he gazed over the imaginary crowd and began. "Ladies and gentlemen, I have found that audiences in Maine and Georgia and Missouri and California and, I hope, Nebraska"—he paused to allow for the expected smiles and chuckles to ripple through the crowd—"all share the same curiosity about speakers they have not heard before." He made a joke about himself and then mentioned the article about himself in the *Daily Dispatch*. William Rhodes should appreciate that. It never hurt to befriend a newspaper editor.

He'd just segued his introduction to the Shepherd's Psalm—he'd recite that at the opening exercises—when he thought he heard a scream. He glanced toward the river. A coyote? He was imagining things. But the second scream convinced him. Very real. And coming from—the direction of that row of little cottages he'd walked past earlier. Empty cottages, he'd thought, although now, as he jumped down off the stage and trotted out from beneath the overhang, he saw a light glimmering in a window. And heard another scream. A woman.

Noah ran.

—∞—

Emilie had been standing, frozen with fear, but with the second scream, she managed to move. She'd barely managed to keep from dropping the lighted oil lamp when the flickering light revealed that thing. *I could have burned the place down.* At least she'd managed to set the lamp down atop the old table. But now what?

Her heart pounding, her eyes on the vile creature curled up in the opposite corner of the cottage parlor, she stepped back. And back. And back until, finally, she sensed the closed door behind her and grasped the glass doorknob. And there she stood.

She couldn't just leave the lamp burning, but there was no way on earth she would be able to muster the courage to reverse her steps.

Even if that thing didn't seem inclined to attack. She shuddered. She would step out onto the porch and regroup. Maybe it would leave. She would keep the door open and watch from a safe distance. Maybe she could outwait it. Maybe the light from the lamp would make it do. . .something.

Slowly, she turned the doorknob and felt the catch release. Taking a deep breath, she stepped to one side, flung the door open, and whirled—directly into the arms of a stranger. She screamed again, before clinging to him like a five-year-old girl welcoming her father home from the newspaper office.

When the stranger rumbled that things were "all right," Emilie backpedaled away from him, nearly tripping off the edge of the porch. He reached out to catch her lest she fall. She waved him off and pointed at the open door. "S–s–snake."

The stranger stepped to the doorway and peered in. "It's just a bull snake."

He was tall. Very. . .tall. And rather good-looking—at least based on the side of his face illuminated by the lamplight. Emilie hugged herself and took another step away. "Who are you? And what are you doing out here in the middle of the night?"

"Noah Shaw," he said. His voice was deep, but gentle. Calming. "And prior to charging across an open field to rescue a damsel in distress, I was practicing one of my monologues over on the Tabernacle stage."

"In the dark?"

Mr. Shaw shrugged and glanced back into the cottage before answering. "I'm accustomed to tents. I wasn't certain what it would be like—how to project." He paused. "And I assumed I'd have the grounds to myself at this hour."

Shaw. After hearing Father talk about Noah Shaw, she'd envisioned spectacles and a bald pate, not someone so young. So handsome. Not someone like the man standing before her. She glanced down at the faded calico dress she'd donned before riding over here. Thankful for the low light, she said, "This is my parents' cottage. I came out here to get a head start on setting up camp." She shivered. "I didn't expect slithering company."

"If you didn't have the snake, you'd likely have mice or rats."

"You can set traps for mice," Emilie said. She looked past him toward the cottage door. "Are you sure it's safe? I mean—it isn't poisonous or anything?"

Shaw made a show of inspecting the snake, bending at the waist to rest his hands on his knees, pondering. Finally, he stood back up. "I'm quite sure it's safe. This one looks exactly like the ones that used to wreak havoc in my mother's larder when I was a boy."

"I suppose you rescued her, too."

He grinned. "I was quite the hero." He stepped into the room. There was a brief pause, and then he called out, "I've got him. Now what?"

Emilie crept to the doorway. The thing must be over three feet long. "What do you mean 'now what'? Kill it."

"Why? I daresay the poor snake has had nearly as bad a fright as you. How about I take him down to the river and let him go?"

Emilie sighed. That's exactly what Calvin would have done—had done, in fact, this past spring when he'd found an entire nest of bull snakes under the front porch at home. "If you must."

"I'll go out the back door. After I've let this one go, I'll return and inspect the premises to make sure he didn't have a companion—if you'd like me to, that is."

"Th–thank you." Emilie lingered in the doorway, watching as Mr. Shaw opened the back door and stepped into the darkness stretching between the cottage and the river. She should have asked him to take it farther away. What if it slithered back? She couldn't imagine staying out here now. What if there were other surprises lurking in the night?

She gazed up toward the bare rafters, and the lamplight reflected off the silken threads of a spider web. A large one. Its creator similarly large, poised right in the center of the web, waiting for a nocturnal feast. She brushed her forearms with her palms to rid herself of the imaginary sensation of an encounter with silken strands. With another shiver, she stepped back outside. Perhaps part of the reason Mother would linger over breakfast in the morning would be to allow Calvin plenty of time to come back out here and eradicate spiders and snakes. Suddenly, lingering over breakfast with Father and Mother had a certain appeal.

Mr. Shaw returned. She heard him close the back door, heard his footsteps as he inspected the premises. She thought of the Bee Hive and her cousins. The idea of a newly pitched canvas tent with a wooden floor sans crawlspace sounded grand.

Mr. Shaw appeared in the doorway. "All clear." He followed Emilie's gaze up toward the beams overhead. "Except for that."

"I'm not afraid of spiders." She didn't like the idea of Mr. Shaw knowing she was going to let a "little thing" like a three-foot snake scare her away. Even if it was true. "I'm all right now. You can go back to your practice session."

"Actually, I'd finished and was just about to head back into town when I heard you scream. Are you certain you're all right Miss—?"

Emilie reached up to tuck an errant curl back beneath the kerchief she'd tied about her head to keep her hair out of her way. Goodness. She was dressed like a washerwoman. Swallowing, she stammered, "R–Rhodes. Emilie Rhodes. Y–You met with my father earlier this evening."

And what did that smile mean, anyway? The Cheshire cat couldn't have had a better smile. "Well. Now that I know you're Mr. Rhodes's daughter, I must insist that you allow me to see you home. The man's about to publish an article about me. I shudder to think what he'd have to say if I left his only daughter stranded alone in the night."

"I'm far from stranded," Emilie said. "My horse is over at the stables."

"Stables?" He gazed off into the darkness.

"At the west end of the grounds. Just a short distance through those trees." As Emilie peered in that direction, an owl swooped out of a tree and alighted nearby. Its golden eyes flashed as it looked toward the cottage. Then it was gone, leaving the pathetic squeal of the poor creature clutched in its talons in its wake. Goosebumps prickled. Now that she really gave it some thought, she wasn't all that excited about walking over to the stables in the dark alone. She swallowed. "I suppose if you'd want to walk me over there—"

"Delighted. And then I'll see you home."

"It's in the north part of town. Past your hotel, in fact. I'll be fine. Really." She had stepped back into the cottage as they spoke. Now she bent to retrieve the key she'd dropped when she first saw the snake.

Shaw pointed to the carpetbag on the floor by the table. "May I?"

As he bent to retrieve her bag and then passed by on his way to the front door, Emilie realized how very tall he was. She turned the lamp down and followed him outside, locking the door and tucking the key in her apron pocket. *Apron. I'm wearing faded calico and one of Dinah's aprons.* She was a lot more embarrassed than she'd been earlier today when Father discovered her in the press room.

Mr. Shaw offered his arm. "Not to denigrate your Chautauqua grounds, but I nearly fell headlong running over here. Stumbled into a hole. You don't want to turn an ankle."

The moon came out from behind a bank of clouds, casting silver light all around. They could both see well enough to avoid any holes. Still, Emilie took his arm.

"So," he said after they'd walked a short way in the moonlight, "A Mr. Tomkins handed your father a folder while I was there—something about your column in the paper? I imagine he's very proud to have you take such an interest in his business."

Emilie grunted a short *hunh*. "Actually, the column was something of a consolation prize. I'd attended a year at a female seminary in Illinois, and I wanted to go back for the second year, but my mother objected. So Father created the Ladies' News. It gave me hope. At first."

"But hope didn't last."

She looked up at him. "What makes you say that?"

"Voices are my business. I hear disappointment in yours." He paused. "I know what it's like to long for an education you can't have. Although in my case, it was a matter of finances. My mother would have been thrilled to know I was attending a university somewhere. Anywhere."

"She might not have felt that way if you'd been a Norah instead of a Noah."

"I'm very sorry you were denied that second year. But that doesn't mean you can't learn. After all, that's what Chautauqua is all about, isn't it? Education for the masses. Including aspiring lady journalists."

Perhaps it was the fact that he didn't pry or that his voice was warm with what sounded like sincere interest; perhaps it was the combined effects of his rescuing her and being so kind; or the fact that he didn't make excuses for Mother. Maybe it was a little bit of everything, combined with the moonlight and the soft breeze rustling through the trees. Whatever it was, as they walked past the Tabernacle, Emilie said, "Actually, I turned in my last column today." Then she allowed a bitter laugh. "Mother didn't approve of my writing for the newspaper. And so I've been fired. By my own father."

"I am so sorry."

The sand that had been spread across the expanse of the earth beneath the Tabernacle roof glowed in the moonlight like a halo. For a brief second, Emilie envisioned Miss Ida Jones up on the stage, speaking on the topic of women's influence over a nation. She blurted out the question. “Do you know Miss Jones?”

“I beg your pardon?”

“Miss Ida Jones,” Emilie said. “She’s on the program with you. She’s supposed to give an address this week. Something about women’s influence over a nation.”

“Sounds fascinating. I’ll have to make sure I hear that.”

Emilie laughed. “It’s all right, Mr. Shaw. You don’t have to pretend.”

“Who’s pretending?”

He sounded sincere. But then voices were his business, and he probably had expert control over his. They were at the stables. Royal whickered and thrust his head over the stall door. He snuffled the carpetbag in Mr. Shaw’s hand. Emilie patted the gentle bay’s soft muzzle, slipped the bridle on, and led him out of the stall. “You were very kind to call me an aspiring journalist just now. The Ladies’ News is just a list of events. All I did was put the list in order and correct spelling errors and the like. There was very little real journalism involved.”

“Yet you’re sorry it’s ended.”

She handed Mr. Shaw Royal’s reins while she shook out the saddle blanket, then settled it on the horse’s back and smoothed it into place. “It’s my own fault. As I said earlier, my mother never really approved. And today at the newspaper office I finally committed the unforgivable sin.”

“Surely not unforgivable.”

She smiled in spite of herself. “I’m being melodramatic. Still, I lost the column.” She hoisted the saddle into place, tightening the girth strap as she explained. “I asked the man who runs the press to let me help him set type today. Father caught me at it.” She allowed a sad laugh. “I had ink under my nails, smudges on my face, my hair was a mess, and poor Father was horrified. He said I looked like ‘some hapless immigrant mill girl.’ And that was that. I’ve been replaced.”

"So soon?"

Emilie shrugged as she led Royal out of the stables and toward the arched gate in the distance. "Mother had a name in mind. I think she'd been hoping to end what she called my 'experiment with journalism' for quite a while. At any rate, I wrote the final column, left it for Father to take with him to the office in the morning, and here I am."

He stopped walking and looked down at her. "You ran away from home."

True or not, the comment made her sound like a spoiled child throwing a tantrum. "I left a note so they wouldn't worry. If it hadn't been for that snake, I'd have been ready to work at first light, and by the time Mother drove over, I would have had a nice surprise waiting for her."

"Peacemaker."

If it weren't for the gentle laughter accompanying the word, Emilie would have thought he was calling her a name. She chuckled along with him. "Don't give me too much credit. Conquering the dust motes and cobwebs in the cottage were also a means to an end."

They passed beneath the arched gate and turned onto the road. He looked down at her again. "You still want to write for the newspaper. Something more than a list of events."

Emilie let go of his arm. "You could not possibly have heard *that* in my voice."

"A slight change in tone," he said. "A little lift at the end of that last sentence that hints at renewed hope."

Was she really that easy to read? "When I asked if you knew Miss Jones, it was because I left a note with Alan Crenshaw at the Paddock before I rode out to the ground tonight. He's the night clerk. We went to school together." She was babbling. How embarrassing. "Anyway, I've requested an interview with Miss Jones. I'm hoping to convince my father to let me do a series for the *Chautauqua Express*, the paper he prints especially for those who attend the Interstate Chautauqua. From the ladies' point of view, as it were." When he said nothing, she defended the idea. "Don't you think the ladies in attendance would like to know more about the speakers?"

"Don't you think *everyone* would? Why assume only ladies would be interested in what you have to say?"

Emilie could feel herself blushing and was thankful that it was dark. "That's very kind of you."She paused. "I was going to suggest Ten for Ten as a series title. Ten questions asked of ten speakers for the ten editions of the *Chautauqua Express* to be published over the ten days of the event."

"That's a very creative hook," Mr. Shaw said. "Any chance you'd want to try your questions out on me?"

"It's probably not a good idea to imply that my Father didn't get the scoop on 'The Man of Many Voices,'" Emilie said.

He gave a dramatic sigh. "You 'crush me under the weight of your rejection,' mademoiselle."

Emilie laughed. "Don't be hurt. And it isn't fair to scold me with Shakespeare. Besides, for all you know, I can't write a complete sentence without four misspelled words and a dangling participle.

"And for all you know," he rumbled, "the real reason I'm here in Nebraska has almost nothing to do with the stage I was standing on when I heard you scream." He pointed up at the night sky. "I do love walking at night. When I was a boy, my mother used to tell me a story about the bear in the sky. . ."

Emilie listened, but she didn't really hear what he was saying about the sky. She was circling the hook Mr. Shaw had dangled before her about why he might really be in Nebraska. And thinking that interviewing him might not be a bad idea, after all.

CHAPTER 6

By the time he and the charming Miss Emilie Rhodes had crossed the bridge south of Beatrice and ambled on into town, Noah really didn't want to say good night yet. He couldn't explain it, but it was as if the curtain that usually existed between strangers didn't exist with her.

"It's only half a mile more," Miss Rhodes said. "I don't want you to have to retrace your steps in the dark."

"But it's nearly midnight, and I wouldn't be a gentleman if I let you go on undefended."

"It's Nebraska, Mr. Shaw." Miss Rhodes laughed. "There are no highwaymen waiting in the bushes to steal my carpetbag. And besides that, you'd regret your kind offer once you had half a mile of dark road facing you on the walk home."

"Who could object to half a mile of moonlight?"

"Half a mile of moonlight?" She shook her head. "All right, Mr. Shaw. How can I reject someone with such a creative bent for describing a walk down a dirt road in the dark."

He laughed. "I believe you've just summarized the difference between your desired profession and mine."

"Really?"

"I look north and see half a mile of moonlight. That's drama. You see half a mile of a dirt road. That's realism. Theater and journalism.

So tell me, which courses did you enjoy most at Rockford? I'd wager it wasn't the course on the romantic poets."

"Gambling is a sin, Mr. Shaw," Miss Rhodes said. Still, she gathered her horse's reins and began to walk north.

Noah caught up to her and asked about Beatrice.

"The accent is on the second syllable," Miss Rhodes said. "I know it sounds wrong—especially to a world traveler like yourself, but it isn't. It's from Julia Beatrice Kinney, one of the founder's daughters, and that's the way she pronounced her middle name, so that's the way we pronounce it. Put the accent on the first syllable, and everyone will know you're a stranger."

"Bee-AT-trice," Noah said and repeated it three times.

Miss Rhodes laughed. "Very good."

"Tell me more."

"Well, let's see. We're the third largest city in the state, and to hear my mother tell it, Father's a big part of the reason. In fact, sometimes I think that if she had her way, the town would be renamed Rhodesville."

"And what would Miss Kinney say to that?"

"Maybe she wouldn't know. She never did actually live here. I think she's somewhere out in California, lucky woman." She turned east on another road. "It's not far now. Just up ahead, actually." They'd only walked a short way when she stopped and muttered, "Oh no."

"What is it?"

It was as if the air around them trembled when Miss Rhodes looked toward the mansion silhouetted against the night sky. Even the horse seemed to sense the change in her mood, tossing its head and dancing away. She ordered it to settle down before speaking to Noah. "That lighted window on the second story? That's my mother's room." She picked up the pace a bit, and when the front of the house came into view, she sighed. "And that second light? That's Father's."

Someone exited the side door and hurried toward the carriage house just visible beyond the porte cochere. Emilie groaned. "And there's Father. I had so hoped to just slip in, retrieve the note I left for them, and sneak upstairs the back way. Now it looks like someone's raised the alarm. They probably haven't even seen my note." She sighed. "If you'll give me a hand up, Royal and I will catch up to Father before he gets the buggy hitched."

"I'll come with you," Noah said. "We can explain where you've been—and they'll know you weren't in any danger. Unless—but your Father knows me. Why would they be angry?"

"Mother will be upset because I was 'gadding about' alone at night, and Father will be angry because I've upset Mother. Again."

She sounded so miserable. Noah almost reached out to offer a comforting hug. Instead, he set her bag down, circled her waist with his hands, and boosted her into the saddle. With a surprised *oh*, she found the stirrup with the toe of her boot, then gathered the reins and motioned for him to hand her the carpetbag.

"Go on ahead," he said. "I'll bring it."

"Please just hand it over. I know you mean well, but your showing up will only create more trouble for me. The last thing I need is for my parents to think I've been wandering around with a strange man on a dark night."

"Your father knew I was headed out to the grounds to rehearse. I don't see how—"

She interrupted him. "You don't see how because you haven't met *Mrs.* Rhodes, the absolute queen of making mountains out of molehills. If you stroll up that drive with my carpetbag in hand, all my mother will see is her daughter and a man to whom she has not been properly introduced." She waggled her fingers in the direction of the bag. "Please. I really do need to hurry."

Noah gave her the bag.

The horse danced in place, seeming to sense her urgency. She held him back just long enough to say, "Thank you for rescuing me from slithers in the night. And don't think this means I'm letting you out of an interview."

"I won't. I still want to hear the rest of the story about BeATrice, the town born on a Missouri sandbar."

"And I'll be happy to tell it," Miss Rhodes said. "Assuming my parents don't lock me in my room as punishment for tonight."

Noah smiled as she cantered toward the house, her apron strings waving in the moonlight. He looked back toward town and then after Miss Rhodes. Was this really going to turn into a crisis for her? Or did a streak of the dramatic reside beneath that lovely exterior, after all?

Your father knew I was going out to the grounds. He'd thought that a good thing just now, but with Miss Rhodes hurrying off to explain her absence—and not wanting Noah with her—a flicker of worry niggled. If Emilie's mother really was in the habit of making mountains from molehills. . .if Emilie let it be known the way the two of them had met. . . *Emilie.* He was thinking of her as Emilie? He was. And he felt oddly protective of her. As if he should defend her somehow.

He looked down at his hands, touching fingertip to fingertip. Her waist had fit perfectly into that circle just now when he lifted her into the saddle. He wondered what color her eyes were by the light of day. If he ever expected to find out, he could not allow the remotest chance that Mr. and Mrs. Rhodes would think he'd sneaked away into the night.

Taking a deep breath, he headed up the drive toward the house.

—∞—

Emilie called, "I'm home," as she pulled Royal up just outside the wide double doors on the back side of the carriage house. Father had already opened them so that he could drive the buggy out, but by the time Emilie had dropped her carpetbag to the ground and dismounted, he'd turned Dutch back into his stall and latched it shut.

As he walked toward her, Emilie could see his face dimly illuminated by the one lantern he'd lit—the one hanging on the iron hook by the small door facing the house. He was furious. Again. As angry as he'd been earlier today when he dragged her out of the press room.

"Apparently you didn't see my note?" She tried to keep the tone just right. She didn't want to fawn. Then again, she did feel apologetic. She hadn't meant to worry them. This time, she'd actually planned things out and taken pains to explain her behavior.

"What note?" Father snapped.

The *t*s were emphasized. Not good. "On the breakfast table in the nook." She reached up to smooth Royal's mane as she talked. Maybe it would keep her hands from trembling so. "I finished the final Ladies' News. It's there, too—along with a note. I left everything where you'd see it first thing in the morning. So that you wouldn't worry."

"Your Mother was concerned after our talk. She went to check on you—and discovered your absence." He raked his fingers through his hair. Took a deep breath. "Do you have any idea how weary I am of trying to translate you to her—and her to you?"

"There's nothing to translate," Emilie said. "If you'd read my note, you'd know. I decided to ride out to the grounds and spend the night so that I could get to work cleaning the cottage at first light. I wanted to surprise Mother."

"Mission accomplished. I am surprised."

Emilie whirled about. Royal danced away, and there stood Mother. Fully dressed, albeit somewhat disheveled.

"I left a note," Emilie repeated.

Mother glanced at Father. Something passed between them, and

Father's scowl relaxed a bit. Mother's tone seemed almost conciliatory when she said, "After the way we ended things, I couldn't sleep. I lay there thinking over how you must be feeling—I just couldn't leave it that way. And so I knocked on your bedroom door. Imagine my surprise when I discovered you'd run away from home."

"But I didn't," Emilie insisted. "How many times do I have to say it? Here," she said, and held Royal's reins out to Father. "I'll prove it. You take Royal, and I'll go get the note I left."

"No." Mother waved for Father to join her. "You tend to Royal, Emilie. Your Father and I will go in. After all this excitement, I'll need a cup of tea before my nerves calm down, anyway." She bent to retrieve Emilie's carpetbag. "We were headed to Cornelia's first. I told your Father it was likely you would have confided in May."

Emilie sighed. For Mother to suspicion some plot with May wasn't all that unreasonable. But this time, May was innocent. "It was just an idea that came up tonight, while I was writing my final piece for the paper."

The three of them stood, looking at one another like combatants who wanted to call a truce but didn't quite know how. Royal pricked his ears and turned his head to stare into the shadows just past the house. He snorted and shook his head. When Noah Shaw emerged from those shadows, Emilie saw Mother put her hand to her hastily arranged coiffure and step back.

Mr. Shaw spoke first to Emilie. "You were very kind to release me from my duties escorting you home, but it just didn't seem right not to see you all the way."

Before Father could say a word, Mother had dropped Emilie's bag in the dust and blurted out, "You!" And then she looked at Father. Her tone was scolding as she said, "You didn't tell me that Mr. Shaw had already arrived in Beatrice. You should have invited him to dine with us this evening." She smiled at Mr. Shaw. "A dear friend of mine was at the Lake Mohonk Conference last year when you presented your paper. She could not say enough about you—about your lecture."

Mother was practically gushing like a nervous schoolgirl. Apparently, Noah Shaw was more of a celebrity than Emilie had realized. If he'd delivered a paper at the Lake Mohonk Conference on the plight of the Indian, there was more to him than a handsome face and a magical voice.

Father cleared his throat. "Mr. Noah Shaw, may I introduce my wife, Mrs. Henrietta Rhodes." He looked over at Emilie. "It appears that you have already made the acquaintance of our daughter, Emilie Jane."

Shaw smiled as if it was the most natural thing in the world for him to be standing outside a barn in the middle of the night with a young woman and her barely presentable parents. Did he have experience making amends with flustered parents? Emilie hoped not. Oh, she hoped not.

Shaw bowed over Mother's extended hand and thanked her for her kind words about the paper she'd referenced. Then he spoke to Father. "As I mentioned at the newspaper office earlier, I meandered out to the grounds to try out the stage. Of course I assumed I was alone. But then I heard a scream." He turned toward Emilie and motioned for her to take up the story.

Emilie repeated her plan to surprise Mother by cleaning the cottage. "But when I lit the lamp—" She shuddered. "A huge snake was curled up in one corner. I did manage not to drop the lamp." She glanced at Mr. Shaw, and he took the stage back.

"I arrived just after the second scream," he said.

"And he removed the snake." Emilie smiled at him.

"A bull snake," he explained.

"Not poisonous," Emilie added. "He carried it out."

"Let it go by the river." Shaw grinned at her. "Although there was mention of my 'killing the vile thing.'"

"But he convinced me to let it be," Emilie added. "And I suppose he had a point." She glanced at Father. "I remembered what you said to Calvin this past spring about the nest beneath the porch."

"So," Mr. Shaw explained, "the snake dispatched, I convinced Miss Rhodes to allow me to walk her home." He looked over at Father and then at Mother. "I wasn't blessed to have a sister, but if I had been, I know my mother would not have wanted her left alone on a dark night after such an episode."

"And so here we are," Emilie said. "And I'm so sorry for causing a stir." She looked once again from Mother to Father. "Truly sorry." She glanced at Mr. Shaw. "For inconveniencing everyone." Those dark, kind eyes. Looking at. . .the kerchief about her head. The worn calico skirt. The faded cotton apron. Looking away, she reached into the apron pocket and began to toy with the cottage door key. She dared a glance over at Mother.

Mother addressed Mr. Shaw. "William and I offer our sincere thanks to you. Emilie is a capable and brave young woman—except when it comes to snakes."

Brave? Mother thought she was brave? And capable?

Father was still annoyed, though. It sounded in his voice as he asked, "How is that you have Royal, Emilie? I told Hartwell to ride him home."

"Bert thought I might need him tomorrow. In case our plans changed."

Father just shook his head before reaching for Royal's reins and offering them to Mr. Shaw. "Thank you for seeing our daughter home safely. You're welcome to the horse if you'd rather not walk back to town at this abominable hour." He glanced at Emilie. "I'm pleased that you've finished the Ladies' News, but your plans for Wednesday have not changed."

Mother spoke up. "Now, William, there's no need to growl at the poor girl like a bear roused from his cave. Emilie's home, and all is well." She smiled at Mr. Shaw again. "In addition to helping me ready the cottage, our daughter has a rehearsal as soon as a piano is delivered to the Tabernacle stage. She's quite an accomplished pianist. She accompanies the Spring Sisters trio. I doubt you've heard of them, but the girls—Emilie's cousins—really are quite good and very popular. In fact, they are on the program at the Long Pine Chautauqua in the western part of the state in just a couple of weeks. It's to be their swan song, now that Emilie's eldest cousin, April, is engaged to be married."

Emilie felt like a third-grader being shown off to company. She was blushing as she grabbed her carpetbag and took a step toward the house. "Thank you again, Mr. Shaw. I hope the rest of your evening enjoys a distinct absence of screams and bull snakes."

As Emilie scooted past Mother, the older woman caught her free hand as she said, "You must allow us to show our appreciation for all you've done this evening, Mr. Shaw. Would you agree to join us for supper over at the cottage Thursday prior to the opening ceremonies?" She hesitated. "Of course we can only offer simple fare when we're camping—perhaps this evening would be more appropriate. Here at the house. Yes, I believe it would. Please say you'll come."

Father, who'd just returned from putting Royal in his stall, added his approval to the plan. "Superb idea, my dear. In fact, since you've just mentioned the Springs, why don't we invite them, too? The girls can give Shaw, here, a bit of a preview." He actually clapped Shaw on the back, and then he invited him inside for "a bit of refreshment to fuel your walk back into town."

Mr. Shaw accepted, and after he'd bowed to Mother and Emilie, he and Father headed inside like two old friends.

Mother put an arm around Emilie's shoulders and hugged her. Then with a low laugh as they headed inside, she said, "Imagine. My daughter screams, and who but Mr. Noah Shaw comes running out of the night to rescue her." She opened the screen door and waved Emilie inside ahead of her. "I'll have Dinah make her lemon pie. Or maybe rhubarb. Which do you think?"

Emilie shrugged. "Does it matter?"

"Well of course it does, dear," Mother scolded gently. "We want Mr. Shaw to enjoy his time with us." She pulled the door closed behind them. "Cornelia is going to be positively green with envy when she realizes who our dinner guest is." At the foot of the back stairs, she paused and gazed toward Father's study. "And Hazel? Oh, my goodness."

Emilie frowned. "Hazel?"

"Yes, dear. Hazel Penner. She's the friend who heard his lecture at the conference in New York. And she is going to be beside herself when she learns that the handsome Mr. Noah Shaw has been to dinner at our house."

Emilie continued up the stairs and on to her room. She might not be as angry as she'd been earlier about the Ladies' News, but that didn't mean she wanted to think about Mother's friend Hazel Penner—or chatter about Noah Shaw as if he were a prize to be won.

"He is very handsome," Mother said. "*And* unmarried."

CHAPTER 7

As the night sky began to pale in the east, Grace Jumeaux slipped out of bed and lit one of the gas lamps on the wall by her hotel room door. It had been a long night. A very long night. And now—it was time. She had to leave before the hotel manager arrived at work and learned that she still had not paid for her room. She remembered him well. Bushy eyebrows and a permanent scowl. Unlike that sweet young man who worked the desk at night, the day manager would have no hesitation when it came to pounding on her door and demanding money.

Quickly, she stepped into the dress she'd spent half the night remaking, removing yards of lace and replacing the expensive French buttons with simple jet. The newly attached buttons fastened, she rummaged in her trunk for a velvet-lined box and nestled the French buttons in place. If things did not go well today, perhaps a local dressmaker would buy them. They might bring enough to cover a simple meal. Maybe something besides eggs.

Reaching up to adjust her collar, Grace crossed the room and stared at herself in the mirror. Normally she would spend the next few moments camouflaging those circles beneath her eyes. She would redden her cheeks and lips and restyle her wig. Today, however, she would let her pale face and weary expression stand. As for the wig—she parted her thinning gray hair down the middle and brushed it until it shone before twisting it into a demure bun at the back of her head.

When it came to a proper bonnet, she'd done her best, covering over bright purple trim with a length of black ribbon she'd removed from another gown. She settled it atop her head, bringing it forward so that it would shade her pale forehead and tying the ends of the black ribbon beneath her chin. She stood back, barely recognizing the demure middle-aged woman in the mirror. The thought made her smile. For a brief moment, she was tempted to walk past the front desk just for the sake of seeing how complete a transformation she'd accomplished. She really didn't think the hotel manager would recognize her. But she didn't dare take the chance.

At the last moment, she opened the bottom drawer of the trunk. Bending down, she reached far to the back, feeling her way beneath the mounds of feathers and ribbon until she found the last bit of costume she needed for today's role. Closing the trunk, she locked it, then dropped the key into the small tatted bag that hung from her wrist.

She returned to the mirror once again, this time to try out several different ways of carrying the black testament. It needed to look natural. Like she was accustomed to toting a Bible along on morning calls. Finally, though, she laid it aside. Even the talented Madame Jumeaux would have difficulty making that seem believable.

She spoke to the woman in the mirror. "You look sufficiently pathetic. Josiah will either pull you into his arms or slam the door in your face. It's time to find out which it will be."

—⁓—

Grace looked down at the paper in her gloved hand and then back up at the simple, two-story white frame house. She'd walked right past it yesterday on her way to the hotel from the train station. Right past Josiah's house. How strange life could be. She'd been so close to him and yet, as Madame Jumeaux, she'd been entire worlds away.

An abundance of red geraniums bordered a brick walkway leading from the street up to the porch stairs. The porch itself boasted a white swing at one end and two rocking chairs near the front door. Grace could not imagine Josiah being content to while away the hours sitting on the front porch. Perhaps his wife—if he had one—had forced the issue. It made her smile to think of Josiah giving in to a woman. It would take quite a woman to make that happen. Someone strong-willed and independent. *Someone like me.*

Now that Grace was here, looking up the walk leading to the front door, she didn't know if she could go through with it. She almost turned away. But then a woman about her age opened the front door. She came to the top of the porch stairs and rested her hand beside a pot of geraniums sitting on the pedestal at the end of the porch railing. "Is there somethin' I can do to help you, ma'am?" she called out. "You been standing out there watchin' this house fer quite a spell."

Grace swallowed and took a few steps closer to get a better look at the woman. She couldn't imagine Josiah taking up with someone who spoke like a country bumpkin. "I—I was wondering if Mr. Barton—what I mean is—is this Josiah Barton's home?"

The woman smiled. She was missing one of her front teeth, and when she said, "This is," Grace imagined a fine spray of saliva exiting the woman's mouth. "I'm the colonel's housekeeper," the woman said. "Is there somethin' I can do to help you? The colonel's not here. But I expect him back in a few days."

Grace's hand went to the top button of her dress. All that trouble to look respectable, and Josiah wasn't here? She looked back up the street toward the hotel, and then the other way, in the direction of the railroad station. Fatigue and hunger washed over her, and for a moment she felt faint. Her hearing must be fuzzy. The housekeeper was talking, but Grace didn't quite catch the words. And her eyes weren't what they used to be, either. Or maybe it was the spectacles. Maybe she needed to have her eyes checked.

The housekeeper clomped down the steps and hurried to Grace's side. "Here now, you come up on the porch out of the morning sun and let Ladora get you a glass of water."

Grace let herself be led up onto the porch. While the housekeeper clucked her way back inside, she settled into one of the creaking rocking chairs and looked about. The porch floor had been painted in a pattern that replicated a tile floor. The ceiling was sky blue. A white wicker planter on either side of the front door boasted an abundance of ferns so healthy they hardly looked real. Of course that would be the case. The Josiah Grace remembered would never have allowed a less than perfect plant in a position of prominence on his front porch. What would people think? Which begged the question of a housekeeper with bad grammar, a missing tooth, and a rumpled apron in serious need of ironing.

The housekeeper stepped back onto the porch. She had a glass of water all right, but it wasn't in her hand. It had been positioned in the exact center of a blue-and-white saucer. Spode. The exact pattern she and Josiah had dined on in the house she'd sold a few months after he'd headed west as a private in the United States Army.

"There now." The housekeeper held the plate before her, waiting for Grace to take the glass of water. When she did, the woman sat down in the other rocking chair, setting the now empty saucer on the small round table between them.

Grace forgot to sip like a lady. Instead, she drank the water down in one long draught, then set the glass back atop the Spode saucer. "Thank you," she said. "I'm sorry I bothered you." She started to get up. "I'll be going now."

"Just like that?" The housekeeper leaned forward, her gaze steady. "What should I tell the colonel?"

"He's a colonel?"

The woman shrugged. "Never heard him called anything else."

"I thought—he was always quoting the Bible," Grace said. "I expected he'd be a minister by now."

The housekeeper shook her head. "Not so as he'd climb into a pulpit regular-like. He ministers a-plenty, though. In his way."

What a curious thing to say. Grace put her hand to her midsection, hoping to muffle her stomach's demands for more than water. A train whistle sounded. People would be milling about at the station. Perhaps she could manage success enough to buy breakfast. No one would pay any mind to a battered, gray-haired old woman. She rose from the rocking chair. "Thank you for the glass of water. I really should be going. I apologize for bothering you."

"Didn't bother me a bit," the other woman said. "The colonel's been gone nigh onto a month now. There's only so much a woman can do with a house without its people in it. No washing, no cooking—and about the third time I dusted the parlor I started feeling like some kind of fool." She laughed a mellow, low laugh. "Ladora," I said, "you are some kind of fool. The colonel don't care if you dust when he's here. Sure don't care about dust when he's gone."

Grace paused at the top of the porch stairs and looked behind her at the house. She knew all about rattling around in an empty house, waiting for a man to return. In fact, she and that housekeeper had waited for the same man, although if Josiah didn't notice dust on furniture, he'd changed some.

The housekeeper rose from her seat and picked up the empty glass and the Spode saucer. "A house is a strange place with its people gone. But the colonel? I've worked for him for nearly ten years now, and he never leaves it really empty. Gives me my time away when he's got no plans for travel. Makes sure I stay put when he's gone." The woman shook her head. "Would you believe he has me leave a note if I so much as go up to Klein's for groceries? It's like he's waiting for someone to show up. You had breakfast yet this mornin'?"

Grace almost missed the question, added as it was on the end of a monologue, almost as an afterthought. "Wh–what? I mean, excuse me?"

"You had breakfast yet? Because I wouldn't mind a bit of company. My sister—her name's Lila—sometimes she comes by and keeps me company awhile, but she's got some big doin's out at the house where she works today. Said she wouldn't have no time for it. I was sittin' there in the parlor just waitin' for the morning *Dispatch* when I seen you staring up at the house. And I wondered. So, you want some toast and eggs? Colonel Barton, he likes his eggs almost raw." The housekeeper shuddered. "Can't stand it. But I fix 'em just so's he likes it. When he's gone? Not on your life. Ladora likes her eggs cooked through. You like scrambled?"

"Well I—I don't—no, actually." Eggs. Again? If God was paying any attention at all to this conversation, He had to be laughing.

"Don't know? Never met a person don't know how they like their eggs. You don't have to eat 'em scrambled. I can fix eggs any which way, ya know. Or oatmeal. We got our own oat mill right here in Beatrice. Maybe you'd rather have oatmeal?" When Grace's stomach growled, the housekeeper laughed another rich, warm laugh. "Well now. To my mind that was a yes to oatmeal and a no to eggs." She nodded. "All right then. You come on in. I'll cook, and you can tell Ladora why you been standin' out there at the end of the walk afraid to come up and see the colonel."

She opened the screen door, then peered through the screen at Grace. Her voice softened. "You don't have to be afraid of him, you know. Some folks seem to think he's fearsome, but they don't know him. He's a right fine man, the colonel is."

The woman paused. Her countenance changed, and her gray eyes watered. "You one of the mothers? Oh my, I bet you are, and here I am going on and on like some idgit. I am so sorry, ma'am. You come right in here with Ladora. You can write it all down while I make that oatmeal, and then we'll have us a nice talk. And you know the colonel will do everything he can. If your boy can be found, he'll do it."

Grace had no idea what the fool woman was blabbering on about, but it didn't appear that she was going to have to worry about saying much to get a free breakfast of something besides eggs. After that—well. Josiah wasn't home. Maybe that could work to her advantage somehow.

Cinnamon. The aroma had wafted up the stairs and seeped beneath Emilie's bedroom door in the early morning hours, but she'd resisted its call, pulling the sheet over her face, trying to ignore the morning light pouring in her east-facing windows. Finally, though, she couldn't resist any longer.

Slipping out of bed, Emilie padded across to the door that opened onto the small balcony that looked out over the beginnings of a flower garden. Several of Mother's new plants had succumbed to the punishing heat this past month. And it was going to be hot again today. Already Emilie was dreading donning petticoats and chemise, white hose, and a long dress. Closing her eyes, she concentrated on the feeling of the cool morning air against the bare flesh of her feet and ankles.

She thought of the day ahead and how miserable it was going to be to clean the cottage and set up. At least Father had had screens installed on the windows for this season. How would people housed in tents stay cool? Would the Bee Hive have windows? Or would they have to roll up the sides of the tent to get so much as a breath of fresh air into the place? Thank goodness April had landed the spot beneath a shade tree. At least she said she had.

A constant stream of wagons would haul supplies and tents across the river today. Scores of men would swarm over the Chautauqua grounds, erecting the tents campers had reserved in recent weeks and much larger tents to house things like the park grocery store, a post office, and Taylor's photography studio. Last year there'd been a bookstore and a meat market, too. And then there was the dining hall, almost as big as a circus tent and claiming to seat three hundred, although Emilie had her doubts about that number.

By the end of the day, rows of benches would fill the space beneath the Tabernacle roof, and the groundskeeper would have finished planting the host of flower beds and planters scattered about the grounds. Thoughts of the Tabernacle made Emilie wonder if Noah Shaw would go back out there tonight after sundown to practice. She wouldn't mind hearing that wonderful voice recite one of her favorite poems. . .by moonlight.

He'd be surprised if, after teasing her about the romantic poets, he learned that Wordsworth was actually one of her favorites. She could almost imagine Shaw reciting the poem that had first drawn her to the beloved English poet's work:

She dwelt among the untrodden ways
Beside the springs of Dove,
A Maid whom there were none to praise
And very few to love:

A violet by a mossy stone
Half hidden from the eye!
Fair as a star, when only one
Is shining in the sky.

She lived unknown, and few could know
When Lucy ceased to be;
But she is in the grave, and oh,
The difference to me!

Would Noah Shaw laugh if he knew how much Emilie loved that poem? How would he spend his time today? And what should she wear to dinner this evening?

The thought surprised her. She'd never been one to primp before a mirror, and she'd never given much thought to the way she was dressed—until last night. First, when Bert commented about a hair ribbon matching her eyes. And then beneath the steady gaze of Noah Shaw's mesmerizing dark eyes. What was happening to her?

Stepping back into her room, she opened the doors of her cherry wood wardrobe and stood back, gazing at the rainbow of colors representing her dinner gowns. Emilie had always thought it ridiculous that Mother insisted they "dress for dinner." Today, though, she was actually looking forward to the chance to erase the image Noah Shaw had of her dressed like a cleaning lady, complete with a kerchief over her hair.

Reaching into the wardrobe, she drew out her white lawn skirt and a ruffled blouse, then gathered white hose and her white shoes. At least she could look nice for the rehearsal, just in case anyone happened by the Tabernacle. She grimaced. With her luck, Shaw would come to the cottage, right when she was in the middle of sweeping. She would wear the indigo gored skirt from last season. And a half-apron. Easy to snatch off if he showed up. Between the stylish skirt and the blue-and-white striped blouse that matched it, perhaps she could replace the image of a washerwoman in his mind. And there would be no kerchief about her head today, but rather a bit of red ribbon holding her hair in a loose French braid.

The aroma of coffee joined that of cinnamon biscuits. Dressing quickly, Emilie headed downstairs, hoping that she was right and that the cinnamon biscuits meant that Mother was still in a conciliatory mood. She really needed the prevailing winds to blow in her favor today. She nearly had her ten questions ready, and somehow she needed to find time to interview Miss Jones. And write an interview.

And present it to Father.

Hope faded when Emilie set foot in the kitchen. Dinah and her sister Ida, who worked for Aunt Cornelia, were already at work. The kitchen counters were barely visible beneath mounds of potatoes and carrots, stalks of rhubarb, bags of flour, cake pans, roasting pans, and a bucket filled with wildflowers. Emilie's heart sank. Even if they did finish over at the cottage, Mother would want Emilie to return home and help with preparations for this evening.

"You've gone and done it, now, young lady," Dinah said, as she measured flour into the massive bowl before her.

"Me? What did I do?"

Dinah didn't answer. She nodded toward the stove. "You'll have to serve yourself. Ida and I have too much to do to think about cinnamon biscuits."

Emilie retrieved a small plate from the pantry and did just that. What did Dinah mean that she had "gone and done it"? What had she done? She decided it best not to ask. Instead, she served herself two biscuits and then, setting the plate down, retrieved a coffee mug from the pantry. "I hope there's coffee left."

"Does my kitchen ever lack for coffee?" Dinah almost snapped the reply, then quickly apologized. "I'm sorry, miss. Of course there's coffee. I'm just a bit flustered. Mrs. Rhodes is in quite a dither. Pot roast won't do. It's got to be leg of lamb. And that means mint jelly, and we used the last of it at Easter."

Emilie gazed around her. All of this because Noah Shaw was coming to supper? Ah. So that was what she had "gone and done." She'd brought all this work down on Dinah's head. "Klein's probably has mint jelly," Emilie offered.

"And what if they do?" Dinah hefted a mound of dough out onto the floured table and began to knead it. "Calvin is already out at the grounds cleaning and scrubbing, and I can't exactly call up Mr. Rhodes and tell him to pick up mint jelly on his way home, now can I."

From where she stood at the sink, peeling potatoes, Ida let out a shout of laughter. "Ha! Wouldn't that be the day." Then she grinned at Emilie. "Men have no idea what it takes to serve up a meal, now do they? They just lap it up and ask for more—like some magician says 'poof' and there it is in the kitchen."

"I could get it," Emilie said. In fact, she wanted to get it. That might give her a chance to stop by the hotel and speak to Miss Jones. "I'd be happy to help"—she motioned around the kitchen—"with all of it. Anything you need. If Mother will allow it."

Dinah gave her "the look." The one that meant, "I don't know what you've got up your sleeve, Missy, but there's something there." She nodded toward the breakfast nook. "Mrs. Rhodes has been waiting for you to come down. Ida and I will see to the mint problem." She looked over at Ida. "Got some nice mint growing out in my kitchen garden. Think we could come up with a sauce?"

CHAPTER 8

Emilie left Dinah and Ida discussing mint sauces and substitutes and headed into the breakfast nook, relieved when Mother looked up with a smile. Still, she apologized for sleeping so late.

Mother only chuckled and laid her recipe book aside. "Not to worry, dear. You aren't in trouble. I've sent your grumbling bear of a father off to the office with my assurance that you and I are fully capable of having a civil discussion without him to referee." She looked pointedly at Emilie's ensemble. "That's last season's skirt, I believe?"

Emilie swallowed. "Yes. I thought—"

Mother didn't wait for her to finish her sentence, "As you know, I've never been one to approve of wearing out-of-date fashion, but that really is a classic line. It accents your tiny waist." She handed over the piece of paper she'd been perusing when Emilie joined her. "Tell me what you think of this evening's menu."

Emilie sat down and scanned the menu. Mother clearly didn't consider tonight a last-minute supper with a few friends. She'd listed oyster soup to be followed by boiled salmon with cream sauce, followed by leg of mutton served with fried apples and mashed potatoes. "I see you settled on rhubarb pie for dessert."

"Yes, but I've added the pound cake with whipped cream. Just in case anyone doesn't care for rhubarb pie. I'd hate to end the meal on a negative note."

At the bottom of the page, Mother had written a reminder to Dinah about "the usual condiments." That probably meant pickled beets, olives, piccalilli, dilled green beans, and at least two different jams or jellies for the Parker House rolls. And a plate of sliced tomatoes, cucumbers, and onions from the garden.

"You're—I mean we—we're asking a lot of Dinah on short notice."

Mother nodded. "I know. Which is why I talked Cornelia into sharing Ida for the day, in spite of her needing to set up camp out at the grounds. I promised her I'd help her all day tomorrow if she needs me, but Calvin is already over there." Mother paused. A smile played about her lips as she said, "Your father is going to ask Mrs. Fielding, the woman who cleans the newspaper office, if she'll take on the cottages for us. You and I have more important things to attend to."

"We do?"

"Well of course we do, dear. You have your rehearsal. And I can't be lollygagging about the Chautauqua grounds when I've a house full of guests arriving this evening. We have to put the leaves in the dining table and press the damask tablecloth—the gold one, I think. And all those napkins. We're going to have to work very diligently, or things will never be ready for Mr. Shaw."

She glanced out the nook windows. "And here come the girls now." Rising, she headed for the side door. "Cornelia's staying here to help me. You girls can go on over to the grounds in the buggy." Mother paused. "And I know you want to help them with their Bee Hive, but I really must insist that you get back here in time for a nice bath. A good soak—with lavender oil. Your father hauled a bucket of rainwater up to the powder room before he left this morning. Your hair will simply glow, dear." Mother smiled. "And please stop looking at me as if I've sprouted horns—or a halo. Aside from May's tendency to be a bit rowdy, your cousins, overall, are a very good influence."

"Does that mean I can—"

"Yes, yes," Mother said. "It means that you can join the girls in their adventure in independence. Just please try to maintain some sense of decorum. One never knows who one might encounter. I imagine all the men—people—on the program will be out and about today."

"Thank you, Mother," Emilie enthused. "Thank you so much." She popped the last bit of cinnamon biscuit in her mouth, delivered her plate and her coffee cup to the kitchen, and hurried outside.

This was Josiah's house. Grace stood in the entryway and looked around her while his housekeeper prattled on about the colonel. He'd taken the room to the left of the front door—the one obviously intended to be a formal dining room—and made it his office. Barrister's bookshelves lined the walls. Two desks claimed much of the space, one piled high with stacks of paper and rolls Grace assumed to be maps. None of that surprised her. It looked exactly as she would have expected. What she did not expect was the large portrait of a girl and a boy hanging by a length of black braid in a prominent place just behind Josiah's desk.

"I'm taking you both downtown to have you shot." That's what their father had said. He'd been joking, but Grace had been particularly naughty the previous day, and she'd been terrified by the possible meaning of being *shot*. Of course Pa had meant he was having their photograph taken. And there it was, hanging on her brother's wall. The sight of it brought tears to her eyes. If Josiah had hung their photograph, maybe there was hope, after all. Maybe he'd forgiven her for selling their parents' home.

"Oh, I know what you're thinking," the housekeeper said. "It's a horrible mess, but the colonel doesn't want me touching a thing in this room—except for dusting the bookshelves, of course. He's working on his memoirs, and he says he knows where everything is." She gave a low laugh. "The amazing thing is, I think he does."

She cupped Grace's elbow and turned her about. "Now, this room, on the other hand, is quite lovely." The formal living room featured a small grouping of chairs and a sofa gathered into a cozy conversation area around a fireplace in the center of the wall opposite the arched doorway. "That's all there is on this floor. The formal parlor, the colonel's office, the kitchen, and my room at the back of the house." She led the way past the staircase, up the hall, and through another door, which opened onto a simply furnished kitchen. "The colonel takes his meals here when he's home. I told him it isn't proper, but he doesn't listen." She pointed to the small rectangle of space jutting out from the back wall of the kitchen that was, to Grace's mind, a bit of heaven, what with the morning light pouring in the multi-paned windows on each wall.

"Now you just set yourself down," the woman said, "and I'll have us a breakfast cooked up in no time. Meanwhile, suppose you tell me about your boy?"

"My—boy?" Grace frowned.

"The boy you want the colonel to help you find. What company was he in? Any battles? When did you last hear from him?" She took a coffee grinder down off a shelf, poured beans in, and turned the crank.

"There's no boy," Grace said. "Is Josi—I mean, is Colonel Barton on some special commission that has to do with the military?"

The woman shook her head. "No, ma'am. Nothing official. It's his own calling, he says. Helping the mothers and wives find their men—the missing ones from the Indian wars. The colonel's been all over the West, and he has a way of remembering faces and names that's very nearly miraculous." She glanced Grace's way before filling an enameled coffeepot with water and setting it on a burner. "The Lord has given him a gift to remember faces and names, and he uses it to help people. Of course some of the missing don't want to be found. The colonel tries to be sensitive to that, too. When he finds a live one, he sends them a letter first. He's learned that not every wife or sister is a saint who wants to be reunited out of the kindness of their loving hearts."

Well. Grace couldn't remember the last time the walls around her conscience had been pricked, but Josiah's unwitting housekeeper had just done it. She shifted in her chair and looked around the kitchen. "You look like you're planning a lot of preserving today." She nodded at the piles of rhubarb on the far counter.

The housekeeper talked as she plopped two blobs of oatmeal into two bowls and put them on a serving tray. "That? Oh, my yes—lots of work in coming days, but that's not for preserves. I've promised five pies a day for the full run of Chautauqua. We have a dining hall on the grounds and serve hundreds every day. The profits fund some of our missionaries. We serve pie for lunch and cake for supper. The colonel's not much for cake, so I didn't promise cakes. I never did get the knack for icing."

So. Josiah hadn't changed in that regard. He'd never cared much for cake. But pie and pastry? Oh, my. His housekeeper added an array of oatmeal toppings to the breakfast tray. Once she was settled opposite Grace, she bowed her head. "Come, Lord Jesus, be our guest." She poured molasses over her oatmeal and added a blob of butter as she talked. "You said you don't have a boy you want the colonel to find," the housekeeper said. "So what brings you to Beatrice? And from where, if you don't mind my asking."

"This is so good," Grace said, and added a tablespoon of raisins atop the oatmeal she'd just tasted. "I don't know when I've had better." She took another mouthful, reveling in the taste of warm butter, cinnamon, and sugar. She was ravenous. It took all her self-control to set the spoon down and answer the woman's questions. "I'm from everywhere. I grew up here, but I've been away for a very long time." She could have made up a wonderful story, but for some reason Grace didn't want to lie to this talkative, generous woman.

"You on the faculty at the assembly? Teaching, maybe? Is that how you know the colonel? He's given his share of lectures hither and yon."

"As it happens," Grace said, "I am familiar with his talent. He's a very persuasive speaker." Josiah had talked her into more than one escapade when they were young. "Is the colonel on the program, by chance? I haven't had an opportunity to see the plan for the entire event. I did make the acquaintance of a Mr. Shaw on the train. I believe he'll be very impressive on the stage."

"Never heard of Mr. Shaw," the woman said. "I'm not much on the speakers. What I like is the music. Our Spring Sisters are going to be singing. Now that's good entertainment. You wait until you hear them. The angels are probably jealous."

Two cups of coffee and a bowl of oatmeal later, Grace was feeling fortified and almost hopeful. She'd listen for the train whistle, and when another train arrived, she'd head to the station. And if luck was with her, who knew? She might even be able to pay for the hotel today. It was high time luck showed its face in Grace Barton's life. High time.

The housekeeper rose from the nook and, without asking, grabbed Grace's bowl and refilled it. "You don't mind my saying so, ma'am, you need to put some meat on those bones of yours. Now eat up." She slid back into her seat and was quiet for a moment before taking a deep breath and launching into a new subject. "Chautauqua brings a lot of folks into town. A lot of money, too. Hotels fill up fast. Some folks rent out rooms—and I mean folks who never do such things otherwise." She paused again, seeming to ponder whether or not to say whatever was circling in her mind. Grace lifted her coffee cup to her mouth, inhaling the rich aroma before taking a sip.

Finally, the housekeeper said, "Now don't take this wrong, but if you're of a mind to earn some extra money while you're in town, they's plenty of chances for it. In fact, might be I could help you with that." She looked over at Grace. "Not keeping house. I don't mean that. I can tell you're not used to scrubbing floors and such."

Grace set the coffee cup back down. "How could you possibly know that?"

"Yer hands. Don't take a genius to see you ain't had to work hard labor. And besides that, you talk real smart. Not like me."

Grace looked down at her hands. Her hideous hands, boasting paper-thin skin stretched across swollen knuckles. And age spots. How she had mourned the loss of her beautiful young hands. But then the housekeeper put her own red, chapped ones on the table, palms down. "Them's a working woman's hands."

Grace shrugged. "You're right. I haven't much experience with 'real work.' I'm an actress. I suppose that shocks you."

The woman laughed. "Takes more than that to shock Ladora Riley." She got up and refilled Grace's coffee cup. "You at the Opera House? I heard there's a comedy troupe expected in."

Grace shook her head. "No. I–I'm not here for that." Without warning, tears filled her eyes. She'd made her way up and down the East Coast begging for roles. Any role. But age had robbed her of the beauty that had once made directors willing to overlook her less than stellar talent. Embarrassed, she looked down at her bowl, poking around in the oatmeal with a spoon and trying not to cry.

"There now." Mrs. Riley patted Grace's pale, wrinkled hand. "It's none of my business anyhow. The colonel will help you if he can, no matter why you come to him. You don't have to say another word."

Grace swallowed. "It's just that I was counting on—" she sighed. "It was very kind of you to invite me in and serve breakfast. It was delicious. And now I really must be going. I'm at the Paddock, but I need to arrange to have my things moved this morning."

"People are pouring into town from all points today and

tomorrow. Those who have good rooms had best not let them go."

"I know you're probably right, but the manager demanded payment in advance, and my most recent income was in francs and marks, and—the banks here—there's been a delay." Again, Grace spoke carefully so as not to tell an outright lie. She did still have a few francs in her trunk somewhere, and presenting foreign money to any of the local banks probably would cause a bit of a delay. It would take a teller at least a few minutes to consult someone, wouldn't it?

"Why don't you just stay here and keep me company for the next few days?" It was obvious the woman had just blurted it out, but once the words were out, she didn't take them back. She picked up steam. "It's just me rattling around in this big old house, and they's times I'm about to go crazy from bein' lonely."

"I wouldn't want to impose," Grace said, even as a faint hope sprung up. Whether she could face Josiah or not, she could get a few days to really rest—and to eat well, if Ladora Riley's breakfast was any indication.

"They's no imposition," Mrs. Riley said. "All I got to do is bake pies every day. I'd welcome the company."

"I should probably admit that I couldn't make a pie crust if my very life depended on it," Grace said. "But I can wash and chop. I'm willing to help, if you're sure the colonel wouldn't object to my staying a couple of days."

"Object? He's not even here. And he would object to my sending a lady away when there's likely not a room to be had in the whole city." Mrs. Riley retrieved a blue-and-white sugar bowl from behind a pile of rhubarb. Setting the lid on the counter, she withdrew a roll of bills, peeled a few off, and held them out to Grace.

Grace shook her head. "Absolutely not. I cannot allow you—"

"The colonel leaves a little in the sugar bowl so's I can help them that comes to his door when he's away. I may be nothing but a housekeeper, but he trusts me. And we don't turn people out. We do what we can."

Grace took the money. Things were looking up.

—w—

Emilie had barely gotten settled between May and Junie on the buggy seat when April snapped the reins and the buggy lurched forward. As she guided the gray mare around and out toward the road, she told the girls they could talk about anything they wanted—with the exception of Emilie's adventure last night, which had to be saved until they could *all* hear the story. As the buggy reached the business row where Klein's Market and the Paddock Hotel and Opera House stood, Emilie couldn't help but look that way.

"Looking for *Noah*?" May teased, practically singing the name.

Emilie shot her cousin her best don't-you-dare look. "Actually, I was just wondering if a Miss Ida Jones might have checked in yet. I'm hoping to interview her." Her interest in the hotel didn't have a thing to do with those dining-room windows looking out onto Sixth Street. And a lingering hope of catching a glimpse of a certain person. She was only wondering about Miss Jones. She was only thinking of the interview. With Miss Jones. Noah Shaw hadn't entered her mind. *More than a few hundred times since waking.*

May frowned. "But isn't Mrs. Penner doing the Ladies' News now?"

June nodded. "She stopped by the house early this morning. Something about double-checking the details of Mama's Ladies' Aid announcement."

"Any excuse to gloat," May grumbled.

"Don't feel bad on my account," Emilie said. "I have an even better idea for a series." And she told them about Ten for Ten. She didn't even mention the title "Another View." Noah Shaw was right. Everyone *would* be interested in the answers to her ten questions, and she would make Father see just that—if only she could get to

Miss Jones and finish the first article. Today. In time for Will Gable to set the type and get it into Friday's *Chautauqua Express*.

"So did you ask Mr. Shaw your ten questions?" May asked. When Emilie shook her head, May teased, "Why not?"

"Because," June chimed in, "they were otherwise engaged." She leaned over and added a breathless, "In the moonlight."

Emilie felt herself blushing. "If you two don't stop that"—she glowered at Junie—"I won't tell you what Bert wants."

Junie was instantly serious. "What does Bert want?"

"Promise you will never tease me about Noah Shaw again."

Junie put her hand to her heart. "I promise."

"Bert wants to sit with us tomorrow night during the opening exercises."

Junie's expression saddened. "What's so special about Bert wanting to sit with *us*?"

"*You* are the best part of us. And before long Bert's going to realize that, and when he does. . ."

"She can make him another roast beef sandwich," May said. "With the famous goblet of milk on the side."

Emilie could tell from Junie's expression that there was more to this story than roast beef and milk. She nudged May.

"Mother was fit to be tied when she saw that Junie had gotten out the good china. That's all."

"All? That's all?" Junie shivered. "You would have thought I borrowed her tiara without asking."

April called back from the driver's seat. "Since when does our Mama have a tiara?"

"I thought you said you couldn't hear what we were saying from up there," Emilie called.

"Just enough to be confused," April shot back. "And you just hold all the chatter. We are nearly there."

But instead of guiding the buggy beneath the entryway arches unimpeded, April had to pull up. Emilie, May, and Junie stood up, holding on to the back of the buggy seat and exclaiming over the long line of wagons ahead of them filled with benches, canvas bundles, and an upright piano.

"If that's the piano for the Tabernacle," May said, "we are definitely early enough." She smiled over at Emilie. "It'll take a while for Mr. Tilden to get it unloaded and tuned. We'll have time to show you our camping spot before we rehearse."

And so it was. The wagon with the piano was waved through the gates and headed off toward the Tabernacle, but the same man who had waved that wagon through, directed April to "pull over to the side" and "let these other wagons by."

"But we've a rehearsal at the Tabernacle," April protested. "We're the Spring Sisters."

"Yes'm," the man said, tugging on the brim of his cap. "I recognize you. But we've got to control the traffic today. You ladies will have to park the buggy out here and walk in. We're only letting the workers hauling supplies onto the grounds today."

April hesitated. "Can we at least drive over to our parents' cottage and hitch up there?" She pointed at the pink cottage gleaming in the distance. "I'll pull around back. Completely out of the way." She smiled down at the man. "The thing is, we're spending most of the day out here, and my father will have my hide if I don't take good care of his old mare." She nodded at the dappled gray buggy horse.

The man waggled the toothpick jutting out from the corner of his mouth as he thought about it. When someone in the line yelled a protest about the delay, he looked up at April. "The point is all the road apples, ma'am. Got to keep them cleaned up."

April didn't miss a beat. "I promise you there won't be a single road apple left behind our cottage. We'll see to it before we leave today. You have my word."

The man nodded. "All right, then." He waved her through.

Emilie heard him call after them. "I'm counting on you ladies to keep your promise."

She nudged Junie and May. "Ah, the Spring Sisters. Vocalists Extraordinaire and Road-Apple Specialists." Even April laughed at that one.

CHAPTER 9

April parked Aunt Cornelia's buggy behind the pink cottage. The girls worked together to unhitch and picket the gray mare and were making their way across the grounds toward the Tabernacle, when May linked her arm through Emilie's and slowed her down a bit.

"I only heard Ma's side of the telephone conversation with Aunt Henrietta this morning," she said. "Did you really run away last night?"

Emilie sighed. "No." She explained her side of things, ending with, "I wanted to make peace with Mother so that maybe, just maybe, I'd be able to be a drone in your Bee Hive these next few days. And it seems to have worked, at least based on her mood this morning."

May laughed. "As if you'd ever be a drone."

"A worker bee, then," Emilie said. "This is April's year to be the queen."

"It's going to be very strange having her married," May said.

"It's already strange. And you know what I mean."

May nodded. "I agree with you, but what do we know about falling in love? Maybe April's common sense approach is the way it's supposed to be."

"I hope not," Emilie said. "It's a shame to be bored before you've even said 'I do.' Honestly, most of the time it seems to me that *Junie* is more in love than April." She paused. "I know everyone says it's just a crush, but if I ever fall for a man, I hope just looking at him makes me blush the way Junie does when she looks at Bert."

"Speaking of blushing," May said, "did this Mr. Shaw who's coming to dinner really come running out of the night to rescue you?"

"It wasn't nearly that dramatic."

May grinned. "Maybe not, but look who's blushing now."

Emilie pointed toward the Tabernacle stage. "It looks like Mr. Tilden's finished tuning the piano."

"So," May teased, "we aren't going to talk about Mr. Shaw?"

"The sooner we finish rehearsing, the sooner we can get over to the campground and see if the tent's set up."

"Not even a little?"

"I have an idea for our Bee Hive sign."

"Okay, then," May groused. "Not even a little."

—∞—

Emilie closed her eyes, savoring the last notes of the arpeggio she always played to finish the Spring Sister's last song. April, May, and June, had been facing Emilie as they sang, their crossed arms resting atop the upright piano, but when applause sounded, their heads turned toward the back row of benches. Emilie followed their gaze. And gulped. Noah Shaw—with a woman on his arm—was standing beneath the overhang at the back of the Tabernacle.

Emilie pinched herself to prevent the blush she could feel creeping up the back of her neck. She brushed an imaginary bit of dust off one of the bass piano keys and then took great pains to close the lid over the keyboard. Almost in slow motion. Finally, she got to her feet and looked over at the couple approaching the stage. They were both smiling, and Emilie realized that for the first time in her life she had just experienced a bolt of good old-fashioned jealousy—and it didn't feel good at all. How ridiculous. She barely knew Noah

Shaw. Still, when she realized that the hair peeking out from the woman's hat was snow white, Emilie's jealousy dissolved into relief. Which was even more ridiculous.

Noah Shaw introduced himself to the cousins, making reference to William Rhodes and the *Daily Dispatch* and how he'd already heard wonderful things about the Spring Sisters and now he knew why. Then he smiled up at Emilie and, motioning to the lady on his arm, said, "I've brought you Miss Jones."

"Your note was waiting for me when I checked in to the hotel a while ago," Miss Jones said, "but then Mr. Shaw sought me out on your behalf, as well. I am honored to be at the top of your Ten for Ten list. It isn't every day a newspaper editor of Mr. Rhodes's reputation encourages our cause in print."

Oh dear. Miss Jones thinks Father is championing a cause? And what, Emilie wondered, *would that cause be? Suffrage, you idiot. What else could it be?* She cleared her throat. "To be quite frank, my Father doesn't know about Ten for Ten yet. And I honestly don't know if he'll be a champion or not."

Truth be told, she didn't even know if Father would print it after last night. Surely, though, if the content was good enough—surely she could make a case for a special Chautauqua series. That wasn't the same thing as a regular column. She'd even offer to publish with a pseudonym. Wouldn't that make it easy for Father to say yes? When she glanced over at Noah Shaw, his smile gave her courage. She looked back to Miss Jones. "I can, however, promise to do everything in my power to convince him to print the series."

Miss Jones didn't say anything for one very long moment. Finally, though, she nodded. "Then we shall do everything in our power to make certain that your piece is so riveting he can't resist it."

With a smile, Emilie introduced her cousins. To their credit, neither Noah Shaw nor Miss Jones laughed when April, May, and June Spring introduced themselves. Why on earth Uncle Roscoe had gone along with the idea of those names for his three daughters, Emilie could not understand. It might have been cute when they were little girls, but now—now it was just embarrassing.

The introductions complete, Miss Jones patted Noah Shaw's arm and said, "Mr. Shaw suggested we conduct the interview over afternoon tea at the Paddock. Does that suit?"

Emilie hesitated. She was supposed to be helping her cousins. And she didn't have her own transportation. "A–actually—"

Much to Emilie's amazement, April interrupted and offered the buggy, with only one admonition. "Just don't forget to fetch us later."

"No Royal today?" Mr. Shaw asked.

Emilie shook her head.

"Then why not accompany Miss Jones and me when we drive back to town? I have to return the hack I rented around two o'clock. You can conduct your interview over tea in the hotel dining room. You might even have time to write up the article and take it to the newspaper office before it's time for me to escort you home in time for our evening engagement."

Emilie hesitated. If she went to tea with Noah Shaw and Miss Jones, there would be no time for the lavender bath and rainwater hair rinse Mother had recommended. Then again, if Mother really was trying to throw her at Mr. Shaw, maybe she'd be happy to see them together. It was hard to predict what Mother might think or do.

"Then it's settled." May spoke for Emilie and abruptly changed the subject. "We were headed over to the campground just now," she said to Mr. Shaw and Miss Jones. "Would you like to walk with us? We can give you the grand tour on the way."

"I'd love to come along," Miss Jones said, "but I have a meeting over at Willard Hall in just a few minutes." She looked up at Shaw. "See you at the gate at one forty-five?"

While April, May, and Emilie made their way to the stage stairs, Junie hopped down beside Mr. Shaw and began to pepper him with questions. Where was he from? Did he always have such a deep voice? How was it he came to be out here last night when Cousin Emilie screamed? What did he think of Beatrice? Did he like boating? Did he play baseball? "Because," Junie said, "if you like baseball, you should sign up to play on Bert Hartwell's team."

"June Elizabeth Spring," April scolded, as the rest of them caught up to her. "It's rude to ask such personal questions."

June shrugged. "Well, he looks like he could be a good baseball player. He's tall and strong." June turned back to Noah Shaw. "Bert's the best hitter on the team, but he doesn't run very well. Sometimes they let someone else run for him, and I bet you'd be hard to beat." She looked over at April. "There's nothing wrong with wanting to help Bert, is there? If Mr. Shaw played on his team, maybe they could win for a change."

"*Mr. Shaw* does not play baseball," Noah said. "He's much too dignified. On the other hand, *Noah* loves the game."

June sent an I-told-you-so look in April's direction as she said, "Really? Do you really play baseball, Noah?"

"You're looking at the home-run record-holder from St. Charles, Missouri." He smiled and tapped June on the nose. "And I've been known to win a footrace or two. So if your friend wants me on his team, I'll do my best."

~

Noah couldn't remember enjoying himself as much as he did for the few hours the Spring sisters and Emilie Rhodes led him on a tour of the Chautauqua grounds. By the end of their time together, he couldn't decide which of them he liked the most: April, with her carefully constructed dignity; May, with her easy laugh and unbounded energy; or June, who wore her heart on her sleeve and obviously longed to give it to Bert Hartwell. As for Emilie Rhodes, she had won a unique place in his mind—a place he hadn't taken time to analyze. Yet.

Hartwell joined the group unexpectedly, not long after Noah and the young ladies had meandered past the bandstand and toward the row of cottages.

"That's ours," Junie said, pointing to a pink structure which seemed small compared to the elaborate tree house off to one side. She glanced over at Noah. "Isn't it hideous?"

"It's—unique," he said.

"No," April chimed in. "*Hideous* is the correct word. Mama insisted, on the grounds that 'pink is such a cheerful color.'"

"We're lucky our house isn't pink," Junie said. "Pa put his foot down at that. So Ma contents herself with pink flowers. Ever–y–where." The words were barely out of her mouth when a young man emerged from the pink cottage and called a hello.

June did her best to sound nonchalant when she called out, "Bert Hartwell, what are you doing in our cottage?" It didn't quite work, though. The tone was a bit off. She was trying too hard. And when her cheeks blazed red, Noah realized why. June Spring was a girl in love.

June put a hand on Noah's arm. "This is Mr. Noah Shaw. Mr. Shaw is one of the speakers this year." She lowered her voice. "But if you agree to call him *Noah*, he just might join your team and see to it that they win this year. He's a home-run king. And a fast runner."

Hartwell extended his hand. "My boss interviewed you for the paper." He grinned at Emilie. "I'm checking the cottages for the old man. He asked me to come out here and do one more eradication tour. Spiders. Snakes. Crickets. Ants. Anything that might cause a poor, defenseless woman to scream in the night." He grasped his lapels and thrust out his chest. "Nothing to fear, now. Hartwell is on the job, defending the defenseless and ridding cottages of vile creatures."

"Are you *quite* finished?" Sarcasm dripped from Emilie's every word.

"I'm not sure," Hartwell said. He pursed his lips. "No, I don't believe I am. In fact, now that I think about it, I should probably ask Mr. Shaw here to show me where he released that bull—"

Noah barely saw her move, but in a flash Emilie had knocked Hartwell's hat off his head.

By the time Hartwell had yelled her name and snatched up his hat, Emilie had taken off like a shot in the direction of the campground.

May nudged June from behind. "Betcha I can beat you over there." And she took off with June on her heels.

April just shook her head. "You'll have to forgive them, Mr. Shaw. One Bert Hartwell plus two Spring sisters and a dash of Emilie Rhodes never ceases to be a recipe for unsophisticated nonsense."

Emilie's laughter sounded in the distance, and then June shrieked as Hartwell jumped out from behind a bush, clasped her in a bear hug and swung her about in a circle before setting her down and, with an exaggerated bow, offering his arm.

April sighed. "Family. There's nothing to be done but love them, even when they misbehave."

"I was just thinking how lucky Hartwell is to be related to such a fun-loving bunch of ladies," Noah said. "And really hoping that he will ask me to play on his team—especially if you four will be present, cheering us on."

April chuckled. "Oh, we have an understanding when it comes to Bert. We never miss a chance to cheer him on. He isn't actually related, but we all adopted one another years ago when Bert's family died."

"How terrible," Noah said. "Not the part about his being adopted, of course—but he lost his entire family?"

April nodded. "Bert calls it his 'terrible miracle.' He and Emilie have always been good friends—and they've gotten into more than their share of trouble over the years because of it. When they were twelve, Emilie dared him to climb a tree. He fell and broke his leg, and the doctor insisted he stay in the clinic for a couple of days. While he was gone from home, his family contracted something awful." April swallowed. "The doctor was never quite certain about the diagnosis, even though he quarantined the house. Anyway, within a few days, Bert lost his mother and father, two sisters, and a baby brother."

They walked along in silence. Finally, Noah said softly, "I make my living with words—but honestly, what does a person say in such a moment?"

April gave him a little smile. "Sometimes nothing is exactly the right thing."

Noah and April had just walked past the bandstand when June Spring came trotting back from the direction of the campground. "You'd better hurry," she said. "May is fit to be tied. The land rush has started, and our tent isn't up yet."

"Land rush?" Noah frowned.

April explained. "It's what we call today and tomorrow. A rush to get set up—and sometimes there's a bit of a fight over prime camping spots for those who didn't prearrange things with the superintendent. But I reserved ours." She spoke to June. "Pap Green promised me that spot."

"What size tent did you order?" May was bent down reading the tag on a canvas bag.

"The biggest," April said. "Twelve by fourteen, is it?"

May shook her head. "They've left us an eight by ten."

Emilie nudged a board with her toe. "And look at this. The flooring's all warped. Are you sure we're in the right spot? Maybe the name is wrong on the tag."

April pointed above them. "See that branch? Perfect for a swing."

She walked over to a couple more small trees. "And these are for the hammocks. This is definitely the spot. Pap Green promised."

Noah looked down the long row of tents already in place. Here and there a family scurried back and forth between a tent and a wagon, unloading camp chairs and, in one case, a rocker. Just then a man stepped up from behind a nearby tent and, without saying a word, began to help himself to the pine boards stacked near the hackberry tree.

"That's *our* tent floor," June said and grabbed the board.

"Doesn't have a name on it," the man said, and held on.

"Doesn't have to." Hartwell rushed over. "The lady said it's spoken for."

The man glowered, but he backed off, and June's face glowed with delight as she gazed over at Bert.

"Our knight in shining armor," Emilie joked, "and guardian of the tent floor."

Bert rolled his eyes. "Tell you what. How about you ladies guard your spot while Shaw and I take the tent over and make the exchange with Pap Green. We'll find out about the flooring, too." He smiled at Noah. "And maybe talk a little baseball?"

Noah readily agreed and suggested that he and Bert could pitch the tent when they got back. He looked at the four ladies. "And I resent those expressions of disbelief. As it so happens, I spent the better part of one entire summer pitching tents for Sells Brothers' Circus."

June spoke first. "The circus? Really? You've been with the circus?"

Noah nodded, then grinned. "And I'd appreciate it very much if you didn't broadcast that part of my résumé to the Chautauqua board. I doubt they'd be impressed by the fact that I count Chuckles the Clown a personal friend."

Hartwell laughed. "Your secret's safe with me." He nodded

toward the ladies. "But I can't speak for them. The little one there once had a crush on a circus clown."

"Bert Hartwell!" June scowled at him. "I was six years old."

"Seems like yesterday," Hartwell said, and together he and Noah headed off in search of Pap Green.

—∞—

Less than an hour after Bert and Noah went in search of Pap Green, Emilie lifted the tent flap and, along with April, stepped inside their newly raised tent, also known as the Bee Hive. Not only had Bert and Noah arranged for the exchange, but they'd also returned with one of the larger tents that boasted two small sleeping areas on each side of the peaked-roof portion of the canvas.

"This is positively luxurious," May said, stepping inside and twirling about. "We may never want to go home."

"I wouldn't go that far," April said. "But it is very nice." She smiled at Noah and Bert. "Thank you *very* much. We'll be able to get all moved in this afternoon." She nodded at Emilie. "While you meet with Miss Jones and write your article."

"You two had better get going," May said. "We'll see you at supper."

Emilie took Noah's arm, and together they headed toward the gate to meet Miss Jones. "It was very kind of you to set aside your plans this afternoon," she said.

"I enjoyed every minute," Noah said. "You're very blessed."

"In what way?"

"To have good friends. Cousins. Family." He sounded wistful.

"I imagine it's hard on your family," Emilie said, "to have you traveling so much. Do you get homesick?"

"Not in the way you mean," Noah said. "I don't really have any family. I've been on my own since I was about thirteen. As to home, well. . .that's another subject."

"I didn't mean to pry. I apologize."

"There's no need to apologize." He changed the subject. "I only hope I didn't talk myself up too much when it came to baseball."

"Oh, don't worry about that. No one really expects you to hit a home run every time you come up to bat." She paused. "Three or four per game should be sufficient."

"Thank goodness," he said. "For a minute there I thought I was in danger of disappointing my new friends."

Friends. He considered them friends? They walked along in easy silence. *Friends.* Emilie decided she liked the idea. Very much.

—w—

Noah hitched the rented rig up just outside the Paddock and escorted Emilie and Miss Jones to a table in the hotel dining room before excusing himself to ask after Madame Jumeaux at the desk. Before he could say a word, the clerk waved him over and handed him a note. "Madame Jumeaux left this for you when she checked out."

"She checked out?" Noah frowned.

"Yes, sir. Midmorning. Lock, stock, and barrel, as they say."

Noah crossed the lobby to the window by the door and opened the envelope:

Mr. Shaw,

You are very kind to have been so solicitous of one you barely know. As it happens, I would have been unable to accept your invitation to dine this evening, even if your own schedule had not changed. Fortune has smiled on me, and I have accepted a unique opportunity which will afford me not only comfortable lodging but also companionship and a small income until the situation I mentioned before corrects itself. I hope that I will have the opportunity to hear one of your upcoming addresses. Sincerely, Mme Grace J.

Her first name was Grace. Not very French. Noah folded the paper and tucked it back into the envelope, then crossed back to the desk. "Was madame distressed when she checked out?"

"Isn't her kind always distressed about something? The woman makes her living in the theater. Seems like being distressed would be a way of life." The clerk looked over at Noah. Cleared his throat. "Not that there's anything inherently wrong with the theater, of course. It's just that—well, sir. You know what I mean. There's theater and then theatrics. And she seemed to have more of a gift for the latter. You don't need to worry over her. Turns out she was in town to talk to Colonel Barton."

"Colonel Barton?"

"Yes, sir. You haven't heard of Colonel Josiah Barton?"

Noah shook his head.

"Famous around these parts and beyond," the clerk said. "Fought with the North brothers and their Pawnee Scouts back in the '60s. Got religion somewhere along the way. He's retired now. Makes it his business to help mothers and such find their long-lost kin—sons, brothers, and such. When he can." The clerk paused. "Anyway, when the colonel's gone, his housekeeper has orders to take them in until he gets back. So your lady friend? She'll be just fine."

"And if I wanted to check in with her—just to make sure? Where would I go?"

"You'd head to the colonel's house. You passed right by it on your way here from the train station. White house. Lots of red geraniums out front."

Noah remembered the house, mostly because of the flowers. Ma had loved red geraniums. "This Colonel Barton," Noah asked, "he served in the West?"

"All over the West, from Fort Kearny to Fort McPherson and beyond. Fought with the Pawnee against the Sioux and Cheyenne. Word is he's writing his memoirs. If he gets it done, it'll be something to read, I can tell you that."

Fort Kearny. Ma had mentioned Fort Kearny. She'd been there, both on the way out with Pa, and then on the way back, alone. Of course there was almost no chance Colonel Barton would remember one woman in a sea of faces. For that matter, he probably hadn't been anywhere near Fort Kearney when Ma was there. And yet, a man who decided to write a memoir. . . You never knew what he might recall. Or whom.

CHAPTER 10

It was late Wednesday afternoon before Emilie made her way to the *Daily Dispatch* office, her first Ten for Ten article in hand. Relieved when she saw Dutch still hitched out back behind the newspaper office, she hurried in the back door and up the few steps that led to the double doors opening into the newsroom. As expected, most of the reporters who occupied the desks in the large room had already turned in their columns and were either on their way home for an early dinner or tracking down a story. Her heart pounding, Emilie paused just outside the newsroom doors and looked down at the neatly written pages in her hand.

She couldn't imagine a more receptive or enthusiastic subject than Miss Ida Jones. Miss Jones had worked hard and found success in what was, on the whole, a man's world. She was intellectual, articulate, and charming. And for all her firm beliefs, Miss Jones displayed nothing of what Father called "the typical suffragist's strident voice and pushy ways." Miss Jones displayed a keen intellect and ready wit. The first installment of Ten for Ten was very good reading—for men and women alike.

The manager at the Paddock Hotel dining room had allowed Emilie the use of a corner table for nearly three hours. She must remember to send him a thank-you note. Perhaps she would do so beneath her byline. There was nothing like a little free advertising to win support.

My byline. Just thinking about it made her smile. *A special report from E. J. Starr. First in a series.* For a moment, she wavered, but then she convinced herself—again—that this wasn't the same thing as requesting a regular column in the paper. And besides, she'd used a pseudonym. Of course she knew she couldn't expect Father to print her name in the paper only hours after he'd agreed with Mother about the Ladies' News. She'd come up with a way to keep everyone happy—and to offer the *Dispatch* a scoop. Taking a deep breath, she pushed through the double doors and headed for Father's office.

He looked up and frowned. "Why aren't you at home, helping your mother get ready for our guests?"

"Because she said she didn't need me. Aunt Cornelia came over to help, and Mother sent me off to the grounds with the cousins to rehearse." Emilie paused. "She even said I could help them prepare the Bee Hive—and stay with them during the assembly. You must have had a hand in that. Thank you."

Father laid the pen in his hand down. "You're welcome. But don't give me too much credit. Your mother would never stand in the way of something that would strengthen family ties. We want you to remain close to your cousins." He glanced at the papers in her hand. "You did a nice job with the Ladies' News. I appreciate the way you handled it."

"Working on the last edition convinced me that, in the end, it was the *idea* of writing for the paper that I liked rather than the Ladies' News. Which is why"—she looked down at the article in her hand—"which is why I've come to ask you about this." She held the papers out.

Father took them and glanced at the heading. "Ten for Ten?"

"Ten questions for ten speakers over the ten days of Chautauqua."

Father's eyebrows shot up. "That's a very good hook."

"Thank you. That would be the first of the ten. I spoke with Miss Jones this afternoon. Mr. Shaw agreed to be the second, and

I think Colonel Barton would be an excellent choice for the third. Reverend Talmage, if I can get through the throngs to speak with him. And Miss Willard, of course. At least I'll try. Miss Jones said she would put in a good word for me. You'll see there that her own story includes many elements people love to hear about—rising from poverty, overcoming obstacles, believing in oneself. As for Mr. Shaw's interview, my article won't be a repeat of the one you've already planned. It would complement it."

Father laid the papers atop the others on his desk. "You've given this quite a bit of thought."

Her frayed nerves calmed a bit. At least they were talking about it. "You'll see I've chosen a pseudonym. It's a veiled tribute to Miss Starr, the woman who helped Jane Addams open the settlement house in Chicago." She and Father had had long conversations about the settlement-house concept. He'd even said that perhaps one day they could visit Hull House. Still, something in his manner prevented Emilie's relaxing enough to sit down on the chair she'd occupied after the "press room incident."

Father rose from his chair and crossed to the windows. As he looked out onto the street, he reached up to smooth the tips of his mustache. Then, quite calmly and without turning around, he spoke one forceful word. "No."

The word seemed to hang in the air between them. Emilie was so surprised that it took her a moment to react. Finally, she managed. "No? But you haven't even read it."

He turned back around, sounding weary when he said, "We had this conversation just last evening, Emilie Jane. Frankly, I'm somewhat appalled at the idea that you've spent the better part of the day pursuing something that your mother and I clearly forbade."

"But you didn't—"

"Yes. We did." He walked back to his desk and picked up her article. "It's unfortunate that you weren't really listening." He frowned. "Exactly how did you manage this, by the way? You said you rode out to the grounds with your cousins. But here you are back in town, having completed an interview and written a news article."

Emilie rattled off an explanation. "Miss Jones had a meeting over at Willard Hall. Noah had met her, and he rented a rig and brought her out to the grounds. The two of them stopped by the Tabernacle just as we were finishing our rehearsal. Then the cousins and I showed Noah the grounds while Miss Jones had her meeting, and then I rode back here with them to do the interview and to write it up. Noah's waiting to drive me home."

"Noah," Father muttered and set the article back down atop the papers on his desk.

Oh, dear. Clearly, he didn't care for that familiarity one bit. And it had just slipped out. "He asked us to call him that."

"So you spent the afternoon here in town with Mr. Shaw and Miss Jones, in lieu of helping your cousins prepare that tent you were so eager to inhabit?"

She willed herself to look him in the eye. "Bert and Noah pitched our tent for us. Pap Green had delivered the wrong size, and they got things straightened out. Bert even invited Noah to play on his team for the baseball tournament. And no one minded my leaving to do an interview." She grasped a bit of her skirt between thumb and forefinger and began to worry it while she waited for Father to say something.

"So now you've managed to get your cousins, Bert Hartwell, *and* Mr. Shaw to support your going against your mother and me."

"I didn't—it wasn't like that." Emilie swallowed. "It just happened. Noah said he enjoyed getting to know us better. He's actually very nice. Even funny sometimes. I think he's lonely."

"We are not discussing Mr. Shaw, Emilie Jane." Father sighed. Shook his head. "I can't imagine what your mother would think if she knew about all of this nonsense."

Mother. It was always about mother. Just once, couldn't he care about her? Be concerned about what she was thinking? She let go of the bit of her skirt and took a step back. "She'll be thrilled," she snapped. "That rainwater she made you haul up to the bathroom this morning? That's to make my hair look especially nice. She's planning on throwing me at Mr. Shaw. What's she going to think? I'd say she'll be *delighted* to see the two of us together. She'll probably call all her friends tomorrow morning and crow about how 'taken' Mr. Noah Shaw is with her Emilie Jane. How he went all the way out to the grounds to hear her play. How he escorted her about town for the better part of a day. And then waited to drive her home." Angry tears threatened. Emilie swiped them away. She grabbed the article and held it up to him. "Won't you at least read it?"

Father shoved his fists in his pockets and stood there, staring at her, his jaw working, his lips pressed together. "No. I told you that your foray into journalism was over."

It was sunny outside, but a chill coursed through her. Something had changed between her and Father. And with that change, something fundamental in her world shifted. A curtain lowered between them. She drew the article to her. Took a deep breath and let it out, slowly. "Well, then," she said and left his office without another word.

The woman who answered Noah's knock on Colonel Barton's door had clearly been busy. She wore a burgundy calico apron spattered with flour and what appeared to be bits of dough. "I'm very sorry to bother you," Noah said. "My name is Noah Shaw. The manager at the Paddock said that Madame Jumeaux had moved over here?"

The woman pushed a lock of auburn hair back from her damp forehead. Before she could respond to Noah's question, another woman stepped through a doorway at the far end of the hall and called out, "I'm here, Mr. Shaw."

As she hurried to the front door, Noah wondered at Madame's complete transformation. He recognized the voice, but that was all. She wore a rust-colored calico dress. Her gray hair was pulled back in a bun, her face devoid of makeup. Had Noah seen her on the street, he probably would have walked right by without recognizing her. The difference left him speechless.

Madame Jumeaux, on the other hand, was unusually talkative. She sent an unspoken plea his way as she chattered, "It's all right, Ladora. Mr. Shaw is on the Chautauqua program. I told you about meeting him on the train. He and I enjoyed a late supper last evening at the hotel." She looked up at Noah. "I don't think I mentioned that the assembly itself wasn't really my principle reason for coming to Beatrice. I was hoping to speak with Colonel Barton. Ladora is his housekeeper, and she's been kind enough to offer me lodging until he returns."

Madame sent a fleeting smile in the housekeeper's direction before adding, "I'm going to help with Ladora's baking. She and the other Methodist women run a dining hall over on the grounds to support their missionaries. Isn't that a fine cause? I'm so pleased to be able to help."

Why was she so flustered? It was almost as if she wished he'd never come to the colonel's house. "I just wanted to make certain that everything was all right," he said. "I'm glad to see that it is." He turned his attention to the woman who'd answered the door. "I understand Colonel Barton spent time at Fort Kearny, Mrs. . . ?"

"It's Riley, but everyone just calls me Ladora, and you should, too. As to Fort Kearny, oh my, yes. The colonel served all over Nebraska Territory and on up Dakota way. Fort Kearny will be mentioned often in his memoirs, you can be sure of that."

"I'd very much appreciate being able to speak with him upon his return. May I leave a note?"

Mrs. Riley stood back and motioned him inside. "The colonel's office," she said, pointing toward the room lined with bookshelves. She spoke to Madame Jumeaux. "I'll trust you, Grace, to rustle up paper and pen for Mr. Shaw whilst I tend to my pies. Top right drawer of the desk for note paper." She looked back up at Noah. "I just filled the inkwell on the desk set this morning," she said. "You may use it, but I'll ask you to take care. It was a gift from General Dodge himself."

Mrs. Riley headed back up the hall toward the back of the house, while Noah followed Madame Jumeaux into the office, gazing about as she retrieved note paper from the desk drawer. "I'm very glad to see that you've found comfortable quarters," he said. He might not have recognized the name General Dodge, but the desk set itself was quite impressive. Polished stone set into a footed brass base held a cut-glass inkwell with a faceted stopper and an ebony-and-filigreed gold pen. Noah hesitated, thinking a hastily scratched note requesting a meeting hardly worthy of such a pen. On the other hand, depending on what Colonel Barton might be able to tell him, this note might change Noah's life.

Madame Jumeaux interrupted his musings with a question—asked in a wary tone of voice. "You have business with Colonel Barton?"

"I have an interest in Fort Kearny," Noah said. He returned the pen to its place in the desk set. "Learning about the colonel was a serendipity. When I learned that you'd checked out of the hotel, I expressed concern for your welfare. The hotel manager sang the colonel's praises by way of reassuring me. He only mentioned the fort in passing."

"I didn't mean to pry."

"Nor did I."

"I do appreciate your kindness. It's just that it's been some time since anyone took notice of me—with kindness as a motivation."

"I'm very sorry for that. I only wish you well, Madame Jumeaux."

"Grace," she said. "Please call me Grace." She reached up and ran her palms over her hair, smoothing it back. "I suppose you're wondering at the change. The wigs and furbelows make no sense for a place such as this. This seemed the right—costume, as it were."

"What's that about wigs and fur-blows?" Mrs. Riley pushed through a small door that obviously led into the kitchen. She had a dessert plate in her hand, which she held out to Noah. "It's rhubarb. The colonel would want me to extend his hospitality in his absence."

Noah took his watch out of his vest pocket, glanced down at it, and winced with regret. "I have to say 'no thank you.' I promised to meet a young lady and—"

Mrs. Riley grinned. "You'd best be on your way, then. It never suits to keep a young lady waiting." She handed the pie to Grace Jumeaux and showed him to the front door.

"Thank you for understanding."

As Noah stepped out onto the porch, Mrs. Riley said, "You get a hankering for a piece of rhubarb pie, you know where to find it. Costs you a dime over at the Stewart Dining Hall. Maybe twice that at the hotel. The colonel's kitchen serves it up free. You remember that."

"I will. And thank you."

"Bring your young lady along if you'd like."

"I just might do that."

He was at the bottom of the porch steps when Mrs. Riley called through the screen. "You can set on the front porch together. That porch swing's just right for sparkin'." She looked over at Madame Jumeaux, who was standing next to her in the doorway, the pie plate still in her hand. "Now, Grace, don't be shocked. Neither of us is so old we don't remember sparkin'."

Noah laughed, tipped his hat to both women, and took his leave. Out at the street, he paused and looked back at the porch swing. He remembered the swing that April Spring had mentioned for "the Bee Hive." And he wondered if Emilie Rhodes had ever engaged in "sparkin'."

CHAPTER 11

Emilie managed to get through the newspaper office's double doors and out onto the street before the tears came. She folded her arms across the sheaves of paper representing her first bit of real journalism and walked along, hugging them to herself. Silent tears coursed down her cheeks. She kept her head down as she skirted around the corner and ducked into the hotel lobby, where she nearly bowled Noah Shaw over.

"We have to stop meeting like this," he joked. Then he noticed the tears. Quickly, he guided her back outside and to the rented rig. Without a word, he helped her up onto the driver's seat. Handing over his handkerchief, he hurried to unhitch the rig, climbed up beside her, and headed north on Sixth Street, past the high school, past the county courthouse construction site, and on toward the north edge of town.

After a few moments, Emilie finally managed to say, "Well. That's that." She gave a rueful laugh, then closed her eyes, willing the tears to stop. And failing. "I feel like such an idiot."

"For crying? Why? There's nothing wrong with crying. Obviously, things did not go well with your father. That has to hurt."

She wasn't really embarrassed about crying in front of Noah. Which was odd. Oh well. Her life seemed to have taken a turn toward odd since last night when she screamed and a gorgeous man came running out of the night. "I feel stupid because apparently I didn't really hear what Mother and Father were saying when they took the Ladies' News away from me." She shook her head. "How could I have been so dense?"

"You are the opposite of dense. It's only human nature to resist bad news about something that really matters to us—to listen between the words and hear what we want to hear instead of what's actually being said."

" 'Listening between the words,' " she muttered. "That's an interesting way to put it." She shrugged. "Father would say that I wasn't listening at all." She held the article up. "He was amazed I even brought this to him."

"He really said no?"

"He barely looked at it."

"I'm so sorry, Emilie."

"I honestly thought I had a chance—especially if I used a pseudonym. I thought that would give him the excuse he needed with Mother." She sighed and looked over at him. "You're right, though. I was listening between the words. I only heard the end of my writing Ladies' News. Now I realize what that really meant. Father's decided he agrees with Mother. Or—even if he doesn't completely agree, he's decided to follow her lead."

She looked down at the few pages of handwriting in her hands. "What upsets me more than anything is the fact that this is good work. Father even admitted that I had a good hook for the series. I just know that if it were submitted by anyone but me, he'd print it." She sighed. "If only he would have thought with the business side of his brain instead of the side that caters to my mother."

Noah was quiet for a moment. Finally, he said, "I never knew my father. My mother died when I was only a boy, and I've never been in love. So what I'm about to say may be worthless in this situation. But it seems to me there's another way to look at what you call your father's 'catering' to your mother. Maybe he feels caught between the daughter he loves. . .and his wife, whom he also loves. That's a tough spot for any man to find himself."

"Well, he's found a way out of it." She took a deep breath. "Just now? It was like he pulled a curtain down between the two of us." Her voice wavered. "And he and Mother are on the other side."

"I can understand why you feel that way right now," Noah said, "but while you're deciding what you're going to do about the series idea, take time to think about all the people who'd give anything to have parents who care about them. To have a family and friends like yours." He leaned over and nudged her shoulder. "To have a Bee Hive during Chautauqua."

Emilie looked over at him. He envied her her family and friends. She'd been right about him. Handsome as he was, talented as he might be, Noah was lonely. "You're right," she said. "I do have a lot to be thankful for."

"So. Do you want to risk the good relationship with your parents over Ten for Ten?"

Emilie looked down at the article. "It's not just this article. They don't realize how important writing is to me. In fact, I've already submitted some of my stories to *Leslie's* and *Godey's*."

Noah looked surprised. "So you're already published?"

"Not yet." She paused. "I don't think fiction is where I belong in the writing world. I tried those stories and poems, but it never felt right. When Father gave me the Ladies' News, I realized why. I have notebooks filled with essays and reports and studies. The kind of writing that I've really loved to do isn't fiction."

"Have you told him that?"

"I'm just beginning to realize it. And do you really think he'd want to hear it? Now?"

"Maybe not now," Noah agreed. "But someday." He smiled. "I can't imagine a parent not wanting to know they've inspired their child."

Emilie looked over at him. "Did your mother do that for you? With the theater?"

He thought for a moment before answering. "I hadn't thought about it. Maybe she did." He laughed. "Although it doesn't take much for a mother to like the idea that her child always gets to be Abraham Lincoln in the school pageant."

"Impressive," Emilie said with a smile.

"It was the height."

"And the voice."

"Neither of which had a thing to do with talent."

"When did you know you were destined for the stage?"

"I'm not sure *destiny* is the right word for what happened in my case. I was the muscle for a traveling theatrical company. One of the older members had taken me under his wing. Someone couldn't go on one night, and Professor Gordon talked the manager into giving me a chance. My ma wouldn't call that destiny or fate. She'd say God led me there. She'd say He gave me the talent, and then He took me to the place where I could use His gift."

Emilie thought for a moment before saying, "I'd love to think that my writing comes from God."

"Why would you doubt it?"

She shrugged. "I don't know. It just feels. . .natural, I guess. It's something I've always done."

"Exactly," Noah said. "And I had my first theatrical role in first grade, playing Abraham Lincoln."

"You really think God did that?"

Noah shrugged. "The Bible says He cares about sparrows and lilies. It doesn't seem all that unreasonable to think He'd care about a boy."

"I suppose when you put it that way. . .maybe writing is something He gave me to help me figure things out. When I have a problem, I write about it. When I get angry, I write it out. I write and write and write until I know how to think about whatever is going on." She sighed. "But neither of my parents are going to be willing to think that what I want to do is anything but my being stubborn. Mother doesn't even try to understand that part of me. She's too busy worrying about poor Emilie Jane who doesn't have a man."

She blanched. Had she really just said that out loud? Goodness. She sat very still and made herself concentrate on the article in her hands, while she willed herself not to turn bright red.

Noah was quiet as well. When he finally did speak, it was to chuckle. "And here I thought that invitation to dine was a tribute to my charm." He grinned over at her. "It wasn't my charm at all. It's a plot. And I must say that it was very clever of Mrs. Rhodes to plant that snake in the cottage so you'd scream and I'd come running. Very clever indeed."

"Don't make fun," Emilie muttered. "I'm already embarrassed enough."

Noah chirruped to the horse, who had nearly stopped in the road. "Do you really think I thought that invitation to dinner was all about some paper I delivered at a conference last year?" He shook his head. "It was a good bit of work, but it hardly merits a middle-of-the-night invitation to dine." Taking a deep breath, he continued. "I probably sound like the most arrogant man alive right now, but the truth is, mothers seeking eligible marriage material isn't new to me."

Emilie braved a glance his way. "If you suspected the real reason behind the invitation, why'd you say yes?"

"You." He paused. "And I rarely turn down an invitation to get a home-cooked meal. And for another. . ." He lowered his voice. "You." He continued. "And I meant what I said about meeting your cousins and Bert Hartwell. I like them. So please, may I still come to supper, even though it might also be a mother's ploy to get me to fall in love with you?"

She looked over at him. He was looking straight at her with

those dark eyes of his, and there wasn't one hint of embarrassment in his expression. Until he frowned. "Unless—?"

"Unless what?"

"Unless your Father is going to bounce me out on my ear for encouraging you to write that article."

"I doubt Father will even mention Ten for Ten. As far as he's concerned, the matter is settled."

"And what do you think? Is it settled?"

Emilie sighed. "I don't know. What do you think I should do?"

He pulled the buggy over to the side of the road and held out his hand. "I think you should get a second opinion. May I?"

She handed the article to him.

He handed her the reins and began to read.

"I said it was good, but I'm not exactly objective."

"Unh-hunh." He kept reading.

"I wasn't sure about that one question." She pointed at a question midway down the second page.

"Hmmm." He kept reading.

"It's very difficult to be truly objective about one's own work. I know that. Maybe I was overly confident when I said it was good and that Father—"

"Stop interrupting."

Emilie held the reins for what felt like half an hour.

Finally, Noah finished and looked over at her. "I think *Daily Dispatch* readers would enjoy this—and look forward to more from this E. J. Starr person."

"Thank you." She was surprised at just how much his praise meant. "And so I ask again, what do you think I should do?"

He shrugged. "What I think is irrelevant. They aren't my parents, and I don't have to live with the consequences of the decision."

"You're no help at all."

"No help?" He leaned back, pretending to be shocked. "How can you say that? For you, mademoiselle, I bring Miss Jones to rehearsal. For you, I pitch tent. For you, I read article and say it is very good. For you, I come to dine with notorious matchmaking mother. For you," he said with a wicked grin, "I face giant snake."

He'd taken on some kind of weird accent and syntax, but it worked. Emilie laughed. "All right, all right. Thank you for all you've done and for all you are about to do." She handed the reins back and took the article. "But I still don't know what to do with this."

"Maybe Ten for Ten is only a symptom of a bigger issue." He guided the rented horse into a turn that sent them back in the direction of town.

They were approaching the turn that would take them to her house before Emilie spoke again. "You're right. There's more to what just happened than just one series of articles." She swallowed. "Lecturers like Miss Jones inspire people to think. She has things to say about the cause that people need to hear. Because the world needs to change the way they treat women. I told Father I wanted to interview Colonel Barton, too. He has things to say about the way we've treated our Indians. People need to hear that, too, because policies should change." She shook her head. "But I'm one girl from Nebraska who can't even get her own father to let her write for his newspaper. Who am I to think that what I report would matter to anyone?"

Noah was quiet for so long that she thought maybe he agreed with her and just didn't know how to say it. Finally, he mentioned a name. "Susette LaFlesche Tibbles. Have you heard of her? A girl from Nebraska, if I'm not mistaken"

"Of course."

He nodded. "And Clara Colby?"

Emilie looked over at him. "What do you know about Mrs. Colby?'

"Enough to know that ladies from Nebraska shouldn't be underestimated."

"I'm not that gifted."

"How do you know? You're as bright as anyone I've ever met."

"But. . .my parents."

"Yes," he agreed. "Your parents. Exceptional parents. Very good people."

Listening to Noah agree with everything she said tempted Emilie to go back to "you're no help at all." Except that, in an odd way, he was helping. He was listening as she shared her heart. He wasn't laughing at her for thinking she could "make a difference" in the world. And he believed she was smart enough to decide what to do—for herself.

They were back at the turn to home. Emilie shook her head. "Not yet. Head back into town."

In the short time they'd been driving, things had changed back in Beatrice. Now, both sides of Sixth Street were lined with carriages and buggies, mounted riders and farm wagons. Two omnibuses were pulled up at the Paddock Hotel, both dropping passengers off. The effects of Chautauqua were beginning to show on the streets of Beatrice. Over the next ten days, excursion trains would disgorge hundreds at the three railroad stations on the west side of town. Farmers would drive in from miles around. Eventually, thousands of people would descend on Beatrice and the Chautauqua grounds just across the Blue River. *Thousands of readers.*

Emilie sighed. Once again, she looked down at the article she'd written. The idea that had flickered to life when she stormed out of Father's office an hour ago took hold. She'd been angry when it first surfaced. This time, the thought was borne of her talk with Noah and her subsequent thinking through what he'd called the "bigger issue" behind hers and Father's disagreement over Ten for Ten.

The buggy passed by Klein's Market. She looked through the windows. The interior was teeming with shoppers. Could it really have only been this morning that she'd offered to fetch mint jelly for Dinah? She felt so much older.

As Noah drove the buggy past the Paddock Hotel, Emilie gazed up Court Street toward the *Daily Dispatch* office. At the next corner, she asked Noah to turn right. "One stop and then you can take me home."

CHAPTER 12

Emilie stood beneath the porte cochere, looking after the surrey bearing all their dinner guests save one back to town. Aunt Cornelia had seen to it that Bert sat beside June at the rear of the three-bench surrey that was Aunt Cornelia's pride and joy. It was a fine vehicle, with padded seats upholstered in deep green and gold fringe along the edge of the canopy. The last thing Emilie saw before the surrey disappeared into the night was Bert reaching over to tug on June's blond braid and her slapping him away. She sighed and shook her head. Someone needed to open that man's eyes to the love that was sitting right next to him.

Laughter dragged her attention away from the departing guests and back up to the top of the stairs where Noah stood talking to Mother and Father. He shook hands with Father and bent to kiss the back of Mother's proffered hand as Father opened the screen door, clearly intending for them both to go back inside and leave Emilie alone with Noah, who was headed toward her now. As Father held the door open, Mother flashed a smile in Emilie's direction and flexed her wrist, ending in the flick of a forefinger indicating Noah. She nodded. Pointedly. Father pretended not to notice as he put his arm around her and pulled her inside.

Noah grinned. "And so the dastardly matchmaker departs, her evil web growing ever more inescapable."

"You're incorrigible." Emilie laughed in spite of herself. "It was a nice evening."

"It was." He hesitated. "Are you certain you don't want me to wait while you speak to your Father about that extra stop we made this evening?"

Emilie shook her head. "Don't worry. I'll make it clear that you didn't put me up to it."

"That's not why I'm offering to linger. I was offering moral support. As a friend." He paused. "You still have time to change your mind, you know. There's an amazing new invention called a telephone. It's not too late to stop the presses."

"I don't want to do that." It was true, even though the prospect of talking to Father about what she'd done made her stomach hurt.

"You barely ate. And that was a delicious meal. I've never heard of sauce instead of jelly with lamb, but it was wonderful."

Emilie chuckled. "You should have heard the panic in the kitchen this morning when Dinah realized she was out of mint jelly. I'm glad you didn't realize it was a substitute. I'll be sure and tell her."

Noah checked the rented buggy horse's feet for stones. He went over the harness carefully. Finally, he walked around and prepared to climb aboard, but then he hesitated. "Emilie."

"Yes?"

"Do you think it would cause too much of a stir if I were to reserve a seat for you at the opening ceremonies tomorrow evening?"

"Do you think I'd care if it did?"

He glanced toward the house, then back at her. "And if I were to kiss you on the cheek right now?"

She stood on tiptoe and kissed his cheek. "Now you don't have to worry about it." And she hurried inside.

The house was dark. Expecting to see light spilling into the hall from Father's office, Emilie was surprised to hear laughter floating down the back stairs from the upstairs hall. Ah. She wasn't going to have a chance to talk to Father, after all.

She moved quietly, padding across the carpet to a window that looked out on the drive, being careful not to disturb the drape as she watched Noah climb up into the buggy. Once seated, he paused and looked toward the house before flicking the reins and heading up the drive toward the road. Emilie hurried to the front of the house, turning down the gas lights in the entry hall and perching on the window seat to catch a last glimpse of him.

She started and got to her feet when she heard the click of a door sounding from the upstairs hall.

Mother appeared at the top of the stairs. When she saw Emilie, she descended. "He is a lovely, lovely man," she said. "I just wanted to caution you about moving too quickly, dear. You don't want to be too forward."

"What are you talking about?"

"A kiss is hardly appropriate. You've known Mr. Shaw for one day. You don't want him to think you're anything but a lady."

Had it really been only one day? In some ways, it felt like she'd known Noah Shaw for years. What did that mean? "It was only a kiss on the cheek, Mother. And it was his idea."

She was silent for a moment. "I see."

No. You don't. How could she. Emilie herself didn't really "see." All she knew was that tomorrow evening seemed far too long to wait to see him again.

Father's voice sounded from the dark at the top of the stairs. "Etta. Come to bed."

Mother looked over her shoulder, then back at Emilie. "We'll talk more tomorrow." She called up to Father, "Coming, Will."

—ᴥ—

Noah turned the rig in at the livery and headed back toward the hotel, but instead of going in and up to his room, he kept walking, thinking about Emilie Rhodes. How was it possible to feel so comfortable with someone you'd just met? How was it possible for a woman wearing faded calico and a ragged apron to look adorable? He'd teased her about those apron strings, but what he'd said wasn't far from the truth. He could no more have walked away from Emilie last night than he could have flown back to town. It was as if a magnet drew him to follow her up the drive to her house.

As for today, he was tempted to think that God was arranging things so that he and Emilie would spend more time together. Miss Jones had immediately agreed to let Emilie interview her. Then, there was the coincidence that he and Miss Jones had arrived out at the grounds just as the Spring Sisters were beginning to rehearse. As for Miss Jones, she'd liked Emilie at once. Emilie's cousins and Bert Hartwell included him in their activities without hesitation. And then she'd trusted him after her father rejected the article. It all made him feel like he'd been given a precious gift.

He looked up at the night sky and, once again, located the Bear. *Do you see me, Pa? Do you see me, Ma? These people. . .they're so welcoming. Do you see her? What do you think?* He liked to think that God sometimes peeled back the sky and let his mother and father see their son. It made him feel less alone. He thought about Colonel Barton, and reminded himself that the likelihood of learning anything more about his parents was slim.

As he shoved his hands in his pockets and headed back toward the hotel, he thought about the changes in this part of the country since Ma and Pa and thousands of people just like them had crossed rivers and creeks and thousands of miles on their way to a better life. Thousands had made it. . .and thousands hadn't. Walking by Colonel Barton's place made him think of poor Grace Jumeaux. What was really behind her desire to meet with Colonel Barton? She was an odd woman. Probably accustomed to lying, although it made Noah feel guilty just to think the words. He hoped Ladora Riley's years of experience as the colonel's housekeeper had made her wise to the ways of "wayfaring strangers."

You're a wayfaring stranger. Be careful about looking down your nose at others. It was a good reminder. A man shouldn't think too highly of himself. That was in the Bible. He smiled, thinking of Ma's gift for quoting chapter and verse of the Good Book. Somehow, she'd always known exactly which ones he needed to hear. If she were with him right now, she'd smile up at him as sweetly as could be as she said, "'Pride goeth before destruction, and an haughty spirit before a fall.'"

He wished Ma was here with him. He'd take her to the opening exercises tomorrow evening, and she'd meet Emilie Rhodes. Maybe she'd help him figure out what was going on in his heart and soul over the girl he couldn't seem to stop thinking about. He'd been arguing with himself about it since standing at the back of that Tabernacle, watching her play the piano today. She was just a girl he'd met because of a bull snake. Then again, Ma had always said that sometimes God was doing His best work when it seemed that He wasn't paying any attention at all.

Emilie wasn't "just a girl." He didn't really need Ma to tell him that. He knew it because it had taken everything in him to keep from pulling her into his arms when she stood on tiptoe to kiss his cheek a little while ago. He knew it because even now, as he walked toward the Paddock Hotel, he could remember the faint scent of the roses pinned in her hair and the sensation of her lips against his cheek. He knew it because he was worried about what would happen when her father found out what she'd decided to do with that article she'd written. He knew it because. . .because he knew.

—∾—

Emilie started awake. She felt a moment of panic, thinking that she'd overslept, but then she realized that what had awakened her was the sound of wagon wheels crunching on the drive. Apparently

Dinah had ignored Mother's directive to sleep a little later after the previous night's entertainment.

Slipping out of bed, Emilie padded to the window. The indigo sky had barely begun to lighten just above the eastern horizon. It couldn't even be five o'clock yet. How did Dinah do it? She and Aunt Cornelia's Ida had worked until nearly midnight, with Dinah insisting that every dish be washed and returned to its proper place in the pantry, every kitchen counter scrubbed, every damask napkin treated for stains and ready to be washed in the morning.

Emilie knew this because she and the cousins had helped clear the table after dessert. They'd seen the mounds of dishes on the counters, carried the coffee and tea tray into the formal parlor, and witnessed Mother's insistence that she would deal with the coffee cups herself and that Dinah and Ida were to go home *now*.

Now that Emilie thought about it, Dinah and Ida were probably looking forward to Chautauqua for very different reasons than the family. Gathering eggs, milking the cow, and preparing and delivering a picnic supper to the cottage once a day amounted to a holiday compared to what those two women managed most of the time. Maybe she should interview a housekeeper for Ten for Ten.

She chuckled when the idea first arrived, but the more she thought about it, the more she wondered if maybe it was one of her more original ideas. Mother had often said that she'd be lost without Dinah. Now that Emilie thought about it, Dinah and Ida were the reason that Mother and Aunt Cornelia had time to champion their causes. What would happen to those causes if the women who supported them had to do without their housekeepers and maids and gardeners? Emilie had never stopped to think about the layers of society and what would happen if they stopped cooperating. Maybe the concerns of the labor unions were more important than temperance. Maybe she should think less and get dressed for the day.

She dressed in the dark, donning a simple green gored skirt

and a white blouse. She brushed her hair and tied it back with a ribbon, then waited until she heard Dinah leave to gather eggs before descending to the kitchen to make coffee and set up the silver serving tray in the nook in preparation for Father's appearance.

She was seated in the breakfast nook waiting when she heard him head down the front stairs. She stirred sugar into her own coffee to try to give her trembling hands something to do.

She spoke before he had a chance. "There's something you need to know."

Father sighed as he settled opposite her. He lifted the silver coffeepot and filled the shaving mug he drank coffee out of every morning. It was his silent protest against the minuscule cups that were part of the delicate porcelain breakfast set Mother loved and he despised. "I don't want to get between you and your mother on this, Emilie. Discussions about such things are for daughters and their *mothers*."

Emilie frowned. "What are you talking about?"

He seemed surprised. "This isn't about your. . .behavior. . .with Mr. Shaw before he left last night?"

"What behavior?" The words were out of her mouth before she realized what he meant. "Is Mother really so upset about a peck on the cheek?" She held up her hand. "Never mind. You're right. Not something I want to discuss with my father. Besides, that's not why I got up early. I wanted to talk to you about my article."

He grimaced. "I want to talk about that even less than I want to talk about the other matter."

"I don't want to fight about it."

"Thank God."

Dinah came in from gathering eggs. While the door was open, Emilie heard the sound of a horse cantering up the drive. "That'll be Billy Towle. I'll see to it." Sizing up the competition had been part of Father's routine for as long as Emilie could remember. He'd hired a boy to bring him the *Dispatch* and the *Journal* as soon as the first copies came off the presses in the morning. She supposed that Carl Obrist of the *Journal* had a similar arrangement.

As she opened the side door, Dinah said, "Tell Billy I'll scramble some eggs if he wants them."

When Emilie relayed Dinah's message, Billy said no. "Tell her thanks, but Mr. Obrist told me to head straight out to the grounds this morning. I'm to help set up the correspondents' office." He reined the horse about and took off.

Emilie stepped back inside, lingering in the kitchen just long enough to scan the front page of the Journal. Not seeing anything of particular interest, she rejoined Father and handed him the *Dispatch*. She kept the *Journal* for herself. And there it was, at the top of page three. Not the front page. Still, very good placement. Right where every subscriber would see it the minute they opened the paper. She stifled a smile.

"Since when are you interested in the competition?" Father poured his second cup of coffee. "And what's making you smile about the *Journal*?"

Emilie moistened her lips. "I came down early so that if this happened, you'd hear it from me." She folded the paper and laid it between them so that he could read the headline: TEN FOR TEN. FIRST IN A SERIES.

He snatched the paper up and glared at the page.

"It's good work, Father. I wanted to see if someone else would be interested."

"And so you decided to go behind my back." He slammed it down with her article facing away from him.

"My motive was never to hurt you. That's why I used a pen name."

Father snorted. "And just how long do you suppose it will take for E. J. Starr's true identity to be broadcast all over Beatrice?

"I submitted the article inside a plain envelope containing

nothing but that article and a note. All it said was that if the first in the series was printed, subsequent articles would be submitted featuring—and then I listed the nine names. I didn't even put the envelope in the *Journal* mail slot myself. Noah did it for me."

Father glowered at her. "So I have Noah Shaw to thank for this?"

"No. It was my decision. He and I talked on the way home, but he refused to give advice in the matter."

Father snorted. "I'll bet."

"I'm telling you the truth. After I left your office, I cried all the way over to meet him. He put me in his rented buggy and took me for a drive, waiting for me to calm down. And then, when I asked him what he thought I should do, he told me how grateful I should be that I have such a wonderful family."

"How noble of him."

"He said that since I was the only one who would have to live with the consequences of what I decided to do, I was the only one qualified to decide."

Father took a drink of coffee. He smoothed his freshly waxed mustache. Finally, he said, "And I suppose the fact that you dreamed up this E. J. Starr and enlisted Shaw to sneak the article into the *Journal* office makes you think I'll recant and offer my support?"

Emilie took a deep breath. "You've made it very clear that if I force you to choose sides, you're backing Mother." She forced a smile. "A girl can't fault her own father for loving her mother, now can she?" Clearly that wasn't what he expected to hear. She met his gaze. "I'm not throwing down a gauntlet like some spoiled child throwing a temper tantrum. But this is important to me. I'm going to continue writing, and I'm going to continue to seek publication." She looked down, tracing the rim of her own coffee cup with her index finger.

The newspaper rustled. Father laid the *Journal* aside. Picking up the *Dispatch*, he opened it and began to read. Presently, he said,

"Would you please inform Dinah that I'd like poached eggs this morning?"

Emilie rose and went into the kitchen. She relayed the message about Father's breakfast and offered to make his toast while Dinah poached eggs and fried a slice of ham. She retrieved a jar of peach jam from the pantry.

"That's the last one," Dinah said. "I was saving it for a special occasion."

"It's Father's favorite," Emilie said, and opened the jar. As far as she was concerned, this was a special occasion.

CHAPTER 13

It was barely light enough for Noah to see the street below his hotel-room window when he dressed and descended to the lobby. The dining room wasn't yet open, and the newsstand held only copies of yesterday's news. Exiting into the predawn light, he paused for a moment and closed his eyes, appreciating the quiet city which, he knew, would soon transform as crowds of people descended from hotel rooms and houses to dine and shop and rent carriages and, eventually, pay fares to ride out to the grounds. Many would want to go early and stake out their place on a bench beneath the Tabernacle covering in anticipation of the evening's opening exercises. But Noah was focused on only one thing at the moment—today's *Beatrice Journal*.

As he paced, he thought his way through first one and then another of the poems in his repertoire. He murmured the Shepherd's Psalm to himself and had just begun with one of his favorite orations, which involved selections from the Old Testament book of Job, when a wagon came into view, turning onto Court Street from the direction of the *Journal* offices.

When the wagon rolled up to the Paddock door, Noah was waiting. He offered to carry a bundle of papers in, disappointed as he scanned the front page and did not see the words *Ten for Ten*. At the sound of a key in the dining-room door lock, he tucked the paper beneath his arm and headed in to breakfast, greeting the waiter and choosing a seat near a window. As the first rays of morning light spilled over the tops of the buildings and into the street, he searched the paper, finally locating Emilie's article. Good placement, in the upper right-hand corner of page three. Right at the top. Right where the eye would land. Superb placement, actually.

He glanced toward the northeast. Emilie was probably standing just inside the front windows at the foot of the mansion's front stairs right now, watching for the lone rider who would deliver the paper to the Rhodeses' home this morning. How would Mr. Rhodes react to seeing her column in his competitor's paper? What would Emilie say to him? *And how would he react to the idea that I delivered the article for her?* That part of the equation wasn't the most important part, of course. He reminded himself that he was leaving town in less than two weeks. And then smiled at the thought of having more time to get to know Emilie during the Long Pine Chautauqua. Would she want to do a second round of Ten for Ten interviews while she was there?

Voices sounded out in the lobby, and hotel guests began to filter into the dining room. Two waiters entered through the swinging door that connected the kitchen to the dining room. One brought Noah his coffee; the other welcomed other diners. And in what seemed like only moments, the dining room resonated with the familiar sounds of a busy restaurant and the aromas of freshly baked bread, frying bacon, brewing tea, and percolating coffee.

Noah ate heartily, but all the while his mind was on what might be happening over breakfast at the Rhodeses' mansion. He wished he could have been there to see the look on her face that first moment, when Emilie opened the paper and caught sight of the name E. J. Starr in print. And if there were to be more tears shed after she talked with her father, Noah wanted to be there for that, too.

—∾—

"I talked Dinah into letting me open the last jar of peach jam." Emilie set Father's breakfast before him and refilled the shaving mug.

Father didn't look up, although he did mutter *thank you.*

She almost sat back down across from him, but then she thought better of it. Perhaps that wasn't fair. Perhaps an uneasy peace was all she should expect for now. Father was, at least, talking to her. She'd almost decided to retreat to her room when Mother descended the stairs and came to join them.

"My, but you're up early," she said to Emilie, as she bent to kiss Father on the cheek.

"I'll bring your tea," Emilie said. She glanced back from the doorway just as Father nuzzled the back of Mother's hand, and then pulled her to him for a different kind of kiss. Emilie's cheeks flamed, and she looked away, embarrassed—not by the show of affection—but by the realization that seeing her parents' kiss had made her think of Noah Shaw.

By the time she had Mother's tea brewed, Father was leaving for the office. "You two have a lovely day together," he said as he headed out the door. He paused and looked over at Emilie, seeming about to say more. Instead, he gave a slight shake of his head and continued on outside.

Emilie gave Mother the cup of tea, then carried Father's breakfast dishes out to Dinah—along with Mother's request for a soft boiled egg and toast. She'd headed up the stairs to her room, intending to begin laying out what she would move over to the Bee Hive later this morning, when Mother called her back downstairs.

About that kiss.

—∾—

Awakened by the doorbell, Grace pulled on her wrapper and headed downstairs to answer it, but before she so much as reached the first of the steps leading down, Ladora had opened the door and spoken to whoever it was. When Grace heard the word *telegram*, she stood as if rooted to the bare wood floor in the upstairs hall, her hands clutching the railing, her heart thumping. Ladora had said that Josiah always telegrammed when he was headed home. How much longer would she have before facing him?

Grace listened as Ladora thanked the messenger and closed the door, then retreated to the kitchen. Finally, the back door closed. That was her cue to move. Ladora would be gone for a few minutes, gathering eggs.

Descending the stairs, she headed into Josiah's office. Facing her brother would perhaps be the most challenging role of her life, and she didn't know how to play it. Returning prodigal? Repentant prodigal? Desperate prodigal? There were nuances to be considered if she was going to get what she wanted, and from her brief time in this house, it was clear to Grace that she didn't know the man Josiah had become. For one thing, his housekeeper called him "devout." For another, he apparently spent a great deal of time helping others—at his own expense. She would study Josiah, just as she'd always studied for any role.

The photograph of the two of them drew her across the room. Skirting her brother's desk, Grace stared at it for a moment, surprised to realize that something had changed for her over the years, too. She wasn't bitter anymore. Josiah had promised their dying mother to "take care of Grace" and then, only a year later, reenlisted. He'd promised to send money when he left. "I'll write," he'd said. But he never did. She worried for weeks. She feared him dead. And then... then she read his name in a newspaper article about Major Frank North and the Pawnee Scouts. And she got angry. Finally, she sold the house and left to follow her own dreams. She'd had her revenge and then some, she supposed. For whatever reason, she wasn't angry anymore. Was Josiah?

She looked away from the photograph and over at the roll of maps and the stacks of papers covering nearly the entire surface of the second of two desks in the room. He was writing his memoir. Why did he believe people would want to read it? What had he done and seen that was so important? Ladora said he'd been "all over the West." Well, so had thousands of other men.

She looked around the room at the books. The shelf nearest her held several Bibles. The rest of that entire bookcase contained theology books and sermon collections. Charles Wesley, John Wesley, George Whitefield, David Brainerd. And Charles Spurgeon.

Grace smiled at the idea that Josiah had several volumes by Spurgeon. She'd gone to hear the man preach. More than once, actually, in London. When had Josiah been converted? And by whom? Had redemption mitigated his anger toward her? Did she have the courage to find out? She'd come all this way, but now that she was here in Beatrice, standing in her brother's study, she wasn't certain. Could brotherly love survive twenty years of estrangement?

She reached for one of the volumes with Spurgeon's name on it. It would behoove her to refresh the vocabulary of the saints before Josiah got home. Intending to take the book up to her room before going into the kitchen, she made her way back toward the stairs, pausing briefly to peer at the two other portraits hanging on the wall to the right of the door. She hadn't really paid them any mind. Now she was glad she'd stopped to look them over. One showed Josiah in some sort of frontier garb, looking more like a character in a Wild West show than the brother she'd grown up with. Was that a young William Cody? It was. Again, Grace smiled. Josiah, with Buffalo Bill. Perhaps she would learn that story one day. Perhaps she'd tell him about meeting Rosa Bonheur in Paris.

The other photograph appeared to be some kind of Indian delegation. A ramrod-straight Colonel Josiah T. Barton in full dress uniform graced this one, and my but he did look impressive. So did the dozen or so Indians in the photograph. Grace supposed she was looking at their version of "full dress uniform" as well, what with their bear claw necklaces and ornate headdresses, their beaded moccasins and government medals.

She glanced back at the desk laden with materials. These photographs explained the memoir idea. Apparently, Josiah knew some famous people relatively well. Buffalo Bill was a sensation. People would love reading about him. And Indian chiefs? Maybe these men weren't chiefs, but still—she squinted at the portrait. With a sharp intake of breath, she removed her spectacles. Leaned closer. She really must have her eyes checked. Or clear her mind with a cup of strong coffee. It couldn't be.

The sound of the back door closing sent her scurrying back up the stairs with the theology book in hand. She had dressed and was halfway back down the stairs when Ladora stepped into the hall. "There you are," she said. "I could have sworn I heard you come down earlier. I have good news. Did you hear the bell ring earlier?"

"I did," Grace said. "I heard the word *telegram*." She shuddered a bit. "I have trouble getting used to the idea that they can bring good news."

"I know what you mean," Ladora agreed. "Not that long ago, telegrams only meant bad news. Now things are changing all around. Colonel wants one of those newfangled telephones. I told him he could install anything he wants, it being his house and all, just not to expect me to use such a ridiculous invention." She led the way back toward the kitchen. " 'Telegrams are just fine,' I said, 'and besides that, Colonel, why would you want to be spending your hard-earned money on a telephone? Think how many books you could buy, and you do love your books. Think how many meals those Indian children you seem to love so could eat for what that contraption would cost.' " She paused. "Not that it's any of my business, of course." She sighed. "Well anyway, he's listened so far and he just telegrams, but I expect he'll want the telephone one of these days, especially once he publishes that memory book of his and gets even more famous than he already is. Anyway, the telegram said he'll be home Monday afternoon."

The prospect of facing Josiah in less than a week put all consideration of Indians and showmen out of Grace's head. While she made coffee, Ladora scrambled eggs, waxing especially eloquent about the performance of the Rhode Island Red hens housed in the chicken coop out back and various other "local news items" that Grace barely listened to.

Her day of decision was definite now. Sometime between now and Monday, she would have to decide what to do. She'd arrived in Beatrice with no alternative but to throw herself on her brother's mercy, but then Chautauqua added an intriguing alternative—especially with the very respectable duties involved in baking pies and helping to deliver them to the Stewart Dining Hall. Of course Grace could still face her brother and hope to reconcile, but even so, it would be nice not to have to do so as a penniless prodigal begging for mercy.

"Beautiful morning out," Ladora said. "I was thinking we might take our breakfast out to the porch. Newspapers have probably arrived by now, and there will be a regular parade going by for most of the day." She paused. "What say, Grace? Shall we be the two old biddies on the porch, watching after other people's business?"

In a matter of moments, the two women had carried a breakfast tray out onto the porch and settled down, first to eat and then to read the papers that, as Ladora had predicted, had arrived. Ladora had also predicted a parade out on Ella Street, and she was right about that, too. First came the empty omnibuses, headed toward the three train stations only a few blocks away. Two boasted hotel names, the Paddock and the Grand Central. A third advertised Hamaker & Skinner Livery & Feed. It wasn't long before the train whistles blew and Ladora said, "You watch, now. A whole parade headed back the other way." She rose. "But first, let me get us more coffee." She grabbed up the breakfast tray and headed inside, calling back over her shoulder, "I'd be much obliged if you'd let me read the *Journal* first. The colonel prefers the *Dispatch*, but I cannot for the life of me understand why.

Grace retrieved the newspapers from where they had landed at the base of the porch stairs and unfolded first one, then the other. She settled back in her chair with the *Dispatch* just as Ladora returned with steaming mugs of coffee. "And so it begins," she said, as she handed Grace's mug to her and nodded toward the street as a family hurried past. A man, a woman, and five stair-step children, all girls, all wearing dresses made from the same dark blue calico, all wearing straw hats with streamers, each one carrying a pasteboard bandbox.

"Don't imagine they'll be camping," Ladora said. She paused. "I think he sells real estate," she said. "Probably up Lincoln way. And the wife is hoping to get him to listen to that Mrs. Willard and to see the light when it comes to demon rum."

Grace looked over in surprise, and Ladora grinned. "Well, you got a better story?"

"As a matter of fact. . ." The small group was almost out of sight when one of the omnibuses came in sight, packed with passengers. "She isn't his wife. She is his sister. And she had to give up her dream of becoming an opera singer in order to return to the Midwest and mother her brother's five motherless children. And they hate her." She paused, then said quickly, "Except for the youngest. The youngest does not remember her own mother, and she is devoted to the opera singer. Which is the only thing that keeps the poor woman from running away."

"Land sakes. Marion Harland's got nothing on you."

"Who?"

"Don't tell me you haven't heard of Marion Harland," Ladora

said. "*Jessamine*? *True as Steel*? *Sunnybank*?"

Grace shook her head. "I'm afraid those names don't mean anything to me."

"Well we will fix that while you are here," Ladora said. "I know there is some who think that novels just aren't fit reading for a Christian lady, but you can't be one of them, you bein' an actress and all. And Missus Harland writes the best stories." She opened the newspaper. "But for now, let's see what the news is for the day."

Grace smiled at the huge letters right beneath the newspaper heading. Some store was closing its doors and offering "ridiculous bargains." She turned the folded paper over so that she could see what was at the bottom of the front page. "Noah Shaw: First Impressions." The first line quoted a review of one of his performances somewhere in Illinois. "With keen black eyes, with a wealth of jet-black hair, with a face to woo the masses, and with a powerful and magnetic voice, he holds his audiences like no other orator has been able to do."

Ladora glanced over at Grace's paper. "That's a good likeness," she said. "Did Mr. Shaw say what he wanted with the colonel? Not that I'm a busybody or anything. But you said you talked on the train."

"The first I knew of his interest in anything military was when I heard him ask you about the colonel yesterday morning." Grace stared down at the image that had been reproduced in the *Dispatch*. Ladora hadn't said anything about it, but then maybe Ladora hadn't looked at those photographs in Josiah's office in a very long time other than to brush over the frames with a feather duster.

The resemblance was uncanny. Truly uncanny.

CHAPTER 14

Mothers. Who could explain them. They worried if you didn't show an interest in any of the young men they paraded past you over the years, and then when you finally did show an interest, they worried.

Mother had kept Emilie in the breakfast nook for what felt like half the morning, reminiscing about when she and Father courted, sharing fond memories of how everyone had known that William and Henrietta would be a "good match," because, after all, their families had *known each other for years and years*. She said that even when people know each other really well, there are surprises in relationships that lead to a "period of adjustment." How thankful Mother had been for the protection of her parents and their guidance during those early *years*.

All in all, breakfast had amounted to a motherly monologue on marriage. Which might make a good news column, now that Emilie thought about it. On the other hand, the point of Mother's motherly monologue had been that, while from all indications Mr. Shaw was a fine man, Emilie should exercise caution in regard to the obvious "high regard" in which *he* seemed to hold *her—so soon after they had met*. When Emilie reminded mother that another version of her parents' courtship and marriage included the term *love at first sight*, Mother frowned.

"Well, yes," she'd said. "But I only thought that in *hindsight*, when I realized how very compatible your father and I seemed to be. Compatibility must be tested by an appropriate span of time, dear. In some cases, a *great deal of time*."

Half an hour later, as Emilie packed for the next few days of camping on the assembly grounds, she was still upset by the conversation. To her mind, it was a perfect example of one of the things that drove her to distraction about Mother. If there was something about Noah Shaw she didn't like, then why in heaven's name didn't she just come out and say it? What did she want Emilie to *do*? Why didn't she just tell her?

Yanking three summer blouses off their hangars one by one, she tossed them onto her bed. She followed the blouses with three skirts, two pairs of sensible shoes, and various and sundry unmentionables. After she shoved everything into the Gladstone bag Father had brought her from one of his business trips, she added the leather travel set that held her brushes and combs. Finally, she added pens, paper, and two bottles of ink, the latter wrapped in a towel for extra cushioning and tucked safely into one corner of the bag, then held in place with a pair of her shoes—and not her favorite ones. All the while she packed, her emotions simmered as she replayed the scene with Mother at the breakfast table.

"We don't want Mr. Shaw to think you aren't a lady," she'd said. "You must guard your reputation."

As if Noah Shaw were some vagabond. As if he's suddenly sprouted horns, after all Mother's fawning over him that first night.

"There's nothing to worry about," Emilie reassured her. "Noah Shaw is a consummate gentleman."

"Not if he was already speaking of kissing when you'd only just met."

"Well, he only spoke of it," Emilie said. "He didn't do anything about it."

"He didn't have to, did he?"

Emilie's cheeks flamed. "I don't know what got into me, Mother, but I can assure you it won't happen again. Now may I please go upstairs and get packed? What time did you say we were supposed to meet Aunt Cornelia?"

Mentioning the busy day ahead finally got Emilie out of the uncomfortable conversation. Mother gave up and went into the kitchen to speak with Dinah about the meal plans for the days ahead.

Now, as Emilie put the last of her things into the bag and snapped it shut, she stopped long enough to look at herself in the mirror and to wonder exactly what it did mean that Noah had requested to kiss her cheek—and, more importantly, that she had so readily kissed his. What did it mean that right now, right this minute, all she wanted to do was saddle Royal and gallop into town and talk to Noah? Had he seen the *Journal*? Did he know they'd printed her article? He would understand how she felt about that. And besides that, he was the second name on the list for Ten for Ten. She needed to interview him and get the article written and submitted—all while moving in to the Bee Hive with the cousins and, if they insisted, going through this evening's music selections again. April was famous for demanding "just one more run-through." Or infamous, depending on a person's mood at any given rehearsal.

Emilie peered at herself in the mirror and smiled. Time with Noah had to be at the top of her list of things to do on this busy, busy day. Life as a fledgling reporter was good. Very good.

Emilie hitched up the buggy and drove up under the porte cochere. Dinah helped her put the portable desk Grandfather had used in the war in the back. Emilie put her bag on the seat. And then she waited. And waited. And waited. Finally, she went back inside.

"She's all a-flutter," Dinah said, lifting her eyes to the second story to indicate Mother.

"About what? There's so much less to do than last year. Calvin's probably done most of the hard work already. And Father hired extra help."

Dinah nodded. "I know."

"And I'm not going to be staying there, so that's even less work."

"I didn't say she was overwhelmed with work," Dinah said, and added the potatoes she'd been peeling to the large roasting pan setting on the stove top. "I said she's all a-flutter." She paused. "It's 'bout that gentleman."

At that moment, Mother came down the stairs with all three of her needlework bags in hand and several books balanced on one arm.

Emilie took the books out of her arms. "Do you really think you're going to have time to read?"

"One never knows," Mother said. "Cornelia's bemoaning the long evenings without our young people about. I just want to make sure I'm prepared to join her if she decides to become some dowager, rocking and knitting."

Emilie laughed. "I can't imagine Aunt Cornelia being content to sit in a rocking chair and watch the world go by." She led the way outside. "Besides that, I doubt that wild horses would be able to keep her from coming over to the Bee Hive at least once a day, just to make sure that whatever we're doing meets with her approval."

"What's this?" Mother pointed to the field desk as she settled her needlework bags on the seat.

"The cousins and I want to make some signs for the Bee Hive," Emilie said. "The way this folds down will work perfectly. And the cubbyholes will give us all a nice, organized way to keep track of our music and the notes we'll be taking at the sessions each day."

Mother looked doubtfully at the old wooden box, with its drop front and fold-out legs. "Do you really need it?"

"Perhaps not," Emilie shrugged. "But I thought I'd offer it, just in case. You don't mind, do you?"

"I suppose not."

"It was just stashed in a corner of the basement back by the coal bin. I'll take it back in if you don't want us using it."

"No, it's all right." Mother climbed up beside her. "I didn't realize the Bee Hive was going to involve actual furniture. I thought—well, in spite of all my needlework and those books, I suppose I thought—or hoped—that you girls might still spend the greater part of your time at the cottage." She shrugged. "I made a point of telling Dinah to be sure she brought enough food for everyone—just in case."

Emilie glanced over. Mother looked sad. "Well, if they really do end up with the predicted eight *hundred* tents pitched over on the campground, who knows but that we'll all come running back the first night."

Talk turned to the traffic in town and the weather, the music the Spring Sisters would present this evening, and eventually it wound its way back to the subject of Noah Shaw and Mother's seemingly harmless musings on what he might present this evening.

"He thought he'd try to do something that complements our first song."

"And what will that be?"

"The new arrangement April wrote that combines 'Let Party Names' and 'Blest Be the Tie.'" Emilie smiled. "April thought it would be a good idea to remind everyone of the need for unity and Christian charity before the fights start over turns at the table or who gets the last piece of Mrs. Riley's pie at the dining hall."

Mother chuckled, and Emilie began to sing in a low voice, "Among the saints on earth, let mutual love be found; heirs of the same inheritance, with mutual blessings crowned," then, as they were pulling up into the drive at Aunt Cornelia's, she finished with, "Blest be the tie that binds, our hearts in Christian love; though lines be long and pie be gone, remember Christian love." She grinned over at Mother. "We aren't really singing those words, of course. But you get the idea." She tied off the reins and climbed down. "Noah's doing the Shepherd Psalm and the Lord's Prayer."

"So simple?" Mother sounded surprised. "I would have thought he'd be bent on impressing everyone with something less well known."

Emilie shrugged. "He said it's best to keep it simple on the first night—and that there are no greater words than the ones in the Bible."

"He said that?"

"Yes, Mother. And now you know he isn't a heathen."

"I never thought him a heathen, Emilie Jane. But I don't recall the Bible being a topic of discussion at supper."

"It came up when we sneaked off behind the carriage house to have that secret romantic interlude." Emilie watched for Mother's reaction before laughing. "He's a good man, Mother. You don't need to worry about us." *Us.* There was no "us." Feeling flustered, Emilie was thankful when May came out the front door and bounded down the steps. Mother went on inside, leaving May and Emilie to transfer things from the back of the buggy to the already-loaded farm wagon parked alongside the house.

May grunted as the two of them lifted the camp desk down from the buggy and began to make their way around to the wagon. "Do we really need this?"

"*We* might not," Emilie said. "But *I* will."

"Really?"

Emilie nodded. "Really." They loaded the old camp desk into the wagon, and then Emilie motioned for May to follow her. Together, they ducked into the barn. Emilie made a show of making certain they were alone. "I have something to tell you."

"Well, there's a surprise." May rolled her eyes. "I thought you were just doing your weekly check of the barn."

"I'm serious," Emilie said.

"And I'm in a hurry," May replied, "so tell me and then let's get back inside so we can finally get out to the grounds and get set up."

"I took my article to Father."

May frowned. "But it wasn't in the *Dispatch*. I looked as soon as it arrived."

"He said no. Very firmly. But then—" Quickly, she told May about what had happened.

"It's in the *Journal*? And Noah did that for you?"

"I used a pen name."

"I heard that part," May said. "And Noah did that for you?"

"If you heard the pen name part, you heard the part about Noah putting it in the mail slot."

"Yes," May said, "but the Noah part is more interesting—at the moment." She nodded. "So you need the camp desk because you have a series to write now." She arched one eyebrow. "Is Noah going to continue helping you?"

"I don't know. That's not important. What is important is that I'm going to need your help."

"Help with what?" Junie appeared in the doorway.

"Help with the sign for the Bee Hive," May said, without missing a beat.

June frowned. "And you had to sneak out here to the barn to discuss that?"

"There's a surprise involved," Emilie said.

"And to make it work, Emilie needs to stay in town for a while today." May grabbed Emilie's hand. "We both do, actually. But you can't tell Ma or Aunt Henrietta what we're up to. Because the surprise involves them."

May pulled Emilie after her, and somehow she convinced Mother to let the two of them linger in town instead of following them out to the Chautauqua grounds right away. In moments, Mother and Aunt Cornelia, April and June were headed south in the family's wagon, while May and Emilie pulled the Springs' buggy over in front of Klein's.

Emilie climbed down. "Tell me when they're out of sight. I need to find Noah, and that search begins at the Paddock."

"You also need to figure out where to get more ink and paper. I suppose we could buy it on credit at Crowell's."

"That's a good idea," Emilie agreed. "By the time Mother notices the charge, we'll be in Long Pine. She'll have forgotten all about it by the time I get back."

"I'm helping you with this for now," May said, "but you have to tell Uncle Bill and Aunt Henrietta everything—and before we leave for Long Pine. It isn't right to keep them in the dark. And besides that, it's a sin to lie."

"Of course I'll tell Mother," Emilie promised. "Just not yet. I want to let Father get used to the idea first."

"He knows?"

Emilie nodded. "I couldn't just let him read it in the *Journal*."

May looked over at her. "That explains that strange sound we heard this morning at breakfast."

"What are you talking about?"

"Papa said it was likely just the *Queen of the Blue*'s whistle. I'm thinking it was more likely Uncle Bill blowing off steam."

"Ha. Ha. Ha." Emilie looked toward the hotel. "I'll be right back if I don't find Noah."

"Find who?" Noah strode toward them from the opposite direction. "I've been pacing around the block, hoping you'd get here before too much longer." He held up the *Journal*. He'd folded it to reveal E. J. Starr's interview of Miss Ida Jones. "Have you read this? It's excellent." He winked at Emilie.

May said something about his being on the front page of the *Dispatch*.

"That—oh—yes. Of course. Thank you." He smiled up at May. "I was hoping you might be able to introduce me to this E. J. Starr. I'd like to see if I could wrangle my way onto his list of ten—although I suppose it's nine, now. You wouldn't happen to know him, would you?"

"*Him*?" Emilie looked up at May. "Did you just hear that? The man reads an article he likes and automatically assumes the author is a man." She looked over at Noah. "Chauvinist."

"Reporter," Noah said back. "Journalist. Writer."

Emilie bobbed a curtsey "Thank you." She motioned at May. "May came up with a way for me to stay in town just long enough to get the next interview accomplished. I hope you're available?"

"I've been waiting for you, with just that in mind," Noah said. "And I've been thinking that you probably still want to maintain anonymity?" When Emilie nodded, he continued. "I have an idea to that end. Is Colonel Barton still on your list?"

"Absolutely. He's the perfect subject for Independence Day."

"I stopped by his house yesterday about another matter," Noah said, "and his housekeeper invited me to return."

"Mrs. Riley tried to feed you." May laughed. "She's famous for that. Every guest must eat. It's her motto. Some of us wonder if she's worked it into a sampler to hang on the kitchen wall."

Noah smiled. "Well, she said I'd be welcome to bring company and enjoy the ambiance of the colonel's front porch." He looked down at Emilie. "So I was thinking that you could leave word with Mrs. Riley about wanting to interview the colonel as soon as he's back—and conduct my interview over pie and coffee."

"Perfect," May said, and moved over into the driver's seat and gathered the reins.

"But—aren't you coming with us?" Noah asked.

May shook her head. "I really do have to help my sisters get set up at the Bee Hive. Don't worry. I'll come up with a reasonable explanation for why Emilie had to stay behind for a little while."

"Composition books," Emilie said. "Don't we all need them to take notes at all the sessions? And we probably need something else for our C.S.L.C. demonstration."

"Your *what* demonstration?"

"May and her sisters host a Chautauqua Scientific and Literary Circle every Monday evening at their house," Emilie said. "The board asked us if we'd demonstrate what goes on at a meeting. Monday at four o'clock."

"The Penner twins are presenting papers on the sovereigns of England," May explained to Noah. "And trust me, once you've seen those two speak on a literary subject, you'll never forget it." She looked over at Emilie. "You know, thinking of Fern and Flora, wouldn't it be nice if we made special corsages for them? Doesn't Klein's carry some kind of special ribbon we'd need to make them?"

Emilie nodded. "I'll get a couple of yards."

"I'm so glad we remembered," May said. "It'll be much easier to have all the supplies before things get going out at the grounds. It's very good of you not to mind running those errands for us." She paused. "In fact, now that I think about it, would you mind walking over to Young's and getting a set of mandolin strings? And a set of strings for June's guitar wouldn't be a bad idea, either."

"I think we've come up with enough reason for me to stay in town." Emilie laughed. "At this rate, I'll have to buy a market basket to carry everything."

"One more stop. We can use a market basket. And for the record, Ms. Reporter, I really would like a spare set of strings. And so would Junie."

Emilie laughed. "All right. I'll see to it."

"Thank you. Just please don't take a second longer than is absolutely necessary to get Two of Ten turned in and to get to the Bee Hive."

"I won't," Emilie said.

"I'll drive her out," Noah offered.

"Unless you've already reserved a rig," May replied, "there'll be no chance of that. And honestly, it might be faster just to walk. The bridge slows things down quite a bit when there's a crowd, and there's sure to be a crowd all day long—only to get worse as time gets closer to the opening exercises." She glowered at Emilie. "And you had better make sure that the Spring Sisters have their accompanist."

Emilie put her hand to her heart. "I promise. I'll be there no later than four."

May slapped the reins across the buggy horse's rump and headed off. As she crossed Court Street, someone shouted her name. Bert Hartwell trotted over to the buggy and climbed aboard. He said something to May, then turned about and waved at Emilie and Noah.

"You have wonderful friends," Noah said. He offered his arm then. "Which way, Madame Reporter?"

"Up Court Street," Emilie said. "We can stop at Crowell's Stationers before going on to the music house to get the strings May wants. It's only a short walk from there to Colonel Barton's. And on the way, you can tell me how it is that you know our illustrious colonel."

Noah smiled down at her. "Do I sense the beginning of an interview?"

"You do."

"In that case, ask me something else."

Emilie looked up at him with a frown. "Really?"

"Really. Ask me something else." When Emilie didn't speak, he finally said, "I'll tell you anything you want to know about that, but not for your article. Just for you. And anyway, we've got over a week for those kinds of conversations—in fact, we have even longer than that if we consider Long Pine."

He is thinking about Long Pine. Emilie's heart sang.

CHAPTER 15

Grace and Ladora had finished their morning coffee on the porch, retreated to the kitchen, and donned aprons in preparation for the baking day ahead, when the front doorbell rang. Grace listened carefully, relaxing measurably when she heard a familiar voice. Not another telegram. Not Josiah returned early. Noah Shaw. . .and a young lady.

"It's Mr. Shaw." Ladora bustled back into the kitchen. "He's takin' me up on the offer of pie on the front porch." She chuckled. "And from the look of things, I wasn't too far off when I teased him about sparkin' on that porch swing." She grabbed a knife and prepared to cut into once of the fresh-baked pies. When Grace looked over with regret, Ladora said, "Now, Grace. It never hurts to taste-test. We can always make another."

"Just how many pie plants do you have growing out back?" Grace smiled.

"Nigh on to a forest," Ladora said. "No need to worry about that. I'll be able to keep my promise to the Methodists. You mind settin' up a coffee tray?"

In just a few minutes, the two women were back out on the front porch, welcoming Mr. Shaw and his friend. *Friend.* Ha. Noah Shaw might be ignorant of the real state of affairs, but it was obvious to Grace that more than friendship was blossoming—at least on the part of the young lady. There was something about the way she looked up at him that reminded Grace of—a memory she'd rather not indulge at the moment. And so she concentrated on setting the coffee tray on the table between the two rocking chairs while Ladora welcomed Miss Rhodes—whom she'd obviously met before.

"I'm doing a series of articles for the newspaper during Chautauqua," Miss Rhodes said. "When I told No—Mr. Shaw that I was hoping that Colonel Barton would agree to be my subject for Independence Day—"

"I suggested we come here for Miss Rhodes to leave a note for the colonel." Shaw finished the young lady's sentence.

She picked up where he had left off. "And then I thought perhaps I could interview Mr. Shaw—if you'd indulge us with the use of the front porch?"

"I assured her that you'd already extended an invitation," Shaw said.

"And since I need to turn in that interview before we go out to the grounds—"

"We thought we'd 'kill two birds with one stone,' as they say." Shaw continued. "Miss Rhodes is writing with a pen name, and she preferred not to conduct the interview at the Paddock."

"I'd like to protect my anonymity if at all possible," she said.

Grace smiled at the two, each one finishing the other's sentence, much like a couple who'd been married for decades. Did they realize what they were doing? She supposed not.

"If you subscribe to the *Journal*," Mr. Shaw said, "you might have already read the first in Miss Rhodes's series. She interviewed Miss Ida Jones yesterday about her life 'on the road,' so to speak."

"The *Journal*?" Ladora sounded surprised.

"I read that article," Grace said. "Enjoyed it very much."

"Thank you." Miss Rhodes smiled.

Ladora looked confused. "Why'd you want to go and write for

the other newspaper? And hide your real name? Rhodes is the best newspaper name you could want around these parts. And the *Journal*?" She sounded a bit like a mother scolding a child when she said, "I wouldn't think Mr. Rhodes would think kindly of his own kin helping the competition." And then she hurried to add, "Not that it's any of my business, of course. But I got to be careful I don't allow somethin' the colonel wouldn't approve."

"I understand, Mrs. Riley," Miss Rhodes said. "And I well remember Colonel Barton's filling in for Reverend Philips this spring. He spoke about personal integrity and the importance of telling the truth."

Ladora looked surprised. "You got a good memory."

"It was a fine sermon," Miss Rhodes said. "One of the reasons I'm using a pen name is that I didn't want to be published because of who I am. Everyone knows that I had the opportunity to write the Ladies' News precisely because my father is. . .my father. It had nothing to do with whether or not I can write. I did take this series to my father first, but he rejected it. And so I decided to try with the *Journal*. But it's important to me that it be accepted or rejected on its own merits. I didn't want it in the *Daily Dispatch* just because Father was making allowances, and I didn't want it in the *Journal* because Father's competitor wanted to get his goat. Hence, the pen name. Which only a few people know about."

Grace looked over at Ladora. "You've got to admire her spirit. She's not giving up."

Ladora still wasn't convinced. "Does Mr. Rhodes know you took it to the other paper?"

"He does," Miss Rhodes said. "When I saw it in the *Journal* this morning, I showed it to him myself." She paused. "And in the spirit of Colonel Barton's talk this past spring, I will admit that Father is far from thrilled with the idea of my writing for a newspaper. But he didn't forbid it. I suppose you could say that we have agreed to disagree on the matter."

Grace avoided Ladora's gaze. In some ways, Miss Rhodes reminded her of herself—strong enough to try to make her own way in the world, even if doing so meant some would disapprove of her choices. Miss Rhodes hadn't mentioned what her mother thought of it all. Grace suspected that the mother had a role in the issue of a pen name as well. She dared a look at Ladora, who seemed to be working hard to reconcile her mother-hen tendencies with her "upstanding Methodist" beliefs.

If Ladora was going to split hairs over something so insignificant as a pen name, what would happen when she finally learned the truth about her houseguest? Finally, Grace spoke up. "All kinds of people in the creative arts take on other names, Ladora. I'm Madame Jumeaux in the theatrical world. Samuel Clemens is Mark Twain to his readers." She looked up at Noah Shaw. "For all we know, Mr. Shaw here is really Mr. Cornswaggle J. McSnapencrackle."

The ridiculous name made Shaw laugh. "What a fabulous name. I may just have to create a new character." He snatched his hat off and held it over his heart. Grasping one lapel with his free hand, he then hitched one shoulder higher than the other and lisped, "Cornssswaggle J. McSssnapencrackle, Esssquire, at yer ssservice."

Laughter broke the tension, and Miss Rhodes said, "I only need to impose on you this one time, Mrs. Riley. I'll have my own office set up out at the grounds by this evening."

Ladora's expression softened. "And Mr. Rhodes knows all about this?"

"Yes, ma'am. I haven't told Mother yet, but I will. Soon."

Ladora glanced over at Grace. "So it ain't really lyin' then, is it? And don't you get offended, Madam Joo-mo. I'm not callin' names. I just never thought on pen names and stage names and such before. I guess I knew Mark Twain couldn't be a real name. Too much of a coincidence, a man with a name like that writin' 'bout steamboats and such. Had to be made up."

The shadows of doubt that had furrowed Ladora's brow cleared. The "upstanding Methodist" and the mother hen melded, and Ladora became her whirlwind self again, shooing the young people into the porch rockers, then alternately recommending the swing and even Josiah's office if Miss Rhodes needed a nice desk. Then, without warning, she asked Mr. Shaw how they were planning on getting out to the grounds and offered them a ride.

"Thing is," she said, "Grace and me have these pies to deliver." She looked up at Shaw. "If yer of a mind to do it, you could hitch Babe up for us and then ride out. It's no trouble at all to detour by that newspaper office. A free ride instead of twenty-five cents or whatever they're chargin' people this year for the horse cars."

Miss Rhodes and Mr. Shaw exchanged what amounted to an unspoken conversation and they both said *thank you* at once. Back at work in the kitchen, Ladora said to Grace, "We'll get there early enough, we'll have prime seats. Miss Rhodes plays piano for the Spring Sisters, and those girls sound sweeter than anything. Wait till you hear. And while I'm not much on lectures, I'll admit to lookin' forward to hearing what Mr. Shaw has to say from up on that stage. My but he is a handsome thing, isn't he?"

Grace busied herself with chopping rhubarb, grateful that Ladora was doing fine holding a conversation without her saying a word. How was she going to take advantage of a Chautauqua crowd if she was expected to keep company with three other people all evening? She might have to claim a headache when it came time to leave. Maybe try to recomb that mousey wig into something more conservative. And a cane. Yes. Definitely. A cane.

Ladora had stopped talking. Knife poised in midair, Grace looked over at her. "I–I'm sorry, Ladora. What did you say?"

"I was just wonderin'. What awful name did you Frenchify?"

"Wh–what?"

"You said Joo-mo was for the theater."

Grace nodded.

"That's French, ain't it?"

"Y–yes."

"So. . .what awful name did you Frenchify?"

Barton. Which wasn't all that awful, unless you were a young girl consumed with anger and resentment. Grace took a deep breath. "I just thought French sounded more glamorous." She nodded toward the front of the house. "Do you think we might offer the young people a little lunch instead of just pie? And if we're going out to the grounds early, did you intend to buy supper out there?"

"Buy supper? Land sakes, no. I can't be spending money like that. You all right with us making ourselves a picnic? Lovely day like today would be a good one to take in the sights and then maybe have a picnic over by the river. The *Queen of the Blue* is running now. She's a pretty sight."

"*Queen of the Blue*?"

"The steamboat. She don't run far. Just from the grounds downstream to the paper mill dam at Glen Falls and back. Costs a dollar. I'd never spend such money. But she's a pretty a little thing. You should see her when they take her out for a torchlight excursion. Oh, my." Ladora glanced toward the front porch. "It's about the most romantic sight I've ever seen."

Relief flooded through Grace as Ladora segued from the topic of romantic steamboat excursions to boating to the new natatorium and other assembly attractions without noticing that Grace hadn't really answered the question as to the real name behind Madame Jumeaux. She'd avoided two things now. Revealing her real name and admitting that just paying the entry fee onto the grounds would leave her penniless. If things went well, the latter problem would be solved tonight. In regards to her being a Barton, she just didn't know. But she had nearly three days to decide. Josiah's train wasn't due in until Monday.

—∞—

Grace stood at her bedroom window, looking down as Ladora drove Josiah's small farm wagon out onto Ella Street. They'd left the tailgate down, and Miss Rhodes and Noah Shaw were perched on the back, their legs dangling, the five rhubarb pies nestled in the thin layer of straw behind them. Just seeing the two talking to each other made Grace smile. Her own experience with love at first sight hadn't worked out, but that didn't necessarily mean that Miss Rhodes and Mr. Shaw were headed down that road. It would depend on Miss Rhodes's ability to adjust to a life she hadn't been prepared for—in her case life with a traveling man who turned women's heads wherever he went. A woman inclined to jealousy would never last with a man like Noah Shaw. *Maybe you should warn her. Or him.*

"No," Grace muttered aloud and turned away from the window. "You should mind your own business is what you should do. And get to work." And there was work to be done. Thankfully, she hadn't lost her touch when it came to playing a role. The sudden emergence of a sick headache had been played just right. She'd convinced Ladora that, while she was too sick to attend opening exercises, Ladora should definitely go. Grace would be fine. She just needed to rest in a quiet room with the shades lowered. Now, as the wagon disappeared from view, Grace took up her comb and brush and began to restyle her dark brown wig.

When the sun dipped low on the western horizon, she got ready, donning the wig and a rural-style blue chambray bonnet. Next came a gray knit shawl and a cane. As shadows lengthened, Grace made her way downstairs and out the back door, avoiding the busiest part of town as she hurried south toward the river. Emerging from behind a lumberyard on Bell Street, she joined the stragglers headed toward the only bridge crossing this part of the Blue River. By now she was using the cane.

She knew her disguise was a good one when a couple driving a buggy pulled over and offered her a ride. She thanked them in a wavering, aged voice. When the driver helped her up, it would have been easy to check his coat pocket for a money clip, but she decided not to. Safer to wait until she was out on the grounds where she could get lost in the crowd. That's how she'd always worked. Get the cash fast and use the crush of people to obscure the act of discarding money clips and coin purses.

It took a moment to convince the young driver and his pretty wife to leave her just outside the entrance to the assembly grounds. No, she really didn't need any assistance. Yes, she really did wish to wait here. Her friends would be along any minute; she was sure of it. She'd promised them she would wait at the gate, and she wouldn't want them to worry.

Finally, the couple believed her and went on their way. Grace waited for a few moments before making her way to the gate. She fumbled with her coin purse as she withdrew her twenty-five-cent entry fee with a trembling hand. The ticket-taker probably associated her shakiness with age, but it wasn't an act. Parting with that last quarter made it real. She was now officially destitute. In spite of the warm evening, she shivered and pulled her gray shawl close.

As she tapped her way through the grass toward the lighted pavilion in the distance, Grace hunched a bit and leaned on the cane. She had transformed into a crabbed old woman. It was time to get to work.

The sad truth of it was that she had lost her nerve. Emilie Rhodes, who had never had a nervous bone in her body when it came to playing the piano in front of a crowd, couldn't seem to play a simple hymn tonight. With the sounding of the last note—she didn't dare try an arpeggio—Emilie braved a look over at her cousins, taking a bow as the evening crowd offered polite, but decidedly restrained, applause.

The set of April's jaw said it all. Emilie was in for a tongue-lashing later tonight. May just looked confused. And Junie—well, Junie was too intent on pretending not to seek out Bert Hartwell's face in the front row to worry about the accompanist who had missed a few notes during the performance.

I don't miss notes. What is the matter with me? The weak applause died down. Emilie felt like slinking into the night. April relied on a strong piano to keep her on pitch. A weakness in her voice to be sure, but not something that the Spring Sisters had ever had to worry about, thanks to Emilie. Until tonight.

She kept her head down as she descended the stairs from the stage to the sand-covered earth. Thank heavens they were seated in the front row. At least she would only feel eyes boring into the back of her head instead of feeling like she was surrounded by people sending either sympathetic or disappointed looks her way. Still, as she settled on the chair next to Noah, she could feel those eyes. Especially Mother's and Father's. Was it possible for mere looks to give someone a headache? She certainly had one.

The Spring Sisters had barely regained their seats when Reverend E. S. Smith rose to give the invocation. Then the town band played, and happily for them—and the crowd—the Beatrice Band was much better this year than last. Maybe their improvement would obscure people's memory of the fiasco that was the Spring Sisters this evening. On the other hand, if that tuba player missed one note or six—*Emilie Rhodes, that is just mean.* Wishing missed notes on a fellow musician. What was wrong with her, anyway?

As she sat, blinking back tears of shame, Emilie gripped the edges of the bench on either side of her lap and hung on, willing herself to sit with her back erect and her chin held high. She pretended fascination with events on the stage, when all she really cared about was getting the night over with so that she could retreat to the Bee Hive, wallow in her failure—and think about tomorrow's interview.

But then Noah leaned close and whispered in her ear, "Everyone has an off night. You'll be wonderful tomorrow." Then he covered her hand with his. . .and left it in place. Not that anyone else could see. Her white lawn skirt hid both their hands. Which made it even more scandalous, she supposed. She looked up at him. Like her, he was concentrating on what was going on up on the stage. And yet. . .his hand stayed put. And then, he was being introduced so that he could introduce the evening's lecturer, Professor C. M. Ellinwood of the Nebraska Wesleyan University.

Noah rose and strode up onto the stage. He looked out over the crowd of several hundred and complimented those in attendance for "choosing Professor Ellinwood's fine lecture on 'The Six Days of Creation' over the Sells Brothers' Circus." The latter, as everyone knew, had had the audacity to set up camp this evening in competition with the Interstate Chautauqua. He mentioned that he and Professor Ellinwood had something in common, this being their first opportunity to share an assembly platform. And then he explained that, since the professor's presentation included "grand and beautiful colored lantern pictures of theological and biblical subjects," darkness would be required before the beginning of his lecture.

He looked over at Emilie. "And so I am hoping that the Spring Sisters will grace the stage once again and delight us with another number."

He was giving her a chance at redemption. The girls rose to a smattering of polite applause, and on the way up to the stage, sweet May leaned in and said, "Just imagine them all in their unmentionables. That always works for me."

May meant well, of course, but Emilie's mind went straight back to its usual subject. She was fairly certain that Noah Shaw looked amazingly good in anything he wore—or didn't. And that thought made her blush again. Finally, though, she decided to imagine what April would say and do if Emilie let her down again. Dread of that had the desired affect. Emilie concentrated on the hymn. She didn't miss a single note. She even dared an arpeggio. This time, the applause swelled.

As the girls made their way back to their seats, Noah moved to the edge of the stage, and as twilight fell and the Tabernacle crowd faded from view in the gathering dusk, he began his recitation. " 'The Lord is my Shepherd, I shall not want. . . .'" The crowd stilled. Emilie turned her head just enough to see a few rows of the crowd. People had lifted their heads and were staring, mesmerized, as Noah's rich voice resonated beneath the Tabernacle roof. With a few quiet remarks, he transitioned seamlessly into the Lord's Prayer and, finally, back to Psalm 22. Then he ended with one phrase. " 'The *Lord* is my Shepherd. I shall not want.' "

When Noah's voice died away, it was as if the crowd gave a collective sigh. There was no applause, just silence as Professor Ellingham's magic lantern projected a colored slide intended to illustrate Genesis 1:1, "In the beginning. . .God."

CHAPTER 16

The moment the opening meeting concluded and Noah stood up, he was surrounded. Someone held a program up and requested his autograph. While he was signing the program, someone else asked where he'd studied elocution. The program said he was from the St. Louis area. Did he happen to know that wonderful orator Garrison Richards? Another program was thrust forward for his signature. He took the pencil, all the while scanning the crowd for Emilie. Where had she gone? She'd been right beside him only moments ago. Now. . .now he was in a conversation with overzealous redheaded twins, essentially trapped here at the bottom of the stage stairs.

"We've heard so much about you from our mother," one twittered, "and now we know why."

"Indeed we do," the other said. "We're the Penners. Flora and Fern." The speaker glanced at her sister. "And we've never heard such a beautiful rendition of the Shepherd's Psalm. Your voice—you project so well."

"Girls, girls." A woman—obviously the twins' mother—pushed her way through the small group gathered around him. "Let Mr. Shaw take a breath." She beamed up at him, "You must forgive Fern and Flora their zeal. It's my fault, I'm afraid. I've been singing your praises ever since I learned that you were the same lecturer I heard at the conference last year." She paused. "And I must say I'm more than a little envious of my friend Henrietta Rhodes. She's out-paced everyone with last evening's dinner party. I'm hoping to convince you to join the Penner family for a meal at some point during the assembly. We've one of the cottages here on the grounds."

Noah nodded without really listening. Finally, he caught a glimpse of Emilie heading off in the direction of the campground with May. She wasn't even looking his way. What did that mean? Was she upset?

The twins' mother was still talking. Noah nodded while he signed other programs. It had begun. Anonymity would be impossible now—at least insofar as the few hundred people who'd attended this evening's session were concerned. And all he wanted to do was follow Emilie back to the Bee Hive.

But then he noticed a young girl standing back a bit, clutching a program, waiting. Hardly daring a glance in his direction, and yet. . .waiting.

"Wonderful," the twins' mother was saying. "We'll look forward to it." She spoke to her daughters. "Come along now, girls. We mustn't monopolize Mr. Shaw's time. There are many others who wish to speak with him." She headed out into the night, the two girls following along.

Even as he wondered what he'd just agreed to, Noah moved toward the girl, noting her simple calico dress, which was clean but faded. He bent down. "May I help you, miss?"

The girl nodded. "I liked your 'Lord is My Shepherd.' " Noah had to strain to hear the words. "My mama used to say it every night for prayers." Tears gathered in her eyes.

Used to say it. Everything else faded away as Noah concentrated on the young girl remembering a mother who was, for whatever reason, no longer saying prayers with her.

"My mama taught me," Noah said, as quietly as possible. When the girl looked up at him, he gave a little nod. "She's been gone since I was about your age. I miss her every day. But I'm glad she taught me that psalm. Every time I recite it, I pretend that God has opened a window in the sky and she's looking down on me, smiling. Sometimes that makes me cry, but mostly it makes me feel better."

The girl nodded. She started to hold the program out to him, but then she sighed and took it back. "I don't have a pencil."

Someone handed Noah a pencil. He asked the girl her name and wrote, *For Elizabeth, Psalm 119:92, Noah Shaw.* "That's another verse that helps me," he said and recited, " 'Unless thy law had been my delights, I should then have perished in mine affliction.' " The girl looked over at him with a little frown. He smiled at her. "You'll understand it better when you get older, but one of the things I think it means for you and me is that even when we feel sad, we should keep on saying the Shepherd's Psalm."

The girl nodded and thanked him in a shy, half-whisper. Noah watched her make her way across the pavilion and to the side of a work-worn man in a battered hat, who was waiting just at the fringe of the light. When the girl looked up at him and said something, the man looked over at Noah and tugged on the brim of his hat. Then he and the girl disappeared into the night.

Could a poor child be an angel in disguise? Feeling humbled—and convicted that he shouldn't be so self-centered when it came to these moments after a performance—Noah shut all thought of Emilie out of his mind and took up the work. He signed programs and conversed with strangers about everything from the beautiful assembly grounds to the new courthouse being erected up on Sixth and Grant Streets to Mr. Wilde's new novel about a surreal portrait of a man named Dorian Gray. And then he caught up with the redheaded Penner twins over at one of the cottages. He apologized for not paying better attention and learned than he'd agreed to a Sabbath-day luncheon with the family. They would collect him directly after the eleven o'clock service.

It was ten o'clock by the time Noah could seek out the Bee Hive. The campground had been set up like a small town, with named streets and numbered tents, both of which facilitated the moving of people and the mail, the latter delivered daily. As Noah walked up one street and turned onto another, the sounds of voices and the glow of lighted lamps shining through the canvas made him think of the Indian tepees Ma had embroidered on his quilt. She had described the glow of campfires on the prairie. He didn't think she'd ever described glowing tepees, but as Noah looked around him, the effect of lamps lighted inside the canvas tents was almost magical. Did tepees glow this way on winter nights when snows kept their owners close to home?

Ma had said someone told her that among the Indians, the woman owned the tepee. It was the woman's job to take it down and put it back up again, and the woman was the one to haul it across the prairie when the tribe moved. She'd seen a long line of Indians go by once. She said the women were walking alongside ponies dragging a conveyance made by attaching the tepee poles to either side of the pony, and then suspending the household goods on a blanket or buffalo skin between the poles. A travois, they called it.

Low thunder in the distance made Noah looked toward the west. Ma had heard that tepees could stay in place even in a very high wind. She'd thought about that the night a storm blew her wagon over. That was the night Pa died, although Ma had never said that, exactly. She just didn't talk about Pa all that much. It was as if one night she was on the trail with him, and the next she was headed the other way with a freighter who'd agreed to give her a ride back to where she came from.

A lot of people at the assembly tonight had expressed a wish for rain to relieve the heat. They might get their wish tonight. Noah looked about at the campground. What would happen to all these tents if a storm blew through? He frowned, thinking of the huge tree branch arching over the place where Emilie and May would be sleeping. On a hot summer day, such a thing was a boon because of the shade. But on a stormy night?

The sound of laughter brought him back to the moment and interrupted the worry. Group laughter. And above the laughter, the strumming of a guitar from the direction of the Bee Hive. He knew a quote about bees. Benjamin Franklin, he thought. What was it? Something about a spoonful of honey catching more flies than vinegar. Why anyone would want to catch flies, Noah wasn't sure. He remembered the quote. "Tart words make no friends; a spoonful of honey will catch more flies than a gallon of vinegar." He didn't like thinking of himself as a fly, but one thing was certain. He was being drawn to the Bee Hive.

Grace made her way back to Josiah's house through darkened, quiet streets. She'd thought she had plenty of time to become Grace Jumeaux again, but she was only halfway up the stairs when she heard the back door creak. She paused just long enough to realize that Ladora was heading this way. As quietly as possible, she scampered up the remaining stairs and into her room. Grimacing as she literally ripped the wig off her head, she stuffed it beneath the bed, along with the cane and the gray shawl, then leaped beneath the covers, still fully clothed. Turning on her side and away from the door, she huddled down, willing her breathing to even out as she listened. As expected, the door creaked open.

Adding just the right tone of confusion—after all, she was supposed to have been asleep—Grace croaked, "W–who's there?"

With a sigh of regret, Ladora opened the door a bit farther. Her voice just above a whisper, she answered. "I'm sorry, dear. I didn't mean to wake you. I just couldn't settle in until I was certain you were all right. Did those headache powders help at all?"

Grace waited before answering. "Y–yes. I believe so." She turned over to face the door—and Ladora. "Now that I'm awake, I think—I think the pain is less. Thank you."

"Has your stomach settled? I could make some mint tea if you'd like."

"Thank you, but that's not necessary. I'm sure I'll be fine in the morning. How was the opening?"

"Oh, it was fine. Just. . .really. . .so fine. Mr. Shaw's voice. . .and the music. I wish you could have been there. The magic lantern show was beyond anything I could have imagined. The professor asked Mr. Shaw to read the creation account from the Bible, and when he said, 'And the Spirit of God moved upon the face of the waters,' the professor actually made the waves up on the screen *move*. I've never seen anything like it. It was mighty near to miraculous. It made me think of all the places you've been in your travels. You've been blessed, Grace. I'm not complaining, mind you. Old Ladora Riley's got herself plenty to do right here at home. But the ocean. That must be something."

"It is," Grace said. "I'm glad you enjoyed the evening."

"There's another one Sunday. You'll get your chance to see for yourself."

Grace said nothing.

"I'll let you rest now. I'm glad you're feeling better. Heat should be letting up in the night. There's a bit of lightning in the west. We just might get rain."

"I'll be down in plenty of time to help chop more pie plant," Grace said.

"Now don't you give that another thought. You just rest. You need anything, give the floor a *whop* with a shoe, and I'll come running. In fact, give the floor two *whop*s when you're ready for breakfast, and I'll bring it up. You remember that, now. One *whop* for help and two for breakfast."

"That's very kind of you, but I'm quite certain I'll be mended by morning. Good night, now."

Grace waited a moment after the door had closed before throwing back the covers. She hoped Ladora was right about the rain. Goodness but it was a hot night to be lying under even one light comforter, let alone with all these clothes on.

She sat in bed, listening until she was certain Ladora had finally retreated to her own room at the back of the house. Slipping out of bed, she knelt on the carpet, grunting as she fished her things out and stowed them in her costume trunk. Next, she retrieved the exquisite little box where she'd stowed the French buttons. She would have to sell them now. It was the only way for her to pay her way onto the grounds again. And she had to return, even though she had little interest in a magic lantern show.

Of course the businesses would stay open to take advantage of all the people in town, but the owner might want to take advantage of the Chautauqua sessions—and only an owner was likely to be aware of the value of French enamel buttons. A town this size should have at least half a dozen women in the dressmaking business. Surely there would be one owner who would choose business over pleasure. The right woman should be willing to pay a dollar a button for the matched set, and she'd know she was getting a bargain in the process.

Laying the button box atop the dresser beside the door, Grace slipped out of her dress and donned her nightgown, scolding herself for tonight—which had amounted to an abject failure. She might not have had a headache earlier this evening, but she was getting one now. She sighed. Of all the things that had changed in her world of late, of all the things that she had lost as her youth waned, she didn't think she'd ever lose her courage. There'd been ample opportunity to resupply her empty purse tonight out at the assembly grounds. People were so naive. It would have been easy. Why hadn't she taken advantage of it?

She turned away from the window and, in the process, knocked the book she'd borrowed off Josiah's shelf onto the floor: *Illustrations and Meditations* by Charles Haddon Spurgeon. Intended to help her remember the right vocabulary for her current role as a respectable old maid. Confound Charles Spurgeon for his blasted meditations, anyway. And confound Ladora Riley and Noah Shaw and Emily Rhodes and their blasted niceness. Because of them, a part of her she'd thought long since dead and buried seemed to be resurrecting itself. Because of them, she was going to have to sell her French buttons. And she didn't appreciate it. Not one bit.

This was no time for a woman alone to grow a conscience.

—w—

Wakened from a deep sleep, Noah launched himself out of bed and stood barefoot in the middle of the room. For a moment, he couldn't quite remember where he was. Which town, which event. . *.June.* It was June. He was in Nebraska. On his way west.

A flash of lightning brought him fully awake. Raking his fingers through his black hair, he hurried over to lower the hotel-room window just as the heavens opened and sheets of rain poured from the sky. The air in the room had dropped several degrees. Good. All those people who'd bemoaned the heat would get some relief, and once the skies cleared—crashing thunder and another bolt of lightning was all it took to draw Noah's attention south. All those tents. In this wind? Another bolt of lightning flashed. And another. A close one. It had struck something. Something tall. A windmill or a tree. A tree. *No!*

The fire bell began to clang. Scrambling to get dressed, Noah didn't even take time for socks, just pulled his shoes on over his bare feet. Stuffing his shirt into his pants, he threw open the door to his hotel room and joined the other men hurrying into the hall and thundering down the stairs. Most seemed to come to their senses in the lobby where they stood, milling about, talking, staring out into the pouring rain, worrying aloud about crops at home—had it hailed anywhere; where the fire was; hope the fire hose company is well-equipped—and a range of other topics. Noah didn't care about any of them. Shouldering his way past them, he dodged into the rain and took off running south.

—∞—

Drenched to the skin, half-blinded by the rain, Noah staggered through the assembly grounds gates. He was one among many making his way past farm wagons and buggies parked along the fence. A couple of young boys had taken shelter beneath one of the farm wagons. Every time lightning flashed, Noah saw more of the scene. One or two farmers dressed in overalls held on to the bridles of staid draft horses they'd apparently hitched up for the drive home. Now they stood in place, waiting for the storm to pass.

The main pole to one of the larger tents—one of the stores, but Noah didn't know which one—had collapsed. Apparently no one was hurt, because the few people standing around observing the damage remained huddled beneath their umbrellas. A gaggle of young people were floundering in the rushing waters of the creek that meandered through the grounds, shrieking with laughter, ignoring the possible dangers hidden in the rushing water.

The grounds didn't seem to have suffered much damage. Still, Noah couldn't erase the thought of that huge branch stretching over the very place where Emilie had planned to lay her head tonight. He slowed to a trot but kept going, past the Tabernacle and toward the campground. Shouts and an occasional screech carried above the wind, which did seem to be dying down.

By the time he'd found Kinney Street, he was beginning to feel stupid for chasing over here half-dressed. But then he came around the corner. For a moment, he didn't believe it. He swiped at the rain blurring his vision as he lumbered forward. But cleared vision didn't change the view. That tree limb had been ripped away from the tree. And it had landed right where it could do the most damage to the girl he loved.

CHAPTER 17

Noah? Noah!"

Noah looked down at whoever was pounding him on the back. "What are you doing out here?"

Swiping at his face again, Noah recognized Bert Hartwell. The downpour was letting up.

"I was—I—" He gestured toward the ruined tent.

Bert raised the umbrella he was carrying high enough to shield Noah from the rain. "I know." He shook his head. "Emilie is not going to be happy. Nor is Mrs. Rhodes. The field desk her father carried through the war is under that limb. In pieces, I imagine. I told Em I'd check on the tent. I didn't expect this."

"Emilie. . .Emilie's all right?"

"Of course. They all high-tailed it over to the cottages as soon as the rain started." Hartwell looked back over at the ruined tent. "You thought—no, no, old man," Bert clapped him on the back again. "They're all having a high old time over at the Springs' cottage. They'd just started a game of Authors when I ducked out to come over here."

Relief washed over him. Noah reached up and swiped at his face. "Thank God." And thank God his hair was sopping wet. The rivulets of water would hide the tears of relief. He took a deep breath. Gestured at the tent. "Think we can move that branch, just the two of us?" A break in the clouds overhead revealed the night sky. It grew wider until finally, moonlight spilled out. All over the campground, people began poking their heads out, calling from tent to tent, checking up on one another.

Bert closed his umbrella and leaned it against the tree. "We can try."

"Maybe the desk can be salvaged somehow," Noah said, as he circled the tent. "I don't think it'll be too difficult to put this back up once we move that branch."

For the next few minutes, Noah and Bert worked together, dragging the branch out into the street, and raising the tent again. Several other men joined the effort, and before long the task was done. Together, Bert and Noah stepped inside to survey the damage. Sopping wet bedding could be remedied. But the camp desk was another matter.

"Too many pieces," Bert said, shaking his head.

"Maybe not." Noah wasn't convinced. "A good carpenter can do wonders."

"You talking about that carpenter who used to have a business in Nazareth? Because I'm thinking we're talking miracles if we expect to put this thing back together."

"I want to try," Noah said. He looked around. "We could wrap the pieces in that blanket. She won't mind if we tell her why the blanket is missing. Think we could round up some twine or rope?"

"You really want to haul the pieces all the way back to town? On foot?"

Noah shrugged. "I ran all the way out here on foot."

Bert just stood there, looking up at him with a dumb grin.

"What?"

He shook his head. "Nothing. There's twine over at the newspaper tent. I'll be back in a minute."

While Bert was gone, Noah did what he could to resurrect the

Bee Hive. Apparently Emilie had taken all of her writing materials with her when they ran for cover. At least that hadn't been lost. The girls' luggage was gone, too. Aside from soaked feather beds and the camp desk, the Bee Hive had survived relatively unscathed.

Bert returned. "You don't have to use one of those wet blankets to wrap up what's left of that desk," he said. "I found a gunny sack that should do the trick."

Together, Noah and Bert filled the gunny sack, then tied the bag closed with twine.

"You sure you can handle this?" Bert asked.

"I'm sure. After I've seen to this in the morning," he said, "I'll buy some work clothes and come back out. I expect there'll be more cleanup to do once the sun's up."

"Just remember that in exactly two days the Bugeaters are depending on you to win a baseball game or six for them. The championship game is at high noon on Independence Day. Don't do anything to hurt your home-run potential."

"Bugeaters?"

"Don't blame me. I didn't name the team. I'm just the captain."

"I'll be ready," Noah promised.

"You're a good man, Noah Shaw. And a lucky one, too."

"What makes you say that?"

"Because the girl feels the same way."

Should he deny his feelings? There didn't seem to be a point. Bert was a good man, too. "And you know that because. . . ?"

"You musical?"

"Not particularly."

"Then maybe you didn't notice all those missed notes tonight."

"Everyone has a bad night now and then. I told Emilie as much."

"Maybe, but when it comes to playing the piano, Em doesn't have bad nights. I wondered if she was feeling sick. So I kept an eye on her."

"Hartwell on the job again?"

Apparently Bert understood the reference to his being asked to check the cottages for unwanted critters. He laughed. "Exactly. Hartwell on the job. And once again, there was nothing to fear. Em wasn't sick. She was just nervous. Feeling self-conscious. When I realized why, I knew I didn't have to worry."

"You don't?"

"Nope. Like I said. You're a good man." Hartwell grinned. "If you really do come out to help with cleanup, that house to the left of the gates would be the place to check in."

Noah nodded. "And thanks."

"For what?"

"Putting me on your team." Noah hefted the bundle to one shoulder and headed for town.

Friday morning was overcast. A scud of rain passed through around breakfast time, and hearing from Bert the night before as to the status of things over at the Bee Hive, Emilie and her cousins were content to have breakfast with their parents and attend morning prayer as a family before reclaiming their rain-soaked abode.

No one was prepared for the sight of the tree limb that had ripped away from the tree. It was still lying to one side of the street running between two long rows of tents.

"Oh, Em." June looped her arm through Emilie's. Her eyes filled with tears.

"Can you believe there were people out playing in that storm? Papa said one group was riding the current down the creek." May shook her head. "Foolish. I'm glad we had the cottages to run to."

Emilie didn't know what to say. She could have been killed. Lesser storms had killed people—without ripping huge tree limbs off trees. Just this past spring, a young woman in Wymore had been killed sitting in her own parlor when lightning struck the house and traveled down the chimney. Thinking about how close to death she'd been last night made Emilie shiver.

"We should get to work," May said. "The storm's gone, and no one got hurt. Thank the Lord and move on. That's what I say."

June was first to duck inside, and the first words out of her mouth were, "Bert Hartwell!"

When the others joined her, Junie was beaming. "Look at all this. Bert said all he did was get help to put the tent back up. He's got us almost ready to move in!"

"Not quite," April said, nodding to the pile of wet bedding in the middle of the floor. She smiled at June. "But he did do a lot." She looked around them. "You'd never know it was a wreck last night."

"And look at that." Junie pointed to Emilie's side of the tent. "He even brought in a new desk. That Bert. He's a gem." The words were no sooner out of her mouth than Junie flushed bright red. "Well he is," she said, defensively.

"It's all right, June," Emilie said. "We all agree with you. We love Bert. And he *is* a gem."

"Even if he is nearsighted when it comes to my little sister." May dodged the pillow Junie flung at her.

Emilie ran her hand over the surface of the small table Bert had set up by her cot. He'd even brought out a coal oil lamp. Emilie looked over at May. "When did he have the time? He must have been up half the night."

"He probably felt bad about throwing out the desk," May said.

Emilie sighed. "Mother was *not* happy. I had no idea it meant so much to her. It's just been sitting in the basement by the coal bin ever since we moved to the new house." She paused. "Do you think there's any chance I could find another one? I know it wouldn't be the same, but it would at least show her how sorry I am about what happened."

"You could ask around at the encampment on the Fourth. Maybe some G.A.R. gent will take pity on you."

"That's a good idea." Emilie stood up. "Let's get this bedding hung out to dry. Then I need to see if I can find Professor Ellinwood. He's next on my interview list, and according to the program, he'll be lecturing over at Tennyson Hall this morning."

"Think you'll be finished in time to go boating with us later today?"

"I certainly hope so," Emilie said, "but even if I can't go out on the water, I'll meet you at the boat dock so you don't have to wonder." She ducked out of the tent, just as Bert and another man hefted the tree branch that had come down in the storm. It took her a moment to recognize Noah, dressed as he was in overalls and a chambray work shirt. "I suppose now I know why you missed morning prayers."

"I didn't miss praying," Noah said. "I just didn't come to the Tabernacle to do it."

"So Bert hornswaggled you into helping with cleanup?"

"Did not hornswaggle," Bert said. "He volunteered. Although the city boy had to go buy himself some real work clothes before he could lend a hand."

"Bert told me about the boating later," Noah said. "Mind if I join you?"

Not only did Emilie not mind, her heart rate ratcheted up at the idea that Noah would be there. "Not at all," she said, hoping she sounded much more nonchalant than she felt.

"See you then." Noah nodded. "Hope E. J. Starr has a good day. If you see him/her, give him/her my best."

"I'll be certain she/he gets the message."

—∞—

The storm seemed to have sapped momentum out of the usual Chautauqua crowds. It took most of Friday and Saturday for the campground to return to normalcy. Attendance was thinner than usual at the events scheduled at the Tabernacle, and Emilie heard more than one person wonder if attendance predictions had been exaggerated.

A general atmosphere of frustration and worry reigned, although events went forward as scheduled. The Penner twins read their papers on the sovereigns of England as part of the C.L.S.C. meeting demonstration, but only a handful of people signed up to receive more information about forming a new circle. Miss Jones's instruction in elocution proceeded as scheduled, although Emilie was privy to her private disappointment in regards to poor sales of her self-published booklets. Only a few hundred people attended Sabbath services at the Tabernacle, when at least two thousand had been expected.

Emilie, who'd been largely soaring above the disappointment thanks to a combination of her reporting life and her romantic life, finally settled into the gloom with everyone else after the Sunday morning service, although it had nothing to do with poor attendance and everything to do with the news that Noah was having dinner with the Penners.

When Flora and Fern came to fetch him as soon as the *amen* sounded at the closing prayer, Noah looked what Emilie hoped was an apology her way. The twins pointedly did not invite her—or anyone else—to join the luncheon party. Emilie assured her cousins that she had no particular claim on Mr. Shaw's time. She wished them all a delightful afternoon and retreated to the Bee Hive to get some writing done.

"Here you are," May said, moments after Emilie had plopped down on her cot. "Don't sulk. He can't spend every minute with you."

"I don't know what you're talking about," Emilie retorted. "I have work to do." She reached for a pen, nearly knocking the ink bottle over in the process. A mild curse escaped her lips. She looked over at May, who was sitting, wide-eyed, staring at her.

"Whoa. You really are in love if you're this upset over one meal."

Emilie just shook her head. "I cannot possibly be in love with Noah Shaw. I haven't even known him for a week. What an absurd notion."

" 'Methinks thou dost protest too much.' " May fluffed her pillow and lay down on her cot facing Emilie. "Remember how you said that you hoped that if you ever fell in love, you'd want to feel like Junie does about Bert?"

"That was completely hypothetical."

"Maybe, but it seems to me you do feel that way about Noah." She grinned. "Maybe you could make him a roast beef sandwich and serve it up on good china. That's what Junie did to rope Bert."

Emilie looked over. "Has Junie roped Bert?"

"You haven't noticed?"

"Noticed what?"

"All weekend long he's been different. He wanted her in his boat when we went rowing. And he took her on the torchlight cruise last night."

"He did?"

"You'd know that if you hadn't been mooning over Noah. Where were you last evening, anyway?"

"Noah walked me into town to submit tomorrow's journal article."

"And then he walked you back, I suppose."

"What if he did? Today he's having dinner at the Penners'. Next you'll be thinking he's courting Fern or Flora."

"Well it had better not be both." May laughed. Emilie threw her pillow at her. "All right, all right. But take it from me, Em. You have nothing to worry about. I wouldn't be surprised if he speaks to Uncle Bill this week."

"About what?"

"Oh, puh-leeze, Emilie Jane." May sighed and shook her head.

"Why do men speak to fathers about their daughters, anyway? Who started that custom?"

"I have no idea," Emilie said, "and any man who has a notion to do something like that had better speak to me first."

"Duly noted."

"We're strong women, remember? We want something different—a man who respects us for our minds as well as our ability to produce little replicas of themselves."

"Preaching to the choir," May said. "I personally have turned down three proposals since the beginning of Chautauqua for the purpose of proving my sincere devotion to the cause of a woman's right to choose her own destiny." She counted on her fingers. "One: Will Gable proposed that I skip choir practice and take a walk with him. I went to choir like a good girl. Two: Bert proposed that I trade my piece of Mrs. Riley's pie for an unknown glob of something he'd gotten stuck with. I declined. And let's see. . .oh, yes. Three: Mother proposed that we all abandon the Bee Hive and come home to the cottage where it's safe. Three proposals. Three refusals. I think, therefore I am. . .woman."

The two friends whiled away the Sabbath together. May read while Emilie worked on another article—this one a behind-the-scenes discussion of all the hard labor by mostly unseen folks that enabled the Chautauqua to proceed. They took a nap, and Emilie mostly managed not to obsess over Noah, who was likely charming the daylights out of Hazel Penner and her twins even as he impressed Mr. Penner, who taught English, with his knowledge of literature. Noah had dozens of quotations stuffed into his handsome head.

CHAPTER 18

She might have wandered from the fold, but even Madame Jumeaux had her limits. When a plethora of opportunities presented themselves on the Sabbath, Grace looked the other way. Once, she even warned a particularly inattentive young lady. "You should keep a better watch over your bag, dear." When the young lady in question scowled at her, Grace handed her the coin purse she'd just lifted. "This practically fell right out of it."

"Th–thank you, ma'am," the girl said.

When Ladora looked over with surprise, Grace shrugged. "Wherever there are crowds, there are pickpockets. Unfortunately, the larger the crowd where people are inclined to assume goodness on the part of their fellow event-goers, the more tantalizing the prospects. Have you heard of London's Metropolitan Tabernacle?"

"Who hasn't?" Ladora said. "The colonel dreams of hearing Spurgeon speak there one day."

"I have had the honor," Grace said, "and I was warned that those crowds are considered prime targets for some of London's less savory elements."

"I suppose you're right." Ladora sighed. "But I don't like to think on it. Someone who would take what's not theirs from the Lord's own people on the Sabbath must have a very dark heart, indeed."

Exactly, Grace thought. Even Madame Jumeaux had her limits.

And so she stayed with Ladora and listened to Noah Shaw re-create the confrontation between Satan and God in the book of Job.

She supposed she'd heard the story before, but when Shaw recited the opening, it was as if it were new material. "'Hast not thou made an hedge about him, and about his house, and about all that he hath on every side? thou hast blessed the work of his hands, and his substance is increased in the land. But put forth thine hand now, and touch all that he hath, and he will curse thee to thy face.'"

Of course Job had done no such thing. The thing was, though, most of the people Grace had ever known seemed to agree with what Satan was saying. That was obviously the wrong side of the heavenly conversation, but it had always seemed to Grace that people were pious because they believed that if they were good, God would respond in kind. The reverse side of that coin was true, too. If you weren't good, you were on your own.

As Shaw's monologue proceeded, things got beyond what Grace remembered of the story—and, in more ways than one, beyond her experience and understanding. First of all, God let Satan wreak havoc in Job's life, which was strange enough in itself, but then Satan was proven wrong, because Job wasn't at all like the pious people Grace had known—the ones who treated God like a celestial banker.

Even without anything to his name, even when his own wife told him to "curse God and die," Job held on to faith. Oh, he whined and stomped his feet for a bit, but at the end of the book—and the end of Noah Shaw's monologue—Job was still believing. And God hadn't even told Job that the whole thing was an experiment and that Job was going to get everything back. In fact, without getting one thing back—except a good talking-to by the Almighty—Job stayed true.

Grace had never known anyone like Job, and something about all that "where were you" passage at the end made her squirm. Did Josiah espouse the kind of faith Job had, or did he "get religion" in order to earn God's favor? And which kind of faith would be best for

Grace when it came time to face Josiah? Wondering made her head spin. The idea of facing God made her tremble.

Maybe she should just take the money she'd gotten for those buttons and whatever else she could get while she was here and buy a ticket for as far away as the money would take her. By the end of the evening she'd decided that was the best idea yet.

—∞—

"Land sakes!"

The shout and resulting crash from below brought Grace fully and immediately awake. For a moment, though, she remained disoriented. It was still pitch dark outside. What on earth?!

It's Monday. Josiah would be here this evening, and one way or the other Grace was going to have to decide once and for all what to do.

Ladora had talked even more than usual last evening on the way back from the Tabernacle service. Noah Shaw's reciting Job didn't seem to have affected Ladora one bit. Her concern centered around preparations for Josiah's return. You would have thought it was up to Ladora Riley to single-handedly prepare the residence for the Queen. She had an absurd list of things she wanted to accomplish. Grace sincerely doubted that Josiah would care whether or not there was fresh straw in the nesting boxes in the chicken coop. On the other hand, after Ladora turned in and Grace couldn't sleep, she was glad for the knowledge that if she could make it until dawn, she would be too busy to think.

More noise from below set her nerves on edge. Today was the day. With a sigh, she slipped out of bed, combed her long gray hair, wrapped it up, dressed, and padded downstairs.

"I suppose I woke you with all my crashing about," Ladora said. She was standing at the counter pouring water over the lard she'd added to a bowl of flour. "Thought I should get these pies out of the way. I just couldn't sleep another wink."

Grace donned an apron before grabbing a handful of rhubarb and heading to the sink to rinse it. "What's on your list that I can do besides washing and chopping the pie plant." She looked over. "Did you really pick this in the dark?"

"Wasn't all that hard," Ladora said and settled a thin sheet of pie dough into the first of the five pie plates. "As to what you could do, there's the nesting boxes—but that has to wait until daylight. So does scrubbing the front walk and the porch. Oh—and those cushions on the rockers need to have the dust beat out of them. That one fern in that planter to the right of the door looks a little peaked. Might get a replacement if there's time. The geraniums need to be dead-headed. I suppose that's all for the outside."

Grace smiled as she worked. "Unless you want the siding to the house and barn scrubbed?"

Ladora looked over at her with a frown. "You think it needs it?" And then she broke off. "You're joshin' me."

"Only a little."

"I just want things to be nice. Don't want the colonel thinkin' I've spent these weeks he's been gone lounging about."

"How long have you worked for him?"

"Nigh onto ten years."

"Then I suspect he knows that you're about as far from being the type who plays when the cat's away as Beatrice is from London."

Ladora plopped another lump of dough onto the counter and began to roll it out. "Wish it didn't take most of an hour to get pies delivered out to the dining hall."

"If you had a telephone"—Grace didn't look up as she washed the last of the rhubarb—"you might be able to call one of the other ladies on the committee and ask them to do it for you."

Ladora didn't respond for a moment. "And if I was the Queen of England, I'd be having tea and crumpets and my livery man would be baking my pies."

Grace laughed. "I doubt even the Queen of England can get her livery man to bake pies for her." She looked over at the housekeeper. "I'll deliver them for you. In fact, I'll do all the outside work. Even the nesting boxes, if you'll agree to let those two hens that hate me so much out in the yard first." She shuddered. "They scare me."

"Colonel wouldn't like it, my treating a guest like a maid."

"You've let me be in charge of the rhubarb," Grace said.

"That's different. It's for the missions. Even high-toned ladies in town do such as that for missions."

Grace sighed. "I'm not a high-toned lady, Ladora. Let me help. Please."

"You know how to drive a wagon?"

"I wouldn't offer if I didn't." And so, a little before noon, Grace nestled five freshly baked pies into the straw scattered over the wagon bed, climbed up to the driver's seat, and headed the plodding draft horse named Babe to the grounds. The gatekeeper peered over the side of the wagon and then up at Grace.

"Those Mrs. Riley's pies?"

"They are," Grace said.

"Thought so." He smiled. "You staying for the W.C.T.U. meetin' today?"

Grace shook her head. "Just delivering these to the dining hall."

The man nodded and waved her through. "No charge."

Things were chaotic at the dining hall when Grace arrived. Apparently the original tent had been all but destroyed by the storm the previous Friday night. Supplies were depleted and now the dining hall was only partially sheltered. Over half the tables would be out in the sun if the ladies maintained the original setup. The woman in charge of things was ill, but someone had made the obviously necessary decision to change that original setup as the sun emerged from the clouds. Now, over a dozen people scurried about with a common goal but no organizer to see that it was achieved efficiently.

No one seemed to notice Grace, waiting to be told what to do with the pies. Finally, she climbed down from the wagon and went in search of the answer. It presented itself when she made her way beneath the awning and saw a table covered with a white sheet. Flies swarmed over the sheet. Clearly, that was where today's pies were being kept.

Someone shouted *thanks* from the opposite end of the dining hall as Grace, pie in hand, headed for the sheet-covered table. "You're welcome," Grace called back. "These are from Mrs. Riley." She lifted the sheet to slide the pie into place. And that's when fate presented temptation. Right there beneath the sheet. A black money pouch.

Grace dropped the sheet and headed back for the other pie. One by one, she transferred pies into place. Four times she ignored the money pouch. But the fifth time, she did what any number of people in her position would do. She accepted fate's offering.

—∞—

Her heart pounded all the way back through the Chautauqua gates. At any moment she expected someone to come running after her. But no one did. The money pouch remained where she'd put it, nestled in the straw behind her, covered over by the sheet used to protect Ladora's pies.

All the way back to Josiah's, all the way up the drive, Grace worked at hardening her resolve. All day long, she worked, deadheading geraniums and replacing faulty ferns in the porch planters, and sweeping the floor, and beating the dust out of the rocker cushions and giving fresh straw to the pesky hens. And for once she missed Ladora Riley's chatter, because working outside meant swirling thoughts about things that Grace did not care to ponder.

It was all well and good for people like Ladora Riley and Noah Shaw to wax eloquent about matters of faith. Ladora had no worries at all as housekeeper to a man who was apparently a paragon of virtue, and people fawned all over men like Noah Shaw. Grace doubted he'd ever had a hungry day in his life. If Josiah had taken his responsibility seriously years ago, she wouldn't have been left on her own. If she'd had Noah Shaw's looks, she would still be in the theater. Some golden-hearted sop would likely replace the money. It probably wasn't even that much. And besides that, the deed was done. She couldn't exactly take it back, now, could she?

It was late afternoon before Grace had finished everything that Ladora had wanted done outside. She even picked enough pie plant for tomorrow's pies. With her arms laden with rhubarb it was easy to hide the money pouch from view as she carried it inside. Hopefully, it would provide the answer she wanted about facing Josiah.

She wouldn't have to.

—∞—

Ladora was still upstairs when Grace went back inside. She laid the rhubarb in the sink, then snatched a clean apron off the hook by the back door and used it to hide the money pouch as she headed upstairs. She was halfway up when Ladora leaned over the railing. "Finished already?"

"I brought in tomorrow's pie plant," Grace said. "And I thought I should put on a clean apron before I help inside."

"Well aren't you just the nicest thing," Ladora said. "I've just finished with the colonel's room. Thought I might get a bouquet of flowers from the field next door and put them on his desk. After that, I'll rustle us up some supper. I'm plum tuckered."

"Don't worry about feeding me," Grace said as she continued on into her room. "I'm really not all that hungry."

"Not hungry? Nonsense. You've just been too busy to notice, I reckon. Hard as you've worked, by the time you get that clean apron on, your stomach will be growling loud enough to raise the dead.

Mine already is." Ladora headed on downstairs, prattling away about how the colonel should be here any minute now, and she'd just get those flowers and then maybe they'd have some cold roast beef sandwiches or maybe. . ."

Ladora's voice faded as she headed toward the back of the house. Grace closed the bedroom door. She placed the money pouch on the bed and stared at it while she removed the soiled apron and donned a clean one. Finally, she opened it. And gasped. She hadn't expected so much. Was it the entire earnings from the weekend and beyond? What fool would leave it all in one place? They should have known to deposit it at the bank at the end of every day.

She sat on the bed for a moment, willing herself to avoid the obvious. Finally, though, conviction settled over her like a cloud. *Conviction.* Where had that come from? She had what she'd wanted all along. Enough money so she wasn't at anyone's mercy. She could leave if she wanted to. Leave and look for honorable work and maybe write to Josiah—or return when she'd had time to—*honorable.* What a word. A good word, just not a word she should use in regard to herself.

She closed her eyes against the memories of every little step she'd taken away from honor and into all kinds of things. She hadn't planned to wander. It had just happened. She'd never planned to lie or cheat. But sometimes a girl alone—and then a woman alone. When she'd heard Charles Spurgeon preach about "the dangers of sin" and the "wiles of Satan," she'd smirked. Anything she'd done was petty compared to real crime. She'd made sure of that, always treading just along the edge of the pit, making sure not to slip and fall in a way that would make recovery impossible. She had rules. She didn't steal on the Sabbath, for example. She didn't steal from the poor, and she never took more than what she absolutely had to have to survive. She'd never done anything that would hurt someone truly good. *Until today.*

As she looked down at the money pouch, conviction and fear settled over her like a cloud. She would go to jail if they caught her. What had she done?

Although the western sky was still light, the eastern sky had darkened to a cobalt blue and the evening star had appeared on the horizon when Emilie finally finished her next article and managed to sneak it into editor Carl Obrist's bag at the newspaper tent. She'd felt oddly out of sorts all day long because, even though the interview had gone well and she felt good about the article, she hadn't seen Noah today. Unless one counted passing by the children's class this afternoon when he was telling Mark Twain's story of a certain celebrated jumping frog.

Perhaps he would make his way to the Bee Hive this evening, but if he did he'd find an empty hive, for the Spring Sisters and Emilie had promised their parents to spend the evening at the cottage with the new double-decker tree house. It was, to hear Mother tell it, the "talk of the entire assembly." Something of an exaggeration, Emilie thought. On the other hand, she imagined that the view of the grounds from the higher platform was probably quite spectacular. She was already looking forward to joining the family up there for the torchlight processional and the fireworks display on July 4th.

Bert Hartwell was standing outside the Bee Hive, almost like a sentry.

"Waiting for Junie?"

"Wh–what?" Bert frowned. He took a step sideways to keep her from entering.

"It's all right, Bert. She won't mind. And I have to get changed, too."

He actually grabbed the tent flap so that she couldn't get in.

"Hey. Give a girl a break. I've had a long day, and I'm in no mood."

"Wait. Just. . .wait."

She heard an odd sound and looked over at the wing she shared with May. "What's going on in there?"

"Something you'll like. Just trust me and wait a minute."

Finally, a familiar voice sounded from inside. "Ready, Hartwell."

Noah? Emilie looked up at Bert, who grinned. With a flourish, he stepped aside and raised the tent flap himself. Emilie ducked inside. Looked. Looked again.

"It isn't perfect," Noah said. "But at least it isn't in some trash pile."

"That can't be the same camp desk," Emilie said. "It was smashed to smithereens."

"Not quite," Noah said. He nodded over at Bert. "Hartwell helped me pack up the pieces. And I talked a carpenter in town into trying to mend it." He looked over at the desk. "I think he did a good job."

Emilie stepped closer. She ran her hand over the surface of the desk. Peered at the cubbyholes.

"The legs that fold out had to be replaced. They weren't much more than toothpicks. Everything else is the same though—well, with several pounds of glue added." He chuckled.

"I—I don't know what to say." She looked up at him. "Does Mother know?"

"We didn't say anything," Bert said, "in case it really was impossible." He nodded at the desk. "You'll want to check that lower left-hand cubbyhole."

Emilie reached into the cubby and withdrew a clear glass paperweight. It was the small rectangular kind made popular as a way to frame and preserve photographs or post cards. This one contained carefully pieced-together fragments of the *Journal*. The date of the edition, the words *Ten for Ten* from her first article, and the byline for E. J. Starr.

"I don't know what to say," Emilie repeated, as she hugged first Bert and then Noah.

"It's the most wonderful thing anyone's ever given me."

"Even better than a pony?" Bert joked.

"Much better." She gazed down at the desk. Shook her head. "I don't know what to say."

"For a woman of words, you're kind of stuck," Bert teased. He looked from Emilie to Noah and back again. "Tell you what. I'm going to head on over to Aunt Henrietta's. I hear there's a taffy pull in the works, and I've got my eye on the perfect partner. You two already have yours, so you just take as long as you need."

CHAPTER 19

Finally, Ladora gave in to fatigue. As late afternoon turned to early evening and the hour of Josiah's arrival loomed, Grace began to feel more panicky. When Ladora said that she was just going to go "prop her feet up for a minute," if Grace didn't mind, Grace didn't mind. She'd been desperate for Ladora to do just that. It would give her the chance she needed to get away.

"Now, I don't plan on falling asleep," Ladora said as she lumbered toward her room. "But if I do, you don't let me sleep long, y'hear? Half an hour is all I need. You pound on the door and get me up. It won't do to have the colonel arrive home and me lollygagging with my feet up."

"I promise I won't so much as close my eyes," Grace said.

"Thank you for all your hard work today." Ladora smiled. "You've been a blessing."

A blessing. The word stung. Ladora closed the door to her room, and Grace climbed the stairs to Josiah's guest room for the last time. Opening a drawer in her costume trunk, she withdrew the special belt she hadn't needed in a very long time. Laying it out on the bed, she transferred the contents of the money pouch over, separating the bills and change into the various pockets so the belt would be evenly balanced. She kept out just enough to buy a ticket to—where?

Strangely enough, New York held no allure. St. Louis would do.

Big enough to get lost in. Big enough to have a theatrical scene where an aging actress might be able to find work back stage. This time she wouldn't hold out for a part. She'd take anything they would give her. Wardrobe assistant, ticket-taker, mender, prompter... anything. She'd scrub floors if she had to. Toilets if it came to that.

She changed clothes. The traveling suit was a decade out of date, but a fuller skirt was necessary. Once ready for the road, she paused before the mirror, twisting and turning to make sure the money belt wasn't visible. She gazed with regret at the open theatrical trunk poised in the corner of the room. If those costumes could speak. They'd attended balls in Europe. Curtseyed in the presence of royalty. *Don't be maudlin. You should be glad they can't talk.* They might have walked the storied halls of Europe, but they'd also witnessed things that would make even the old Josiah blush.

With a sigh of regret, Grace crossed the room and retrieved the book she'd left on the small table by the bed. Spurgeon's sermons didn't belong in a thief's room, and Madame Jumeaux didn't belong in this house. She'd tried to learn the vocabulary to make it work, but she'd failed. All she'd learned from reading Spurgeon was just how far she had missed the mark, and if she'd ever doubted the true condition of her soul, the money belt around her waist was all the damning evidence she should ever need.

Cradling the volume of Spurgeon in her arm, she retrieved her cane and crept downstairs. She returned the book to the shelf in Josiah's office. Tears glimmered in her eyes as she looked up at the portrait of a naive brother and sister, unaware of the looming disaster that would soon destroy their happy existence. What a fool she'd been to think she could redeem the past.

At the last minute, she removed a bit of notepaper from Josiah's desk drawer and scribbled a parting message. As soon as the ink dried, she held the portrait out from the wall and tucked the note behind it. It only had to stay put for a few hours. Just long enough for her to catch a train.

The note tucked in place, Grace took one last look around the office. She paused again before the portrait of Josiah and those Indians, wondering at the mystery of the man who looked so much like Noah Shaw. She'd never know the truth about that now. But then the truth was not something Grace Jumeaux was known for, anyway.

"You sure you're all right, ma'am?"

Grace started. She looked up at the stationmaster. Or the conductor. Or was he just a freight handler? It was hard to tell, what with these spectacles blurring her vision so. She nodded. "Yes, yes. I'm fine. Just fine."

"That was the last train, ma'am. Where was it you said you were headed?"

Where was she headed? It didn't really matter. "St. Louis."

"But ma'am—you missed the train. You can't sit here all night."

"There aren't any hotel rooms." She grasped the handle of the cane she'd leaned against the bench when she sat down. "I can defend myself if I must. Now leave me be." The money belt was heavy. That was it. That's what had kept her from getting up to catch the train. It weighed her down. And so she'd sat here and let the first train leave. And the next. And then the next. And the longer she sat, the less will she had to move.

Ladora would be awake by now. Grace should have left her a note, too. She could have said she went over to the assembly grounds to hear the evening lecture. Why hadn't she thought to do that? It would have been the perfect cover. Josiah wouldn't have thought a thing about it. He didn't even know who his houseguest was. Both he and his housekeeper would have retired, and it would have been morning before they suspected anything was out of order.

At least the railroad worker had left her alone. But now he was coming back. Why couldn't a woman just sit on a bench and be left to her thoughts?

"I'm sorry, ma'am, but Jeffrey was right. We can't let you sit here all night. You were right about all the hotels being full, but there's likely to be a cot available over on the assembly grounds. One of the church groups offers lodging."

"The Methodists again?"

"Ma'am?"

Grace just shook her head. It probably was the Methodists. Lodging beneath the very roof she'd wronged. Would history continue to repeat itself? She'd sold the house out from under Josiah, only to return and be sheltered beneath his roof. She'd stolen from the Methodists, and now, here was someone suggesting she take shelter with them. If God was paying attention, He must be amused. Again.

"We've asked the last horse trolley to wait for you. Only ten cents one way." The man reached for her carpetbag. "Here, let me—"

She slapped his hand away. "I don't want to go to some tent run by a bunch of pious do-gooders. Can't you just leave me be?"

"It's all right, Jeffrey. I'll help the lady."

Grace blinked wearily and looked over to see who was going to bother her now. Her breath caught. She looked away.

Josiah crouched down before her. "It is you, Gracie. Isn't it?"

She couldn't bear to look at him. She shook her head. Closed her eyes against the tears, but they rolled down her cheeks anyway. "No," she whispered. That, at least, was the truth. She wasn't the sister he remembered.

"Oh, Gracie." Josiah's voice broke. "If you knew how I've prayed you'd come home."

He reached for her hands, but she pulled away. "I can't. Can't stay."

"Then just come back for tonight. Jeffrey's right. There won't be any more trains until morning." When she still didn't move, he sat beside her on the bench.

"How did you know it was me? At the house, I mean."

"I knew the moment I heard your name. How old were we—six?—when Nanny Jess started calling us her *jumeaux*?" He chuckled softly. "How we hated it when people asked if we were twins."

"You remembered."

"Of course I remember." He paused. "Mrs. Riley thought maybe you'd walked over to hear the evening program. When you didn't come back, she was quite concerned—as was I." He paused. "And that brought another memory to the surface. As I recall, I was always the one to come after you when you ran away." He reached over and squeezed her hand.

"Then you also remember that I was always the one in trouble." She moved her hand. Any moment now, he would expect her to confess to whatever it was she was talking about. What new trouble had she brought home. Any moment now, his kind, gentle voice would take on a different tone, and he would move away.

He let go of her hand, but his voice didn't change, and he didn't move away. "I remember that you were the one I ran to when I got hurt," he said. "And I remember you taking more than one spanking for me." He took a deep breath. "I remember you begging me not to leave after Mama and Papa died, and the selfish way I just bulled ahead, doing what I wanted to do, without regard for what I was doing to you." His voice wavered. "I'm so sorry, Gracie. Can you forgive me?"

He was apologizing—to her? After all she'd done? "I shouldn't have left that way. I shouldn't have sold the house. I—I was just so angry. I wanted to hurt you." She swallowed. "I'm sorry, too."

"*Have* you forgiven me? Is that why you came home?"

She closed her eyes, trying not to wail the answer. "I didn't have anywhere else to go." Tears flowed again. "I just couldn't face the poor house. I was going to beg you to take me in." The money belt weighed on her like concrete. If she were only younger she would run into the night. Anywhere. Just away. But the "run" had gone out of her. She was tired of running. Sighing, she let her head droop forward, her shoulders sag. "The trains kept coming. I meant to go. But I couldn't make myself get off this bench. They kept coming, and I kept thinking about the next one. I'd take the next one. But then I couldn't. I just. . .can't."

"Shhh, now, Gracie. Shhh. . .it'll be all right. I'm so glad you came home." Josiah stood. Grasping her by the shoulders, he helped her up, wrapped his arm around her, and together, they headed back toward the house with the red geraniums.

—∞—

The last thing Grace remembered was leaning into Josiah at the train station. The next thing she knew, she was waking up back in the bedroom with the rose wallpaper. A soft tap sounded at the door.

The money! She sat up. Her hand went to her waist. It was still there. She'd just been settled on the bed and left to sleep, fully clothed. Someone had removed her tattered bonnet and covered her with a light blanket. She sat up. "Come in."

Ladora.

The housekeeper smiled as if nothing had happened. As if guests misleading her and then running off in the night were all part of a normal day. She pulled the dressing table bench out and set a breakfast tray on it. One look at the tray and Grace's eyes filled with tears. Wildflowers. Ladora had put a little vase of wildflowers on the breakfast tray.

"The colonel wanted me to tell you that you're to rest as long as you want. There's no hurry about anything," she said. She seemed about to say more, but then she merely nodded and headed for the door.

Grace found her voice. "Wait. Please."

Ladora turned about, but she stayed by the door.

"I–I'm sorry I lied to you."

Ladora shook her head. "But you didn't. I studied on it half the night after the colonel brought you home. Seems to me you were real careful not to lie. I appreciate that, Grace. And I understand your wanting the colonel to be the first to know you'd come home. It's only fitting."

Grace blinked with disbelief. Where was the woman's outrage at being duped? "B–but I—tricked you. I wasn't forthcoming."

Ladora shrugged. "I decided to think on all the hard work you did instead. How much you helped me with the pies and all. And how nice it was to have company instead of being alone all day, every day. Like I said, I understand your wanting the colonel to be the first to know. It wasn't your fault he wasn't here when first you knocked on the door. I don't know what I would have done in your place, but you just picked up a knife and started chopping rhubarb." She smiled. "It's all right, Miz Barton. I'm not one to hold a grudge."

"Grace. Call me Grace."

"Don't seem fittin'."

"I don't care."

Ladora opened the door a little farther. "I'll think on it." She pointed at the breakfast tray. "Don't let that get cold. Nothin's worse than cold oatmeal." She slipped out and closed the door behind her.

Grace's stomach growled. Her hand went to her midsection. And she knew what she had to do. Slipping out of bed, she hurried to change, then downed a few bites of oatmeal. It took only a few moments to retrieve the black money pouch from the depths of the theatrical trunk.

One by one, she unrolled the bills, then arranged them in dimensions, from small to large. People must be in the habit of adding a donation amount to their luncheon tab. That would explain the number of five-dollar "woodchoppers," and perhaps even the ten-dollar "rainbow" note. It also made her feel even worse about what she'd done. But she was going to make it right. Today. First, she would chop up the rhubarb she'd picked last night. Then she would make another pie delivery. And no one would ever have to know the rest of that story.

—∞—

"Saints alive and praise be! Ladora! Ladora Riley, would you look at this!"

Ladora tugged on the reins and Babe stopped, almost in midstride, as a red-headed woman came trotting up to her side of Josiah's farm wagon from the direction of the dining hall. The woman held a black money pouch up, her face beaming. "I told Dorcas it would turn up. Land sakes but things were such a mess yesterday, what with trying to move everything over to capture the shade of a few trees and Pearl not here to head things up. I just knew someone had set it aside and it got tangled in a bundle of tablecloths or something. And I was right. Here it is. Whoever found it must have felt so bad about it they just set it right there with the pies. Can you imagine? And Dorcas so upset she was going to have Mr. Rhodes make it a headline in the newspaper. As if someone stole it." The woman rolled her eyes. "Aren't we glad we didn't do that. Our Chautauqua doesn't need bad publicity such as that."

Ladora agreed that a newspaper article would have been a bad thing. But for a different reason. "You don't want folks thinkin' the ladies are lax when it comes to the money box," she said. "I hate to think on it, but the colonel's sister reminded me—"

"Sister? Colonel Barton has a sister?"

"Now where are my manners," Ladora said. "Miss Grace Barton"—she nodded at Grace—"Mrs. Opal Safford." The introductions finished, Ladora continued. "As I was saying, Miss Barton has traveled the world, and she reminded me the first time she saw these crowds that the world isn't as kind as it once was. Some people see such an event as our assembly as little more than an opportunity for thieving."

The woman held the pouch up to Ladora. "Which is why I'm giving it to you. Can you stop at Nebraska National and deposit it for us? We've all decided we'll keep only the smallest amount of change on hand and make regular deposits so this can't happen again."

Ladora took the money pouch and handed it to Grace to hold until they got back into town. It was a wonder it didn't burn her hands.

As Emilie hurried to prepare for Thursday evening's meeting, the Bee Hive tent flap waggled and a deep voice called her name.

"Just a minute," she answered, wiggling her way into first one and then the other of her white lace-up shoes. Tying each one quickly, she stood up and smoothed her skirt, then hurried to open the flap, talking as she untied the closure. "I'm sorry I'm taking so long, but. . .Father?"

He smiled. "Your cousins were beginning to look worried, and so I offered to fetch you. Of course Shaw would have been more than happy to do the honors, but I convinced him to let me have a moment alone with my daughter."

Oh no.

"And no, I have not been recruited by your mother to raise further concerns in regards to Mr. Shaw. Although I will say that it has been noted that the two of you are spending quite a bit of time together."

"We're interested in the same things," Emilie said. "And Noah's being very careful about protecting my reputation. And—"

Father held up his hand. "Do you remember what I said at breakfast last week?"

"About topics of conversation? Mothers and daughters and all that?"

Father nodded. "Exactly. I haven't changed my mind, but if I had, you would know about it. It is not in my nature to talk *around* things instead of *about* them. I have no objections to the company you are keeping, and anyone who does is quite likely motivated by sentiments other than true concern for you."

He means whoever's been talking is jealous. Emilie nodded.

Father reached inside his coat. "This is the reason I wanted to see you alone for just a moment." He handed her a small folder. "I had the honor of seeing Miss Willard to the train yesterday. She was most complimentary in regards to a certain young woman who'd interviewed her. She was also quite pleased with the resulting article. She asked if I would mind seeing that Miss Starr received this."

Emilie opened it. Below her portrait, Miss Willard had written, *Kind regards to E. J. Starr—Frances E. Willard, July 2, 1890.* "What a treasure! Thank you, Father."

Father nodded. "Yes. Well. . .I wanted you to know that after she'd given me the portrait, I told Miss Willard that you are my daughter." He held up his hand. "Now, there's no need to be upset about that. Only Miss Willard heard me say it. I thought you might also want to know that when I told her you'd chosen a pseudonym expressly because you wanted to be published on your own merits—and that you are writing for my competition—she expressed admiration for your determination." He paused. "As I've had time to ponder the situation, I've come to realize that I. . .well. I may wish that the matter had been resolved differently, but that doesn't change the fact that I am proud of you."

"You are?"

He nodded. Then he pointed at Miss Willard's gift. "Now put that somewhere safe and let's get going before I have to face the wrath of the Spring Sisters for making you late."

CHAPTER 20

The Beatrice cornet band's "national salute" sounded through Noah's open hotel room window at six o'clock in the morning on Friday, Independence Day. He was already half awake, and hearing the music made him smile. Emilie was hearing the same music. Like him, she'd get ready for the day to the tune of the "Star Spangled Banner."

Humming the tune as he crossed the room to the wash stand, Noah pulled his nightshirt off and poured water into the bowl. As he rinsed his face and combed his hair, he wondered if he would still be smiling at the end of this Independence Day. He peered at himself in the mirror. How he wished Ma could somehow telegraph advice to Nebraska. Do this. Say that. Too soon. Time flies. Hold her hand. Let go. Tell her. Don't.

With a sigh, he shrugged into a clean shirt. *Do you see me, Ma? What would you say? What should I do? Am I being foolish? Is this what it's like to be in love?* He'd never felt this way about a woman before; never spent time thinking about ways to please her; never counted the minutes until he could see her again; never felt his own mood change just because she smiled—or didn't. And he had most certainly never lain awake obsessing over how to propose.

Was it even possible to be in love after knowing a woman only—he looked at his watch—nine days, six hours, and twenty minutes?

What would he say to Mr. Rhodes? The man would think him a fool. *I'd like your permission to court Emilie.* Noah could just imagine the reaction. Mr. Rhodes would take his own watch out of his vest pocket and mutter something about those nine days. *Wait*, he'd say. *Wait*. But at the end of the Long Pine Chautauqua, Noah would only have known Emilie for twenty-eight days. He'd counted. From a parent's perspective, that was still a ridiculously short period of time—at least in this place, at this time.

In some cultures, a man met his bride on the wedding day. In others, a man didn't even *see* his veiled bride until after the ceremony. He and Emilie had already spent more time together than those couples. True or not, pointing out foreign marriage customs was unlikely to persuade Emilie's parents to alter their expectations for their daughter's future. The best Noah could probably hope for would be a suggestion that he and Emily conduct a long courtship that would involve writing letters and more visits when his travels allowed for it. But he didn't want to write letters and he didn't want to wait. He wanted to share his life with the girl who'd been able to finish his sentences since the first night they met.

He glanced over at the quilt Ma had made. *Can you see her, Ma? Isn't she beautiful? I love her, Ma. I wish I knew what you think I should do.*

With a sigh, he finished getting ready.

—∾—

Grace was halfway down the stairs on the morning of July 4th when Josiah called a greeting from his place behind his desk. "How long have you been down here?" she said. "You should have awakened me. I could have made you breakfast."

"Mrs. Riley fed me well before she departed for the grounds."

"She's already left? I should have helped out."

"You're not a servant, Grace. You're my sister, and this is your home—if you want it to be. No one resents your taking a well-earned rest. You've been under a great strain. Don't feel guilty for sleeping past dawn."

"And how long have *you* been at your desk this morning, Colonel Barton?"

He smiled even as he tapped a letter on the stack to his left. "Touché. But there was quite a bit of mail, and I'm especially glad that I read these. There's an interview request from the daughter of a friend, who is apparently writing for her father's competition—and then a note from a young man I believe I'll be sharing the stage with today."

"That would be Noah Shaw," Grace said. "I met him on the train. He has an interest in the West, although he didn't say why." She told Josiah about the hours Miss Rhodes and Mr. Shaw had spent at the house. And then she stepped into his office and pointed to the portraits hanging to the left of the doorway. "I can see why reporters want to interview you," she said. "Buffalo Bill? And this one appears to have been an important event."

"It was," Josiah said. "Although like so many other delegations to Washington, the results weren't what we'd hoped for."

"Ladora says that you've helped a great many people as a result of your years in the army."

"I like to think that."

"She said you'd been at Fort Kearny?"

"Yes. Why?"

"Mention of Fort Kearny is what brought Mr. Shaw to your doorstep." She smiled. "Well, that and following the lovely Miss Rhodes." Josiah laughed when Grace told him about Ladora's matchmaking.

"I'll look forward to meeting Shaw and hopefully answering his questions. Which brings up the topic of today. There's sure to be a huge crowd, and thousands of people plus only one good bridge across the river equals a monumental challenge. If it isn't too much of a strain for you, we'd be much better off walking there and back."

"Just because I wasn't up at dawn doesn't mean I need to be coddled."

"Don't take a tone, Gracie. I was only trying to be thoughtful—and diplomatic. You had a cane with you at the station, remember?"

Of course. The cane. Grace shrugged. "A poor replacement for a good pistol, but still serviceable if a lady needs to defend herself."

Josiah chuckled as he rose from his chair. "I should have known. Well, in any case, I'm pleased that the cane wasn't a symptom of decrepitude." He nodded toward the kitchen. "Mrs. Riley left a plate of flapjacks in the oven. As I said, I've already eaten, but I'd like a second cup of coffee. May I join you?"

—∾—

By the time the cornet band sounded the final notes to the "Star Spangled Banner," Emilie and her cousins had accomplished the camping version of their morning toilette. Soon they'd had breakfast and joined the rest of the campers trimming their tents with flags and red, white, and blue bunting.

Emilie was as patriotic as anyone, but this year she was far more interested in how the day might end than in the speeches—except, of course, for the reading of the Declaration of Independence by Mr. Noah Shaw. She wondered how long Colonel Barton would speak. He hadn't contacted her about her request to interview him, but then he was probably very busy after being away from home. Today was not the day to follow up on that request, anyway. Today was about hearing Noah read and watching Noah play baseball and, if she was fortunate, being at his side when the fireworks display began. . .and then again when the illuminated parade began on the river.

"Emilie!"

"What?" She looked over at April, who had apparently said something to her more than once.

"Have you decided to be the centerpiece of your very own tableau for the day?"

Emilie looked down at the small flag in her hand.

April just shook her head. "When you've finished daydreaming, come on over to the cottages. Those of us who aren't daydreaming about Noah Shaw are going to help Mama and Aunt Henrietta decorate."

Emilie and May were nearly finished draping bunting across the front of the pink cottage when Aunt Cornelia, who was planting small flags in her window boxes, sighed. "I do regret the disharmony between my lovely little cottage and the national colors."

"Really?" May teased. "You don't think Lydia Pinkham is a good match for Old Glory?"

"Lydia Pinkham?" Aunt Cornelia looked horrified. "Miss Pinkham's medicines aren't this color."

April looked over. "We know, Mother. That's not why we call it 'Pinkham.' "

Aunt Cornelia looked up at the cottage. The truth dawned. She seemed honestly surprised as she murmured, "It makes you ill? Is it really so hideous as that?" She planted the last of the small flags in the window box before her and then stepped back to take a look at the decorations. And then she began to laugh. "I see what you mean." She shrugged. "Oh well, there's nothing to be done about it now." She summoned June to help her decorate the new tree house.

Noah arrived at the cottages just in time for everyone to make their way to the Tabernacle. Early attendees filled every seat available beneath the roof, with the exception of the front row, which had been reserved for the immediate family of today's speakers. As Emilie and Noah picked their way through the patchwork of quilts and blankets used by the ever-growing crowd to stake claims on the lawn, Emilie said, "I'm glad the Spring Sisters aren't expected to sing today. Only half the crowd would have any chance at all of hearing them." She paused. "When Father said there might be as many as fifteen thousand on the grounds by this evening, I didn't believe him." She pointed toward the entrance in the distance. "But look at that. There's a solid line as far as we can see. Does it make you nervous, looking out on such a sea of faces?"

"I don't know that I'd say I'm nervous," Noah replied, "but I am definitely thankful I'm *reading* instead of *reciting* today. People might not be upset if I misquoted a poet or faltered in the middle of a story, but I doubt that would be the case with our Declaration of Independence."

"There's Colonel Barton." Emilie nodded toward the opposite side of the Tabernacle. "And isn't that Madame Jumeaux on his arm?"

"It is."

"I wonder what their story is."

Noah chuckled. "Give a woman a byline, and she sees a news item everywhere."

Emilie nudged his arm. "Well, whatever her story is, it's probably played a role in the fact that I didn't get the interview I wanted. There won't be a Ten for Ten article tomorrow—unless I corner someone else today."

"Did you plan to do that? I was hoping we could spend the day together."

And just like that, Emilie decided that either her series title would have to change, or Ten for Ten would continue at least one day past the closing ceremonies of Beatrice's 1890 Interstate Chautauqua.

—ꟽ—

Grace and Josiah had covered only half the distance to the grounds when she realized that, in spite of Ladora's glowing praise for "the colonel," Grace hadn't truly realized just who her brother had become.

Not everyone recognized him, of course, but many did, and they greeted him—and her, because she was with him—with deference and, in some cases, thinly veiled awe.

When Josiah approached the Tabernacle stage, a smattering of applause followed in his wake. Grace's heart swelled with pride—and then the pain of regret and shame threatened to smother it. What she had almost done. Would regret ever stop hounding her? At least she could be thankful that she'd had a chance to give the money back. No one suspected. No one knew, save God, and since Grace and God hadn't been on speaking terms for a very long time, she didn't expect that to be a problem.

Josiah guided Grace to one of the reserved seats on the front row and then made his way up the stairs and onto the stage, just as the chorale filed up the opposite set of stairs at the far end. Miss Rhodes and the Spring Sisters were part of the chorale, but before the singing commenced, Noah Shaw stepped forward to call the crowd to order with the reading of the Declaration of Independence.

Josiah hadn't seen Shaw at first. But when he did, Grace knew that she wasn't the only person to have noted a resemblance between the man standing next to Josiah in that delegation photograph and Noah Shaw. Surprise transformed to shock as Josiah looked and then looked again.

When Shaw had finished the reading, Josiah rose to shake the younger man's hand, leaning close to speak with him as he did so. Shaw smiled and nodded and then took his seat. Josiah pulled two sheets of paper from his inside coat pocket. As he was unfolding them to place them on the lectern before him, he glanced over at Noah Shaw. Once. Twice. And yet again.

As for the speech, for a man who was, according to Ladora, in demand as a public speaker, Grace assumed that what she had just heard was not her brother's best effort. He seemed distracted, and he lost his place in his notes more than once. But the crowd didn't seem to care, and toward the conclusion Josiah seemed to regain his balance. The closing few moments were really quite good. So much so that, when Josiah stepped back from the podium, the crowd rose as one to applaud warmly. There were even a few cheers.

The chorale stepped forward to lead the singing of "The Battle Hymn of the Republic." Cannon fire provided a rousing—and deafening—conclusion to the assembly. Grace thought that Josiah might speak further with Mr. Shaw as the chorale filed out, but Shaw moved quickly in the opposite direction, clearly bent on catching up with Miss Rhodes.

Josiah stared after him.

—w—

"Yes!" The crack of the bat brought Emilie and her cousins to their feet. Noah took off, loping easily along as he watched the ball he'd just whacked arch high above the heads of the outfielders. It finally came down somewhere in the brush along the river bank. The left fielder made a valiant attempt to retrieve it, but finally emerged from the weeds empty-handed, just as Bert Hartwell rounded second. The Bugeater who'd been on third had long since crossed home plate, but no one stopped cheering as Bert shuffled his way home.

Once Noah had stepped on home plate, the jubilant Bugeaters threw their caps in the air and swarmed about the man who'd just brought in the winning runs—and the captain who'd recruited him. With pats on the back and a few hurrahs, the players went their separate ways to ready themselves for the next part of the day—food.

Bert and Noah caught up with Emilie and her cousins as the girls made their way toward the cottages to help their mothers get set up. When Noah fell in beside Emilie, Bert interrupted. "Come on, Shaw. If we don't hurry to get cleaned up and get back out here we'll miss the food."

"It's only a light supper," Emilie said.

"Right." Bert nodded and looked over at Noah. "Allow me to define the meaning of the term *light supper* in the context of Mrs. Rhodes and Mrs. Spring. The former will fill six feet of table to the point of collapse. And then, not to be outdone, the latter will fill an eight-foot table." He grinned. "It's also a contest between Dinah and Ida, the two cooks—who are also sisters. I really cannot say enough about the advantages of being invited to a meal when those four women are competing for compliments." He headed off toward the Spring cottage where he'd left a change of clothes.

"Guess I'd better take Bert's advice," Noah said. "You'll save me a seat?"

"Don't worry." Emilie laughed. "We won't run out of food."

"I'm not worried about the food," Noah said. "I just want to make sure that I get to dance with the prettiest girl at the ball—metaphorically speaking."

"Well, since you asked so nicely, I'll be sure to put your name at the top of my dance card."

"And if I asked that you make mine the *only* name on your dance card?"

Emilie pretended to ponder the question. "I suppose I could be convinced to say yes to that."

"And what would it take to convince you?"

Two familiar redheads came into view. "A promise that no matter how enticing the Penners' invitation, you'll stick with the Bugeaters. . .and me."

"Done," Noah said, just as the Penner twins came fluttering by.

Emilie was standing with May on the lower level of the Spring family's tree house when she caught sight of Noah headed their way from where he'd changed in the Tabernacle dressing room. He'd donned a white suit and a straw hat, and Emilie thought him the most beautiful thing she'd ever seen. She wasn't alone. Numerous heads turned as he strode across the grass toward her.

"Wow," May muttered. "Are you quite sure he doesn't have a brother?" And then she gave Emilie a little shove in Noah's direction.

"Promise kept," he said, as soon as he was within earshot. "And you?"

Emilie smiled. "Dance card filled."

As darkness fell, everyone lent a hand with putting away the last of the food. The Spring Sisters climbed the stairs to the second story of Aunt Cornelia's tree house, but when Emilie moved to follow, Noah put his hand on her arm.

"Do you mind if we find our own spot?"

Emilie didn't mind. "Just give me a minute," she said, and slipped into the Rhodes cottage to retrieve a clean blanket. Draping it over her arm, she returned to Noah's side. "Something to sit on so you don't ruin that gorgeous suit."

"How about you lead the way," Noah said, and took the blanket—and her hand. "Pick a spot where we'll be in a good situation when it's time to head for the river. I've never seen a 'procession of illuminated barges,' and that steamer really does look beautiful when she lights the lanterns on board."

When Emilie decided on the perfect spot from which to view the fireworks and then get a front-row seat for the river display, Noah spread the blanket on the ground. Emilie sat down, feeling self-conscious and more than a little awkward. "Did you get enough to eat?" *Stupid.* What a stupid question. She looked toward the cottages in the distance. She hadn't realized they'd come this far. Wonderful. Mother would undoubtedly feel it her duty to have another little chat.

"Look at that," Noah said, and pointed toward the tangle of brush along the river. "Fireflies. Ma used to call them God's fireworks. She let me catch them in a jar, but she never let me keep them for long.

She said they should be free to dance."

"What a lovely image."

"Thank you," he said.

"For what?"

"For welcoming me the way you have. Introducing me to your friends."

"They like you," she said and chuckled. "Some of them a little too much. What did the Penner twins want, anyway?"

"Just to say hello." He looked over at her. "You don't have to be concerned about the Penner twins."

The cornet band began to play. Everyone looked toward the sound, and as they did, the torchlight processional came into view from the direction of town. They marched in pairs at first, but as they approached the Tabernacle, they moved through an intricate and obviously oft-practiced routine that had the crowd applauding in appreciation. Finally, with a clash of cymbals, the first of the fireworks erupted, and for the next few moments, the sky was ablaze with color. At some point, Noah planted his arm just behind her. To provide a backrest, Emilie assumed. And so she leaned back, resolutely fixing her eyes on the sky, as if it were nothing to be almost in his arms.

When the fireworks concluded, he rose and helped her up, shaking out the blanket and draping it over his arm. She took his hand again and led the way to the river and a spot where he draped the blanket over a fallen limb and then lifted her up to a new perch in full view of the river. It was a wonderful spot. He folded his arms and leaned back, and when the first lighted "barge" came into view, it seemed only natural for Emilie to put her hand on his shoulder and lean close to say, "What do you think?"

He turned to look at her. The golden light reflected off the water and illuminated his face as he said softly, "I think I'm falling in love with you."

Emilie caught her breath. Was this what it felt like? Did everything fade away. . .everything except dark eyes a girl could get lost in. . .and arms to lean into. . .and lips that, when they were pressed to hers made her believe that this was what she'd been waiting for all her life?

CHAPTER 21

Land sakes, Miz Barton! You got no call to be out here in the half dark like this, working like you was the housekeeper!"

As Grace pulled another stalk of rhubarb from the dangerously thinned row of pie plant in Ladora's garden, the older woman chugged down the back porch steps and across the lawn, scolding all the way to Grace's side. Grace added to the bundle of rhubarb already lying in the wide basket she'd set on the ground before answering Ladora's protest. "It would appear that my first inclination was the correct one. I'm going to have to leave Beatrice."

Ladora frowned. "Leave? What are you talking about? You can't leave. The colonel is downright giddy to have you home, and hasn't he proven it? Why, you should have heard the ladies at the dining hall talking about it yesterday. Not a one of them any less than thrilled to see the smile on the colonel's face every time he introduced you." She paused. "Saving Mrs. Patterson, of course. She's always had a notion in regards to the colonel and her—which of course she finally realizes is nothing more than ridiculous, especially now that the colonel has you to keep him company, but—why'd you say such a thing as you ought to leave? You'll break his heart, Miz Barton.

"Why, didn't you notice that when we left for the grounds yesterday, he told me I didn't need to leave a note on the door? And what did that mean but that for all these years, I been leavin' notes in case you was to come home. He didn't want you finding an empty house and getting away."

Grace had learned that if she set her theatrical ear to listen for the tell-tale lift in tone toward the end of one of Ladora's long speeches, she could sometimes stop listening to specifics in the middle. This time, though, she'd listened all the way through, and what she heard brought tears to her eyes. Josiah had had Ladora leave notes because of her?

"So you see," Ladora was saying, "you can't leave. Although I suppose if you got business to tend to, the colonel will just have to understand."

Grace shook her head. "I don't have any business to attend to. That's my point. Madame Jumeaux is upstairs in that theatrical trunk, and I am more than happy to have bade her a fond farewell. But Ladora, I can't just sit in that big house like some newly appointed lady who folds her hands in her lap and observes, while you do all the work."

The housekeeper blinked. "Well I—but you're the colonel's sister. Folks would think I was putting on airs, tryin' to be friends with the colonel's sister."

"Putting on airs?" It was the ultimate irony—or perhaps a good dose of reaping what she'd sown over all those years as Madame Jumeaux. She hadn't retired to applause. Instead, she'd sneaked off into retirement and used what little talent she had to steal. Oh, she'd restored the money pouch to the Methodist women, but that hadn't dispelled her persistent, lingering guilt. And now Ladora Riley—of all people—had erected a wall that Grace couldn't seem to get past. More reaping what she'd sown, Grace supposed. Except that she wasn't going to put up with it.

"Ladora. Have you stopped to think that if I'd stayed put instead of running off after Josiah, *I* would most likely be Josiah's housekeeper? I'm trying to make up for the past, but you won't let me. You won't let me be Grace Barton. Won't you at least try to see the situation from my point of view?"

Ladora looked toward the house. "Oh." Frowning, she sucked in her lower lip, obviously thinking hard about what Grace had just said. "Well, now, I didn't think on it that way. But now that you mention it, I guess I do see what you've been trying to say."

"Thank God." Grace bent to pick up the basket of rhubarb. "I'll get started on this while you gather the eggs."

Ladora nodded, but then she called after Grace. "I. . .uh. . .do you think you and the colonel could see your way to letting me stay on for a few weeks more? Just until I find something else?"

Now it was Grace's turn to be confused. She turned back around. "Why would you want to find something else?"

"Well, if you're wanting to take over as housekeeper."

"What?! No! I—" Grace started to laugh. "Oh no. That's not what I meant at all." She shook her head. "Goodness gracious, Josiah would either starve or drown in a pile of clothes I'd ruined trying to do the laundry. No, no, no." She took a deep breath. "I've forgotten the very little I ever knew about cooking or housekeeping. I just want to help the woman who does those things so well." She hesitated. "The truth of the matter is that I don't know how this is all going to work out—my coming home, I mean. I'm not really good for anything." She smiled. "Although I do like to think I was a first-rate rhubarb chopper before you got so prickly about letting me work in the kitchen."

Ladora laughed. "Well, all right, then. You can help as much as you want. We've got double the baking to do today. Can't be baking on the Sabbath. The colonel isn't quite so strict on the rules about all that, but the Good Book says we ought not to be a stumbling block, and some of the ladies would question my status with the good Lord if I was to bake a passel of pies on the Sabbath. And that might reflect poorly on the colonel. Can't have that." Ladora took a deep breath. "Now I'll get to the eggs, and you get to the kitchen." She bustled off.

Grace had lined up the pie pans on the kitchen counter and commenced to processing the pie plant when Ladora came in, her apron pockets bulging with fresh eggs.

"You said you'd think on calling me 'Grace,'" Grace said. "Have you thought on it?"

"Fact is, I asked the colonel what he thought about it before I chased you down this morning."

Grace looked toward Josiah's office. "He's up?"

"He is." Ladora nodded. "And fit to be tied. I headed to the front porch to fetch his newspapers, and there he was, going through his papers like they was a haystack and he'd lost the only needle known to mankind in the midst of 'em. That's when I asked him about what I should call you."

"And he said?"

"He said I should do whatever it takes to make you feel to home 'cause he don't want you running off again ever." Ladora smiled. "So, *Grace*, if you'd want to make the colonel his coffee this mornin', that would allow me to get to the business of the piecrust—not that I'm giving orders or anything."

—∾—

Grace stood in the doorway with Josiah's coffee in hand. "Ladora was right," she said, as she held out the mug of steaming coffee. "She said you were searching for the proverbial needle in your haystack of papers."

Josiah took a sip of coffee with a grateful sigh. "Actually, I found what I was looking for the first time, but reading through it reminded me of something else." He set the coffee mug down on his main desk. "And it would appear that that *second* needle in my research haystack may have gone permanently missing."

"Can I help?"

He gestured at the research desk. "I was sure it was right here, but if I don't find it soon, yes." He smiled. "Just don't let me be the one to make you abandon Mrs. Riley today. Talmage is sure to bring out the largest crowd yet tomorrow. That means the ladies have the opportunity to take in a good deal of money for their missions projects." He gazed across the room at the portraits hanging on the wall. "Mr. Shaw will be by Monday morning. And I really do need to locate a specific report so that I'm fully prepared for his visit."

Grace followed Josiah's gaze across the room. "Who is the man standing next to you in the one on the left?"

Josiah didn't answer right away. "What, exactly, do you know about Noah Shaw?"

"Only what I've already told you. I met him on the train, when I was in full 'Madame Jumeaux' mode." She sighed. "I was quite insufferable. Looking down my nose at everything, waxing braggadocious about my European tour. To his credit, Mr. Shaw was patient, kind, and generous." Again, she asked about the man in the photograph.

"That's Kit LeShario. He was one of Luther North's scouts. The last I heard, Bill Cody had hired him to work out at Scout's Rest—that's Bill's ranch out in Lincoln County."

"And you know him because. . . ?"

"*Knew* him," Josiah said. "Over twenty years ago." He took another gulp of coffee. "Did Shaw say anything to you about his family? Where he's from? Anything at all?"

Grace thought back. "Nothing that isn't already in the brief commentary printed in the Chautauqua program."

"The program!" Josiah glanced over at the other desk. "I haven't so much as looked at it."

"And there was an article in the *Dispatch* about him last week. It would have been Wednesday. Miss Rhodes did her second Ten for

Ten interview with him, as well." Grace motioned to the stack of newspapers in the corner. "I'll find them for you, but first, come and eat breakfast before it gets cold. Ladora has had enough upsets for one day."

"Mrs. Riley is upset?"

"Not anymore."

"But she was?"

"She thought it would be putting on airs for her to call me 'Grace' and allow me to help with chores now and then. Thank you for setting her straight on the matter, by the way. And I took care of the other issue."

"Which was?"

"Convincing her that I don't want her job." With a soft laugh, Grace motioned Josiah toward the kitchen.

—∞—

"Grow old along with me! The best is yet to be, the last of life, for which the first was made. . . ." Noah lingered in his room on Saturday morning, replaying last evening in his mind, reveling in the memory of Emilie Rhodes's kiss, and realizing that Robert Browning's familiar words would never again be just another beautiful piece of literature. He, Noah Shaw, had found someone he wanted to grow old with, and Browning's declaration that the first of life was made for the last resonated in a new way.

In the first part of his life, Ma had done her best to teach Noah things that would prepare him for the last part. *Learn to be content. Don't long for things you cannot have*, she'd said on that long ago day when he'd tried to lighten his skin to please Sally Bennet. *Thank God for all you do have.* Wasn't it nice to be so tall? And wasn't he thankful for all that thick black hair? Just think of poor Mr. Cooper at the general store and the ridiculous way he combed his thinning hair, trying to make people believe he wasn't half bald.

Even after Ma died and life got hard, Noah did his best to be thankful. Self pity was an ugly thing, and for all the hardships he might have had, he only needed to look around him to realize he'd also been blessed. He'd never gone hungry. God had provided people like Professor Gordon to teach him how to comport himself in society, and when the chance came to be on stage, Noah had been ready. And now, now he was ready for this. Ready to share his life with a brave girl—except, of course, when it came to snakes. The memory made him smile.

Every time he'd felt lonely, every time he'd longed for family ties and a real home, Noah had remembered Ma's lesson. *Look around you. Thank God for all you have.* And he was thankful. It was just that meeting Emily and her family and friends had resurrected the old longing. Kissing her and holding her in his arms had whispered promise and hope. Now, as he lay in bed and relived last evening's kiss, joy flowed through him.

I might not have to be alone, Ma.

A promise like that was enough to make a man smile. To make him want to sing, even if he was nearly tone deaf. And if the walls of this hotel weren't so thin, he'd have begun his day with a rousing chorus of. . .something.

He might need to take another walk tonight.

CHAPTER 22

She'd done her best to sleep, and now Emilie was doing her best to act as if she cared about Saturday's highly lauded "Grand Joint Debate" to take place this afternoon on the Tabernacle stage—a debate over the "prohibition question." It was easier to be enthusiastic about hearing the celebrated Reverend T. De Witt Talmage tomorrow afternoon. His article on "The Despotism of the Needle" was a special favorite of hers. Still, everything associated with the Chautauqua assembly seemed inconsequential in light of that fact that she'd been thoroughly kissed by the most handsome man in the universe—a man whose very presence thrilled her right down to the pointed toes of her white summer boots.

Noah had wanted to speak with Father today. "I may be a traveling man, but I'm no heathen, and it's only proper that I request his permission to court you."

She'd actually giggled. "No one thinks you're a heathen, and I've just given you the only permission that really matters." She'd stepped into his arms again and encouraged another kiss, but Noah captured her hand instead. "I want more than stolen kisses by the light of the moon, Emily Jane." He smiled down at her. "Does the idea of being courted by a man you barely know horrify you?"

She shook her head. "I already told you that you're the only name on my dance card. And I feel as though I've known you for most of my life."

He'd walked her back to the Bee Hive then. There'd been no good-night kiss—unless Emily counted the one to the back of her hand—so here she sat at her desk on a sweltering July morning, trying to work. As if her entire world hadn't been turned on end just a few hours ago.

She'd awakened when April and June got up and headed out to replenish the Bee Hive's water supply. Now she was struggling not to daydream about Noah. She had only managed to write an introductory sentence to her article about Professor Davidson, who was providing an evening lecture and lantern show titled "From the Italian Lakes to Vesuvius."

Mother and Father had gone to Italy on their wedding trip. Of course she and Noah wouldn't be able to afford any such thing unless Father gave them a wedding trip. *Wedding. Honeymoon.* The former word made her smile. The latter caused a blush.

May's voice sounded from the direction of her cot on the opposite side of the tent wing they shared. "So. Tell me."

Emilie didn't turn around. "April and June? They went to get water."

"That's not what I mean, and you know it."

"It isn't?"

"Turn around and talk to me," May said, "or I'm going to make a sign that says 'The Bee Hive, temporary office of E. J. Starr' to hang outside."

Emilie spun about on her stool. "You wouldn't."

"Of course I wouldn't," May said as she sat up. "But it got your attention." She grinned. "Did you even *see* the fireworks?"

"I liked the ones that changed from green to white best. What about you?"

"It was all beautiful," May said. "The Penners preempted us in that spot on the river where we all planned to watch the river parade. They were waiting when we got there. Bert stuck by Junie all evening long, though. She was so happy, I thought she was going to soar right up into the sky. He even walked her back here to the Bee Hive. With April and me as chaperones, of course. But I think he's finally beginning to notice that June has blossomed."

"It's about time." Emilie looked down at the blank piece of paper before her. "I can't seem to think what to write."

June ducked into the tent. "You have to come quick. April and I stopped by the post office, and there was a letter from Elwood. April was so pleased—at first. And then she just went pale." June gulped. "He's broken their engagement."

May blurted out, "In a letter?!" She hopped up and went to the tent flap and peered out. "Where is she?"

"She said she needed some time alone," June said. "She's gone home."

"Should we tell Mama?"

May and Emilie both said no at the same time. "It's not our news to tell," May said.

"I agree with that, and I understand her wanting to be alone, but I hate the idea—"

"We should follow," May said.

Emilie gathered up her papers. "I can finish my article at the dining-room table. And aren't we glad that we aren't on the program again until Monday?" She paused. "I'll stop and leave a note for Noah at the hotel. If he comes looking for me and I'm not here, he might worry."

"Maybe you should just stay here and let us handle this," June said.

Emily shook her head. "I'd never be able to act like nothing is wrong if Mother or Aunt Cornelia stop in. Besides that, Noah will completely understand. He'd want me to go to April. Family is very important to him." She scrawled a note.

I'm at Aunt Cornelia's with my cousins. April received a letter this morning. Her fiancé has broken the engagement. We didn't think she should be alone. I'll finish my article there. April doesn't want anyone to know, but you aren't "anyone."

Fondly. E.

Noah stared down at the note Emilie had left with the hotel desk clerk. It would take him twenty minutes to walk out to the Springs' house. He'd want time to change before catching a horse trolley out to the grounds for this evening's performance, and he really should be in place fifteen minutes before the evening program was slated to begin. He would need to leave the Springs' house by early afternoon. Still, he wanted to know how poor April was doing.

She'd been so kind to him that first day, trusting him with Hartwell's story, almost as if he were already a friend. Poor April.

On the other hand, if Elwood Sutter was the kind of man who would do such a thing in a letter, perhaps she was better off without him. Of course he wouldn't say such a thing aloud. He'd do exactly what Emily and April's sisters had done. Stand by.

Poor April.

Noah arrived at the Springs', red-faced and out of breath, but when he knocked on the door and Emilie opened it and stepped into his arms, he was glad he'd made the effort. When May and June stepped into the hallway from the direction of the formal parlor, he spoke to them. "I don't mean to intrude."

Emilie pulled him inside, but she kept her arm about his waist. "I'm so glad you came."

"It's no intrusion," May said.

Junie agreed. "We're glad you're here."

Having May and June echo Emilie's sweet thoughts warmed his heart. "I know there's nothing I can do, but I had to see for myself that things were all right before I head out to the Tabernacle. Is there anything you need? Anything I can do?"

April's voice sounded from the stairs. "Be good to my cousin," she said. "And if there's ever a problem between the two of you, don't be a coward about it." Her voice wavered. "Be man enough to handle it face-to-face."

May and June hurried to their sister's side.

"I have time between here and Long Pine to hunt him down," Noah said. "If you want it done, I'll drag him back here and make him face you."

April actually smiled. "I believe you mean that."

"I most certainly do," Noah said. "And your father is going to want to do the same."

April sighed. She looked down at the garnet ring on her finger. "I'm not nearly as brokenhearted as I should be." She shrugged. "I might even be a little relieved." After a moment, she said, "At least he isn't going to parade around Beatrice with my replacement. He's staying in Kansas City." She forced a smile. "There is always something to be thankful for, if we look hard enough. Isn't that what the Good Book says? Or someone—maybe that was Shakespeare." She waved them all toward the kitchen. "Let's have a glass of lemonade."

Junie spoke up. "Ma had the icebox taken out to the cottage."

"There's well water," April replied as she opened a cupboard and took down a clear glass reamer. In a few minutes, they were all sitting at the kitchen table with glasses of cool lemonade.

—w—

April finally delivered her news to her parents and Mr. and Mrs. Rhodes late on Saturday, and Noah had the opportunity to witness the drawing together of a family—Bert Hartwell included—to support April in a way that only strengthened his resolve to do whatever was necessary to earn and keep this exceptional family's respect and, in time, their affection.

When Noah tried to leave "to give you all privacy," everyone insisted he stay. By late that evening, he and Hartwell were playing checkers while May strummed on a guitar. Finally, the Spring sisters began to sing—softly, at first, but as time went on and they ventured into Stephen Foster's songs, Noah noticed that passersby were stopping to listen. Finally, Mrs. Spring and Mrs. Rhodes produced "light refreshments" from the abundance left over from the July 4th bounty, and by the time the moon rose over the grounds, quiet resolve reigned over April's troubles.

"Your family is wonderful," Noah said as he walked Emilie back to the Bee Hive beneath a canopy of stars. "The way they've all united to support April."

"That's what families do," Emilie said. "They support one another when bad things happen." She paused. "To tell you the truth, I really think the sense of relief April mentioned at the house will eventually blossom into full-blown joy that she didn't go through with it. May and I have had our doubts about that engagement ever since it happened."

"You didn't like Sutter?"

"I wouldn't say that. There wasn't any reason to object to Elwood. It's just that there wasn't any reason to be all that impressed with him, either."

"But why would April have agreed to something she didn't really want?"

"April's always been the perfect, conventional daughter—the one who does what's expected. In a lot of ways, she's the standard against which the rest of us have been measured." Emilie paused. "It's a wonder we don't all hate her for it. We probably would if she weren't so resolutely kind."

"Well, I hope people don't gossip behind her back about it."

"I don't imagine it'll be too rabid. And even if people do talk a bit, I have no doubt April will be fine. Beneath that gentle, kind exterior, lives a strong woman. If Elwood Sutter knows what's good for him, he'll stay clear of Beatrice for a very long time."

Noah almost felt a bit of pity for the man—first, for losing out on the chance to have April Spring for a wife, and second, for missing out on being part of her family.

—∞—

The Sunday service that would feature Reverend Talmage wasn't scheduled to begin until midafternoon, but every bench beneath the Tabernacle roof had been claimed long before lunchtime. In fact, those who attended the morning service stayed put, alternating lunchtimes and breaks to preserve their places.

Just when it was time for Emilie and Noah to take their turn at the dining hall, news filtered through the crowd that lines were unusually long and supplies were running out quickly. Several workers—including Colonel Barton's sister—had been ordered home when they grew ill from the heat.

Emilie looked toward the cottages. "Let's raid the icebox over there," she said. "Dinah will have brought something out—if she was able to get here." She nodded toward the entrance and the seething mass of pedestrians and carriages, wagons, and buggies that stretched from the entrance and out of sight toward the city.

Bert walked up, mopping his brow. "There are so many people headed this way that they're actually worried about overstressing the bridge. The Burlington's bringing in five excursion trains today, and there's at least five more specials headed this way. It took me nearly an hour to get here." He smiled over at Junie as he produced a tiny nosegay of wildflowers from the inside pocket of his suit coat.

"Bert Hartwell," Junie said, blushing.

"Sorry they're wilted," he said and settled next to her before waving Emilie and Noah toward the cottages. "Bring us back a drink of water if you don't mind."

Emilie led the way to the cottage, only to find that someone had raided the icebox. "Mother will be incensed," she said as she rifled through a basket sitting atop the icebox. "There's a bit of tea left, but if we take time to make it..."

"It's all right," Noah said. "Let's just head back. We'll be all right. Maybe I'll persuade you to join me for supper at the hotel later this evening."

"Will the hotel have anything left? It must be bedlam in town."

Noah grinned. "We can always throw ourselves on Mrs. Riley's mercy again."

"Dinah would never forgive me. If the hotel can't help us, we'll just head home."

"I thought you said that Dinah essentially had the ten days of Chautauqua as a holiday—save for bringing a picnic supper out for your parents."

"She does," Emilie said. "But just because I *don't* cook doesn't mean I *can't*."

As it turned out, both families ended up back at the Rhodeses' house late that night, talking over the size of the crowd (thirty thousand), the effect of thousands of voices singing "All Hail the Power of Jesus' Name," and the fact that Mrs. Penner had "scooped" everyone when her husband convinced the famous Reverend Talmage to deliver a ten-minute address from the balcony of the Penners' cottage, under the auspices of enabling a few more people to actually hear what the man had to say.

Later that evening, as the family gathered back at the cottages,

Aunt Cornelia produced an issue of *Leslie's Illustrated* and read Reverend Talmage's contribution aloud. "'It is said, if woman is given. . .opportunities she will occupy places that might be taken by men.'"

"There's a terrifying thought," Father said.

Mother nudged him. "Hush, William. You might learn something."

Father didn't try to hide his amusement. "I suppose I have Miss Ida Jones and her talk of suffrage and women's influence to thank for this?"

Aunt Cornelia read more. "'I say, if she have more skill and adaptedness for any position than a man has, let her have it! She has as much right to her bread, to her apparel, and to her home, as men have.' Now what do you think of that!"

Noah spoke up. "I think that Reverend Talmage is clearly one of the most brilliant men in America. No—let me rephrase that. He's one of the most brilliant men in the world."

Emily leaned forward and in a stage whisper, corrected him. "Universe."

"Right." Noah nodded. "In the universe."

Mother joined the laughter before saying, "I wonder what E. J. Starr will say—assuming Reverend Talmage granted him an interview." And then she turned to Father and said, "Which reminds me, William. With the assembly coming to an end, so will that series I've mentioned to you. If you know what's good for you, you'll get hold of E. J. Starr and hire him right out from under Carl Obrist."

When Father only looked at her in shocked silence, Mother nodded. "I know, I know. You don't like to be told what to do, but I can't tell you how many times I heard comments about that series in the *Journal*. You should at least talk to the man and see if he'd be interested in switching over."

CHAPTER 23

At nine o'clock on Monday morning, Noah stepped through the hotel doors and onto the walkway just outside the hotel. It was going to be another very hot day. He glanced off toward the south and the assembly grounds.

Emilie and her cousins were probably already on their way over to the Tabernacle, where various musical groups were rehearsing for this evening's "grand vocal and instrumental concert." She'd promised to meet him for lunch back here at the hotel. And then this afternoon, she had her own appointment with Colonel Barton, during which she would conduct her final interview as E. J. Starr.

As he walked past the *Dispatch* offices, Noah smiled, remembering Mrs. Rhodes's insistence last evening that her husband snag "that E. J. Starr" for the *Dispatch*. Emilie had turned a fabulous shade of red while that brief exchange went on.

Noah hadn't had a chance to talk to her later, but he couldn't help but wonder how that would all play out. How would Emilie tell her mother the truth? And how would Mrs. Rhodes respond?

As far as Noah knew, Mrs. Rhodes and her sister were the only two people in the family who didn't know E. J. Starr's true identity. They were going to be hurt. . .or angry. Or both. He really wished that Emilie had told her mother the truth before now.

Truth. Would Colonel Barton be able to shed light on Noah's past? The very thought made him quicken his steps. Rounding the corner and heading up Ella Street, he cast his thoughts heavenward. *Do you see me, Ma? Everyone says that Colonel Barton is the man to ask if I want to know more about Fort Kearny. I miss you, Ma. I wish you'd told me more. I wish I'd listened better.*

Taking a deep breath, Noah made his way up the geranium-bordered walk and onto the porch, surprised when Colonel Barton answered the door himself. After shaking Noah's hand, the colonel led him inside and into his office. They'd barely been seated when Grace Barton opened the door between the office and the kitchen. Both men sprang to their feet as Miss Barton offered to serve coffee. Noah said that coffee sounded good.

"If she has any in the larder," Colonel Barton added, "I'm sure we'd both enjoy some of Mrs. Riley's spoon-drop biscuits. With a bit of apple butter, if she doesn't mind?"

"She don't mind a bit," Mrs. Riley called from the kitchen.

Grace smiled as she spoke to Noah. "You're a gifted orator, Mr. Shaw. I imagine the Bard himself would have been pleased to hear your *Henry V*. More than one old soldier—my brother among them—grew misty-eyed when you transported them back to the days of their own 'band of brothers.' That St. Crispin's Day soliloquy was magnificent."

"Thank you," Noah said. "That means a great deal, especially coming from someone with your experience in the theater."

Miss Barton waved the compliment away. "Please, Mr. Shaw. My 'experience' didn't really amount to much." She glanced at the colonel. "It's a great relief to finally have a respite from pretending otherwise." She stepped into the kitchen, letting the door swing closed behind her.

"Allow me to echo my sister's accolades," the colonel said, as he and Noah once again took their seats. Sliding the small stack of papers before him to one side of the desk, the colonel leaned forward and said, "And now, tell me how I can help you."

"I don't really know if you can." Noah told the colonel how he'd learned about the older man's helping those who'd lost track of family and friends. "It's a very slim chance—and I do realize that—but I'm hoping you might remember something about my parents. They were part of a wagon train that passed by Fort Kearny in '65."

"Both your parents, you say. Both of them together?"

What an odd question. "Yes. But then my father was killed, leaving Ma stranded. She actually ended up working at Fort Kearny for a while as a laundress. Which is why I'm hoping you might remember something. Because of the unusual circumstances." When the colonel still said nothing, Noah continued. "When Ma talked about the West, there was something in her voice. A wistfulness. She said it changed her forever. I'd like to know why. I've always felt there was more to it than just the fact that I was conceived out here."

The colonel only nodded. He seemed to be thinking hard, trying to remember.

Noah kept talking, hoping that some detail of something Ma had said over the years would stir the older man's memory. "It would have been late in the summer of '65. Ma used to tell me stories about it, but even as a boy I sensed that she was talking *around* some of the details. As I got older, I realized that parts of it were probably just too painful for her to relive. As a result, I'm not really certain what was story and what might have been real family history." He paused. Two images from the quilt back in his hotel room came to mind. He leaned forward a bit. "If it's any help at all, she did mention Turkey Creek. And the Powder River."

Thank God for that quilt, because at the mention of Turkey Creek, the colonel rose from his seat behind the desk and strode across the room, where he began to rifle through the papers piled on the other desk.

"Go on," he said. "Tell me everything you know."

"Well, as I said, she didn't like to talk about the accident itself. I don't really even know how long she was at Fort Kearny. Eventually she got passage back to Brownville with a freighter. From there, she worked her way home to Missouri—as some kind of maid on a steamer." Noah paused. "She told me that she realized her 'predicament'—that's what she called it. Her 'predicament.' Of course she meant *me*. Anyway, she realized she was going to be a mother at some point on the journey home. And here I am, Noah Leshario Shaw, born in the spring of 1865."

The colonel spun about, papers in hand. "Leshario?"

"Yes, sir." Noah nodded. Shrugged. "Sicilian—but not Papist, if it matters." And from the colonel's reaction to the name, it did matter. Inwardly, he sighed. Ma had warned him not to share his middle name with people. There had been a great deal of animosity against "Papists" since colonial days, and things were getting worse, especially for the Irish and Italians in America.

Thankfully, Miss Barton's arrival with the coffee tray momentarily defused the tension in the room. Noah had been too nervous to be hungry for breakfast at the hotel. Just the mention of Mrs. Riley's biscuits had made his mouth water only moments ago. But now. . . now things weren't feeling quite so welcoming here at Colonel Barton's house. Miss Barton sensed it, too. Noah could see it in the way she looked at her brother. He heard it in her voice when she said to let her know if they needed anything else.

"Thank you, Grace," the colonel said. "Just leave us to ourselves, now, please. I'll let you know if we require anything more." He left off searching through his papers, and he even closed the door that opened onto the front hall before returning to his desk.

When the door latch clicked into place, Noah flinched. What was going on?

The colonel seemed bent on letting the suspense build. He spread apple butter on a biscuit and popped it into his mouth. He took a drink of coffee. And all the while, he avoided making eye contact with Noah. At one point, he rested his hand atop the Bible on his desk.

Noah braced himself for whatever might be coming.

Finally, with a little nod—as if he'd just made a decision—the colonel spoke.

"Son, I've commanded men from every imaginable walk of life—among them, men born in probably over a dozen different countries. German or French, Papist or Baptist, druggist or financier, it is of no concern to me." His voice was warm with emotion as he said, "Sadly, your mother was quite right to caution you in regard to revelations about that unusual name of yours. But I'm not one to label a man 'worthy' or 'worthless' based on who his father was." He took a deep breath. "I've had men in my command who, in spite of having had every possible advantage in life, proved utterly worthless. The opposite has happened, too. Men who, because of the circumstances of their birth, wouldn't be welcome in the better homes or institutions in the land, have proven themselves worth their weight in gold to me, both as men and as personal friends.

"The apostle Paul said that there is neither Jew nor Greek in God's eyes. Jesus Himself once reminded the Pharisees that being children of Abraham didn't mean a thing if they didn't have a heart for God. In fact—" He broke off. Shook his head. "Son, I don't care if you're Sicilian or Irish or a blue-blooded direct descendent of King George—" He broke off, chuckling. "And that concludes today's sermon."

When he continued, the colonel's tone was warm with something Noah hoped meant possible friendship. "You were kind to my sister when she sorely needed kindness. Mrs. Riley can't say enough good things about you. I can see that you were obviously a devoted son, and you've earned the admiration of the Rhodes family in record time. That's enough for me." He motioned to the coffee tray. "Now settle back and have another biscuit."

Noah relaxed. While he ate, he told the colonel more about Ma's quilt. "She began working on it before I started school. At some point, she began to tell stories while she embroidered over the lines creating all the symbols and figures scattered about. I'd point to something—a wagon train or a tepee, for instance—and she'd tell me a story about it. That was the beginning of my fascination with the West." He paused. "When I ran off from my cousin's, the quilt was the only thing I took with me. I rolled it up and tied it shut with a piece of rope—imitating a soldier's bedroll, I suppose."

The colonel nodded understanding. "You'd be surprised if I told you about some of the things soldiers keep tucked in pockets or saddlebags just to remind them of home. Everything from once-perfumed lace-edged hankies to gold lockets to a pebble from a creek bed in Germany." He paused. "Women may be the keepers of hearth and home, but we men have ties just as strong as they." He pointed behind him at the portrait of him and his sister. "That's all I have of my family—" He put his hand on the Bible on his desk. "That, and this. My uncle carried it with him from Manassas to Appomattox. I wouldn't take anything for either that portrait or this Bible."

He understands. Noah went on. "Ma didn't know where Pa was buried. That always bothered her. It bothered her a great deal." He swallowed. "I'm thinking of staying out here for a while after I finish up at the Long Pine Chautauqua. I'd like to see Fort Kearny for myself. See if I can find the Powder River and Turkey Creek."

The colonel nodded. "If you'll move this tray over onto that chair in the corner, I'll show you something." While Noah moved the tray, the colonel retrieved a map from the other desk. Unrolling it atop his desk, he weighed down each of the four corners—one with a paperweight, another with the inkwell from the desk set, and then the desk set itself. The small Bible was placed over the remaining corner. The colonel pointed to a place on the map. "Turkey Creek," he said and looked up at Noah. "Tell me what you know about it."

Noah thought for a moment before answering, trying to remember everything Ma had ever said. "Shooting. Indians. Being terrified. And being rescued by the army. Was that the Second Nebraska? Was it you?"

The colonel shrugged. He pointed to another point on the map. Noah leaned close. *Powder River.*

"And your father?" the colonel asked. "Tell me what you know about him."

"Nothing of his background. Ma said he didn't talk about it. But he gave his life to save us. Once, when I was young—" He told the colonel about trying to lighten his skin. "I'd never seen her so angry. 'One of the best men to ever walk the earth.' That's what she said about Pa."

The colonel was looking down at the map as he said, "Your mother gave you her name. She merely dropped out the letter *r*."

It wasn't a question. Noah's pulse quickened. "Yes. That's right. Norah Shaw. You knew her? You really knew her?"

The older man nodded. "I was fairly certain when I first met you. But I wanted to be sure. And everything you've told me confirms it. She was a lovely woman. Kind, tenderhearted. Unforgettable, for many reasons. There was a grace about her—an ability to be at peace in spite of her considerable suffering. It impressed many who crossed her path, including me. Her quiet faith during the days following Turkey Creek spoke to many very roughshod hearts.

"God also used her during her time at Fort Kearny—just as surely as He uses men like Reverend Talmage." The colonel paused. "Now that I think about it, she would have enjoyed the reverend's sermon yesterday." He quoted Talmage's text. "'Seek him that maketh the seven stars and Orion.'"

Noah nodded. "Yes. I thought exactly that when the reverend quoted that verse. Ma stitched stars on the quilt. Stars and campfires and wagon wheels. Tepees and wolves. An elk—or maybe a deer. And a bear. Just outlines in red thread. But they illustrated Ma's stories, and they set my mind to imagining." He gave a soft laugh. "She always encouraged my imagination. When my voice changed—I was young when that happened, and you can imagine the teasing it invited at school—she just said she liked my 'growly voice.' She even called me her 'Little Bear' sometimes."

Again, some indiscernible emotion flitted across the colonel's face. Clearing his throat, he rerolled the map and returned it to the other desk as he said, "Perhaps you'd want to read what I've written about the incidents at Turkey Creek and the Powder River."

"You'd allow me to do that?"

"If you still want to—after we talk a bit more." The colonel motioned for Noah to sit back down. Then he crossed the room and took one of the portraits of himself down off the wall. "The name *Lesbario.*" He cleared his throat. "I think it has far greater significance than you've ever realized." He handed the portrait to Noah. "This was made when I accompanied an Indian delegation to Washington about twenty years ago. That's the White House in the background. I'm on the far left." He put his hand on Noah's shoulder.

Noah looked down at Colonel Barton. He was dressed in full military regalia. Those buttons would have glimmered in the sun. And that sword. Impressive. And then—then Noah saw the real reason the colonel had just handed him the portrait.

The stranger next to Colonel Barton stood broad-shouldered and erect, staring straight at the camera. He wore a long coat boasting a single row of what appeared to be military buttons. A blanket was draped over his left shoulder. Two panels of intricate beading ran from beneath the hem of the long coat, down the front of each leg. He wore his thick, black hair cropped short. And he had Noah's face.

CHAPTER 24

The colonel gave Noah's shoulder a squeeze before retreating to take his seat on the opposite side of the desk. His voice was almost gentle as he said, "His Pawnee name is Blue Bear."

"But how—who—" Noah sat back. "*Pawnee*?"

The colonel nodded. "The tribe consists of four different bands. Kit was part of the Republican band—the Kitkehahki. The word *lesharo* is their word for *chief*. You can see how that might become Leshario. It does sound Italian, but it isn't." The colonel paused. His voice gentled. "He's a fine man, son."

Noah stared down at the portrait. His mind raced. This couldn't be happening. He slid the portrait onto the colonel's desk and sat back. He shook his head. "Ma said my father's dead."

"I'm sure she thought he was. He very nearly did die." The colonel took a deep breath. "I'll tell you only what I know for certain, either because I was an eyewitness, or because I was there when others wrote up their reports on the events. Hostilities were on the rise in '64. I remember seeing emigrant wagons that had been brought together and burned so that nothing was left but the iron work.

"Miss Norah Shaw was with a family group headed west when their wagon train fell prey to the Cheyenne. Later when Miss Shaw was rescued, she said that there were only two survivors of that terrible incident, herself and a young woman. The Cheyenne traded the other woman to the Sioux not long after the initial event."

Noah shivered. His own mother. . .captive? And then left alone. No wonder she hadn't wanted to speak of it. And yet. . .and yet she'd drawn those tepees on the quilt. Why would she have done that? It didn't make sense for her to memorialize such a terrible event.

"In the winter of '64 to '65," the colonel said, "Kit had been recruited to be a Pawnee Scout. They'd gone into winter camp at Fort Kearny but then were ordered to go north and scout for hostiles. It was early February, and the weather was brutal. All the scouts found was a small band of Cheyenne with a woman captive. There was a short skirmish. The Cheyenne fled, leaving a number of fine ponies and their captive behind. On the way back to Fort Kearny, the company got caught in a snowstorm. Separated by the storm, they were left to their own devices. It snowed almost continually for a week. The scouts eventually straggled back in to Fort Kearny—all, that is, except for Kit Leshario and the woman captive. Everyone assumed they'd perished in the storm.

"In March, my company engaged a hostile band of Sioux. That was when I learned that my friend Kit and the woman he'd rescued had taken shelter and survived the storm, but then they'd been discovered and were being held captive—this time by the Sioux. Kit was gravely wounded trying to protect the woman—your mother. He survived, but he wasn't brought back to Fort Kearny with Miss Shaw. I put him on a travois myself and took him to Fort Laramie. I knew the doctor there would see past his skin color and do whatever it took to save him."

"You saved his life," Noah said.

The colonel shrugged. "He would have done the same for me." He waited for a couple of minutes before saying, "Miss Shaw was overwrought. Everyone—including me—labeled it 'hysteria.' She was bundled off in a wagon. And she was hysterical. But now—now I realize why." He paused. "She didn't want to be separated from him."

Noah took a deep breath. He swiped at his forehead with a shaky hand.

The colonel rose from his chair. "I'm going to get us both a glass of water." He slipped through the swinging door and into the kitchen. Noah heard murmuring, but it seemed distant, almost as if it were in another world. In some ways he supposed it was. Certainly the world he'd known didn't exist anymore. Everything was different now. . .everything.

The colonel came back in, a glass of water in each hand. He handed one to Noah and set the other on his desk, pacing back and forth as he talked. "It was early fall by the time Kit was well enough to make his way back to Fort Kearny to take up his duties with the Pawnee Scouts. Your mother had already left for the East." The colonel stopped pacing. He took a drink of water.

Noah just sat, his mind reeling. Mrs. Riley's spoon-drop biscuits had congealed in his gut. For a moment he thought he might be sick. He reached for the glass of water and drank it down. *Can you see me, Ma?* She'd called him *Bear*. Even given him the man's name. *I don't understand, Ma.*

The colonel must have read his mind. "Kit would never have taken advantage of a helpless woman, son. I knew him. I rode with him, and believe me, men in the field have plenty of opportunity to show their true character. Kit's was exemplary." The colonel leaned forward. "They were together for weeks. Alone. In a desperate situation. Your mother would have had opportunity to see all the things that made Kit a 'man among men.' That would have been a powerful attraction. You've told me your mother was devoted to your father's memory. As for Kit—he's lived alone all these years. And he's still alone. To my mind, that's testimony to something extraordinary."

He's still alone. Noah frowned. He'd been so awash in feelings, so shocked over the past, he hadn't taken time to ponder the fact that the colonel was speaking of Kit Leshario in the present tense. His voice cracked when he spoke. "H–he's not dead?"

The colonel shook his head. "He works for Bill Cody."

Noah stared down at the stranger in the photograph. Kit Leshario. Blue Bear. Alive. Within reach. *My father is a Pawnee Indian.* Emotions swirled. Tears threatened. He hung his head. This couldn't be real. Bitterness trickled into his voice. "Why didn't she tell me?"

"Maybe because she would have been risking the life she created for the two of you."

Noah snorted. "So she left me to discover it this way?"

"She thought he was dead, Noah. She didn't leave you to discover anything. If you choose to see it that way, what she did is remarkable. She didn't just survive—she found a way for you to thrive. And for herself, she created a lasting record—the truth couched in a story. Stories that must have given her great comfort."

The colonel made it sound almost noble. Noah shook his head. Ma had given him a life, all right. . .a life based on a lie. He reached for the portrait and held it up, staring at Kit Leshario's face. *Father*. A good man, the colonel said. Someone who'd been willing to give his life for a woman he loved.

All right. Things happened that, in a moment of time, changed their lives forever. People yielded to temptation. That didn't mean they were evil. What was it Jesus had said? "He that is without sin among you, let him first cast a stone. . . . Why beholdest thou the mote that is in thy brother's eye, but considerest not the beam that is in thine own eye?" Extraordinary situations created. . .situations. What had happened was between God and Ma and. . .Blue Bear.

Maybe he could reason his way through all of that. Maybe he could even get to a point where he understood. But that didn't change reality for him today. Because even if he believed everything the colonel had said about Kit Leshario and even if he made peace with that part of the past, he still had to face the present. The present in which he'd been given what he'd always wanted—and, at the same time, lost what he wanted.

He knew why the West had meant so much to Ma. He knew what had caused that wistful tone when she spoke of it. He knew why it had changed her forever and why she hadn't let it go. He knew why she'd preserved the memories, spending hours drawing symbols and outlining them with red thread. He knew. He'd gained a past and lost the future. Because it wouldn't really matter whether Kit Leshario was a good man or not. It wouldn't matter if he and Ma loved each other. It wouldn't matter if Ma fought to stay with him or if they'd planned to marry. It wouldn't matter that Ma had thought Kit dead and been on the way home before she even knew she was going to have a child. None of it would matter when it came to Emilie.

Oh, women like Mrs. Rhodes might support reservation schools. They might even attend conferences and try to influence legislation to improve "the plight of the Indian." Men like Mr. Rhodes might publish articles that encouraged a new day in regards to "the Indian question." They might even dine with the likes of Charles Eastman and Standing Bear. But for all their philanthropy, when it came to Indians, the daughters of people like Mr. and Mrs. William Rhodes did not marry Indians. And they most certainly did not marry men the world labeled "half-breed bastards."

Notebook in hand, Emilie hesitated at the doorway and scanned the Paddock Hotel dining room, looking for Noah. But it was Colonel Barton who rose from where he'd been seated alone at a table along the far wall and came to greet her. "I've left Mr. Shaw immersed in a mountain of reading material at my office," he said. "I hope you don't mind, but I suggested that he continue reading while I came to the Paddock in his place. I thought we could go ahead with the interview while we dine."

A mountain of reading material. That was good, wasn't it? "Of course I don't mind," Emilie said, and took the colonel's arm. "Noah's so fascinated with the West. I just knew you'd be able to satisfy his curiosity."

The colonel nodded and then changed the subject to the interview at hand. For some reason, the segue felt abrupt. As if he didn't want to talk about Noah and what he might be reading. It made Emilie feel unsettled. Which, she told herself, was ridiculous. It was only right that he be reluctant to discuss the details of their meeting.

"Mrs. Riley's seeing to your Mr. Shaw's luncheon," the colonel said. "She's also expecting us back at the house for dessert. She and my sister are in the throes of apple-dumpling baking." He spread his napkin across his lap. "Apparently this year's assembly nearly decimated the stand of rhubarb in Mrs. Riley's garden. She's had to substitute to fulfill her promise to the dining hall out on the grounds."

My Mr. Shaw. Pondering that phrase, Emilie barely heard what the colonel was saying about rhubarb and apple-something. When the waiter brought menus, the colonel suggested the cold tomato soup and the hotel's signature biscuits. Emilie agreed to the selection, requested iced tea to drink, and then, while the colonel ordered for them, pulled out her notebook and scanned the questions she'd prepared.

"I took the time to read some of your other interviews," the colonel said. "Very fine work."

"Thank you." Emilie hesitated. "I suppose you're wondering why I'm writing for the newspaper that competes with the *Dispatch*."

The colonel only smiled. "People wonder about all kinds of things that really aren't any of their business. My compliment was sincere—not a thinly veiled attempt at prying into your personal affairs. And now"—he pointed to her pad of paper—"shall we proceed?"

"Proceed with what?"

Emilie's grasp on her pencil tightened as a familiar voice sounded the question from just over her shoulder. She looked up into Mother's puzzled face—and then over at Aunt Cornelia, who was clearly just as surprised as Mother to find Emilie at luncheon with Colonel Barton. Things got worse as Colonel Barton said, "I suggested Miss Rhodes conduct our interview here at the hotel." He smiled at Mother. "You must be very proud—even if she has adopted a *nom de plume*. It's certainly commendable for a young woman to seek to be recognized for her talent rather than her family ties."

To her credit, Mother carried the situation off with aplomb. "Mr. Rhodes and I have always been proud of Emilie. She has so many talents."

Emilie ducked her head and stared down at the list of questions on her notepad, hoping that Colonel Barton would merely assume that she was playing the part of the embarrassed child being touted by proud parents.

Putting a gloved hand on Emilie's shoulder, Mother leaned in to point at one of the questions on the notepad. "I'll be looking forward to reading the colonel's reply to that one," she said. "Assuming it survives Mr. Obrist's editorial pen."

Emilie swallowed. *Have you witnessed a reunion between a parent and child that you'd want to share with readers?* She could feel her cheeks coloring with embarrassment. Father must have told her about E. J. Starr. The questions was, how long had Mother known? And what was she thinking?

"Carl Obrist?" Aunt Cornelia asked. "What on earth are you talking about?"

"Come now, sister," Mother said with a laugh. "Surely you knew. E. J. Starr of *Journal* fame is none other than our own Emilie Jane."

"She is?" Aunt Cornelia stared at Emilie. "You are?"

Emilie nodded. She dared a glance at Mother, whose smile had taken on a somewhat frozen look. Finally, Mother spoke to the colonel. "Well, it's a happy coincidence to run into you here, Colonel Barton. Your address on the Fourth was quite inspiring." She managed a bit more small talk—even a joke about her and Aunt Cornelia stealing away to the hotel dining room for a respite from "camping"—before excusing the two of them and taking a table on the far side of the dining room, next to the large windows where they could look out on the street.

As soon as they were out of earshot, Colonel Barton sat back down. "I am so sorry, Miss Rhodes. I assumed your entire family knew about E. J. Starr."

Emilie just shook her head. "It's all right. Everyone did know—except for Mother and Aunt Cornelia. I should have spoken with them about it long before now." Her voice trembled. She bit back tears. Shook her head. The waiter approached and settled bowls of soup in place before them.

"I don't imagine you're very much in the mood for lunch at the moment," the colonel said.

Emilie sighed. "I didn't mean to hurt anyone. I just"—she glanced over at the notepad lying on the table beside her—"I just want to write."

For a moment, the colonel said nothing. When he did speak, his voice was gentle. "If you'll allow me to comment?"

Emilie nodded.

"A long time ago, I made a choice that ended up hurting someone I loved very much. But I waited until it was too late to make amends. God has been gracious to me in recent days. I've been given a second chance to make things right with my sister, and for that I am most grateful. But if I had it to do over again—"

"You wouldn't have done it." Emilie finished his sentence for him, and as she said the words, her heart sank.

The colonel shook his head. "No. I felt strongly that I was meant to join the army. I would still have done so. But I would have done it in a way that was kinder to Grace. A way that took her feelings into consideration."

Emilie told the colonel about how she'd revealed E. J. Starr's identity to Father. "I didn't want him to discover it on his own." She glanced over to where Mother and Aunt Cornelia were sitting. Mother had her back to Emilie. "I should have done something similar with Mother. And I really did intend to. But so much has happened in the last few days—"

"Including a young man named Noah Shaw?"

Emilie nodded. "That may be a reason I was distracted, but it still isn't a proper excuse. Mother deserves better. And now it's too late." She shook her head. "One of the things Noah loves most about—us—is our strong family ties." She swallowed. "He misses his mother so much. He told me all about her. It makes me feel even more ashamed about what just happened." Once again, she glanced over at the table where Mother and Aunt Cornelia were sitting.

"You need to speak with her," the colonel said. "And sooner, rather than later."

"I wouldn't know what to say."

"'I'm sorry' is as good a beginning as any." The colonel nodded at the notepad. "If you'll trust me with those questions, I'll write out the answers, and you can pick them up later today." He anticipated Emilie's next comment. "And have no fear—I can keep your young man busy until you come to fetch him." He smiled. "The apple dumplings will keep, too."

Again, Emilie looked over her shoulder. Aunt Cornelia was saying something—with great energy. She glanced Emilie's way, not exactly glaring, but she didn't smile, either. Emilie put one gloved palm to her midsection and tried to take a deep breath, hoping the effort would force her stomach to stop churning.

"If you can manage it," the colonel said, "a little something would do you good."

Emilie forced herself to swallow a spoonful of soup. She took a bite of bread. Washed it down with tea. Another spoonful of soup, and the colonel leaned over and said quietly, "They are leaving." He reached for the pad of paper. "I shall look forward to seeing you later today. And Godspeed, Miss Rhodes."

Emilie caught up with Mother and Aunt Cornelia in the hotel lobby. "Mother, Aunt Cornelia—I—"

Mother held up a hand to silence her, just as Mrs. Penner entered the lobby, exclaiming over the unbearable heat and dabbing at her perspiring face with a lace-edged handkerchief. "There you are, I'm sorry I'm late. I suppose you've eaten. The girls just had to make an extra stop at the dressmaker's." She glanced over at Emilie. "Oh, hello, dear. I didn't know you were joining us." She made a show of looking about. "Where is that nice young man? I declare, one would think the two of you are courting. I don't think I've seen one of you but that the other was nearby." She paused. "The girls were so disappointed not to find you on the Fourth. They really had their hearts set on seeing the river parade with everyone together. Wasn't it lovely? I hope you and Mr. Shaw didn't miss it."

"Now, Hazel," Mother said, "of course we all saw the river parade. Emilie was just telling me her favorite. And Cornelia and I agreed. Why, the Greens outdid themselves. That gazebo poised right in the center of that barge. It was as if a garden were floating down the Blue."

Emilie stared in amazement as Mother deftly managed to divert Mrs. Penner's attention and then literally led her out the door with the promise that they would all have to luncheon again soon. "As soon as we've all recovered from the assembly," Mother said as she led the way around the corner and toward the place where she'd hitched the buggy in front of one of three millinery shops.

To her credit, Mrs. Penner finally got the message that Mother was in no mood for a gossip session. As soon as they were out of earshot, Mother looked over at Emilie and almost snapped, "Don't you have an interview to finish?"

"Colonel Barton took the list of questions. He's going to write out the answers for me. I can retrieve them later this afternoon."

"And will you have time to meet your deadline?"

Emilie nodded. "I wanted to—I'm sorry, Mother."

"Well, I should say you should be," Aunt Cornelia blurted out. "As if our families don't have enough trouble in the wind, what with April's broken engagement. We're certain to be the talk of the town. And now this. My brother-in-law's own daughter, writing for the other newspaper. How could you, Emilie Jane?"

"I didn't mean to hurt anyone."

Aunt Cornelia sniffed. "You failed."

"Really, Sister," Mother said, and glanced about. "This is not a topic to discuss on a public street." She untied the reins and climbed up into the driver's seat. Then she waved at Emilie. "Well. Climb aboard. We'll continue this at home."

"At home? But—aren't you going back out to the grounds?"

Mother shook her head. "Cornelia and I have had quite enough of camping. It's hot and miserable, and I, for one, can think of nothing I want more than to soak in a cool bath."

"We'll go back this evening for the concert," Aunt Cornelia said.

"But I—" Emilie glanced toward Colonel Barton's house.

"Yes, yes." Irritation sounded in Mother's voice. "You have business to conduct. An interview to finish. A young man to catch up to. I know, I know. And it shall be done. You can ride Royal back in to town and have all the freedom you need to carry on." She sighed deeply. "But please, Emilie. Let us have a few moments of privacy while we air our differences and—hopefully settle this nonsense once and for all." She paused. "I really am quite weary of the battle."

CHAPTER 25

Ladora closed the oven with a sigh. She stared at the door that led into Josiah's study for a moment before pouring herself a cup of coffee and retreating to the nook where Grace sat, hemming some new kitchen towels. As she settled into the chair opposite Grace, Ladora sighed again. "That poor boy," she said. "That poor, poor boy."

Grace nodded.

"Don't like him being all alone in there, bearing it all alone. That's not good for a body."

Grace looked up. Ladora was staring at her. Meaningfully. "I hardly know him," she said quickly and looked back down at the handwork.

"But you've got lots in common," Ladora said. "You lived the same life."

Grace sputtered. "Don't be ridiculous. The stage never welcomed me as it has our tall, handsome friend with the booming voice. It was hard scrabble the entire time for me. Hard scrabble and nothing to show for it in the end but a trunk full of threadbare, outdated ensembles."

"But—but you saw the world, Grace. Paris and London and Rome and the Blue Danube. Queens and dukes. And glittering parties. Why, now that I think on it, the colonel's got nothing on you. You could write your own memories down. It would be like taking people on a trip to an enchanted castle."

Glittering parties, enchanted castles. If only Ladora knew the truth. Grace took a few more stitches before looking up. "There was another side to some of the parties I attended, Ladora. To some of the places I've been. A side that fills me with shame." She looked away. "Mr. Shaw's experiences—and his character, I imagine—outshine me and mine as surely as the sun outshines a distant star."

Ladora's voice was gentle as she said, "But you came home. You've made peace with the colonel. And you've helped raise money for missions and helped me bake and clean. Goodness, you worked so hard on the Fourth we had to carry you home because of the heat."

Grace waved the compliment away. "Being a victim of heat prostration hardly warrants praise. I was sincere in wanting to help, but the fact is I failed miserably, and frightened you and Josiah in the process. And I kept you from enjoying the rest of the day out at the grounds because you had to bring me home." She paused. "And don't think I don't know that you'd rather be out at the grounds today, listening to the Grand Debate, instead of minding me." Grace slipped the thimble off her finger and set it on the table, then took a drink of water from the glass Ladora had placed before her.

"I can read about the debate in the paper," Ladora said, fanning herself. "I don't mind one bit having an excuse to stay home. Fact is I was downright relieved when Miz Spring's Ida offered to fetch our baking to the dining hall today. It's been a right busy few days, and I'm content to let Chautauqua wind down without me." Again she looked toward Josiah's office. "I just feel so bad for that boy and the new cares that have settled on him."

Grace shrugged, but the truth was she did feel for poor Noah Shaw. Ladora would not let it rest.

"Maybe you don't see it, but I do. Some of the cares you carried in that front door with you when you first came here have started to fall away. Oh, I know it'll take time for everything to sort itself out, but you know I'm right, Grace. You got to know it. And that's why I'm sayin' that you'd be a good one to give the boy a kind word. To let him know it'll be all right. That God ain't forgot him. Just like He didn't forget you all those years you was wandering."

Grace shook her head. "God doesn't want anything to do with me. And with good reason." She could feel Ladora staring at her, but she didn't look up.

"Why, Grace Barton—that's blasphemy! Why'd you ever say a thing like that? God don't behave that-a-way. He ain't like people. He don't give up on folks. 'specially not folks that turn a corner like you have."

She'd turned a corner, all right. From petty theft to grand larceny—from a church of all things. What would simple-minded Ladora Riley say if she knew that? Grace pressed her lips together. But Ladora wasn't finished.

"Folks ain't perfect. Not a one of us is. And sometimes when we've come to try to walk a new road, we slip a bit. The Baptists even got a name for it. They call it back-slidin'. I don't know that we Methodists ever named it. Just plain old sinning, I suppose. But we've all done it, if we're honest about it."

Grace allowed a grunt. "You don't need to school me on the subject of sin. I know the topic well."

"Don't we all? God says 'be ye holy; for I am holy' and goodness, who can do that? And ain't that the point, anyway? We can't, so Jesus did it for us." Ladora paused. "Least-ways, that's how I came to understand it. After a while."

Ladora glanced toward the room where Noah Shaw sat alone, undoubtedly feeling—what? Who knew what he was feeling? Shaw himself probably didn't know.

"That boy needs to know that he can carry on," she murmured. "That if he'll just keep his face toward heaven, God will carry him—even if he can't carry himself right now."

Grace put the mending down. "If you've a burden to encourage Noah Shaw, Ladora, then you should do it. Stop preaching to me and get in there and tell the boy what you think he needs to hear."

Ladora sat back, almost as if she'd been slapped. After a moment, she rose and, crossing to the stove, bent down and opened the oven door. The aroma of baked apples and cinnamon filled the kitchen. Pulling a shallow bowl off a shelf, she ladled a dumpling into place, then sprinkled cinnamon over it. Next, she poured a tall glass of milk. Finally, without so much as a glance in Grace's direction, Ladora headed into the next room, fresh-baked dumpling and glass of milk in hand.

Grace sat still for a moment. Finally, she gave in. Tiptoeing across the kitchen to the swinging door, she leaned close to listen, like a child eavesdropping on her parents.

—w—

Noah started and leapt to his feet the moment Mrs. Riley pushed the kitchen door open. "'Scuse me for bothering you," she said as she crossed the room. "But these dumplings are always best fresh out of the oven." She set a bowl and a glass of milk before him, then stood back, her hands clenched before her.

When Noah thanked her, Mrs. Riley nodded. "Yer welcome. I. . .umm. . .I know food don't fix everything, but there's something about a warm dumpling that's downright comforting. At least it seems so to me."

Apple dumplings. Just the aroma brought tears to Noah's eyes. How could Mrs. Riley in Nebraska have known about Norah Shaw in Missouri? It was impossible. And yet. . .Noah glanced down into the shallow bowl. "You sprinkled extra cinnamon on top."

"Always do," Mrs. Riley said. "Looks pretty. Smells nice. Tastes good."

Noah nodded. "My mother made apple dumplings every fall.

Almost as a way to mark the passing of summer."

"Wouldn't mind if summer would pass," Mrs. Riley said with a low chuckle. "Sad to say, my kitchen's hot enough to prove that summer is still with us." She motioned to the closed hall door. "You'd have a chance of catching a breeze if you opened that door."

Noah rose and opened the door, rewarded for the effort by a slight breeze that blew in to riffle the papers he'd scattered across Colonel Barton's work desk as he read. For some reason he felt self-conscious in Mrs. Riley's presence. What was the woman thinking? What did she know? Had those murmurs in the kitchen meant that Colonel Barton had told both women everything? Not knowing, he blathered on about Ma and her recipe for dumplings and how he helped her roll out the dough. "One year, she made me memorize President's Lincoln's Thanksgiving Proclamation about 'blessings of fruitful fields and healthful skies.'" He paused. "I think she feared my forgetting God as I grew older."

"Well, you didn't, and she'd be proud to know it."

He looked around him at Colonel Barton's library. "Some days, I'm not so certain about God and me."

"A man that's forgot God," Mrs. Riley said, "don't recite the words of the Good Book like you did at the assembly last week. I never thought much on the book of Job until I heard you recite it. That part about the ocean having to stop because God said so? I've never seen the ocean, but I can imagine it's a powerful thing. And God controls it. And the stars. You reminded me of just how powerful He is."

"Thank you, but any skilled orator could have done the same."

The older woman shook her head. "No, sir. Not so. Not the way you did it. There was life in the words. They came from your heart."

Noah didn't know what to say. He had always loved that passage in Job for the same reason Mrs. Riley had just expressed. It reminded him of God's power—a concept that had comforted him through more than one long night. Today, though, he was more than a little disgruntled with God. Why had He allowed Ma to encounter such a vicious thing as being held captive? And why once she'd been set free, why send a snowstorm? Why trap her with a stranger? And then why leave her alone to raise a boy? In the past couple of hours, questions had piled up until Noah felt like a man facing a mountain range with no chance of scaling the sheer walls.

"I am so sorry for what you must be going through," Mrs. Riley said.

"Colonel Barton told you, I suppose."

"He didn't have to," Mrs. Riley said. "I been dusting that portrait hanging on that wall for ten years. I thought on it the minute I saw you. Wondered at it." Her voice gentled. "Wasn't my place to say anything, of course. I knew Colonel Barton would know what to do."

Noah glanced back at the portrait. "I know it must be true, but I can't quite embrace it yet." He motioned to the papers scattered on the desk. "Any of it. It doesn't seem real."

"You hang on to God, Mr. Shaw. That's what I came in here to say. Even when He's quiet, He's there. And you're a good man. Anybody can see that. As for Miss Rhodes, the way she looks at you? You just give yourself some time. You'll be all right."

Emilie. Noah winced at the thought of her. "You're very kind to say so."

Mrs. Riley smiled. "The dumplings and the milk are for kindness' sake. The words are because they're true." She took a deep breath. "I'm not a learned person, but I've been at the bottom of the heap in my life, and I know that if you'll keep your face toward heaven, God will carry you—even if you can't carry yourself. So you just hang on to God." She turned to go, then hesitated. Turned back to face him. "As for Miss Rhodes, don't you be turnin' into some noble fool runnin' off and leavin' her to wonder what she done wrong. That's not kindness. That's just pridefulness in a new uniform." When

Noah said nothing, she pressed the point. "You respect her enough to let her make her own decision about this." She swept her hand over the two desks. "You been washed over by a flood today. Give the waters time to recede. Give the good Lord time to send that dove with the olive branch." She harrumphed. "That's a fancy way of sayin' don't you go runnin' off. And that's all I got to say. Except for that dumpling's gettin' cold, and you should eat it while it's warm."

With that, she was gone, without giving Noah a chance to say a word. Which was just as well. He wouldn't have known what to say. But at some point during the woman's long-winded speech, just a flicker of hope had been born. Surely God was still on His throne, and if He had, indeed, enclosed the oceans, then He must know about what was happening here in Beatrice, in this moment. He knew Kit Leshario and Mr. and Mrs. Rhodes. He knew Emilie and Noah and whether or not their love would stand the storm that had just swept into their lives. Maybe, just maybe things would be all right.

Noah reached for the apple dumpling. He inhaled the aroma of cinnamon and baked apples. *Do you see me, Ma? I'm trying to understand.* He closed his eyes. *Do you hear me, God? Help me. Please. Help me.*

Emilie sat in the back of the buggy, her head bowed, her hands clenched in her lap. She wished she hadn't forgotten her parasol back at the Bee Hive. It was so hot. As she stared off into the distance, the scenery shimmered. An imaginary pool of water glimmered in the distance.

"I really am quite weary of the battle." That's what Mother had said just before they left town. She'd said she wanted to settle things between the two of them "once and for all." Did that mean she was going to deliver an ultimatum? When she turned the buggy up

the road leading to the new house instead of continuing on to the Springs', Emilie realized that Aunt Cornelia was going to be in on the conversation, too. That did not bode well.

Mother pulled up beneath the porte cochere, and Calvin came hurrying out of the barn. "This evening's concert begins at 7:30," she said to him. "If you can have the buggy ready by 6:30, that should be fine." She hesitated, then glanced back at Emilie. "Would you like Calvin to saddle Royal for you? Then you can meet up with. . . whoever. . . ." Her voice trailed off uncertainly.

"That's a good idea. If you don't mind, Calvin?"

"I'll have him waiting right here at the hitching post, soon as I get old Dutch, here, unharnessed and cooled down."

Emilie climbed down and followed Mother and Aunt Cornelia up the stairs to the side door, through the back hall, and finally into the front parlor which, thanks to Dinah's having drawn the heavy drapes early this morning, actually felt almost cool compared to the rest of the house.

Mother removed her bonnet and dropped it on Father's chair. Aunt Cornelia followed suit. Together, the sisters crossed the room and perched on the couch along the far wall. They simultaneously removed fans from their bags and sat, fanning and waiting. As if they'd planned how to make Emilie as uncomfortable as possible.

Emilie cleared her throat. "As I said, I meant to tell you. I just—there was never a right time."

"You have had an unusually busy few days," Mother said.

"I don't know what else to say, except that I'm sorry. And I am, for hurting you." She took a deep breath. "But I'm not sorry for doing the work. I'm just—sorry—that you found out the way you did today."

"Today?" Mother looked over at Aunt Cornelia. "She thinks I just learned about it today." She looked back at Emilie. "Emilie, dear. I've known since the appearance of the first article. Or perhaps the second. Yes, now that I think on it, it was the second."

"Father told you?"

"Emilie Jane," Mother said, shaking her head. "Do you really think I am so obtuse? I've read everything you've written since you were ten years old. I recognized your style with the first article. By the second, I was convinced. No one had to tell me." She shook her head. "And goodness, but the dancing about each other your father and I did until finally we both realized the other already knew." She paused. "I will admit to being hurt that you didn't trust me in the same way you trusted him. But I forgive you for that. And while I'm reluctant to admit it, I can even understand your reluctance to tell me."

Emilie plopped into a chair. "You knew. You both knew? And you don't mind?"

"Mind?" Mother looked over at Aunt Cornelia again. "Well, yes. I do mind, actually. But apparently some very fine people are in the other camp. Reverend Talmage, for example. And Miss Jones. Mrs. Colby—although I've always thought of her as something of a radical."

Aunt Cornelia nodded agreement. "Radical. . .and yet still quite a lady in every respect. As is Miss Jones." She paused. "I do hope you aren't going to take this newfound independence of yours too far, though. Your mother's been worried all week that you'll be donning reform dress next."

Mother nodded. "I just. . .well. . .of course I'll still love you, dear, but honestly, I don't think it's attractive for a lady to expose her bloomers to the public. Do you?"

Relief set Emilie to laughing. "Reform dress? No. . .I have no plans to raise any hems or expose any bloomers. Writing for publication is all the rebellion I have planned at the moment." She paused. "And I didn't really even plan that. It just. . .happened."

"Thanks in part to Mr. Shaw's assistance, I presume," Mother said.

Emilie sat back up. "No, ma'am. Don't blame Noah. It was entirely my idea."

"I don't doubt that it was," Mother said. "And you're misunderstanding my point. As usual. The thing is, if Mr. Shaw isn't supportive of your writing, that's a problem that needs to be addressed." She paused. "You must realize, dear, that you will be miserable married to a man who doesn't understand your. . .unique intentions when it comes to the future. Goodness, if I hadn't had your Father's unwavering support for all my causes. . .well. I don't know if our marriage would have survived."

"Noah. . .my writing won't be a problem," Emilie said. "He understands me." She shrugged. "We finish each other's sentences half the time. It's almost strange."

"No," Mother said with a gentle smile. "It's wonderful."

"He's your soul mate, dear," Aunt Cornelia said. "Everyone who's seen the two of you together knows it. Even Hazel Penner recognizes it—although those girls of hers are being stubborn."

Emilie smiled at them both. "You approve of Noah?"

"Well, of course I approve of Noah, dear," Mother said. "And don't look so surprised. The very first time I saw your Father, I came home and wrote in my diary that I'd just met the man I was going to marry."

"You did?"

"I did."

"And Father. Was he. . ."

Mother laughed softly. "He took a little convincing."

"And a little display of a finely formed ankle." Aunt Cornelia nudged Mother.

Mother pushed back, then stood up. "Well, I'm so glad we had this little chat. The air is cleared, and Emilie, you can go about finishing that article." She looked over at Aunt Cornelia. "Calvin can drive you home."

"Nonsense," Aunt Cornelia said. "It's a five-minute walk. There's a cool bath in my future, as well. And no more camping—at least until Long Pine." She smiled. "Now that April isn't retiring from the trio, I'm going to see if I can meet with Mr. Bowers while we're there."

"Mr. Bowers?" Emilie asked.

Mother nodded. "Mr. Thomas Bowers, the booking agent for the Redpath Lyceum Bureau," She smiled. "The bureau that manages Mr. Shaw's schedule."

"And if Mr. Bowers takes on the Spring Sisters," Aunt Cornelia said, "you can be our accompanist *and* a roving reporter at the same time."

Mother nodded. "I was thinking that you might do a series titled From the Road. But for now, you should get changed so that you can ride back into town and get to work on your article about Colonel Barton. I'm looking forward to reading it. And be thinking about what you'll do for the *Dispatch*. I know your Father has plans for E. J. Starr, but you mustn't let him dictate too much." She paused. "Although I have found that sometimes it's best to let him think things were his idea." With a soft laugh, she headed for the stairs.

CHAPTER 26

Mrs. Riley and Miss Barton were out back in the yard when Noah returned his empty dish and glass to the kitchen. Rinsing the glass, he refilled it with water and had just headed back toward the office when Colonel Barton came in the front door. When Noah commented on Emilie's notebook in his hand, the colonel recounted their unexpected encounter with her mother and aunt at the hotel.

"I encouraged Miss Rhodes to settle things with them instead of coming back here with me." Back in his office, he laid the notebook on his desk. "I promised to write out the answers for her. She'll be by later to pick them up." He settled back in his desk chair. "I assumed you wouldn't mind having a little more time before you see her."

"I don't mind, but I don't know if more time is going to make any difference. My mind's still reeling. I don't know what to do about any of this."

For a moment, the two men sat in silence. Finally, the colonel said, "How much damage would it do your career if you excused yourself from Long Pine?"

"I've never missed an engagement. I don't really know."

"Then you've established that you're dependable."

"I suppose you could look at it that way."

The colonel nodded. "Can you do without the money?"

"Other than a new suit or two now and then, my needs are

minimal. So yes. I could do without."

The colonel leaned back in his chair, his hands clasped before him. "What if I were to offer to be your guide? I have commitments that will take me east again late next month, but if we were to leave in the next few days, I could take you to see what's left of Fort Kearny. It was abandoned back in '71. I don't think there's anything left but the cottonwoods around the parade ground. Still, it's the place all the wagon trains passed by. And there's something to be said for seeing a place for yourself, even if it has changed."

"You'd do that—for me?"

"Not just for you, son. It would help me, too. Refresh my memories. Energize my writing." The colonel paused. "I'd be doing it for my friend Kit, as well. I am hoping that before all is said and done, you'll want to meet him."

"You're assuming he'd want to meet me."

"I don't have to assume anything. He will."

"You seem very sure."

"He's lived alone ever since he lost your mother. He works on a ranch instead of living on the reservation down in Oklahoma. And he chose Christianity. He's been set apart from the majority of his people for a very long time. It has to be a lonely life. In light of all that, to discover that he has a son? Of course he'll want to meet you."

No wife or family. . .no reservation family. . .and Christianity? The last thing was the most surprising. "Christianity," Noah said. "Really?"

The colonel nodded. "I've seen him reading a little testament by firelight. And on more than one occasion when we were all in a tough spot, Kit quietly reminded me that God was with us. Not that he preached any sermons, mind you." The colonel chuckled. "He always said he'd leave the sermonizing to me."

The mental image of the man in the photograph bent over a testament, reading by a campfire made Blue Bear more real. More tangible. Noah glanced back at the photograph. "I do think I'll want to meet him. Someday. But I don't know when. I just—I don't know."

"Can you ride, son?"

"Well enough." When the colonel looked doubtful, Noah shrugged. "Not very well. Certainly not compared to you. There's never been a need. I grew up in the city. Rode the rails. Learned to drive a buggy, but that's about it."

"If you think you can handle a few weeks in the saddle, we could do the entire trip on horseback. That would enable you to follow the same trail your mother did, from the Blue River here to Fort Kearny and beyond. It's a week to the old fort and about another two days up to Turkey Creek. The city of Kearney is a booming concern these days, thanks to the railroad. There won't be any problem getting resupplied along the way.

"After Turkey Creek, the distances get longer again. Powder Horn Valley is a good ten days to the north—assuming our horses stay sound and we don't run into any problems. Allow another week to get back to North Platte—assuming that you want to meet up with Kit. All told, that's a month." The colonel smiled. "And if we make it that far, I can say with certainty we will both be more than ready to ride the train home." He paused. Tilted his head. "So what do you say? A month, more or less, and a lot of aching muscles. By the time you get back, you'll either never want to see another sand hill, or you'll get that same look in your eye you say your mother always had every time you talk about Nebraska." The colonel looked back over at the portraits on the wall. "We can send word ahead if you want to make a stop at Scout's Rest before catching the train back here. I'm assuming you'll want to come back to Beatrice before getting back on the Chautauqua trail."

Noah nodded. "Yes. To all of it. I'll head to the telegraph office and let my manager know today. He'll just have to understand." He paused. "I hope I don't turn out to be so much of a greenhorn that

I can't keep up with you."

The colonel chuckled. "Don't worry, son. I've had plenty of experience with greenhorns in my day." He paused. "And the truth is, these days my old bones are stiff. I won't mind it if you do hold us up a little." He leaned forward and took up Emilie's notebook. "Ideally, we should go to the livery together. But Miss Rhodes will be here soon. Why don't we go out on the porch where we can catch a bit of fresh air? I'll give you more to read, and I'll work on these questions while we wait. Then when Miss Rhodes comes into view, I'll head over to Hamaker's and do some preliminary planning at the livery while you speak with your young lady." The colonel didn't wait for Noah to agree to the plan before rising and beginning to gather up more of the papers on the research desk for him to read.

Emilie. What was he going to say to Emilie? How to even begin to explain this to her? Noah stood up. "Mrs. Riley said that if I respect Emilie, I won't hide anything from her. She warned me against thinking that 'the noble thing' would be to keep her in the dark." He hesitated. "Again, I just don't know how to think—or what to do."

The colonel turned to look at him. "Things have progressed—rapidly between the two of you."

Noah nodded. "I'd intended to ask her father's permission to court her before leaving for Long Pine." He raked his hands through his hair. "I can't do that now, can I? I mean—really. I thought about little else while you were gone. I've looked at it from every possible angle and—I can't see any other way but to break it off."

The colonel merely handed Noah a pile of papers to read, then led the way out onto the front porch. As soon as the two men were settled in the rocking chairs facing the street, the colonel said, "I don't think you could go wrong to listen to Mrs. Riley on the matter."

"On principle," Noah said, "I agree with you. But I just can't see myself saying the words. Not to Emilie."

"What words are those?"

"Half-breed. Bastard."

The colonel frowned. "Those are strong words, son."

"Well aren't they true? Isn't that what the world says about people like me?"

"Yes. But labels are just that, aren't they? Labels. And to my mind, they say more about the people assigning them than anything. For example. My profession invites labels, too. Soldier. Indian fighter. Friend. That's from one side of things. From the other side, I might be called warrior. Enemy. Killer." He paused. "Let's take the other pursuit I've been drawn into. People call me a minister. Reverend. Gospel grinder. And some use other, more colorful terms not to be repeated in polite conversation."

"But that's all just semantics," Noah said. "Not everyone agrees with all of those."

"And the people who know you aren't going to agree with the labels you just gave yourself, either. The simple fact of Kit's being your father doesn't erase any of the other things about you. It can't unless you allow it to. And the gospel truth is that every single one of us—if we're honest about it—are 'half-breeds' in some sense. I myself am a mixture of English and German. And that's only the part of the family history I know about. Only the Lord knows what else might be mixed in there. My grandfather told me once that there were rumors in his past of an ancestor who loved a slave. But I'm not going to accept any of the pejorative labels attached to that family history. Why should I?"

"That's a fascinating argument," Noah said. "And it would be great material for a debate. But you and I both know that the likelihood of Mr. and Mrs. William Rhodes sharing that philosophy when it comes to their only child. . . Well. The likelihood of that is just about nil." Noah stood up, looking out on the lawn and the red geraniums for a moment before he said, "I want to marry her, Colonel Barton. I love her. And the irony in that has just this moment struck me."

"What irony is that, son?"

Noah turned to face the colonel. "Blue Bear and me. Both losing the women we love because of circumstances beyond our control."

The colonel was quiet for a moment. Finally, he said, "You're racing ahead of yourself, Noah. Give yourself time. Give her time. Give God time. A psalm comes to mind. 'Wait on the Lord: be of good courage, and he shall strengthen thine heart: wait, I say, on the Lord.'"

Noah looked over at him. "You think the Lord is going to solve this for me?"

"Whatever He does, He promises to strengthen your heart. You're leaving for a few weeks. That will give the good Lord plenty of time to keep that promise, don't you think?"

"Maybe. But I don't have plenty of time to decide what to tell Emilie. And I can't just let her think everything is fine—that nothing has changed."

"I'm not suggesting that you do," the colonel said. "Of course you should tell her. But use gentler terms. Don't accept those ugly names you just called yourself a bit ago. And explain the journey."

"She won't want to hear it," Noah said. "Not after she learns the truth about me."

"Then it wasn't meant to be," the colonel said. "And that's not some fatalistic cliché. It's the truth. If that's to be the case, then be thankful you discovered it now. And again, son, don't forget God in all of this. He isn't sitting in heaven wondering what to do now that he's learned that Noah Shaw is part Pawnee Indian. I think He already knew that. And I don't imagine it's upset His master plan for your life."

Noah turned to look down at the colonel. "You think what happened to my mother was part of some master plan?"

"I think," the colonel said, "that every terrible thing that God allows into a life can be redeemed. But don't take that to mean that I minimize the pain mankind causes himself. I don't. I've seen too much of it to just wash it over with some convenient verse of Scripture." The colonel stood up. "Listen, son. I have just as many questions about the rough patches of life as you do. All I know for certain is that there is a God, and He loves His children. He never forsakes us. In my experience, He's often doing His very best work when we don't think He's paying any attention at all."

A master plan. Doing His best work. Could that be possible? Was God in all of this? Did He really have a plan? *Think of all the things you have to be thankful for.* That's what Ma would say right now. He could almost hear her voice. He bowed his head, thinking. He'd been given knowledge of the very things he'd longed for. Not only that, but he had Colonel Barton to guide the way. All those written memories he'd read. All that information. All of it worthy of Noah's giving thanks. He took a deep breath. "All right," Noah said. "I'll try to trust. But I still don't know what to do about Emilie."

"The next thing," the colonel said. "Just do the next thing. And for whatever it's worth, my housekeeper has proven herself to be a repository of wisdom over the years. Good, sound, old-fashioned wisdom. She told you to respect the young lady enough to be truthful. I think that's good advice. So you tell her. And you trust God. In the end, He's the only One I know who can work all things together for good."

Noah snorted softly. "If He can work this for good—"

"Then he must be not only all-knowing, but all-powerful, too." The colonel smiled and patted him on the back. "Lucky for you, He is."

—∾—

Emilie could see that something was wrong the moment she saw Noah. He'd been sitting in one of the rockers on Colonel Barton's front porch, but as she drew near, he stood. Then he seemed to remember the papers in his hand. With a little wave in her direction, he went inside. When he returned, he was empty-handed. But the expression on his face made her call out to him before she'd even pulled Royal to a halt by the hitching post. Noah stepped out onto Colonel Barton's front porch. "What is it? What's wrong?"

Noah descended the porch stairs without answering. His hands circled her waist and he lifted her to the ground. "Did you apologize to your mother?"

As soon as she'd hitched Royal, he took her hand and led her up the porch stairs.

"Would you believe that she knew all along? She said she recognized my writing style." When Noah guided her to one of the rockers on the porch, Emilie sat down, but he remained standing, leaning against the porch railing while she talked. "She was hurt that I hadn't told her, but in the end, she wasn't really all that upset. She said she *understood* why I would have delayed telling her. That I'd been very *busy*." She laid her riding crop on the table beside the chair, smiling up at him. "I think that was a reference to you, by the way."

Noah smiled back, but still. . .there was something lingering behind those dark eyes of his. Something that made her uneasy. She took her riding hat off and smoothed her hair. "The truth of the matter is I'll never understand her if I live to be a hundred." She took a deep breath. "You can imagine I didn't have any appetite at all for lunch—the colonel and I hadn't taken so much as one bite when Mother and Aunt Cornelia waltzed up." She glanced at the front door. "Are we really going to get one of Mrs. Riley's famous apple dumplings?"

Noah nodded. "I'm to let her know when we're ready. First, though, we need to talk. About my ma. The colonel remembered her."

Why wasn't he beaming with joy? Why was he staring down at the floorboards of the porch as if he didn't want to look at her.

What was going on? "So. . .he was able to give you some helpful information?"

Noah shrugged. "Information. Yes. Helpful? I'm not sure. I—" He got to his feet and stood, looking out at the street. "I don't really know how to do this."

Emilie rose and went to his side. "You're scaring me, Noah." She put her hand on his arm. "Please tell me what's happened. You can tell me anything, you know. Just—tell me."

He put his hand over hers and gave it a squeeze. Then he grasped her upper arms and had her sit back down. This time, he sat in the other chair, but he leaned forward, his elbows on his knees, his hands clasped before him as he talked. "I'm going to go away for a while. Colonel Barton offered to go along. That's where he is right now. He's over at the livery making arrangements. We'll follow the trail Ma did when she came here. All the way to Fort Kearny. Then on to Turkey Creek and Powder River. The colonel's offered to show me where everything happened."

"But that's good news, isn't it?"

Noah reached over and took her hand. "Honestly, I don't know. I mean—I thought it would be. But—" He rose to his feet and pulled her after him. "I'll show you. Inside."

He led her through the front door, into the hall, and then into Colonel Barton's office. Her notepad lay atop the colonel's desk. From where she stood, Emilie could see that he hadn't written a thing. She was going to miss her deadline.

"Emilie." Noah grasped her by the shoulders and turned her about. "You need to see this."

She stared at the portraits on the wall, her eyes drawn first to the handsome man dressed in buckskins and standing next to a young Colonel Barton. "That's Buffalo Bill. The colonel and he are friends." She looked up at him. "Are you going to meet him? Is the colonel taking you all the way to Scout's Rest?"

"Look at the other portrait. That's what you need to see. *Who* you need to see."

She saw. Stepped back, aware of Noah's nearness. She tilted her head. "Who is that? You look just like him."

"His Pawnee name is Blue Bear. Mother named me for him. My middle name. Leshario? It isn't Italian, after all. It's for him. Kit Leshario." Noah paused. "He's my father, Emilie."

When she took another step back, Noah put his arm around her. He guided her to the chair beside the colonel's desk and made her sit down. Next, he got a glass of water from the kitchen. She could hear him talking. To Mrs. Riley, she supposed. Perhaps even to the colonel's sister. When he returned, Emilie took a drink before setting the glass down on the colonel's desk with a trembling hand.

Noah pulled the colonel's desk chair out from behind his desk and sat next to her. "I didn't know any of this until today. When I told him what I knew of Ma's story, the colonel remembered her." He paused. Took a deep breath. "There's more, but the point is—he's my father. Colonel Barton knew him, too. They were friends. They haven't communicated in a while, but—apparently he works at Scout's Rest."

Emilie rose from her chair and went back to study the photograph. For a moment, she didn't say anything. This was the real reason Noah hadn't come to luncheon. The reason Colonel Barton came instead. She turned back around. "I can't imagine how you've been feeling. To be alone, learning this." She went to his side and sat down, reaching out to put her hand on his arm.

He covered it with his own, but he only patted it before pulling away. "I spent the day reading part of the colonel's memoirs. Then military reports." Finally, he looked at her. "You have to believe me, Emilie. If I'd known, I never would have. . . I never would have. . ."

"You wouldn't what? Have fallen in love with me? Because that's what I thought we were doing. Falling in love."

He took a deep breath. "They weren't married, Emilie. Do you understand what I'm saying?" He paused. "I'm not coming to Long Pine." He paused. "I might even—I might even meet him. I don't know—I don't know if I want to do that. But maybe—maybe I will. I just don't know." Tears filled his eyes. "I'm so sorry, Em. I didn't know. Please believe me. I never would have—if I'd known."

"You haven't answered my question," she said. "Were we falling in love?"

He closed his eyes and half groaned. "Yes. I love you. But now—" He shook his head. "I don't know what to do. I just don't know."

He loves me. He loves me. The admission was couched in pain, but still. . .the words rang true. She reached for him. Lifted his chin so that he would look at her. "You go with Colonel Barton. See what you need to see. Meet your father. And then you come back to me, Noah Shaw. Because of all the things you need to know—this one is the most important." And she leaned close to kiss him.

CHAPTER 27

What do you mean he isn't coming to Long Pine?" May stuffed the rest of her bedding into the box the girls were using to pack up the Bee Hive while she talked.

"Not coming?" April and June echoed.

Emilie nestled the paperweight Noah had given her in her own packing box, then folded up the camp desk and latched it shut. "I mean he isn't coming to Long Pine," she repeated. "Colonel Barton's taking him to Fort Kearny."

"Well how long does that take?" June asked. "Aren't there several trains a day?"

"They aren't going by train," Emilie said. "They're riding."

"Horses?"

"No. Camels." Emilie looked at her cousins. "Of course *horses*."

"I didn't know Noah rides," June said.

"I'm not sure he does. I suppose he'll learn. He said he wants to experience things the way his parents did." She paused. How she wanted to talk to May about—everything. But she didn't dare. Not yet, anyway. "It's a pilgrimage, and it's important to him. It was Colonel Barton's idea. He told Noah that it will help renew his own enthusiasm for his memoir."

"But—can Noah just cancel out on an event like that?"

Of course April—the responsible one—would ask. "He said that he's never missed an engagement, and his manager will understand."

"Fine," May said. "But what about you?"

"What about me?" Emilie didn't look up. She'd nearly depleted her strength for being nonchalant and supportive. If the questions didn't end soon, she was going to burst into tears.

"Emily Jane Rhodes." May was standing, hands on hips. "What about—you know—" She kissed the air.

Emilie blinked away tears as she bent down to fold up her camp cot. "He'll write. I'll wait." She cleared her throat and feigned a cough. "Now come and help me carry the camp desk out of here."

"Are you taking this to Long Pine?" May asked as they set the desk on the ground beside the growing pile of things Calvin would pick up later this evening.

Emilie shook her head. "Once again, Mother has amazed. She's bought me one of those writing boxes I've been admiring at the stationer's. It's almost as if my having a writing life was her idea. As if our past disagreements never happened."

"You have Noah to thank for that," May said as they ducked back inside.

"How so?"

April chimed in. "Well, thanks to Noah, Aunt Henrietta no longer has nightmares about her daughter the reporter, lingering in the newsroom, smoking cigars and wearing pants so she'll fit in with the rest of the crew."

May nodded. She put a pencil in her mouth, jutted out her chin, and strutted about the tent, her thumbs in imaginary suspenders.

It was a perfect imitation of Tom Tomkins, and it made Emilie laugh. "Like that was ever a danger."

"*You* know that, and *we* know that," June said. "But did Aunt Hen?"

April smiled. "June has a point, Em. You've put our mothers through a lot over the years."

"Well, she's in love now," June said, "so they can stop worrying and start planning a wedding again."

Once again tears threatened as Emilie thought about the next few weeks without Noah. He'd kissed her, but would he really come back to her? If she thought about that question for long—she went to help June fold her bedding.

But April wasn't finished with the discussion of engagements—broken, anticipated, or otherwise. "Thank goodness you've given them a distraction," she said. "I'm sick to death of my role in the spotlight as April of the Broken Engagement." She sighed. "If mother gives me one more of her pathetic, sympathetic looks—"

"I know how to make that stop," May said.

"Pray tell," April countered.

"Accept Will Gable's invitation."

"What's this?" Emilie asked with a fierce scowl. "What invitation? What haven't you been telling us?"

May spoke up. "It's no secret that Will's been pining after April ever since Elwood gave her that *tiny* little garnet."

"May Ophelia Spring," April scolded. "The size of that ring never mattered to me, and you know it."

"All I'm saying is you should give Will a chance. We all like him." May motioned for Emilie and June to support her. "Don't we?"

"We do," June said.

"Absolutely." Emilie nodded. "You should definitely accept his invitation—to whatever it was."

April shook her head. "He asked me if I'd like to go for a walk after the concert this evening. That's all."

"And you said?" May asked.

"I said it would depend on whether or not my family needed me. That we were packing up the Bee Hive and then there were the cabins to attend to." She smiled. "He offered to help."

"Then he's a gem, and you should marry him tomorrow," May

joked. "Any man who is willing to help women pack up a camp"—she glanced over at Emilie—"or de-snake one is a man we can all approve of."

"Here, here," Junie said. "Bert's already said he's helping Calvin load the wagons."

"Well then," May said. "I guess everyone has the perfect man all lined up. Except for poor, pathetic May." She forced a frown and swept away an imaginary tear, then clasped her hands together and leaned toward Emilie. "Are you *sure* Noah doesn't have a brother?"

—∞—

The final evening beneath the Tabernacle roof included a moving invocation and a rousing vocal and instrumental concert. The crowd offered up enthusiastic applause after the Spring Sisters' final song, and when they left the stage, Emilie smiled when Mother and Father nodded their approval. She would have felt wonderful, except for the fact that Noah wasn't there.

There was so much to do, he'd said. He couldn't leave Colonel Barton to make all the preparations. The colonel had suggested that Noah check out of the hotel and board at the house while they got ready for their adventure. Emilie imagined him walking up the geranium-bordered walk to the colonel's house just now, traveling bag in hand, the duffel containing his mother's quilt slung over his shoulder.

The colonel had at least a hundred more pages of material for Noah to read before they left. No, he didn't think he'd be able to come this evening. He couldn't just leave the colonel to do all the work.

As for tomorrow, he didn't know when he would be able to see her. The colonel said his suits wouldn't last a week on the trail, and so he was going to have to shop for sturdier gear. Beyond that, there was the matter of horses. Apparently a greenhorn didn't just choose one of the more gentle horses at the livery. A gentle horse might not have the stamina for the trek. And a horse with stamina might have too much spirit. Apparently choosing any trail horse could be a challenge. Choosing a trail horse suitable for a greenhorn was another matter entirely. The colonel wanted Noah to ride more than one horse. Noah didn't know how long that would take.

All of it made complete sense. None of it helped Emilie feel any less dejected as she sat amidst the Chautauqua crowd, with May on her right and Bert Hartwell on her left and Noah over at Colonel Barton's house doing whatever it was he needed to do.

As the evening wore on, Emilie's nerves wore thin and her mood plummeted. Everything Noah had said earlier today ran through her mind, over and over again. His father was a Pawnee Indian. His parents had never been married. There were labels assigned to people like him. Of course none of that mattered to Emilie. But if she thought it wouldn't matter to her parents—she glanced their way—if she thought it wouldn't matter to them, Emilie knew she was being naive.

She looked over at May. What would May think? What would she say? And Bert. And April and June and Uncle Roscoe and Aunt Cornelia and—Hazel Penner. Well, she could just imagine what Hazel Penner would say. Emilie closed her eyes. In spite of her best efforts, a tear escaped. She bowed her head. Another tear. She bit her lower lip. Raised her gloved hand and feigned a cough. Cleared her throat. Nothing worked.

Finally, she leaned over and whispered in May's ear. "I'm all right, but I have to get a drink of water. Tell Mother I'll be back in time to help over at the cabin." With that, she slipped out of her seat and hurried away.

As she wove her way through the crowd seated on blankets and quilts, Emilie pulled a handkerchief from the small bag hanging from her wrist. It was as if the presence of the handkerchief gave the tears permission to flow. Before she consciously realized what she was doing, she was heading for the arched gates, up the road, and finally, across the bridge to town.

She'd calmed down. The sun was setting, the moon rising just above the trees. Her tears stopped. She looked back toward the Tabernacle. They were singing the closing hymn. *"My faith looks up to Thee, Thou Lamb of Calvary, Savior divine! . . . May Thy rich grace impart strength to my fainting heart."* The words became a prayer as Emilie stood, looking down at the waters of the Blue River. . .the river that had attracted Noah to this place, the river beside which his mother had camped, the river beside which Emilie and Noah had kissed. Had it been only a few days ago? It seemed a lifetime ago.

The words to the hymn rang out, sung by thousands and carried on the wind. Harmony. They were singing harmony, soprano and alto, tenor and bass, the parts blending beautifully in the summer night. *"While life's dark maze I tread, and griefs around me spread, be Thou my Guide; Bid darkness turn to day, wipe sorrow's tears away, nor let me ever stray from Thee aside."*

"Oh God," Emilie whispered. "Oh God, help me. Help us. I love him so." She began to cry again. Someone was coming from the direction of town. She ducked her head and turned away.

"Emilie? Emilie, is it you? Oh, Emilie—" Noah reached her side. He pulled her to him.

"I just—I couldn't just sit there. Without you. Wondering." She choked out the words. "I've had hours to think. I've pretended nothing was wrong. I haven't said a word to anyone. But Noah—are you really going to leave me?"

"I have to go, sweetheart," he said.

"I know. That's not what I mean."

"Walk with me," he said.

They made their way across the bridge, away from the assembly grounds, and toward town. He kept his arm about her, and for

Emilie's part, she wasn't about to let go of him. As they walked, the sky darkened and the stars came out.

"The colonel and I have spent the evening in his office. We've made a terrible mess of it, sorting through all those piles of papers on his desk." He reached into his pocket with his free hand and withdrew a few sheets of paper. "I had to tear them out of your notebook so that I could carry them in my pocket while I looked for you, but Colonel Barton answered your questions."

"I wasn't worried about that," Emilie said. "It doesn't really matter." She choked back another sob.

Noah's arm about her tightened. "It does matter. E. J. Starr has a promising career ahead of her. Neither the colonel nor I want to do anything to hamper it."

Emilie stopped walking. She looked up at him. "Then don't break my heart."

He took a deep breath. "Haven't I already?"

She closed her eyes and leaned into him, resting her cheek against his chest. "I still love you. I don't care about that. Nothing's changed."

He caressed her hair, then kissed her on the forehead. "Everything has changed, beloved. Everything."

Beloved. He'd never said that before. He sounded older. Distant. The music had stopped. He noticed.

"They've stopped singing. Your family will be worried."

He was right, of course.

"I don't know how to behave around them. As if nothing has happened. As if nothing is wrong. How can I do that?"

"I asked the same question earlier of the colonel. He said that we just 'do the next thing.'" He paused. "For me, that's learning to ride a horse. For you?"

She sighed. "Packing. Helping pack up the cabins."

"Beware of snakes," he said. "And wait for me. And pray. The colonel reminded me that God isn't surprised by any of this. I know he's right. But I don't know what it means for the future." He lifted her chin. "Do you see me, Emilie Jane?"

She nodded. "I see enough."

"I love you." He bent to kiss her, and then he said, "If you still want me a month from now—when you've had time to think it through—I'll be back. I'll talk to your father like a proper gentleman. And then we'll see." When she started to speak, he touched his finger to her lips. "Shhh," he said. "We'll see. Now take my arm, and I'll walk you back."

Finally back in her own bed—she had forgotten how luxurious a real mattress could feel—Emilie slept half the morning away on Tuesday, waking only when Mother opened the door and called to her.

"Your cousins will be here in half an hour, Emilie Jane."

Emilie turned over to face her. "Do I have to go?"

"For the last meeting of the chorus class? The closing song? I suppose not, if you really don't want to." Mother stepped into the room. "Are you ill?"

With a sigh, Emilie sat up. "No. I'm just. . .tired of it all." She paused. "I wish we weren't scheduled up at Long Pine. I've had my fill of camping."

"We've a lovely cottage reserved," Mother said. "You'll love it once we're there. I hear the natatorium is much better than the one here." She paused. "And before he left for the newspaper this morning, your father said he has some ideas for E. J. Starr. Something connected to your Chautauqua experiences."

Emilie threw back the sheet and put her feet to the floor. She stretched. Looked over at the bag she had yet to unpack. Sighed.

"Come now, Emilie. I know it's a great disappointment to you that Mr. Shaw isn't going to be there, after all. But really—" She smiled. "He'll be back at the end of the summer. And a little period of separation isn't a bad thing in these matters."

"Tell that to April," Emilie said, crossing to her dressing table and reaching for her hair brush.

"Noah Shaw," Mother said firmly, "is nothing like that Elwood Sutter."

Emilie glanced at Mother in the mirror. "You had doubts about Elwood?"

Mother hesitated. "Of course I didn't want to say anything. But yes. I did. His people have never been particularly. . .oh, I don't know. His family doesn't impress. As for Elwood, he never seemed to be able to muster passion for anything—including April. Your Mr. Shaw is nothing like Elwood Sutter—thank heavens. It's obvious he comes from good stock. I only wish his parents were still living. But as far as I can see, he's more than proven himself in every way that's important. He's made something of himself, even without the support of a strong family behind him. That speaks well for a man." She came up behind Emilie and put her hands firmly on her shoulders. "Allow him his little adventure in the West, dear, and be thankful for Josiah Barton's taking him under his wing. There's no better man for Noah to be around if he's intent on adventure. Josiah will return the boy safe and sound, right where he belongs."

"And where is that?"

"At your side, of course," Mother said.

"Do you really believe that?"

Mother frowned. "In the end I don't suppose it matters whether I believe it or not. Are you having second thoughts?"

Emilie shook her head. "It's just that the next few weeks are going to be the longest few weeks of my life." Her eyes filled with tears.

"What's this?" Mother gathered her in her arms. "Where's my brave girl reporter? It'll be all right, dear. Truly. The young man's completely in love with you."

Emilie took a deep breath. "I'm behaving like a child," she said and stepped out of Mother's embrace. "I'll be fine. Just—let me get ready. There's no good reason for me to sit here at home pining over Noah, especially when he hasn't even left yet." She began to unbutton her chemise.

"I'll have Dinah get a light breakfast ready. You'd better hurry, now." Mother stepped out into the hall and closed the door behind her.

Emilie faltered only once in dressing. *Just do the next thing.* She could do that. She could attend the closing ceremonies and sing in the chorus. She could unpack and plan for Long Pine. And she could go by the newspaper office and talk to father about E. J. Starr's future with the *Dispatch*. Thoughts of writing brought her up short. Made her smile. She would talk to Father about his ideas for E. J. Starr. But first. . .first, she would stop in at the *Journal* and introduce E. J. Starr to Carl Obrist. It couldn't hurt to have more than one egg in one's basket. And now that she thought about it, she had some ideas of her own for E. J. Starr.

CHAPTER 28

At the end of the first day of what Noah had come to think of as his "quest," he swung out of the saddle with a groan, staggering a bit when his feet hit the ground. The bay Colonel Barton had advised him to purchase looked back at him with what Noah could have sworn was disdain. "I know," he said, "I'm embarrassing you. Can't be helped. Everything hurts." The horse shook its head and gave a soft snort. When Colonel Barton dismounted with a grunt, Noah spoke to the horse again. "He's sore, too. And *he* knows what he's doing."

Colonel Barton laughed. "These old bones keep reminding me just how long ago that was." He arched his back and stretched. "I've turned into a city boy, too. Let's call it a day."

It was still dark when the colonel shook Noah awake the next morning.

"Four o'clock, son," he said. "Don't have a bugle and decided to forego the gunfire. Still, it's time to rise and rustle breakfast. Assuming, of course, you still want to re-create your mother's trail experience."

"I do," Noah said. And then he tried to sit up. He knew it wasn't really possible to pull every single muscle just sitting astride a horse. Yet every move hurt something.

The colonel chuckled. "Wait until you're fifty and you decide to pull some fool stunt like this. Then you'll know what it's like to be sore." As he walked past on his way to stir up the campfire, the colonel tossled Noah's hair. "Come on, greenhorn. Buck up and move out. It'll get better in a few minutes after you've stretched out the kinks."

With a loud groan, Noah managed to get to his feet. Staggering like a drunkard, he made his way to the creek. When he crouched down to cup his hands and splash his face with water, he lost his balance, landing on his backside in the grass. His horse had been grazing nearby, but the sudden motion of Noah's fall made him jerk his head up and snort.

"What are you looking at?" Noah groused.

The horse took a step toward him. Then another. Noah lay still, staring up at the predawn sky, hurting. In a moment, the horse loomed over him. Dropping its head, it lipped his hair, then nuzzled his cheek.

"Thank you," Noah said, reaching up to pat the horse's muzzle. "Your sympathy is appreciated. You wouldn't want to help me up, would you?"

By way of answer, the animal stepped away. Seconds later, Noah heard the sound of the grass being watered. Laughing, he once again crouched at the waters' edge, ignoring the pain in his legs as he splashed water in his face, then raked his damp fingers through his hair. Finally, he stood up, leaning from side to side, grimacing with every move.

"You fry the bacon," the colonel called. "I'll show you how we make camp coffee."

Boiled beans completed the meal. They were on the move by seven and rode until noon. Lunch consisted of bread, a hunk of cheese, and water drawn—with permission—from a rancher's well.

"What did you do before the country was settled?" Noah asked. "How'd you know where to find water?"

"At first, we depended on native scouts who knew the land. In a dry year, we sometimes went without, even with a guide along." With that, the colonel was off on a story of a fruitless search for water and men fighting to be the first to put their parched lips to a trickle of water seeping out of a canyon wall.

Not all that far west of Beatrice, rolling hills gave way to treeless prairie, and a landscape Noah at first thought of as empty. But as time went on, he began to see things a different way. Blooming wildflowers made him think of Ma again and her love for something she called a butterfly weed. He wondered if she might have been remembering the bushy plants with orange blossoms that seemed to attract butterflies. In time, he realized there was variety, even in what had at first seemed an endless sea of grass.

One evening as the campfire died down and the colonel and Noah lay looking up at the canopy of stars, the colonel told a story about native men stopping at a lone dugout one winter day. "Frightened some poor homesteader's wife half to death," he said. "Her husband was off hunting, hoping to bag one last deer for winter meat. Anyway, the woman's two boys took ill. She had them in bed, and here came a band of Indians, wanting something to eat." He paused. "You've heard folks call Indians 'beggars,' I suppose?" The colonel didn't wait for Noah to answer, merely continued. "Well, that's just another example of the basic misunderstandings of the culture. You visit a tepee or an earth lodge, and you're going to be given food. Welcomed in. The most respected man in the village is the one who gives the most away. And hospitality? No one is more hospitable than an Indian. So you can see how a brave would just assume that of course a woman would offer them bread. It was their way. Of course, the whites didn't see it that way.

"Anyway, as the story goes, the head man heard the children coughing. Mind you, it was just a dugout, but they'd split it into two rooms with a blanket tacked to the rafters. The Indian peered around the blanket. The poor mother was certain that she was about to see her own children scalped. But all the man did was to touch his palm to their foreheads and grunt. They had a fever. So the Indian left. But not long after, he returned with a handful of weeds. He couldn't speak English, but he made it clear that she was supposed to make tea with those weeds. He insisted. So now the woman was thinking that maybe he'd returned to poison her children. Except that his gestures made it clear that he intended to help them. And wouldn't you know it? Those two boys drank a cup of tea and fell asleep. And that was the end of their fever and their cough."

"How'd you learn that story?" Noah asked.

"The woman told me about it one Christmas at Fort Laramie. Her boys were in the Second Nebraska with me."

"Was Blue Bear the Indian?"

"No. The Indians were Sioux." The colonel was quiet for a moment. "Remind me to write that story down tomorrow when we stop for lunch, will you?"

Noah said he would, and in moments the colonel was snoring softly. The night was still and just on the verge of too hot, but as the stars came out, Noah stared into the expanse of the sky. The vastness of the earth stretching away from the camp site in all directions washed over him.

"What is man, that thou art mindful of him?. . . Where wast thou when I laid the foundations of the earth?" "Grow old along with me. . .the best is yet to be." He sat up, seeking—and finding—the Big Dipper. Orion. The Pleiades. *What is man? What am I? Who am I?*

He laid back down. Surely the God who had made all of this; who kept it in balance; who was not, as Colonel Barton had said, surprised at the news that Kit Leshario had a son; surely this God could make a way for Noah Shaw and Emilie Rhodes.

"Please, God," Noah whispered, "make a way."

—∞—

As the train rumbled along, Emilie pretended to read the newspaper Father had handed over just as Emilie and her cousins, Mother and Aunt Cornelia boarded the Fremont, Elkhorn, and Missouri Valley train for the trip to Long Pine.

"This will give you an idea as to some of the unique aspects of the area that E. J. Starr might want to report on," Father had said. "The Long Pine Chautauqua has quite an active group of boosters interested in making it one of the more attractive assemblies in the state. Perhaps you'll learn something that will help the Interstate Chautauqua right here at home stay ahead of the game."

Emilie had murmured something that she hoped sounded cooperative, all the while wondering at the change in Father—and Mother, for that matter. Both of them had gone from being suspicious of her ambition to encouraging it. She glanced up and realized that April was watching her with a concerned expression. When Emilie force a smile, April smiled back and returned to reading the book in her lap.

"If you aren't going to read that," May said, nudging Emilie and nodding at the newspaper, "hand it over."

"In a minute." Emilie forced herself to concentrate on the article about the Long Pine Chautauqua, which took place "in a maze of woodland scenery formed by grove thickets and shady glens, with foliage of the oak, different species of the pine, and countless varieties of other shade and ornamental trees and shrubbery." The Chautauqua grounds were "in a canyon one hundred feet below the surrounding undulating prairie." The article said it was a "delightful spot for recreation, rest, and keen enjoyment."

As she read further, all Emilie could think about was how wonderful it would have been to be there with Noah. "Nature could not have created a more perfect place. A labyrinth of winding walks and driveways runs among a bower of leafy canopies and ferns and creeping vines. . .thousands of mossy banks and cool nooks. . . ." She blushed to think of spreading a quilt on one of those mossy banks, having Noah join her, being in his arms again, kissing.

The article went on to say that Long Pine offered "a paradise for the angler. Nature's laboratory for the student of geology and botany. Absolutely pure water. Extensive bathing facilities. All kinds of outdoor games," and the "best boating facilities." One strong point that Beatrice would never be able to rival was the fact that the bath houses at Long Pine were served by no fewer than seven natural springs.

A mention of "miraculous cures by pure water" piqued Emilie's curiosity. "Taking the waters" was becoming something of a national pastime. Perhaps E. J. Starr could look into that. If the claims were real, Long Pine deserved more publicity. If they were grandiose, well. . . Was E. J. Starr going to be the kind of reporter who exposed false claims? She hadn't thought about that before. Exactly what kind of reporter did E. J. Starr want to be?

A married one.

Honestly. It didn't seem to matter what she did these days, Emilie's mind always returned to Noah. Wondering where he was. Wishing he'd written. Hoping that whatever was happening with him and Colonel Barton and the West, it would all combine to eventually bring him back to her. What she wanted hadn't changed. But what if Noah did? What if he decided he didn't want to come back? What if his time away from her only served to convince him that everything between them had happened too quickly? What if—

"Emilie!"

With a start, Emilie looked up from the newspaper at May, who was standing in the aisle. "We're going up to the dining car to have something to eat. Don't you want to come with us?"

Emilie gazed toward the front of the car, then back out the

window at the passing landscape. When she hesitated, May sat back down next to her.

"Are you going to tell me what's really going on with you, or are we just going to continue to pretend this is all because you're pining after Noah? I mean—I know you're pining after Noah, but there's something else. Something you aren't saying."

Surprised when tears came to her eyes, Emilie looked away. Shook her head. "I can't. Not yet."

May reached over and grasped her hand. "I hate seeing you so miserable."

"And all the while I thought I was hiding it," Emilie said. May snorted softly. Emilie took a deep breath. "It's—Noah. Something Colonel Barton—something that changed everything." She snapped her fingers. "Just like that." Again, her eyes filled with tears.

June appeared at the front of the car and made her way toward them. "Come on, you two," she said. "Mama's fit to be tied. What do you want to eat?"

"Just order us a sandwich and hot tea," May said. "We'll be along in a bit." She handed Emilie a handkerchief. "And don't say anything about—this."

June rolled her eyes. "As if you had to tell me that." She headed back to the dining car.

Emilie moved to get up. "I'm sorry I haven't confided in you, May. But—I need time to think." She paused. "I have to work it out in my own mind first."

"I could help you with that, too," May said. "If you'd only trust me."

The hurt in May's voice only added to Emilie's burden. "Please don't be angry with me," Emilie said as she set the newspaper on May's seat. *Please, May.* "Everyone will know about it in time. But I'll tell you first. I promise." She pointed at the newspaper. "You can read that next. Long Pine sounds really beautiful." And with that, she got up.

As she followed May up the aisle, Emilie took a deep breath. She could do this. She would do it. She had to. She had to smile and "just do the next thing," as Noah had said. And the next thing was Long Pine. Accompanying the Spring Sisters. Writing as E. J. Starr. And praying.

Mrs. Riley had said to pray, squeezing Emilie's hands and whispering, "Times like these, I ponder on a verse that says, 'Thou wilt keep him in perfect peace, whose mind is stayed on thee.' When I don't have words for a situation, I still hold it up to the good Lord. You do that, Miss Rhodes, and He'll give you some peace while your young man is gallivanting all over creation."

The woman's sweet spirit had been better than a hug—although she'd offered one of those, too. That had been a few days ago. Her conscience pricked, Emilie wondered if maybe the reason she was so troubled was that she hadn't spent much time thinking about "the good Lord" and His part in things. She would try to do better. But first, she was going to have to pretend to be hungry or Mother and Aunt Cornelia would hover like nursemaids.

Nursemaids. Wouldn't it be grand if all it took to heal a person's problems was the right poultice?

In the days following Josiah and Noah Shaw's departure, Grace grew increasingly restless. Every morning was the same. She was awakened by the crowing of Ladora's infernal rooster. Pulling on her dressing gown, she descended to the kitchen, only to be greeted by a cheerful Ladora, who had already gathered the eggs and made coffee and was happily humming her way through a quiet morning. As if boredom was a gift.

As far as Grace was concerned, it seemed that Beatrice had awakened for a few days and, once the brief disturbance was over, bowed its head and gone back to sleep. When she groused about it over breakfast one morning, Ladora stared at her with surprise. "Land sakes, Grace. Aren't you glad to be finished with all that baking? I surely had my fill."

"Oh, well, I don't suppose I mind not having to chop all that rhubarb or peel apples for half the morning. That's not what I mean exactly." Grace sighed.

"You'll get used to the quiet," Ladora said. "And the colonel will be back before you know it, wanting to have this meal or that and waiting on folks that come to visit him looking for his help. And he'll be bent on writing those memories once he comes back, you can be sure of that. He might even need a secretary. Maybe you can help him with that."

"That's all well and good," Grace said. "But what about—" She opened her mouth to complain, then closed it quickly. "Never mind. Forget I said anything."

"You need to get on some committees," Ladora said.

"Why would I do that?"

"'Cause they could use the help, of course. There's the library committee and then the Ladies' Aid."

"I don't quilt," Grace said quickly.

"Well there's nothing to quilting," Ladora said. "And you could learn. It's for a good cause, after all. We've got a project going right now to make comforters and such for the home."

"Which home is that?"

"For the feeble minded," Ladora said. "Now that I think on it, you should come to the meetin' this afternoon. Half the ladies who come to quilting you already met working at the dining hall."

Yes, I know. Those are the women I stole the money from. "I don't know. . . ."

"What do you know, Grace?" Ladora stood up and went to work. Taking the cover off the crockery bowl where she'd put some bread to rise, she snatched the cloth off and punched down the dough, then left it to rise again. "I mean it. I invited you to everything, and you don't want to go. But you're not happy." Ladora paused. Finally, clearing her throat, she said. "You gave it back, Grace. You got to let it go."

"Wh–what are you talking about?"

"The money pouch. It's been nigh on to a month now. You gave it back. It was a lot of money, but that don't matter. You thought better of it, and that's that. God forgave you. Forgive yourself and stop wallowin' in it."

Grace pulled her trembling hands into her lap and sat, unable to speak. Ladora knew. Who else knew? Did Josiah know?

"Nobody knows but me, and I'm not tellin'. You got nothin' to worry about, Grace. Move on. It's done." Ladora returned to the nook and sat back down. After a moment she said, "I guess you're shocked I picked up on it."

Grace didn't move.

"I wasn't always a housekeeper, you know. The colonel pulled me out of a deep and miry pit once. And I ain't never looked back. You don't have to look back, either. That's in the Bible. 'forgetting those things which are behind. . .I press toward the mark.'"

Grace couldn't get past the idea that Ladora knew. Had known. Would always know. "You knew?"

"Not until you put it back," Ladora said. "I really never suspicioned you. But then I saw you put it back." She suppressed a smile. "I thought it right funny of God to see to it you had to take it to the bank."

Grace hung her head. "I've never regretted anything so much. I don't know why I did it."

"'Cause you was scared," Ladora said. "You didn't know what your brother was like. You was remembering someone else. And you was scared about what that might mean for you. But he's changed. God changed him, and God changed me, and God can change you.

You just got to let Him in. Why, truth be told, I think He's already been changing you. You just don't want to admit it."

Ladora rose and went into Josiah's office. Presently, she returned with a book in hand. "Before, when you was reading this, it was so's you could learn how to play-act. So's you could fool us." She set the volume of Spurgeon's sermons before Grace. "You should try reading them again. For a different reason. Start with the one on page ninety-two."

With a little frown, Grace opened the book to page ninety-two. "Sincere Seekers Assured Finders."

"You just read that one," Ladora said. "Over and over. Till it makes sense." She smiled. "You're gonna be just fine, Grace Barton. You just don't know it yet."

CHAPTER 29

No letter. There was no letter waiting when Emilie reached Long Pine. Of course Noah and the colonel wouldn't have so much as reached their first stop on their trek yet. Still, she'd hoped. The colonel had said it would be a week before he and Noah got to Fort Kearny. Even if Noah wrote her then, he probably wouldn't post it until they reached the city of Kearney the next day. The soonest she should expect to receive a letter would be in the final days of the Long Pine Chautauqua. Still. . .she'd hoped. In spite of logical explanations and reasonable observations. She'd hoped.

Noah's body was beginning to acclimate to the demands of the trail about the time the tops of the cottonwoods around what had been the parade ground at Fort Kearney came into view. It had been a week since he and Colonel Barton rode out of Beatrice.

"The military reservation was ten miles square," the colonel said as they rode along. "In fact, we're on it now. The post itself is on a slight elevation. That afforded an excellent view of the surrounding country. This was all Pawnee land before. . .before things changed. Of course the Sioux and the Cheyenne hunted buffalo all across the plains. All three tribes were traditional enemies, and there was always competition for buffalo, for horses, for good grazing. Then we came along and insisted on drawing imaginary lines across the earth, expecting our ideas about things to be adopted and respected." The colonel was quiet for a moment before he motioned around them.

"These trees had already been here for twenty years when I came in the '60s." He began to point to where various structures had been. "Barracks. Sutler's. Post commander. Stables." He paused. "It really was quite a place. Imagine what a welcome sight a busy fort would have been to people who'd been crawling across a treeless prairie for weeks. Especially in a time when hostilities were on the rise and they had to be constantly watchful—constantly fearful of being attacked." He nodded toward the south. "Your mother would have spent most of her time near that copse of small trees and brush. Laundry row was there. Little more than shacks by our standards today."

Noah wondered at the idea of women standing over vats of boiling water when the weather was like it was today—the heat made even more oppressive by a hot wind. "What happened to all the buildings?"

"Sold to the highest bidder, I imagine. Torn down for the lumber—maybe moved intact to some neighboring farms." The colonel nodded to the west. "Ben Holladay had a stage station not forty rods that way. A storehouse, office, eating station—all from cedar logs Holladay hauled in from nearly a hundred miles away."

"It's hard to imagine such a deserted place ever being very important," Noah said.

"All the Platte Valley traffic came by here. Hundreds of wagons a day. Freighters, Concord stages, and the prairie schooners everyone remembers with such romanticism. The Pony Express passed by, too, and then the telegraph." The colonel paused. "Nearly all the military expeditions involved in the territory back then moved out from here. During the worst times of hostilities, we'd hold wagons back until there were a few dozen to travel together. And we stationed squads every few miles along the Platte, all the way from here to Julesburg."

And still, Noah thought, *Ma's wagon train was attacked and burned.*

They lingered at the site of the old fort for just a few minutes before heading for Kearney, where Noah would post his first letter to Emilie. As they rode along, the colonel regaled him with tales of Dobytown. "Fourteen saloons run by six families."

"And you know that because. . .?" Noah teased.

The colonel looked over with a sad smile. "Experience, son. Sad, lasting experience."

As they neared the Platte River, he pointed to a thicket of cottonwoods. "There used to be a house over there. Dirty Woman's Ranch, we called it."

"That sounds bad," Noah said.

"*I* was bad." After a moment, the colonel smiled. "I once was lost, but now am found. Was blind, but now I see."

"Maybe you should write about that," Noah said.

"Maybe I should."

The river was little more than a few rivulets of water meandering between islands of sand peppered with stands of grass and saplings. "Not much of a river," Noah said as the horses made their way across.

The colonel nodded. "We've had a dry year. When snowmelt's rushing down from the Rockies, the water moves fast. I've seen this river run a mile wide. Hard to imagine right now, but at times like that, there's quicksand to be considered. Makes me think of a time when. . ." And the colonel launched into another tale of the West that helped Noah ignore his aching muscles and bruised backside.

The Spring Sisters had been at Long Pine for nearly a week when, late one night, Emilie ducked out of the cabin and stood, looking up at the night sky. Locusts buzzed. In the distance, someone was playing a guitar. And somewhere. . .somewhere Noah was looking up at this same sky. Was he thinking of her?

Try as she would to "just do the next thing," Emilie was failing, and she knew it. Her appetite was nonexistent. She was having trouble sleeping, and she'd botched the piano part on one of the Spring Sisters' songs tonight.

Just before retiring this evening, Mother had put her hand to Emilie's forehead. "Maybe we should check in with the doctor," she'd said.

"I'll be fine," Emilie replied. "Maybe I'll 'take the waters' myself tomorrow, and write a first-hand account of the healthful benefits of the Long Pine springs." But she hadn't sounded very convincing.

A rustling behind her signaled that she wasn't the only one awake. Hurrying down the cabin steps, Emilie headed off into the night in the direction of the creek. Perching in the shadow of a moonlit rock, she drew her knees up and, wrapping her arms about them, rested her forehead against her knees. Trying to pray. *You have to help me. I know I should trust You, but I can't. What if Noah doesn't come back? What if—* Tears threatened.

"You have to stop this." May sat down next to her. "You have to let us help you."

"You can't. There's nothing anyone can do. At least not right now."

"I'll speak with Mama," May said. "I'll go with you."

Frowning, Emilie looked over. "Go with me. . .where?"

"Wherever," May said. "There's the Friendship Home up in Lincoln, although I suppose you'll want to go farther away than that." She touched Emilie's shoulder. "You won't have to be alone, Em. I promise."

"What—what are you talking about?"

May's voice wavered. "The baby." She reached for Emilie's hand.

"What?! Why on earth would you think—a baby!"

May sounded defensive. "Noah isn't writing. You aren't eating. You aren't sleeping. You're half sick. What else could it be?"

"I've only known him for six weeks. That's hardly—" Emilie

could feel herself blushing. "There's no baby. A baby would be easy. We'd get married right away, and no one would object. Oh, they'd whisper behind our backs, but—" A baby. May thought she was *enceinte.* Did Mother? Goodness.

"Don't be angry," May said quickly. "I just thought—I mean—you're a mess, Em. It had to be something bad. And after what happened last year to Garnet Davies—"

Garnet Davies. The classmate who had put on so much weight and then quite suddenly gone on a trip to visit a distant aunt. And come back, pale and thin and. . .sad. So sad. Emilie shook her head. And then, in the midst of tears and sobs, she blurted everything out. All of it, in a rush, with May just sitting there beside her, not moving, not saying a word. "And so he's off on a quest to trace his mother's steps. And maybe to meet his father. I told him it doesn't matter. He said it does. He said it changes everything." She said the ugly words Noah had used. "He said that about himself. And he hasn't written, and I don't know what to think." She hid her face in her hands.

"Oh, Em." May offered a hug. "It's going to be all right, Em. I don't know how, but it will. You'll see. We love you. We like Noah. Everyone does. It's going to be all right. It has to."

Emilie cried for a few more minutes. She talked. May listened. Finally they got up and returned to the cabin. The next morning, Emilie managed to eat something. She and May set off together to take advantage of the "healing springs." Somehow, Emilie felt better. May knew. Emilie wasn't alone in it anymore.

Friday, July 18, 1890
Dearest Emilie,

Where to begin. How I wish you were here this evening with me as I sit beside a dying campfire. The western horizon is marked by a band of rose that fades to pink and then peach and then pale blue that darkens as one's gaze rises to the dark canopy overhead. In moments it will seem as if an inkwell has washed the sky with indigo. How I wish you were here beside me.

Your city boy has become quite the plainsman—at least that's what Colonel Barton says, as he teases me about the way my hair grows over my collar and my hands roughen. My skin grows darker with every passing day—an ever-present reminder of why I'm out here in the first place. The relentless sun inspires an equally relentless search for shade whenever we stop.

After several incidents that sent Colonel Barton into gales of laughter and left me feeling like the most dim-witted man alive, I've taken to calling my horse Phil. You will recall that the Philistines were something of a plague on God's people for much of ancient history. I believe that's all I need to say about Phil's role in my life.

The first week was miserable. Just when I thought that every muscle had already been challenged to its maximum for causing me pain, something new would happen to prove me wrong. Most mornings, I moved like a man many decades past my actual age. By midafternoon my entire body screamed, Stop. On a couple of occasions, my mouth said it aloud, and Colonel Barton took pity on me and stopped early. He said that his "old bones" were glad for the relief, but the truth is he could have gone yet another few hours were it not for the greenhorn tagging along behind him.

General Barton writes many pages at the end of every day. At first I was too exhausted to write. Still, I want you to know what I am seeing. Somehow to feel what it means to me to be tracing my past.

There is nothing left of the fort where Ma worked as a laundress, save the towering cottonwoods ringing the old parade ground. Two have been the victim of lightning. Others show the effects of wind. The most memorable has reached a circumference of probably ten feet. It stands like an old warrior and has witnessed so much. That tree witnessed the passing of thousands of wagons and freighters, Pony Express riders and stage coaches. Most important to me, that tree "saw" my mother when she was young. I wished that I might climb its branches and be transported back in time to somehow understand her life in this place.

I am posting this letter to you in Kearney, and then we journey out to Turkey Creek and beyond. As I am not certain that this letter will reach Long Pine before you leave, I am sending it home to your Beatrice. If the delay in hearing from me has caused you to worry, please forgive me. Not an hour goes by that I don't think of you. Perhaps the favorite image is from that first night when you rode away from me to speak with your parents. The memory of those apron strings waving in the moonlight will ever make me smile.

There was so much more that Noah wanted to write. How beautiful the prairie was. How vast the sky. How a man understood his insignificance in the scheme of things out here in this place, and how the realization humbled him when he stopped to realize that the God who ruled the world also said, "Come now. . .let us reason together." He wanted to tell her just how much Colonel Barton's friendship and wisdom were helping Noah shape his image of himself and the man he would soon meet. But it was late, the campfire was nearly gone, and words were simply not sufficient for some things.

It is dark. I must stop writing. If I can't post another letter, please don't worry. I am ever and always yours.

Noah

Noah's letter had been waiting for Emilie at home. Waiting on the entryway table with calling cards from Mother's friends and a request from Carl Obrist that she stop in the *Journal* office upon her return from Long Pine. That was good news, of course, but it didn't matter nearly as much as Noah's letter. Emilie read it quickly the first time. The second time, she tried to imagine him beside a campfire. She closed her eyes and willed herself to see the sky he'd described. And the third time she traced the words "I am ever and always yours" with her fingertip.

Now, as she stepped out onto the small porch just off her room, she looked west and wondered. What had Noah learned about himself at Turkey Creek? And what effect would the Powder Horn Valley have on him? And then. . .then what? She closed her eyes. *Help him, Lord. Help us all. And thank You for May.*

Fully one month after he'd ridden out of Beatrice alongside Colonel Josiah Barton, a bronzed and trailworn Noah Shaw rode into North Platte, Nebraska. Josiah had warned him that North Platte had "quite a reputation."

"The last time I was there, saloons were the most common business in town. Even the drugstores and general stores sold liquor and wine, and that didn't include all the unlicensed saloons, gambling dens, and other establishments. Cowboys and soldiers on leave rode a long way to have a 'good time' in North Platte."

As the two men rode into town, Noah had opportunity to see exactly what Josiah meant. It was after sundown, and Front Street was alive with raucous laughter and the tinny sound of almost-in-tune pianos.

"It's as if one of the towns in those dime novels I used to read just came to life," Noah said as he swung out of the saddle, then followed Josiah into a livery stable. The horses attended to, the men walked up the street and got a room at the Union Pacific Hotel.

"Time to decide, son," Josiah said. "How many nights do we need the room?"

"At least two," Noah said.

Josiah smiled. As he signed the hotel register, he inquired as to the availability of baths.

"This time of night?" the clerk protested.

"Yes. Tonight. We've been on the trail for nearly a month, son," Josiah said.

Half an hour later, Noah sank into a tub of hot water with a sigh of pleasure. "I should get a haircut," he said to Josiah, similarly lounging in a tub on the other side of the sheet hung from the rafters to create separate "rooms" in the bath house.

"Plenty of tonsorial parlors in town," Josiah said. "You can search one out tomorrow while I ride out to Scout's Rest."

And that's just what happened. Noah got a shave and a haircut while Josiah rode the few miles to the Scout's Rest. Everything was going according to plan. Until Josiah rode back into town, accompanied by Kit Leshario.

—∽—

Noah and Josiah had ridden in to North Platte on the first Wednesday of August. The sun was hot, the streets ankle-deep in dust. They woke to rain, but Josiah insisted that a little rain was no reason for him to delay making contact with Kit out at Scout's Rest. He left right after breakfast. Noah made his way to Jim Davis's Shaving Saloon where he lost a month's growth of hair but kept the beard (albeit trimmed) lest he look "like a paint horse," since the skin beneath his beard wouldn't be as dark as the rest of his face.

On the way back to the hotel, he stopped at a stationer's and purchased letter paper. Next, he had a leisurely breakfast, and then he returned to the hotel, intent on writing Emilie. Instead of returning to his hotel room, though, he lingered in the men's lounge just off the main lobby, drinking coffee and waxing eloquent about the last few days of the trip. Since Powder Horn Valley, he'd encountered a rattlesnake—which Phil stomped to death, seen the distant glimmer of a prairie fire, caught a glimpse of a falling star, and wished that Emilie could have been with them when he and Josiah topped a rise and saw what looked like a giant sapphire glimmering in the valley below.

Of course it was "only" a spring-fed body of water reflecting the blue sky, but the image will linger in my mind for the rest of my life. I'll tell our children about it. Perhaps we'll bring them west to see it for themselves. Of course by then, I suppose the west that Josiah knew and the west that I'm experiencing will be gone. I hope not. Oh. . .I hope not. Every night when I unroll Ma's quilt, the things she memorialized mean more. I'm going to see if he wants to meet me, Em. Will you pray for me? For us? I keep thinking of Ma mourning the death of the man she loved for all those years. She carried that sadness with such grace.

Noah had just raised his coffee mug to his lips when movement in the doorway made him look up. There he was standing behind Josiah, staring at Noah with an expression that defied description.

Noah set the coffee down. He stood up. The man behind Josiah stepped around him. But then he seemed unable to move forward. He was unmistakably Indian, even though he was dressed like any other cowhand. A red bandana tied about his neck. A blue shirt. Chaps. Denim pants. Boots with spurs. When he finally snatched the hat off his head and Noah saw the ragged black hair, he reached up and raked through his own.

Finally, the man moved. Coming to where Noah stood, he paused, looking into Noah's eyes. "I see myself."

Noah nodded.

The man put his hands on his hips. He looked away. Finally, he said, "Barton tells me she has gone to the fathers." He put his hand to his breast. "This grieves me."

"Pneumonia," Noah said. "When I was thirteen. She—" He couldn't say Ma didn't suffer, because she had. He swallowed. "It happened quickly."

The man nodded. Tears glimmered in his eyes as he stepped forward and put his palm on Noah's chest, almost as if he needed to prove the boy was real. "You are a gift I do not deserve," he said and dropped his hand.

And so it began.

CHAPTER 30

Colonel Barton cleared his throat. "We should continue this somewhere that affords privacy."

At the colonel's comment, Noah glanced about. Every one of the handful of men in the room was staring at Kit and him, and not all of them were merely curious. A couple looked downright upset. One was standing beside the table where he'd been sitting, smoking a cigar. Both the angle of the cigar in the man's mouth and the clenched fists sent a threatening message.

Kit glanced at the man and then at Josiah. With a wry smile, he muttered, "No Injuns allowed," and headed for the door.

Noah followed, his heart pounding. "Wait." He caught up to Kit in the lobby. "Can't we—what about we go up to our room?"

Kit shook his head. "Even worse." He headed on outside.

"Is he kidding?" Noah said, incredulous.

Josiah shook his head. "I should have known better, but when we rode up and I saw you in the lounge, I thought it'd be all right. That surely things had changed in the years since I'd been out here." He sighed. "I was wrong. I'm sorry."

"So what do we do?"

"We can head over to the livery." With a slow smile, he added, "In fact, we could pack up and go for a ride. You can impress Kit with your exemplary horsemanship."

By the time Noah and Josiah exited the hotel, Kit had already mounted up. When Josiah explained the plan, Kit nodded. "I'll wait at the edge of town," he said and, without another word, rode off toward the north.

Noah hesitated. "I—wait a minute. I need to get something." He took the hotel stairs two at a time, then loped down the hall to his room, where he grabbed the bedroll he hadn't undone since arriving in North Platte. Back downstairs, he held it up. "It's all I have of her. He should see it. I think it'll mean something to him. She never forgot."

Together, he and Josiah made their way to the livery. In moments, they'd joined up with the lone rider waiting astride a mottled gray horse with white splotches across its flanks. Kit turned west and kicked his horse into a lope. When Noah looked at Josiah in surprise, Josiah merely shrugged and moved out after the spotted pony. When Kit finally held up, he was at the top of a rise. Josiah and Noah caught up, and together the men descended into a valley just like the one Noah had written Emilie about—a bowl of sand holding a pool of water bubbling up from the earth, reflecting the rainclouds that were beginning to separate. An oasis of sorts in the midst of the vast sand hills.

When Kit dismounted, his horse lowered its head to drink. Noah and Josiah followed suit, and for a while, the men said nothing. Noah would look at Kit, and the older man would smile and nod and then look away.

Finally, Noah loosened the cords holding the bedroll behind his saddle. "Ma made this. And she used to tell me stories about it." Josiah reached out for Phil's reins, which Noah gladly handed over. Then he walked to a grassy spot beneath a tree and unfurled the bedroll. Standing back, he watched Kit.

The older man looked. And looked again. He squatted down beside the quilt. A calloused finger reached out and traced something.

His jaw tensed. He frowned. And then a tear trickled down one weathered cheek. He brushed it away with the back of his hand. And then he began to sing. The music rumbled up from someplace deep inside the man as he stared down at Ma's handwork. It was like nothing Noah had ever heard before. Not melodic in the way of the music he was accustomed to, yet beautiful in its own way. At one point, Kit raised both hands to the sky. He sang with his eyes closed, tears streaming down his cheeks. When the song ended, he sat at the edge of the quilt and leaned forward, still studying the imagery, tracing this drawing or that, sometimes smiling. And finally, looking up at Noah and gesturing for him to come and sit beside him. When Noah complied, Kit pointed to the outline of the Big Dipper.

"This is part of the Bear." He pointed up at the sky. "You know the Bear?"

Noah nodded. "She used to call me her Little Bear sometimes." He put his palm to his chest. "She said it was because of this voice."

"The voice is good."

"But that's not why she called me her little bear. She called me that because of you."

Kit pointed to an owl. "Tell me what she said about this."

When Noah repeated the story, Kit smiled. Nodded. "Yes. That is what happened." He paused, then added, "I wished for her to stay with me. I am sorry this has caused you pain."

Noah gestured at the quilt. "Tell me what she was remembering when she drew these things."

For the rest of the afternoon, Kit Leshario told stories. When the last one had been told—as it happened, the turkey wasn't really about Turkey Creek—Noah sat back. "I always believed there was more to these drawings than Ma would say." He looked over at his father. "She stitched a message. Proof that she never forgot. For the rest of her life, she carried your memory with her."

"As I do of her," Leshario said. He looked over at Noah, his dark eyes smoldering with emotion. "And now, give me stories of you, my son. So that I can carry your memory with me, alongside hers."

As the train rolled into the Beatrice station, Noah stood and reached for the treasured bedroll. Next he slung his saddlebags over his shoulder and followed Josiah off the train. It was early evening. He hesitated just a moment, remembering the last time he'd stood in this spot, trying to avoid an aging actress who had made herself something of a nuisance. Back then, he'd excused himself because he needed to meet with an editor. And here he was again, weeks later, needing to meet that same editor again.

"Rhodes works late," Josiah said. "You might catch him if you hurry. I'll see to the horses—and pray."

Noah broke into a trot. He crossed the railroad tracks and headed for Court Street, arriving at the *Dispatch* office a few blocks away just in time to see someone pulling the outer office door closed to lock them. As he got closer, Noah recognized Bert Hartwell and called out.

Hartwell hesitated. Frowned. "Do I know you?" Then when Noah got closer, his eyes grew wide. "Noah?"

"I was hoping to catch Mr. Rhodes before he left for the day."

"Oh, he's still here," Hartwell said. "He just wanted me to lock the front doors." He pulled the door open and motioned for Noah to head on in. "Never took you for mountain-man material," he joked. "But you sure look the part."

"It's a false impression. I can't wait to get shed of these clothes and get back into a suit." He realized it was true. He didn't belong in the "Wild West." He was and always would be someone who loved cities and crowds and all the other accoutrements of civilization.

"Well—see you soon," Hartwell said. "I'd stay and badger you with questions, but Junie's expecting me to stop by.

"That's going well?" Noah asked.

"Better than well." Bert shook his head. "I don't know what happened. It's as if I'd never really seen her before. But I see her now. Do I ever." With a low laugh, he pulled the doors closed, turned the key in the lock, and headed off up the street.

Noah walked up the few steps to the inner double doors. The newsroom was empty, but he could see into Mr. Rhodes's office. The 'old man' was there, bent over something spread out before him on his desk. Rapping on the outer office door to signal his presence, Noah proceeded into the newsroom, past a couple of desks, and waited at the door to Mr. Rhodes's office.

With a grimace, Rhodes rose from his chair and came to the door. "You'll need to make an appointment," he said brusquely. But then he hesitated. He looked Noah up and down. Offered his hand. "Well I must say you certainly look the part. I doubt even Emilie would recognize you at first glance."

"We need to talk. Now, if you're agreeable to it?"

Rhodes retreated to the other side of his desk, but he didn't sit down, nor did he invite Noah to do so. "Let's hear it. Give the speech."

"Speech?"

"The 'I know we've only known each other for a short time' speech. The one where you convince me to let you court my daughter. Isn't that what this is about? My wife's been warning me it's coming." He smiled. "And she's already told me what to say. But I suppose I must wait until you say your part of it. Do hurry, Shaw." He gestured down at the paper on this desk. "I've work to do before I can get home to my supper."

Noah took a deep breath. "I'm afraid it may not be as simple as you reciting whatever Mrs. Rhodes advised."

"I disagree," Rhodes said. "Yes. You may court my daughter. How's that? Saved us both some time."

"Thank you, sir," Noah said. "But—"

Mr. Rhodes reached up to tug on the waxed tip of his handlebar mustache. "There's an addendum?"

Noah took a deep breath. The office windows were open, but the place felt stifling. Claustrophobic. He set his bedroll down on the floor. Then looked at Rhodes for permission to follow with the saddlebags slung over his shoulder. Rhodes nodded and then sat down behind his desk and pointed to the chair in the corner.

"Sit. Tell me what's on your mind."

As many times as Noah had practiced this speech, now that he was actually facing Mr. Rhodes, he felt like a schoolboy trying to think up an excuse for misbehaving. Finally, he took a deep breath. "I do intend to ask your permission to court Emilie. Josiah—Colonel Barton—has asked me to return to Beatrice after this season closes down at the end of November. I'd be his assistant—helping him once and for all organize things and get his memoir written."

"Excellent," Mr. Rhodes said. "I'll call on him tomorrow. I've been badgering him for nearly five years now to let the *Dispatch* do the printing, once he's finished the thing. Glad to know it's finally going to happen."

"I haven't accepted the position yet," Noah said.

Mr. Rhodes sat back. "Go on."

"Before Josiah and I left on our adventure. . ." Noah told Rhodes about the portrait hanging in the office. Once he'd begun to talk, he raced through the entire story like a runner seeking a prize. He watched Mr. Rhodes's expressions but couldn't discern a thing. And with each passing moment, his heart pounded harder, until he thought surely the man must be hearing every single beat. "And so I wanted you to know." He swallowed. "I want a family, and I don't want to do anything to jeopardize Emilie's relationship with you all. If you can't accept me—well. She's said that won't matter. But it does. To me."

Rhodes frowned. "You've told Emilie about this?"

"Yes, sir. I didn't want to seem to be hiding anything."

"Well. I guess that explains her melancholy."

"I didn't mean to cause anyone pain, sir. But once I discovered the truth, I couldn't see any way to move forward without telling her everything."

Rhodes shook his head. "I wish you would have said all of this before you left, Shaw. It would have saved Emilie—and you—a great deal of unnecessary worry." He rose and went to the window, where he stood looking out on the street, his back to Noah.

Noah cleared his throat. "Sir, I love Emilie. I want to make a life with her. I'm not a wealthy man, but my needs have been few over the years, and I have a good amount of money saved up. But as I said earlier, I want a family. I can't tell you what it's meant to be embraced by yours—as a friend. But if, in light of this revelation, you can't accept me, then I'll say good-bye and end things as painlessly as possible."

Mr. Rhodes looked over his shoulder for a moment, then back out to the street. "You do have a flair for drama, Mr. Shaw."

"Sir?"

Rhodes waved a hand in the air, then began to twirl his mustache again. Finally, he said, "Much ado about nothing. That's what I think about all of this." He turned about to face Noah. "What do you know about my parents, Mr. Shaw? My grandparents? What about Mrs. Rhodes's parents?"

"I. . .um. . .I don't know anything about them, sir."

"Exactly. And you probably never will. There's no reason to discuss them. Out here in the West, a man can make something of himself based on who *he* is—not because he inherited a name or a privilege."

"Are you saying—"

Rhodes held up his hand. "Let me finish." He cleared his throat.

"It isn't a subject of polite dinner conversation, of course, but it's also no secret that sometimes in the West, folks entered into commitments to each other and had to wait until spring to finalize things with a circuit rider. I could name some names, but that's not my point. My point is it happened. And when it did, people politely looked the other way. And no one called names when a child arrived 'early.'" He paused. "So here's what I have to say about the situation, Mr. Shaw. I have no intention of using what you just told me as a weapon. In sum, I don't care if your father was a purple pied piper. I do care very much that you make my daughter happy."

"Sir. . .I. . .thank you, sir."

Rhodes nodded. "You're welcome. And listen carefully, now: There is no need to go blathering on about this to anyone else. Emilie knows. I know. Let that be the extent of things. You're the son of a good man. You're a good man. May the tradition continue." Mr. Rhodes bent down and, picking up Noah's saddle bags, handed them to him. "Now get out of my office. I have work to do, and you have someone else to see."

Emilie was sitting out on the little balcony just off her bedroom, Noah's letter in hand, when she heard him ride in. How she knew it was Noah, she couldn't say, but at the first sound of hoofbeats out on the road, she rose and went back inside. Setting the letter down on her writing desk, she flew across the room, into the hall, and down the back stairs, so quickly that by the time he was dismounting beneath the porte cochere, she was waiting on the bottom step—waiting to be taken into his arms. And she was not disappointed.

"I'm a ragged mess, but I couldn't wait to see you." He held her close.

"You're my ragged mess, and I love you." He smelled of dust and sweat, and she didn't care. Finally, she looked past him at the horse.

"So. This is Phil." At the sound of his name, the horse brought his ears forward and turned toward her voice. "How do you do, Phil." When Emilie reached up to stroke the animal's muzzle, he dodged away. "Here, here," she said, and grabbed his bridle. "We'll have none of that." She gently brought his head back around. "You have to get to know me." This time, Phil stayed still. "In fact," she said, "you should probably get to know Royal." She looked over at Noah. "Shall we put him in a stall in the barn? See how the two of them do? You have to come in. I want to hear everything."

"Will it be all right? Maybe it's too late."

"There is no 'too late' for you, Mr. Shaw." Mother's voice sounded from the top of the stairs. "Welcome back."

"Thank you, ma'am." Noah held his arms out. "As you can see, I'm really not fit for human company yet."

"Nonsense," Mother said. "Stable the horse and then come in. Dinah made lemon pie today. I'll get you a piece. And coffee?"

"Yes, ma'am. Thank you."

"Did you have supper on the train?"

"I'm fine, ma'am."

"Why, yes, Noah, I believe you are. But you're probably hungry, as well." Mother chuckled. "I'll see to it." And with that, she moved away from the door.

As Noah led Phil toward the barn, the animal stepped close and butted Emilie away.

"Hey," Noah tightened his hold on the reins. "See what I mean about him being something of a Philistine?" He spoke to the horse. "You're going to have to get over that. Make me choose, and I'll choose her."

Emilie laughed as she stroked the horse's broad neck. "Hear that? This isn't a contest. I've already won."

Phil tossed his head and whickered. Royal answered from the barn. Emilie and Noah worked together unsaddling Phil and brushing him down, then turning him into the stall next to Royal's.

After a few minutes of snorting, the two horses settled down.

"I believe they've declared a truce," Emilie said. Then she turned about and looked up at Noah again. "I knew it was you when I heard the horse out on the road."

"How?"

She shrugged. "I don't know. I just did." She took his hand. "Mother will be wondering where we've gotten off to."

"She'll know." His dark eyes glimmered. He drew her close. "I've so much to tell you, I don't know where to begin. But now. . .at this moment. . .somehow it doesn't seem as important as it did before."

"You came back to me."

His grip tightened. "As long as I have breath in my body, I will always come back to you." His lips found hers.

As their kiss deepened, Emilie stood on tiptoe and wrapped her arms around his neck, drawing him to her, eager. . .willing.

Breathless, Noah broke off and stepped back, taking her hand and pulling her after him as he strode out of the barn and toward the house. He paused at the foot of the stairs leading up to the side door. "All the way here, all the way from North Platte I wondered. And then after I spoke with your father—"

"You've seen Father?"

He nodded. "Yes. Before I came here. You do remember what I said about stolen kisses?"

"That you want more. A family. Like mine."

"Yes. Aunts and uncles and cousins and second cousins and friends and friends of friends. Riotous birthdays, unforgettable Christmases. For you and me and our children."

"How many children?"

"A dozen?"

She laughed. "I think you've skipped a step?"

"Right," he nodded. "Engagement. But I'm not prepared. I don't even have a *tiny* little garnet—"

"I don't want a garnet."

"Emerald? Diamond? Topaz?"

Emilie just shook her head. "All I want is you, Noah Shaw."

"You say that now. But I can just hear the talk among the Spring Sisters. Twenty years from now, they'd still be talking about it."

"They wouldn't. They love you. Bert likes you. Mother and Aunt Cornelia approve. And Father thinks you're fine."

"And E. J. Starr? What does E. J. say to a life with a traveling man?"

"E. J. already has an idea for a series called From the Road."

"From the Road. Good hook. I usually leave around the end of April." He smiled down at her. "Think we could manage a wedding by then?"

"We could manage a wedding tonight."

"I have a feeling your mother and your aunt Cornelia and your cousins might have something to say about that. I'm on their good side. I'd like to stay there." He dropped to one knee. "Your mother's watching out the window. How am I doing?"

"You look ruggedly handsome," Emilie said and extended her hand.

He took it. And then his expression sobered. "'Grow old along with me. The best is yet to be.'"

"'The last of life, for which the first was made. . .'"

Noah rose and put his arms around her. "In case that wasn't quite clear, I'm asking you to be my wife."

"And I'm saying yes," she murmured, "with all my heart."

Together, they headed up the steps. . .and into the house. . .and toward a new life.

The Future I may face now I have proved the Past.
My times be in Thy hand!
Perfect the cup as planned!
Robert Browning

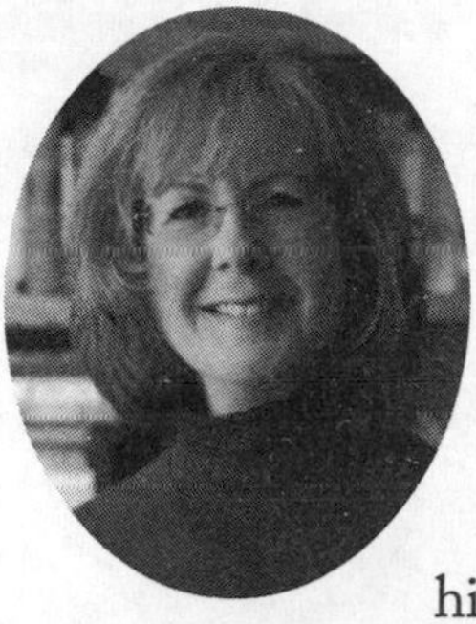

Stephanie Grace Whitson, bestselling author and two-time Christy finalist, pursues a full-time writing and speaking career from her home studio in southeast Nebraska. Her husband and blended family, her church, quilting, and Kitty—her motorcycle—all rank high on her list of "favorite things." Learn more at www.stephaniewhitson.com

Other titles by
Stephanie Grace Whitson

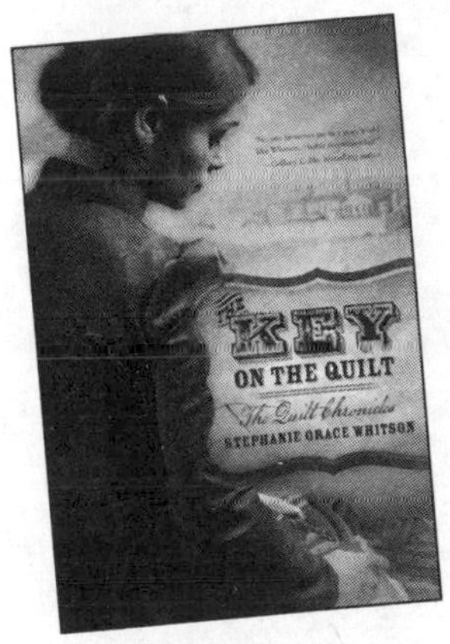

The Key on the Quilt

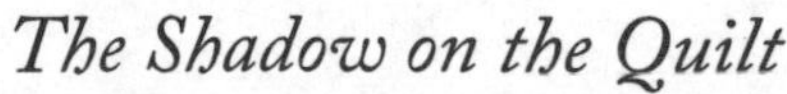

The Shadow on the Quilt

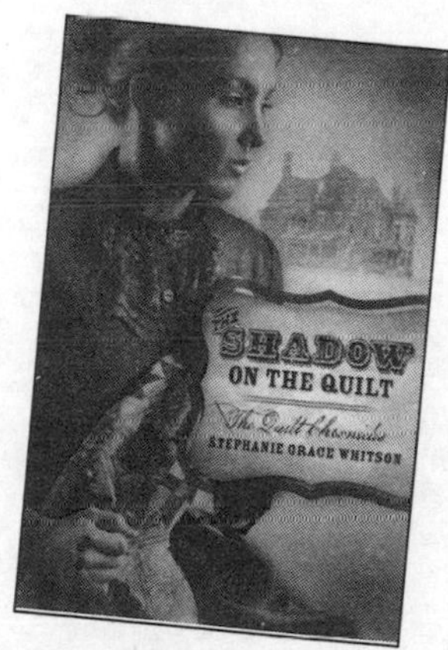